The Shadow of a Noose

Ralph Compton's
The Shadow of a Noose

A Novel by
Ralph Cotton

WHEELER
PUBLISHING, INC.
ROCKLAND, MA

★ AN AMERICAN COMPANY ★

Published in large print by arrangement with Signet, an imprint of New American Library, a division of Penguin Putnam Inc., in the United States and Canada.

Wheeler Large Print Book Series.

Set in 16 pt Plantin.

Library of Congress Cataloging-in-Publication Data Available

Cotton, Ralph.
    Ralph Compton's The shadow of a noose / Ralph Cotton.
        p. (large print) cm. (Wheeler large print book series)
    ISBN 1-58724-225-7 (softcover)
    1. Large type books. I. Title. II. Series.

Prologue

St. Joseph, Missouri, June 15, 1871

"Jed," said Tim Strange to his twin brother, "now that Ma is in the ground, I don't rightly know what to do next. I wish there was some way to get in touch with Danielle and let her know what happened here. But I don't reckon anybody's heard a word from her since she took out after the bastards that killed our pa. That's been over a year ago."

For Jed, looking into his twin brother's face was like looking into a mirror. "It's going to plumb break her heart even hearing about Ma's death from *us*, let alone if she had to hear about it from a stranger," Jed replied, miserably.

They both gazed across the barren, empty garden near their farmhouse. The house was in sore need of repair, and had been long since before their sister Danielle had left.

"Look at this place." Tim sighed. "It's all worn down to dust and sorrow. We don't even have the price of seeds. You and I have been left in sorry straits, brother. If we're going to go hungry, we might just as well do it on the trail. We might even find work out there somewhere, if we kept our ages a secret. We won't find any around here, not with Reconstruction going on. If not for that old double-barreled rabbit gun in the house, I reckon we'd starve."

"I know what you mean," said Jed. "Everybody around here is having it as rough as we

1

are. Never thought I'd say this, but I'm so sick of rabbit, I can't stand it."

"Well, even rabbit is starting to get scarce," Tim said.

Tim and Jed Strange were only fourteen when their sister had left them one year ago on the hard-scrabble farm to take care of their grieving, ailing mother, Margaret Strange. Try as they did, the two boys had not been able to make ends meet for themselves and their mother.

"Then we both know what we have to do, don't we?" said Tim. "We'll have to go find Danielle, and make sure she hears the bad news from us."

Jed looked at his brother, knowing that while neither of them wanted to admit it, they had both been a little bit envious of the fact that it was their sister Danielle who had taken up the vengeance trail, hunting for the murderers of their father, Dan Strange. Both boys shared the thought that hunting for cold-blooded killers was man's work. They had been too young to go after the outlaws themselves at the time. While it was an indisputable fact that their sister Danielle was as good with a gun as any man, her going after the killers alone still didn't set right with them.

But Tim and Jed Strange were a whole year older now, and every spare minute they had was spent practicing their draw and their aim. The Colts they used had been custom-fitted by their father, who had been known as the best gunsmith in Missouri. Before his demise he had seen to it that his children knew how to *use* as well as repair a gun, starting when they were hardly more than babies.

With their sweat-stained, beat-up Stetsons in their hands, the twins looked down at their mother's grave, and at the wildflowers they had placed on the fresh-turned mound of earth. "Ma," Jed said, his head hung down low, "I wish we could of buried you in the cemetery proper-like, the way you deserved. But this is the best we could do."

"Don't talk like that," Tim said. "You know as well as I do that Ma would as soon be here in the yard near this old house as she would in the finest cemetery in the world."

"You're right," Jed said to his brother, holding back the tears that were about to spill from his eyes. "I'll tell you one thing— the men who killed Pa just as well had killed Ma, too. She started dying the day Pa was put down. It just took her longer to do it. I want to find Danielle, and I want all three of us to find the bastards that caused all this."

They stood silently for a few minutes, each mulling over his own private thoughts. A small cool breeze cut through the hot air and made the petals of the wildflowers rustle over their mother's grave. Finally, Tim said with a tightness in his chest, "We still have our Colts, and one tin of bullets between us."

Lifting his eyes from the grave, Jed said, "Yes, and we still have the two good bay horses, except that they're run-down in their flanks from want of grain."

"Then what are we waiting for?" said Tim. "Talking ain't going to get it done." Tim stepped back from the grave with a last sorrowful look. He took down one of the gun belts that they had hung on a stubbed branch of a cottonwood tree a few feet away, rather than wearing them to their mother's grave. Jed only watched his twin brother for a moment as Tim strapped the belt around his hips and began to tie the holster down to his thigh with a length of rawhide.

Jed realized that what they both had dreamed of for the past year was about to come true. He hurried over to the cottonwood tree, took down his gun belt, and strapped it on in the same manner as Tim had done. "You're right. What *are* we waiting for?" Jed Strange said, echoing his twin brother's words.

As Jed and Tim Strange stood inside the barn, saddling the two bay geldings, preparing the gaunt horses for what both boys knew would be a long and treacherous journey, the sound of a buggy rolling into the yard caused them both to turn from their tasks and step back out into the sunlight. At first they thought it might have been one of the many families who had come by earlier to pay their last respects, perhaps someone who was arriving late. But when they saw it was Orville Myers, the new land speculator who'd been plying his

4

profession in the St. Joseph area of late, they knew the purpose of his visit before he stepped down from his buggy and walked toward them.

"Damn," said Jed to Tim, "you'd think he could wait till after the funeral dust settled."

"Men like Orville Myers don't wait for nothing," Tim said. "But he could have saved himself a trip in this case."

Orville Myers seemed to have an idea that they were talking about him, for he kept his eyes lowered, unable to face them head-on, something their father had taught them always to be leery of. Dan Strange always told his sons, "If a man can't face you directly, most likely he's hiding more than just his eyes."

Before Orville came to a complete stop, Tim Strange hooked his thumbs into his gun belt and said, "You weren't here when our friends and neighbors were, so you just as well might have not come at all."

"Boys, I know you don't like me. Nobody around here does. But I don't let them stop me from doing my job. I know the fix you're in, and I felt it only obligin' of me to ride out and make you an offer on this old place before it ends up on the auction block."

"What's he talking about, Tim?" Jed asked, keeping his eyes narrowed on Orville Myers's weasely face.

"I don't know, Jed. What *are* you talking about, Myers? The taxes are paid up on this place. Ma sent Danielle into town to pay them before Danielle left last spring."

"Indeed. But that was for last year's taxes." Orville Myers adjusted the wire-rimmed glasses on the bridge of his long thin nose then took out a folded piece of paper from his black linen suit. "I reckon you boys are too young to realize that taxes ain't a one-time thing. You owe the same amount now as you did then, except this year the government is upping the total by twenty-six dollars to get back some money it spent fighting that blamed war. I guess that's the government's way to make a bunch of yellow rebels think twice before they decide to kick up their heels again."

"Mr. Myers, I don't mean no disrespect," said Tim, "but you best be careful calling these men around here *yellow*. The feelings over the war haven't cooled that much. There's some who'd leave you swinging from a tree over talk like that."

Orville Myers looked startled and quickly said, "Boys, don't get me wrong, I'm a businessman. I took no side in the war, and I take none now. I make my profit no matter who wins or loses. But back to the subject at hand. I'm making you an offer of two hundred dollars for this place just like she sits. It's a fair offer, and I advise you to take it. It'll put a little traveling money in your pockets."

"Why, you snake!" Tim Strange took an enraged step forward, but brother Jed grabbed his arm, stopping him. "We'd stand in one spot and starve to death before we'd sell you this place!"

"Take it easy, Tim," Jed said, holding his brother back. Jed shot Orville Myers a threatening look, saying, "And you best follow your heels back to that buggy and clear out of here!"

Myers backed away, talking as he went, pointing a finger at them. "Boys, you best see the wisdom in taking my offer. If you let me walk away from here today, I might change my mind before morning. If I haven't, you know where my office is. Don't let pride keep you from doing what's best for you."

The twins stood and watched the rise of dust drift away behind the buggy. Only when Orville Myers was out of sight did Tim Strange cool down a mite. Even so, his breath still rose and fell hard and hot. "It's a good thing you were here," he said to Jed, who stood beside him. "I saw red there for a minute. Funny, how the two of us are the same in every other way, yet when it comes to keeping a rein on our tempers, you're always the calmer one."

"Yes, but not by much in this case," Jed said. "It was awfully tempting to let you give that snake a sound thrashing. But let's always remember who we are and how we were raised, especially once we get out there on the road. Try to always ask yourself what Ma and Pa would have us do before we go acting in haste. That's what I try to do, anyhow."

"That's good thinking, Jed," said Tim, "and I'll try remembering it. But there just might be things come up out there where we won't have time to stop and think what Ma and

Pa would expect of us. I reckon wherever Danielle is, she's learned that by now. If she ain't, she might already be dead herself."

"Let's not think that way, brother," said Jed, patting Tim on his shoulder. "Come on, let's get the horses and get under way. We'll go to town and see where we stand on these taxes before we ride on."

Afternoon shadows had begun to stretch long across the land by the time Tim and Jed Strange rode into St. Joseph, hitching their gaunt horses to the iron rings in front of the town hall. Elvin Bray, the tax assessor, had already pulled down the hood on his oaken roll-topped desk and closed up the wooden file cabinets along the back wall behind the counter. He followed the same routine every day before he left his office. His next step would have been to lock the front door, pull down the shade, then count the cash he had collected before locking it away in the small Mosler safe beside his desk. But just as he reached out to lock the door, Tim and Jed walked through it. Elvin Bray jumped back a step and spoke in a startled voice.

"My goodness, young men, I wasn't expecting anybody this late in the afternoon!" Elvin touched his thin, nervous fingertips to his chin, trying not to look too shaken. "Is this something that can wait till tomorrow?"

"Pardon us, Mr. Bray," Tim said, taking off his battered Stetson and, out of force of habit, batting it against his right leg. "Now that Ma's dead, Jed and I are leaving the county for a while. We just wanted to see how much taxes is owed on our place before we head out."

"Head out?" Bray looked back and forth between them. "But your ma's funeral was just this morning. Sorry I couldn't make it out there. My wife Cheryl Kay and my boy Thomas was there though, right?"

"Yes, sir, they was," Tim Strange said, "and we appreciated the turn-out."

"I've been meaning to come out and talk to you boys anyway," said Bray. "Come on in here, and let's close this door a'fore somebody else shows up," said Bray, ushering them farther into the office. He closed the door and locked it. "I always get a might anxious this time of evening when there's money on hand."

"We understand," said Jed as he and Tim moved closer to the counter. Elvin Bray stepped back behind the counter through a waist-high swinging door. He straightened the garters on his shirtsleeves, then spread his hands along the countertop. "All right now, young men. What can I do for you?"

"Well, sir," Tim said, "as you know, our sister Danielle has been gone this past year. We haven't heard from her, nor she from us. We were fixin' to head out searching for her when Orville Myers come by the place. He's talking like we owe some taxes, and if we don't get them paid real quick, we could lose the farm. Can you give us an idea what we owe? We want to find a way to pay it."

9

Elvin Bray raised a thin hand, stopping Tim Strange from saying any more. He said, "Boys, let me ease your minds. As of right now, your taxes are paid in full for this year. They were paid by mail less than a month ago."

"Huh?" Tim and Jed looked at one another, puzzled.

"That's right," said Bray. "I can tell you without looking it up. Neither of you have been to town lately or I would have told you sooner. My Cheryl Kay would have told you today at your ma's funeral, but we didn't think it was the time and place to mention it." As he spoke, Bray pulled up the hood of his roll-top desk, then picked up a ledger book and turned back to them with it. The twins noticed the metal cash box sitting on the desk as Bray spread the ledger open and ran a thin finger down to the name *Strange*.

"See here? You're paid in full for the year." He raised his eyes to them and smiled. "Maybe you haven't heard from Danielle, but we sure have. She mailed a bank draft in a letter to us. In fact, she overpaid by fourteen dollars."

"Well, thank God for that." Jed Strange sighed. "Not only for her paying the taxes, but also for letting somebody know she's still alive."

"Was there a return address on the letter?" Tim asked.

"Hold on, I'll find it for you," said Elvin Bray as he turned to his desk again and rummaged through a drawer full of opened envelopes.

Tim and Jed looked at one another, waiting on Elvin Bray. "Why do you suppose Orville

Myers tried pulling a stunt like that on us, Tim?" Jed asked.

Before Tim could respond, Elvin Bray, hearing their conversation, said over his shoulder, "Because Orville Myers is a cuss. He most likely figured you boys being young, he'd get you scared of losing your home for taxes, then buy it on the spot before you even checked out his story."

"Being young don't mean we're stupid," Tim said defensively.

"I know that, boys." Elvin Bray found the letter and said, "Here it is," handing it over to them. "But somebody like Myers who ain't from here, and has no regard for anybody anyway, just figures you both for a couple of wet-nosed pups." As Tim and Jed inspected the back of the bank draft envelope, Bray went on talking. "If you boys are headed out on your own for the first time, you're going to find a lot of Orville Myers along your way, or worse. It don't matter what you know, or what fine upbringing you've had. Out there you'll meet some unsavory characters who'll be out to snare you, taking advantage of your inexperience."

"Thanks, Mr. Bray, we'll be careful," Tim assured him.

"This letter was mailed from Dallas, Texas," Jed noted, tapping a finger on the envelope, "but it gives no return address. I reckon Danielle must have known she wasn't going to be there long when she sent it." He shook his head. "I swear, it ain't like Danielle to not keep in touch."

11

"If she's moving around a lot on her own," Bray said, "you might be surprised how much she's changed in the past year. She might not want to say much, for fear it'll reveal things about herself she might not want known."

"What are you saying, Mr. Bray?" Tim asked, seeming to take offense.

"Now, don't get your dander up," Elvin Bray said. "I'm only saying people change once they get out there and get knocked around some. Be prepared, boys. That's all I meant by it."

"Not our sister!" Tim said, irritated. "She'll be the same as always, once we find her."

Jed intervened. "Tim, all Mr. Bray is saying is that a year can make a difference in a person. He's not saying anything bad about Danielle, are you, Mr. Bray?"

"No siree. I've known you and your folks too long, and we've always been good neighbors to one anther. I suppose what I'm trying to do is give you some parting advise. I apologize if it's been mistaken."

Tim cooled off and said, "No, I'm the one who needs to apologize. I'm sorry I took offense. I've got a lot on my mind today." He nodded at Jed. "We both do. Jed just don't show it as easily."

"Well," said Bray, smiling patiently, "I won't offer no more advice. The road is the best, yet harshest teacher I know of." Bray sighed and shook his head slowly. "But as for your taxes, you can see you're in good shape till next year. Knowing that ought to make you feel some better."

"Thanks again, Mr. Bray," Jed said. "Suppose we can keep this envelope?"

"Sure." Elvin Bray shrugged. "In fact, if you're in need of some traveling money, I can let you have that extra fourteen dollars."

"Can you?" said Jed. "We'd sure be obliged!"

"Be glad to," Bray replied. "I'll just need one of you to sign a receipt, for our records."

Jed and Tim nodded in unison. Elvin Bray went to the cash box on his desk, counted out fourteen dollars, then picked up a receipt pamphlet and returned to the counter. Once the money changed hands and the receipt was signed, Bray smiled. "There you are. When you find Danielle, you be sure and tell her she's missed by all of us here."

"We will, sir," Tim said, folding the money and shoving it down into his shirt pocket. "She'll be glad to hear you said that."

Elvin Bray stayed behind the counter and watched them leave. At the door, he called out to them, "Will you do me a favor? One of you pull that sash down on your way out?"

"I will," said Jed. But as he took a hold of the long sash cord and pulled down, it broke off in his hand. "Sorry, Mr. Bray," he said, turning to Bray with the cord dangling from his hand.

Elvin Bray raised a hand toward him. "It weren't your fault. That cord was getting old. Just pitch it away for me first chance you get." He smiled, leaning on the counter, and watched them shuffle out through the door, Jed Strange winding the length of sash cord around his finger. When the door closed behind them, Elvin Bray shook his head, thinking of the long trail that lay before the two young men. Then he went back to his roll-top desk, picked up the metal cash box, and pulled the hood down.

Across the street from the assessor's office, in the darkness of a narrow shadowed alley, two outlaws by the name of Duncan Grago and Sep Howard stood watching Tim and Jed Strange as the twins mounted their horses and rode out of sight along the quiet afternoon street. Sep Howard took note of Jed's short-barreled ten-gauge, the butt stock sticking out from beneath his blanket roll.

"What do you think, Dunc?" Sep asked. "We've been eye-balling this sucker for three days. This is the first time we haven't seen him lock the door this late in the evening."

"I believe we better make our run at him," said Dunc. "If we do this quiet-like, there's a good chance the last ones seen leaving the office will be those two." He nodded his ragged hat brim in the direction of Tim and Jed Strange. "One thing I learnt in prison—anytime you can shift the blame to some-body else, do it." He spread a thin, wicked grin.

"Sounds good to me," said Sep Howard. "But we'll have to kill that assessor to make it work that way."

"So?" Dunc Grago squinted at him. "You got any qualms against killing? If you do, I doubt if my brother Newt would have sent you to look for me. He knows that wherever I'm at, there's killing a-plenty."

"I've got no qualms against puttin' anyone under snakes," said Sep. "Just tell me what you want done."

Dunc Grago reached down and drew a long bowie knife from his boot well. He tucked the knife into his waistband, smoothing his vest down over it. "Move these horses closer and be ready in case anything goes wrong. I'll be coming out of there before you know it, so be ready."

Inside the assessor's office, Elvin Bray counted the dollar bills, stacked them neatly, and laid them down on his desk beside the cash box. It was the first time in seven years that he'd failed to lock the door before making his daily tally and entering the figure into his accounting ledger, as the arrival of Jed and Tim Strange had broken his routine. Just as it dawned on him what he'd done, he heard the door ease open quietly, and he turned toward the stranger with his ledger book in his hand. "I'm sorry, sir, but we're closed for the day. If you've come to town to pay your taxes, we'll be open again early in the morning."

"Taxes, huh?" said Dunc Grago. "Never paid any, never will." As Dunc spoke, his arm went behind his vest. He raised the bowie knife by its handle and flipped it around in his hand to where he held it by the blade. "Catch this for me." His arm shot forward as if he were cracking of a whip, sending the blade through

15

the air in a shiny streak. The force of the blade striking Elvin Bray in his chest from fifteen feet away sent him staggering back against the oaken desk. Bray stood frozen for a second, staring down wide-eyed in disbelief at the knife handle pinned to his chest, the blade sunk deep in his heart. His face stiffened, then went slack as he sank to the floor.

"There now, all done," Duncan Grago said to himself, locking the door and pulling the shade down by its broken stub of a cord. He walked quietly over behind the counter, placed a boot on Elvin Bray's chest, and pulled the big knife free, wiping it back and forth on Bray's white shirt. "If you could talk right now," he said to the wide, dead eyes staring blankly up at him, "you'd have to admit, that's the fastest thing you ever saw."

As Duncan Grago had predicted, nobody noticed him and Sep Howard leave town through the back alley, leading the horse slowly through the afternoon shadows until they were a good quarter of a mile from Elvin Bray's office. They had both kept quiet, looking back over their shoulders occasionally. Finally Sep Howard raised his lowered hat brim and spoke.

"I have to tell you," he said, the two of them finally stepping up onto the horses on the road out of town, "that was slicker than socks on a rooster. No wonder your brother Newt wants you back riding with him. I feared you might be a bit rusty, spending four years in stir."

The Colt in the tied-down holster on Duncan's hip streaked up toward Sep Howard, causing the older gunman's breath to catch in his throat. "Does that look rusty to you?" Duncan sneered.

"Lord, Dunc, give a feller a warning!" Sep Howard mopped his gloved hand across his brow, and settled as Duncan spun the Colt back down into his holster. "You know I wasn't making light of you."

"If I thought you was," said Duncan, "you wouldn't be sitting there right now." He offered a thin, tight grin. "Let's get on down to the Territory, see what Newt and his boys have got cooking for us."

"Sounds good to me," said Sep Howard. He heeled his horse forward, yet he purposely kept a few feet back behind Duncan Grago. Sep Howard was getting on in age, and one reason he'd managed to stay alive as long as he had was because he'd learned not to show his back too long or too often to a man like Duncan Grago. When Newt Grago had asked him to ride all the way to Arizona to meet Duncan as he got out of prison, Sep Howard's first thought was why didn't Newt go meet his brother himself? But ever since Newt Grago had more or less become the leader of a small gang of cutthroats and cattle rustlers down in Indian Territory, Sep saw Newt grow increasingly full of himself and staying wound pretty tight. Newt Grago had shot one of his own men for sassing him over a cup of coffee, and Sep and some of the others had watched him do it. So Sep hadn't back-talked him. He'd done as he was told, taking along a spare horse for the young convict. He'd met Duncan Grago as soon as the young man stepped out through the iron gates of the prison with his belongings tied in a bandanna spindle. It took all of about five minutes for Sep Howard to decide that this young man was as wild as a buck, and madder than a slapped hornet. Sep had already given some thought to saddling up and disappearing into the night. But now, seeing how cool and quiet this young man had just breezed in and out of the assessor's office, bringing back close to five hundred dollars, Sep decided to stick around awhile longer and see how things went from here. As he was thinking about these things, Duncan Grago turned in his saddle, looking back at him as he spoke.

"Get on up here beside me, Sep," he said. "I've grown edgy about having an *hombre* shadowing me."

"I don't blame you, I'm the same way, Dunc," Sep Howard said, nudging his horse up a notch. He took a guarded glance at the tight, grit-streaked face beneath Duncan Grago's hat brim, seeing the narrowed eyes, the crooked bridge of his nose, the shaved sideburns—prison style—and even the way Duncan sat loose and easy in his saddle. There was an ever-present tension about him like that of a coiled viper.

"I reckon my brother told you why I was in stir, didn't he?" Duncan Grago asked.

18

"Well, he mentioned a knife fight," said Sep, not wanting to appear too curious about it. "He didn't say what you was charged with, just that you was given five years."

"A knife fight, huh?" Duncan Grago laughed and slapped his thigh. "Yeah, you could call it a knife fight. But after it was over, you could of called it a quilting bee, it took so much thread to piece him back together. I cut him everywhere but the soles of his feet...and that's only cause he was wearing boots. Lucky for me he was part Mexican, or I'd be in that sweat hole the rest of my life."

"You mean the man lived through all that cutting?" Sep Howard asked, feeling a little queasy the way Duncan Grago seemed to relish giving him the gory details.

"Yeah, he lived, if you call that living. Top of his head looks like an Arkansas road map." Duncan Grago spit, then kicked his horse up into a canter, liking the feel of the evening breeze on his face. Posting high in his saddle like a kid out on an evening lark, he shot a glance back at Sep Howard and called out, "Keep up with me, ole man, you might learn a thing or two!"

Under his breath, Sep Howard whispered, "Lord have mercy," and he spurred his horse forward. Sep was getting tired of all the new faces showing up in Indian Territory of late. These younger outlaws seemed wilder than ever, he thought. Most of them were kill-crazy, out looking to make themselves a reputation with a gun. Many of them were bent on revenge of some sort. Sep Howard had seen them come and go. They came from the prisons, the badlands, and from hell itself, it seemed—all of them hot for spilling blood.

He thought about the one he'd been hearing a lot about lately, the one who rode a chestnut mare and carried a crossed brace of Colts on his hips. Dan something-or-other was the kid's name. Sep Howard had never met the young gunman, and couldn't say he had much of a hankering to do so. But he'd heard talk, the kind of talk that got a person's attention. Word of the young gunman had sure enough gotten Newt Grago's attention.

Apparently everywhere the young gunman showed up, somebody turned up dead—usually somebody close to Newt Grago. In the past year four outlaws that Sep Howard knew of had met their match. Sep wondered if his going to fetch Duncan Grago had anything to do with the fact that Newt Grago was getting a little concerned, wondering why so many men he'd ridden with were dying in their boots.

Trying to keep up with Duncan Grago, Sep Howard ran names and faces through his mind. Bart Scovill, Snakehead Kalpana, Levi Jasper, Brice Levan. These were all bold, hardened killers. But now these men were dead. Sep thought this was a good time to watch his back real close and be ready to drop out of sight at a minute's notice. He didn't know if any of the others had made the connection between these men dying and the young gunman on the chestnut mare, but *he* sure had, and he was pretty sure Newt had too.

20

Sep Howard heeled his horse harder, trying to stay by Duncan Grago's side. This was a good time to keep his mouth shut, Sep thought. He was getting older and slowing down, unable to handle himself with these young gun slicks like the one with the crossed Colts. He'd heard enough to know that he didn't want to find himself on some dusty street somewhere, all of a sudden having to look into those icy green eyes he'd heard so much about.

Chapter 1

Sheriff Matthew Connally had taken his supper at a small restaurant off the main street and a block from his office. Oil lamps had already begun to glow in windows as he strolled back along the boardwalk with his shotgun under his arm. While he still wore his Colt .45 making his evening rounds, the ten-gauge was his choice of weapons when it came to searching into darkened doorways and alleys. St. Joseph was not a wild, unruly town at present, but it had long been Sheriff Connally's experience that the only way to keep a town peaceful was with a tight hand and a ready load of buckshot.

In the darkness, Sheriff Connally saw the one-horse buggy pull up out front of the assessor's office, and as he walked closer, he saw Elvin Bray's wife, Cheryl Kay, hurry down from the buggy seat and to the door of the darkened office.

"Elvin, are you still in there?" Cheryl Kay said, knocking on the glass pane in the door. She tried peeping around the edge of the drawn windowshade, but saw nothing in the silent blackened office. "Do you hear me, Elvin? Are you there?" She reached down to shake the doorknob but, in doing so, felt the door give away and swing open a few inches. She gasped, and stepped back.

"What's the problem here, Mrs. Bray?" Sheriff Connally asked, hastening up beside her.

"Oh, Sheriff," Cheryl Kay Bray said, looking at Connally with a hand to her cheek, "Elvin wasn't home for supper. I got worried. I came here and..." Her words trailed as she nodded at the partly opened door.

"I see," Sheriff Connally said, already on the alert, guiding her to one side of the doorway. "You wait out here, ma'am." He slowly opened the door the rest of the way and stepped inside. Cheryl Kay Bray waited in breathless anticipation. In a moment, she leaned slightly around into the open doorway and spoke.

"Is everything all right, Sheriff?" She started to step into the dark office, but when Sheriff Connally heard the floor creak beneath her shoes, he spoke to her from within the darkness.

"Don't come in here, ma'am. Something terrible has happened."

Within minutes, word had spread up and

down the street. The assessor's office was soon brightly lit by lamps and lanterns, and a couple of young women from the nearest saloon stood comforting Cheryl Kay Bray out front on the boardwalk until the minister arrived. Bystanders milled in the street.

A town councilman by the name of Carl Hundly, who had been playing poker at the saloon, now stood in the center of the floor of Elvin Bray's office with his bowler hat in his hand. He rocked up onto his toes and craned a look over the counter to where Sheriff Connally and Doc Soble rolled Elvin Bray's cold body onto a gurney. Councilman Hundly winced at the sight, shook his head, and spoke to Connally.

"Sheriff, I hope you're prepared to act swiftly on this. Hattie McNear said she saw the Strange twins leaving here right about closing time. Said one of them was twirling a length of cord around his finger."

"Which one?" Sheriff Connally asked, riffling through the receipt pamphlet and seeing where Tim Strange had signed his name. "Which one?" Councilman Hundley blustered. "How the hell could she tell which one? They're identical!"

"Oh," Sheriff Connally said, purposely busying himself with the receipts. He'd only asked the question to slow Hundley down, not wanting to let the councilman step in and try to call the shots. "Do me a favor, Councilman," he said, without raising his eyes to Hundley. "Send one of those saloon girls for some coffee. I'd ask them myself but you seem to know them so much better."

"What?" Hundley fumed. "How dare you imply such a thing!"

But Sheriff Connally had already moved around the counter and past him to the door. He looked out into the gathering of people and called Hattie McNear into the office. As Hattie scurried forward, Sheriff Connally said under his breath to one of the saloon girls, "Will you fetch us a pot of coffee, Wanda Lee? We're going to be a while." He also pointed a finger at two men and motioned them inside to carry Elvin Bray's body to the mortician's.

Councilman Hundley still fumed silently as Sheriff Connally spoke to Hattie McNear.

"The councilman tells me you saw Tim and Jed Strange leaving here this evening, Hattie. Is that so?"

"Yes, Sheriff, I did see them whilst I was out searching for my cats," Hattie McNear said, her eyes large and watery behind a pair of wire-rimmed spectacles. "One of them was winding a string around his finger."

"I see," said Connally, cutting a glance to the broken stub of cord on the door shade. "Were they in any hurry, Hattie?" Sheriff Connally asked. "Which direction were they headed in?"

"No, they didn't seem to be in a hurry, Sheriff. They rode south. And I never said a word about thinking they might have done something like this." She cut a harsh glance at Councilman Hundley. "I've known those boys since they were babies. They wouldn't do such a thing."

"I know, Hattie," Sheriff Connally said. "But it's my job to ask questions."

Councilman Hundley interjected, saying, "It's your *job* to get on those boys' tail and bring 'em back here. This looks awfully suspicious on their part."

"Quit acting a fool, Councilman," said Sheriff Connally. "They didn't do this, and if they had done it, they'd be riding hell-bent right now. I'd never track them in the dark."

"Well," Hundley huffed, "just what *do* you intend to do, besides have coffee, that is?"

"I've sent somebody to find the telegraph clerk," said Connally. "The first thing we're going to do is send out a wire to the towns south of here. If Tim and Jed were riding south, they weren't headed home. I know those boys wouldn't do Elvin no harm, but I want to hear what they might know about who *did*. Come morning, I'll get on their trail by myself, and see if I can't locate them in a way that won't scare the hair off their heads."

"I think you're making a terrible mistake, Sheriff," said Hundley. "How in the world do you know those two didn't do this!"

"I just know, that's all," Connally said in a firm tone. He turned to the faces pressing closer through the door of the office. "Let me ask you people," he said, raising his voice above their murmurs. "Do any of you believe Tim and Jed Strange killed Elvin, or had something to do with this in any way?"

"No," the voices replied in unison. "Hell no!" one voice trailed behind the rest.

Sheriff Connally turned to Councilman Hundley. "See? We all know these boys, and until something tells me otherwise, I'll not jump down their backs and accuse them of being murderers."

"We'll see about this," Hundley hissed, his face turning beet red. He wheeled around and left, forcing his way through the throng of onlookers. He went straight to the telegraph office, a pencil stub in his hand, already writing down what he intended to say to the authorities in the surrounding communities.

The South Trail, June 15, 1871

Tim and Jed Strange had made good time before dark. They'd stopped at a small mercantile outside St. Joseph, where they knew the price of grain and supplies would be a little less expensive. They'd taken on some hardtack, coffee beans, three pounds of fresh pemmican, and dried red beans. After they'd left with their supplies tightly packed into their saddlebags, they made twelve more miles before darkness seeped in around them. They struck a camp not far from the banks of a river where they grained their gaunt horses and picketed the animals for the night. With a small fire glowing, the boys drank coffee and ate hardtack, being careful to ration themselves for the long unsure road ahead.

Jed lay the battered ten-gauge rabbit gun on

the ground beside him. "Tim," he said, studying the fire and stirring a hickory stick into the small bed of embers, "do you suppose what Mr. Bray said is right, about how the road has a way of changing everybody, teaching them some hard lessons?"

"I don't know," Tim said, attending to his Colt pistol, which he had disassembled on his spread bandanna close to the crackling flames. "All's I know is Pa taught us how to shoot, ride, and rope, and Ma taught us to respect others and read the Good Book. I reckon all a person can do is take these things and go forward with them. That's what Danielle done. We'll have to get her take on the rest of it. Whatever lessons are out there, hard or otherwise, we'll face them as we go. There's no turning back from life. We both know that already." He held up the Colt's cylinder, having cleaned and oiled it, and rolled it back and forth between his palms, looking through it, inspecting each shiny part in the firelight.

Jed, his own Colt already cleaned, inspected, and reassembled, nodded in agreement, and started to speak. But at the sound of one of the bays nickering low in the darkness, he fell silent and stopped stirring the hickory stick in the fire, looking furtively at his brother.

"I hear it," Tim whispered, his hands already working hastily, clicking parts back together on his Colt, then punching cartridges into it. Jed rose into a crouch, picking up the short-barreled rabbit gun, and stepped back out of the firelight, his thumb over the shotgun's

27

hammers, cocking them both at once. They heard the bays nicker softly again, and now heard the sound of footsteps brushing through a stretch of broom sage. Tim shoved the sixth cartridge into his pistol and purposely spun the cylinder loud enough to be heard, then he, too, rose to his feet.

At the sound of Tim spinning the cylinder on his Colt, a voice called out from the darkness, "Hello, the camp!"

Tim Strange let his hand hang down his trouser leg, shielding the pistol from view. He cut a quick glance at Jed standing in the shadows with the shotgun poised, then spoke to the inky night.

"Hello as well," Tim said, taking a step farther to one side, putting distance between him and Jed. "Come forward," he added, his voice calm and friendly, yet his eyes searching the darkness with caution.

A silence passed, then Sep Howard called out, "It don't sound too friendly in there. We just heard you spin one up."

"Yes, you did," said Tim Strange, "but not until we heard you slipping up unannounced."

"Sorry about that," Duncan Grago called out, putting a short, friendly laugh into his voice. "We're new around here, and don't know the ways yet. Are we welcome?" Tim looked at Jed, not certain what to do, for it was only good manners to invite a fellow traveler in. Jed nodded slowly, then Tim called out, "Come on in. We're having some coffee and hardtack."

"Much obliged," Sep Howard said, stepping closer into the outer edge of firelight, Duncan Grago beside him. Watching them, Tim and Jed both could have sworn the two men had slipped their pistols into their holsters just as the light fell upon them. Sep Howard and Duncan Grago could both see that the two young men had not moved back to the campfire.

Duncan Grago spoke. "Hell's bells, who wants to eat a handful of hardtack this close to town?" He paused and looked back and forth at the two shadowy figures of Tim and Jed Strange. "Are you boys scared or what? Come on into the light. We're pilgrims, same as you."

"No, sir, we're not scared," Jed said. He started to step forward, but then the sound of Tim's voice stopped him.

"Stand fast, Jed," said Tim. He kept his attention on the two rough-looking gunmen as he spoke. Eyeing Sep Howard and Duncan Grago up and down, Tim could tell they were not newcomers to the ways of this country. "If hardtack don't suit you, then I reckon you've come to the wrong place."

"Yeah, I reckon," said Duncan Grago, rubbing his chin, leaning forward a bit, trying for a closer look at Tim and Jed. "Tell me, though, is that a new Colt you're holding down your leg?"

"This?" Tim moved the pistol just enough to make it clearly seen. "No, it's just well kept, in case a rattlesnake raises its head. My pa built this Colt for just such a purpose."

29

"Let's go, Dunc," Sep said under his breath. But Duncan would have none of it, not yet. He laughed, speaking to Tim.

"Then I expect your pa must be Samuel Colt, hisself," he said.

"You know what I mean, mister," said Tim. "Colt made it, but my pa turned it custom to fit my hand and work slick as silk."

"Oh! I'd truly like to see it," said Duncan Grago.

"You're fixin' to," Tim said, his tone of voice taking on a cold edge.

Jed joined in, saying, "Yep, and this double barrel as well."

"Let's go, Dunc," Sep Howard whispered again, his voice growing tight and shaky.

Duncan Grago hesitated for a second longer, then sneered, "Keep your sorry hardtack, then. We're leaving." He backed away a step and added sarcastically, "It's getting plumb dangerous out here, all these plow jockeys carry firearms." He chuckled and faded back into the darkness. "We'll be looking for yas, though."

Tim didn't answer, finding it more prudent to ignore the threat than to spark a shooting. He and Jed stood stone-still, listening to the sound of their footsteps move away through the broom sage. Jed faded backward into the darkness himself, circling to their right, where he put a hand on one of the bays' muzzles, settling it. When he found the other bay, he unhobbled both of them, and led them quietly the few yards to the dark edge of the camp. He stood with the horses beside him, the rabbit gun in his hands. After another moment of silence he spoke in a hushed voice.

"Newcomers, my foot. Did you get a look at them two? They've been on these trails longer than the dirt."

"Shhh," Tim said, silencing him. They stood stone-quiet, the night around them still lying in deathlike silence. Then at length Tim spoke in a guarded whisper. "They're still out there. Back the horses into the dark. I'll kill this fire and bring our saddles and gear. This reminds me too much of what happened to our pa."

With Jed leading their horse, and Tim hurrying a few yards behind, wrestling with their saddles and loose sleeping rolls, they stopped at the river's edge long enough to right their gear and sling their saddles up onto the bays. Suddenly, in the darkness from the direction of their abandoned campsite, came the sound of heavy gunfire. They ducked in reflex, but then stood back up watching the muzzle flashes as the two gunmen fired on the campsite in vain. From fifty yards away, Jed and Tim heard one of the gunmen's voices call out to the other, "Stop shooting! They've slipped out on us!" Tim drew the cinch beneath his bay's belly, speaking to Jed.

"I reckon we just learned one of them hard lessons, didn't we?"

"Yeah," Jed replied, "never trust strangers out here. That's a shame too, because people ought not have to live this way."

"Come on," Tim said, still keeping his

31

voice low, "you can preach on the ills of the world once we're farther away from those varmints."

Tracy Sidings, Missouri, June 17, 1871

The town of Tracy Sidings had a temporary look to it, and rightly so. The railroad company had erected the town primarily for their workers, and as a repair station and water stop along the route between St. Joseph and Kansas City. Not far behind the railroad workers came the drinking tents and gambling shacks. Not far behind the shacks came the whores, the traveling minstrels, and the peddlers. Soon, sparse houses sprang up for the wives and children of the railroaders, who demanded more respectable living quarters. Like all such transient towns, the few residents of Tracey Sidings lived with the uncertainty of knowing that any day the railroad might change its operation and leave them all sitting stranded in its dust.

Standing outside a makeshift telegraph office, the town's acting sheriff, Martin Barr, stood watching the two young men ride in across the open plains from the north on gaunt-looking bays. In his left hand he held two telegraphs that arrived on the night of the fifteenth. Without taking his eyes off the approaching riders, he said to the telegraph clerk beside him, "Looks like this might be our killers coming here, Willard. The horses sure fit the description."

"Killers?" said Willard Chapin. "That depends on which telegram you want to believe. The one from Sheriff Connally said he only wants to talk to these boys."

"Yeah," said Martin Barr, "but the one from the councilman says they're looking pretty good for the crime. I'll just follow my hunch and take them into custody."

Martin Barr hadn't been wearing a badge very long and was only doing so now because the railroad had appointed him sheriff until the town could hold a proper election. Arresting a couple of killers was all Barr figured he needed to make a name for himself, dampening anybody's chances at running against him for the position.

"You might want to go along with Sheriff Connally on this thing," said Willard Chapin. "He knows the people around St. Joe better than some councilman. He's saying these are good boys, and that you better not crowd them. They've had lots of grief lately."

"*Boys* is right," said Barr. "They're fifteen years old if the councilman is correct. I don't think they'll be giving me any trouble."

"Still," said Willard, "you'd be wise to take heed."

"Hush, Willard," Barr said over his shoulder, still watching Tim and Jed Strange riding closer. "Get around to Copley's Tavern, and tell some of them night switchmen and hostlers they've just been deputized. Tell them to bring their guns, if they're sober enough to hear you."

Willard Chapin whistled under his breath

and shook his head, but did as Barr asked him. Within minutes there were seven men with liquor on their breath and weapons in their hands. As the whiskey-lit railroaders showed up, Martin Barr had them spread out and take cover along the rutted street, forming a large horseshoe-shaped trap, into which Tim and Jed Strange would have to ride.

"If that's the sheriff up ahead," said Jed Strange, "first thing we better do is tell him about those gunmen night before last." Both of them had seen the group of railroaders appear then disappear, leaving the man with the large shiny badge on his chest facing them as they rode in closer.

"Hold it, Jed," said Tim, "something ain't right here. Don't go no closer." They slowed their horses down to hardly a walk. Something about the determined way the man stood in the street caused Tim to turn his bay sideways to a halt. His brother followed suit.

Jed sidled his horse a few feet away from Tim, letting his hand rest near his Colt. Tim called out loud enough to cover the distance between them and Martin Barr.

"Morning, Sheriff! We're just down from St. Joe." Tim caught a glimpse of a railroader's cap appear above the edge of a rain barrel, and he suddenly grew wary. Across the street, Jed saw a glint of gun metal, and felt his heart quicken a beat. "Is there something wrong here?" Tim asked Barr.

"Come on in closer, boys, we'll talk about it," said Barr.

"Like hell," Jed whispered to his brother, seeing more signs of men in hiding along the boardwalk. "Tim, we're covered over here."

"I know, over here too," said Tim. "Sit tight." He turned his voice back up, calling out to Martin Barr, "Sheriff, we're not looking for any trouble. We're just passing through."

"Nope, not today you're not," said Barr, his right hand on his pistol butt. "We got a wire from Sheriff Connally in St. Joe night before last. He said to take you two into custody till he gets here. Now ride in here slow-like, raise those pistols with two fingers, and let them fall."

But the twins only cast one another a glance before Tim spoke again to Barr. "What for, Sheriff? We haven't broken any law that we know of."

"Then you better be advised that *murder* is breaking a law. Ride in closer and drop those pistols, right now. I'm not asking again."

"Murder?" Tim gave Jed a bewildered glance. "What's he talking about?"

The lump in Jed's throat kept him from responding right away. When he did manage to speak, his voice wavered. "These men are fixin' to shoot us, Tim. What're we going to do?" As he spoke, the first of the railroaders rose up from behind a stack of nail kegs, the barrel of his rifle starting to swing toward them.

"We're going to shoot them back," Tim said, seeing no room for plea or reasoning. He spun his big bay in a fast, full circle, the Colt

35

in his hand out at arm's length, then fired, the sound exploding hard along the narrow street. The railroader's head snapped back as if it were on a spring hinge. Blood flew. Tim's horse reared as a rifle shot whistled past its ear. As it touched down, Tim's Colt exploded again. Another railroader fell screaming as Tim's bullet tore through the man's shoulder in an explosion of crimson and white cotton coat lining.

"Wait, damn it! Stop!" Martin Barr shouted amid the roar of gunfire, seeing too late that he'd stepped on the wrong cats' tails. But the fight had commenced and there was no stopping now. Jed had sailed from his saddle into the street, a bullet striping up the length of his forearm. His horse bolted away as he rolled to his knee, firing shot after shot in rapid succession. Dust swirled high beneath Tim's bay as he swung it back and forth, taking his shot at one side of the wide street, then the other. But when a load of buckshot kicked dirt high near the bay's hooves, Tim, rather than risk harm to the animal, flung himself from his saddle and slapped the big bay's rump.

Tim's pistol never missed a beat until it clicked on an empty chamber. He worked quickly, reloading while Jed covered him. A bullet grazed Tim's thigh, spilling a streak of blood down his leg.

Two more railroaders had fallen, one as he ran from cover along the boardwalk and was hammered by a bullet in his ribs, another as he jumped out with a loud curse and raised a shotgun toward the twins in a drunken rage.

36

"Damn it to hell! Cease! Stop firing," Barr screamed. Then he made the mistake of running toward the twins with his pistol waving in the air. Tim, unable to hear through the gunfire, mistook Barr's action and stopped him short, putting a slug through his chest.

As suddenly as it had started, the fighting stopped. Tim and Jed were each propped up on one knee, back to back in the middle of the street beneath a lingering halo of burnt powder and dust. "My gawd!" shouted one of the three remaining railroaders, "They've kilt Martin Barr!"

Tim punched out his spent cartridges and shoved new ones into their place, saying over his shoulder, "Jed, are you all right?"

"I'm shot, but not that bad," Jed replied, his voice straining against the pain along his bloody forearm. "What about you?"

"Same here," Tim said. "Let's back away to some cover while they figure out what went wrong."

Chapter 2

Tim and Jed Strange slowly moved away from the center of the street. Tim was limping from the bullet in his thigh. Jed helped him as much as possible, although the bullet that had torn up his own left forearm left him weak and nauseous. With the burnt gunpowder smoke adrift around them, the twins retreated like wounded wolf pups, bloodied but still game. The two frightened bays had backed off twenty yards and milled about in the street. Onlookers had come forward cautiously, making the horses more nervous, until Jed whistled to them. At the familiar sound, the bays ventured over to them at a trot, snorting and nickering under their breath.

"Easy, horse," Jed whispered, helping to support Tim and at the same keeping an eye on the stunned railroad workers, making sure they hadn't yet gotten over their shock and begun to retaliate. On the boardwalk across the street, more men had come running to see the aftermath of the gunfight now that the firing had stopped. One of the three railroaders lifted his head up enough to look from the bodies on the ground over to Tim and Jed, huddled against their horses.

"There they are!" the stunned railroader shouted. "They're getting away!"

Jed struggled, trying to shove his wounded brother up into the saddle. "Help me, Tim, pull up!" he pleaded. But Tim couldn't swing his bleeding leg over the saddle, and together, spent, they both crumbled to the ground. "If they come at us now, we're done for," Jed said in a trembling voice.

But as the railroaders drew together for courage and stalked forward, the sound of a fast-moving horse resounded from north of town. Two pistol shots suddenly sounded. Jed almost turned Tim loose to return fire. But then as the men came closer, Jed and Tim saw them stop abruptly and raise their hands up chest-high. Sheriff Connally slid his big brown paint horse down onto its haunches and slipped from his saddle before the animal righted itself. His pistol covered the men in the street as he spoke.

"I'll shoot the next man that takes a step!" the sheriff bellowed. He gave a sidelong glance to the twins. "Tim? Jed? Are you boys all right?" Neither of them answered, but seeing them both still alive was enough for Connally. He shifted his gaze back to the men in front of him. "You drunken bunch of bastards," he raged, looking into the bloodshot eyes. "For two cents I'd haul back and let them kill the lot of yas!"

"We're deputies!" one railroader offered, pointing at Martin Barr's body in the street. "He deputized us! They kilt him! So don't jump on us! What about them? They're murderers, he said."

"He ain't saying nothing now, though, is he, you gandy-dancing, bo-shanked bunch of peckerwoods!" The railroaders backed off, but not before Connally forced himself through the throng toward the one doing the talking, and swiped a hard blow across his forehead with his pistol barrel. The railroader went down, a thick hand clutched to his forehead. "Get him up and out of my sight!" Sheriff Connally commanded.

The other men reached down, grabbed their dazed friend by his shoulders, and pulled him back. "What about them two, Sheriff?" one man ventured. "They *did* kill Martin Barr."

"As stupid as he was, somebody *had* to kill him," Connally shouted. "I just wish it was his mother on the day he was born! Now git, all of yas, before I cut loose."

The men moved farther away, one of them grumbling aloud, "You've got no jurisdiction here."

"What?" Connally shouted. "*Jurisdiction,* you say?" A shot from his pistol kicked up dirt at their boots. They scurried back like frightened rats until the lot of them stood behind the protection of an abandoned buckboard wagon.

Sheriff Connally hurried over to the twins. "Take it easy, boys," he said, seeing the cocked Colt still in Tim's hand. "This is all a mistake." He moved in and looped Tim's arm over his shoulder, pistol and all. "Let's get him off the street. He's bleeding like a stuck hog."

Willard Chapin hurried in as Jed and Sheriff Connally helped Tim along the dirt street, the two bays following behind them. One of the horses raised its head toward Chapin's buckboard wagon and let out a threatening nicker. "I'm not with them," Willard Chapin said, seeing the cold fury in Sheriff Connally's steel gray eyes. "How can I help?"

"Is there a doctor in this mud-sucking hole?" Connally hissed. "This boy don't know it but he's about to bleed out on us."

"Follow me," said Willard Chapin, ignoring Sheriff Connally's insult. "We'll take him to

Doc Eisenhower's, if Doc ain't already headed out to help those wounded men back there."

"To hell with their wounds! Let 'em pour whiskey on them. These boys have been unjustly bushwhacked, far as I'm concerned."

Propped up between Sheriff Connally and Jed Strange, Tim's head started to droop from loss of blood. Yet he still tried to ask Connally, "What was...they talking about... murder?"

"Shut up, Tim," Sheriff Connally said, still coiled tight in his rage and unable to shed it. "I'm here to straighten things out."

In an upstairs office above a rickety saddle shop, the white-haired doctor stood up from dressing Tim's wound and sighed, shaking his head. Tim faded in and out of consciousness from loss of blood and the short dose of laudanum he'd taken. "You boys are down to feathers and bones, the both of you," the doctor said, turning his tired eyes to Jed Strange. "I'm afraid to give him any more for pain, least it kill him."

"It...don't hurt none...Doctor," Tim managed to say in a weak voice.

"Hell, it never does," Doc Eisenhower said in a gruff, wizened tone. "That's why everybody enjoys getting shot, I reckon." He turned back to Jed Strange, asking, "What have you boys been eating lately? His blood's thinner than mountain air."

"We've been doing all right," Jed responded, his face flushing red with stung pride.

41

"Yes, I can see that." Doc Eisenhower looked at Willard Chapin and said in a blunt tone, "Willard, step yourself over to Gertie's, and tell her I said to cook up a mess of calf liver about half raw. This boy needs something pumping in his veins real quick." He jerked a nod at the bandage he'd placed on Jed's arm while waiting for Tim's wound to congeal, adding, "Tell her to fix double helpings. This one's wounded too, and paler than Cull's mustache."

"I ain't hungry," Jed lied grudgingly as Willard Chapin headed for Gertie's boardinghouse.

"Of course you're not, but indulge me," the white-haired doctor said to Jed Strange. The room was hot, and thick with the metallic stench of drying blood. Doc Eisenhower wiped his hands on a blood-soaked towel, then pitched it on a pile in a corner. "Now then, Sheriff, if you'll permit me, I'll go attend those railroaders, if they ain't gotten drunk and forgot all about it."

"Thanks, Doctor," Sheriff Connally said, rising from his spot against the wall.

"Don't thank me, just pay me," Doc Eisenhower quipped with a faint grin. Rolling down his shirtsleeves and picking up his black bag from his desk, he left the office and walked down the squeaking stairs. On the surgery table, Tim raised his head with much effort and looked down the length of his torn trousers, and at the bandage wrapped around his thigh. "My only...pair of jeans, gone," he offered.

"Don't worry, they still make trousers,"

Sheriff Connally said. "The main thing is you're both alive. I knew full well that you boys had nothing to do with Elvin Bray's murder."

While the doctor had attended the wounded twins, Sheriff Connally had filled them in on what had happened in St. Joseph. Tim shook his exhausted head and let himself slump back down on the table. "I swear...we must've been talking to Bray...shortly before he died. It don't seem right, a good man like him... stabbed to death."

"Don't talk right now, Tim," the sheriff said, resting a hand on Tim Strange's shoulder. "Let your brother tell me." He turned to Jed Strange. "Was there anybody else around when you left the office?"

"No, Sheriff, not that we noticed anyway." His mind went to the two men they'd encountered later that night. "We had some unwelcome company on the river trail. They might have been coming from the same direction. They were definitely the types who might do that sort of thing. They sure tried to kill us. I think they might have been following us."

Connally knew Jed was telling the truth, for he had seen the tracks of two other riders on his way to Tracy Sidings. "All right, tell me all about them," Sheriff Connally said. "But start back, to where you two first rode into St. Joe. Tell me everything—where you were headed, and why. Don't leave anything out. I know you're both innocent, but it's important that I hear everything, in case somebody else tries accusing you."

43

Sheriff Connally listened as Jed told him everything, from the time after their mother's funeral right up to when they'd ridden into Martin Barr's ill-fated trap. Connally looked at both of them as Jed spoke, and couldn't help but feel sorrow for them. They were too young to have had so much go wrong for them, yet they carried it well, he thought. They were just two kids who should still be in school, but were instead sitting here hungry, whip-handle thin, and nursing wounds that were cast upon them for no good reason.

Sheriff Connally sat silent for a long moment after Jed had finished talking. Finally when he spoke, he did so with a wince and a sigh, his eyes cast down at the wooden floor. "Boys," he said, unable to face either of them, "it seems like you two have been handed a raw deal ever since your pa's death."

"His murder, you mean," Jed cut in.

"Well, yes, his murder," said the sheriff. "I know it's been rough on both of you, what with your sister gone and your ma turning sick and dying. I know you've been living on a lick and a promise—"

"We...ain't complaining," Tim offered in a weak voice.

"I know you ain't," Connally said, "but I reckon I *am* on your behalf. Now, I know you ain't going to like hearing this, but I need for you to stay here for a day or two, just till I get this thing ironed out for you. Most likely a circuit judge will want to hear what you've got to say. After that I promise you'll be free to go."

"Free to go?" asked Jed. "You mean you'll be holding us in custody? Why? You know we didn't kill Elvin Bray."

"Because that's just the way the law works, Jed," Connally said. "I don't like the thought of detaining you any more than you do, although to be honest, you'd be better off never stepping foot into the Territory. But the fact is, you can both use some food and rest, and so could your horses. I saw how poorly they look. Holding you here is the best thing that could happen to you, if you'll look at it in the right light."

"Sheriff Connally," Tim said, raising his head slightly, "you have always been...a man we trust. But...we've got to find our sister...and the men who killed Pa. You'd do the same...if it was you."

"I know, boys. You needn't convince me. If it weren't for my responsibilities in St. Joe, I'd be seriously considering riding with you. But back to right here and now. Look, boys, I'm trying to ask you as a favor...to stay here, help me get this thing settled. You want to help see Elvin's killers brought to justice, don't you?"

"You know we do," said Jed Strange.

"All right, then. Will you do this for me?" Sheriff Connally looked back and forth between them.

A silence passed as the twins looked at one another. Then Tim said from his surgery table, "All right, Sheriff Connally, we'll do what you say...but then we're headed to Indian Territory." Tim relaxed back down, then asked, "Sheriff...how did you feel the first time you...killed a man?"

"I felt terrible, Tim, the same as you're feeling right now. But like you, it was forced on me." Something passed over Connally's eyes for a second. "To tell the truth, if I could go back and change it, I'd as soon it be me that laid dead in the street that day." He took a long breath, then let it out with resolve. "But that's what was dealt me, and that's what I done with it. Try not to think about it. That's all I can tell you."

"I—I didn't kill anybody out there, did I?" Jed asked.

"No, but you shot the hell out of a couple, according to Willard. The only one dead is Martin Barr. That's no big loss. The stupid bastard would've walked off a cliff sooner or later, I reckon. Don't worry about the charges, though. Willard Chapin saw it all. Said Barr started the whole thing. The railroaders fired first. If they had a real sheriff here, he'd be charging *them* with assault. Don't worry about it. The ground is full of fools and want-to-be's. Martin Barr was just shining his play badge on the wrong corner."

"Did you know him well?" Jed asked.

"As well as I cared to," said Connally. "He spent the first half of life on the wrong side of the law. The second half I reckon he wanted to spend upholding it. They say he rode with Coleman Younger and his brothers for a while after the war."

"The Younger gang? The James boys?" Jed appeared stunned by the revelation.

"Yep, so rumor has it." He turned his gaze to Tim. "I reckon if there's any truth to it, you can rightly say you dusted down one of the original Boys."*

"I don't want to...say nothing about it. Period," said Tim, his voice a bit stronger now. "To tell you the truth, I feel sick thinking about it."

"That's a good sign, young man," Connally said. "I'd be worried for your immortal soul if I thought you felt otherwise."

Willard Chapin returned with a large platterful of well-done steak and red, rare calf beef liver, covered by a grease and bloodstained white cloth. "Gertie said she holds no responsibility for the rare liver. I told her it was Doc's orders to serve it that way."

"What's the word on the street?" Sheriff Connally asked, ignoring Willard's remarks.

"Just what you'd expect," said Willard. "The railroaders are gathering at Copley's Tavern, cussing, talking about hanging. Saying, how the hell do these boys get steak served to 'em, right after shooting the blazes out of Martin Barr and the night crew."

Connally nodded, thinking things over. "Have they built a jail here yet?"

"Yep. Halfway up the block, a brand-new three-cell beauty, as Barr called it. Why? You can't arrest those men. You've got no jurisdiction..." His words trailed, remembering how

* *"The Boys" was a name commonly given to the original members of the James-Younger Gang.*

47

Connally had reacted to that same statement earlier.

"I'm not planning on arresting anybody," replied Connally. "I need a safe place for these two to hole up and heal till they're well enough to ride."

"Well, it's probably the safest place in this town for them, and you too," Willard said. "Barr had the key in his pocket. I'll go by the barbershop and get it for you—the barber here being our undertaker as well. The night workers will soon go off to their shacks. But it's the ones coming in tonight you'll need to worry about. There's a lot more of them."

"I figured as much," said Sheriff Connally. He looked at the faces of Jed and Tim Strange, and saw the concern in their eyes. "Don't worry, boys, we'll be all right here."

Ordinarily, Duncan Grago would have ridden wide of any nearby town after what he and Sep Howard had done in St. Joseph, but this was different. They'd come upon the hoofprints of Tim and Jed Strange's bay horses near the river where the twins had given them the slip, and had been trailing them ever since. When the two outlaws had heard shooting, they pulled off the trail and took cover in a dry creek bed. From there, they'd seen Sheriff Connally ride toward Tracy Sidings like a bat out of hell as the sound of gunfire continued unabated. After an hour of silence had passed and no more shots were heard, Duncan Grago spoke with a grin.

"I can't resist seeing what happened to those two pumpkin busters, can you?"

Sep Howard was hesitant. He said, "Dunc, your brother Newt is awfully anxious for us to get back down to the Territory. We're supposed to meet Julius Byler on the way. He's waiting on us outside of Fort Smith."

"We've got time," said Duncan. With no more word on it, he jabbed his horse up from the creek bed and urged it on toward Tracy Sidings. Coming into town along an alley that passed by the town dump, the two outlaws rode toward the sound of angry cursing coming from a run-down tavern off the main street. Out front of Copley's Tavern, they reined their horses loosely for a quick getaway if needed, then slipped inside among the gathered railroad workers. As they ordered two beers and a bottle of rye whiskey, a railroader with a pistol barrel welt on his forehead noticed them and fanned three of his fellow railroaders aside.

"What have we got here?" he asked, scowling at Duncan Grago and Sep Howard. "More strangers riding in on us?"

As the others turned to the two outlaws, Duncan Grago lowered his beer mug toward the drunken workers. "Whoa, boys. We heard the shooting from a mile off and just came to investigate." He jerked his thumb toward Sep Howard. "This here is Al Townsend, I'm Earl Jones. We've been tracking a bunch of cattle rustlers all the way from the other side of St. Joseph. Two of them split off from the

49

others and headed this way over three weeks ago. The two we're after are look-alikes, riding a couple of underfed bays."

"Tarnation, that's them!" one of the railroaders exclaimed. The drunken men all looked at one another, then the one with the blue welt on his forehead stepped forward.

"What are you, stock detectives or bounty hunters?"

Duncan Grago shrugged and sipped his beer. "We're a little bit of both, you could say. But that's not important. What was all the shooting about here?"

"I'm Denton Perkins. A couple of wanted killers rode in here a while ago, shot our sheriff down like a dog, and wounded some of the men trying to help him uphold the law. Now the sheriff from St. Joe is protecting them—feeding them steak and biscuits, if you can believe that!"

Duncan Grago shook his head in disgust and said, "I can believe just about anything when it comes to that sheriff in St. Joe. Most detectives like us don't even bother asking his help anymore, for we know we won't get it. But he is a lawman, so what can you do about it?"

Denton Perkins gritted his teeth, running his fingertips across the bruise on his forehead. "You just watch, mister, you'll see what we can do about it!" he said to Duncan Grago. "When the law don't work for decent folks, it's time to get rid of the law! Am I right, men?"

"Damn right!" one of the railroaders shouted. Beer mugs tipped in agreement.

Denton Perkins swiped a hand across the bar, snatching up a half-full whiskey bottle. He threw back a long swig, and when he caught his breath, he banged a fist down on the wet bar top with a look of solemn finality. "Get a rope," he growled at the others.

In a wake of shuffling boot leather and drunken threats, the railroaders spilled from the dirty tavern, busting the plank door off its hinges on their way. At the bar, Duncan Grago turned to Sep Howard and laughed under his breath. "See? Wasn't this worth stopping for?" He raised his beer mug as if giving a toast and added, "I say anytime you can take a few minutes and get some poor bastard hung, it's always worth doing."

"Damn," Sep Howard whispered almost to himself, "and them boys are innocent."

Duncan Grago turned to him incredulously and said, "*Innocent?* Innocent of what?" He cut a sharp glance to Sep Howard. "The last innocent man on this earth was Jesus. You heard what he got for his effort. I ain't worried about innocent men getting hung. It's when they hang the guilty that troubles me."

Chapter 3

Sheriff Connally heard the large rock slam into the door of the doctor's office. He stood up and walked to the small window overlooking the narrow dirt street. "They're quicker than I thought they would be," he said over his shoulder to the twins, Willard Chapin, and Doc Eisenhower, who had returned from tending the wounded railroad workers in the lobby of a small hotel. "Willard, are you sure the horses are safely tucked away out of sight?"

"Yes, Sheriff," Willard replied, moving over to the window beside him to peer down at the angry mob. "I stabled them at the old express station. Nobody uses it anymore."

"How far it is from the jail?" Connally asked.

"Less than two blocks," Willard replied. "But don't worry—when you need them, I'll go fetch them for you and take them around back."

"Much obliged, Willard," said Connally, "but you've done plenty already. You have to live with these folks after it's over."

Another rock hit the door, then Denton Perkins's voice shouted in a drunken rage, "Come on out, Sheriff! Hand them killers over to us!"

Instead of opening the door, Sheriff Connally raised the window a little more and called down to them, "These boys are not charged with anything, and they won't be. You're making a big mistake here. The next rock that hits this door is going to cost somebody their fingers!"

On the street, one of the railroaders holding a rock at his side let it drop to the ground. Denton Perkins saw him and raged at him, "Pick that up, Wilson, you coward! We're not backing off till we've finished this!" He looked around at the other men behind him, and shook the rope on his shoulder. "That goes for *all* of yas! We'll burn them out if we have to!"

"This is insane," Doc Eisenhower said, hearing Denton Perkins shout at the others. "Let me see if I can talk sense to these men."

"Don't go out there, Doc," Connally cautioned him. But Doc Eisenhower wouldn't listen to him.

"I know all of these men, Sheriff, and I'm getting tired of dressing their bullet wounds." He moved quickly to the door and swung it open before Sheriff Connally could stop him. He looked down at the drunken, angry faces from the second-floor landing, then said to all of them, "You best watch your mouth, boys. Torch this building, and I'll leave here and never look back! Then who'll you go limping off to next time you crack your ankle with a bull hammer?"

"Stay out of this, Doc!" Denton Perkins warned him. "Those boys are outlaws! Two stock detectives just identified them over at the tavern. They been on their trail the past month, ever since their gang split up! We're taking 'em to a pole and stringing 'em up!"

As Doc Eisenhower and the railroaders shouted back and forth, Sheriff Connally looked back over his shoulder at Willard Chapin and asked, "What's he talking about? These boys never left the farm except to hire out a day's work when they were lucky."

Willard replied, "I have no idea, but there was two strangers headed into the tavern when I came by there."

"Well, hell." Connally sighed. "There's no telling who that is. Could be the bushwhackers these boys ran into coming here."

"It don't matter who it is," Jed Strange said, pushing himself up from his chair with his good hand, his bullet-creased arm in a sling. He walked over to Sheriff Connally and Willard Chapin by the window. "This is mine and Tim's fight, Sheriff. Just let us go down there."

"That's right," said Tim, trying to swing his wounded leg over the edge of the table, "you've done all you can for us."

"Both of yas, hush," said Sheriff Connally. "Stay back from the window, Jed. I didn't ride all this way just to see you both hang!"

On the landing, Doc Eisenhower had been arguing with the railroaders when his voice stopped short in a grunt as a rock skipped off his head and bounced through the open door. "Damn it all!" he shouted, staggering back inside with his hand raised to a bloody gash. "That's it! I'll shoot them myself, the drunken bunch of gandy dancers!"

"Hold on, Doc," Sheriff Connally said, seeing Doc Eisenhower reach for Jed and Tim's rabbit gun, which Willard Chapin had brought in from the express stables. "Take care of your head. I'll handle this bunch."

"Not by yourself you won't," said Jed, snatching the rabbit gun from the doctor with

54

his good hand. "Not as long as I can swing a load of buckshot."

"No, Jed, trust me on this," Sheriff Connally said, reaching out for the shotgun. "Seeing you armed will only make them madder. This ain't the first time I've had to handle a bunch of drunks. They're whiskey-brave right now, but it won't last."

Reluctantly, Jed turned the shotgun loose when Sheriff Connally closed his hand down over the front stock. "That's good, Jed," Connally offered in a quiet tone. "Now if you'll let me borrow this for about five minutes, we'll all feel a little better."

"Careful down there, Sheriff," Doc Eisenhower warned.

"Is there another way out of here?" Connally asked, checking the action of the short-barreled rifle as he spoke.

"Yep, there's a set of stairs leading down to Pelcher's saddle shop," said Doc Eisenhower. "The shop's closed till Pelcher gets back from Arkansas. There's also a back door out to the alley."

"Good deal," said Connally. "Suppose the two of you can get Tim over to the jail, while I turkey these railroaders down?"

Doc Eisenhower looked Tim Strange up and down, and replied to Connally, "Well, moving him this soon is gonna start that leg bleeding again, but I reckon we're down to slim choices." He looked at Willard Chapin. "You up for it?"

"I'm game," said Chapin.

55

"All right then," Connally said, swinging the rabbit gun under his arm, then lifting his Colt from his holster. "Count to fifty once I step out the door, then make your move."

"But, Sheriff," said Jed Strange, "I can't let you do this—"

"Jed," Connally said stiffly, cutting him off, "it's been years since anybody's *let* me do a damn thing. You can best help by doing like I say. Get ready now, all of yas."

When Sheriff Connally stepped out on the landing, the railroaders greeted him with loud jeers. A rock thumped against the side of the clapboard building then fell at the sheriff's boots. Slowly, Connally looked down at the rock, the butt of the rabbit gun propped against his hip, the Colt in his right hand still hanging down his thigh. The crowd grew quiet for a second, seeing his slow, calm manner as he looked out at them and spoke.

"Count your fingers, boys. What I said about rock throwing still goes." Connally stepped down, one slow step at a time, his calm aura seeming to give the men pause. But as he stepped off the bottom stair, the nine or ten railroaders drew closer together like cautious wolves. Denton Perkins crouched a bit and began slapping the coiled rope on the dusty ground, a noose now tied in the end of it.

"Come on, Sheriff, just try to stop us," he said, the slapping rope raising a low stir of dust. "There's only one of you. You've overplayed your hand."

"I'm sorry to hear you say that, mister,"

Connally said, raising the Colt, eyeing down the barrel at Denton Perkins's leg, "because I know you came all this way to work and make wages. I figure a busted kneecap's gonna lay you up at least six weeks, provided there's no infection. You can spend the rest of your life telling everybody why you limp."

"You won't do it," Denton Perkins sneered. "Those stock detectives told us the color of your stool." He slapped the coiled rope harder and faster on the ground, the sound of it seeming to turn the rest of the men bolder. They all inched forward behind Perkins.

The sheriff's Colt cocked beneath his thumb. "Slap that rope one more time, and it's done, you ignorant peckerwood," Connally hissed through clenched teeth. The conviction in his words caused Perkins's coiled rope to stop midswing, but Perkins hadn't backed down altogether yet.

"Sheriff, we all move at once, we'll plow right over you," Perkins said with a sneer.

"Some of you might," Connally said, pulling back both hammers on the rabbit gun, "but most of you won't feel nothing but a hot blast." He honed back into Perkins's eyes. "Then you won't have to explain the limp. I'll kill you graveyard dead. That's the sum of it." As Sheriff Connally spoke, he made his advance, pressing closer, so close to Denton Perkins that the man had to inch back lest the barrel of the rabbit gun poke him beneath his chin. With Perkins backing up, the men behind him had no choice but to back up too. Those who didn't had to spread to the side, Connally moving into their midst, his eyes and guns fanning back and forth slowly.

Connally saw that second when the whiskey alone wasn't enough to sustain them. The men wanted to turn and run now, he could sense it. Yet there was one more thing he needed to bring it about, and Denton Perkins opened his mouth and gave it to him.

"We ain't going to be—"

Before Perkins could get the words out, Connally dropped low almost to his knees, swinging the Colt a full fast circle and slamming the barrel upward into the big man's crotch. Perkins buckled forward, his arms wrapping around his lower belly. He hung there as if suspended, a long string of saliva swinging from his wide open mouth. The onlookers groaned with him. A couple of them cried out as Connally's pistol whipped around in another hard fast circle and the butt of it crashed down hard on Perkins's thick neck. The force of the blow lifted Connally up onto this tiptoes.

"Lord—God!" a thin man in striped bib overalls yelled. "Don't kill him!"

"Do something, Roberts!" a voice from the crowd called out to the thin man.

Connally stalked toward him now, the rest of the men's spirits breaking fast as they hurried away quarter-wise, still staring back. Connally reached out with his boot and kicked the coiled rope forward. Roberts jumped from it as though it were a snake. "Go on, *Roberts*!"

58

Connally shouted. "Pick it up! This man's down, now you take the lead!"

Roberts broke backward in a run, a startled look on his face. "Sheriff, you can't do this! We're just hardworking—"

His words were cut short as well, a blast from Connally's pistol throwing dirt up against his shins. "Who's gonna take the lead now?" Connally bellowed at the dispersed men. "Come on, somebody pick it up!" He stood for a moment in the echo of his words, his eyes moving from one man to the next as they cowered back a safe distance. "All right, I'll take it myself!" Connally jammed the pistol down into his holster, snatched up the coiled rope, and stepped back to where Denton Perkins lay heaving on his face, his buttocks still raised in the air, his arms still tight across his belly.

"You've...ruint me," Perkins groaned, strained and breathless.

"Not yet, I ain't," said Connally. He dropped the noose over the big man's neck and jerked up, making Perkins raise stiffly to his knees. "Now we're gonna see who your friends really are." He jerked more, forcing Perkins to his feet. "He's going with me," Connally announced to the rest of the men. "You want to see a hanging? Just come give me some guff. I'll swing him off a chair from a jailhouse rafter."

The men only watched, their mouths agape, as Sheriff Connally shoved Perkins forward ahead of him. Perkins staggered in the dirt, his waist still badly bent, his boots dragging and having a hard time staying straight. Perkins heaved up a spray of sour whiskey as they moved in the direction of the new jail.

"My goodness," Doc Eisenhower exclaimed, taking Denton Perkins by his bowed-over shoulder and helping him through the door, "you've nearly nutted this man."

"He's all right," said Sheriff Connally, shoving Perkins forward until the man slammed against a desk and fell into a ball on the plank floor. "He's lucky I didn't kill him." Connally bent slightly, placing a boot down on Perkins's shoulders and yanking the noose enough to make Perkins face him. "Anybody rushes this jail, and I'll take it out on your hide. Because *they* know, *you* know, and *I* know that I will hang you dead. Are we clear on that?"

"I—I didn't do...nothing but try to...see justice done."

"I'll see to it that they carve that on your marker," said Sheriff Connally. "Now, tell me about these two so-called stock detectives. What did they look like? What are they riding?"

"I paid no attention to what they're riding," Denton Perkins said in a strained voice. "They said their names were Al Townsend and Earl Jones. Jones was the one doing the talking. He's young, with rusty yellow hair. Wears his hair and sideburns bristly short, almost shaved. He sports a leather Mexican vest, and a brown beat-up Stetson." Perkins stopped and gulped a

60

breath of air, then continued, his arms still clutched across his belly. "The other is older, heavyset and unkempt. Wears a big drooping gray mustache and a black-and-white checkered shirt. His hat's too far gone to describe."

Willard Chapin cut in, saying, "I looked over at the hitch rail outside of Copley's Tavern on our way over here, Sheriff. Those two horses are gone. One was a line-back dun, the other was a roan with three white stockings."

"Thanks, Willard," said Sheriff Connally. He turned his eyes to Jed Strange standing inside the open cell door, and asked, "Does that sound like the men you ran into?"

"Yep," said Jed, "that's them all right. We didn't see their horses." Jed shot Denton Perkins a glare of contempt, saying, "You took their word that we're outlaws. Mister, my brother and me have gone hungry the past year when it would be easy to walk in somewhere with guns and take what we wanted. I hope you're *damn* proud of yourself."

"Easy, Jed," Sheriff Connally said, seeing the rage in the young man's eyes. "He's only one more fool in a world full of many." Connally straightened up and turned to Dr. Eisenhower, asking, "How's Tim's leg, Doc?"

"It's bleeding again, like I was afraid it would," Doc said, nodding toward the open door of the cell where Tim lay on a bunk. Jed and Willard Chapin stood beside him. "The bullet nicked an artery. I put a stitch down deep in it. I'm going to let it alone for a few more minutes. If it don't stop, I'll cauterize it." He sighed, then added, "My fear is that when the day workers come in off the road, they'll liquor up and start things all over again. If they do, it'll be hard to stop them." He nodded at Tim Strange. "And that boy has no business on a horse, making a run for it."

"Damn it," Connally said under his breath. He looked all around at the small office, the three cells, and the door on the back wall. "Get his leg fixed up the best you can for traveling, Doc. Having Perkins here will buy us some time. I'll hold up this bunch as long as I can, but this evening me and these boys are going to *have* to clear out of here. Once they're safe back in St. Joe, I want to catch up to Townsend and Jones real bad. I'm getting a hunch they're the ones who robbed and killed Elvin Bray."

As the sheriff spoke to Doc Eisenhower, Tim listened from the bunk in the cell. He looked down at his ripped trouser leg and at the blood-soaked bandage around his thigh. Then he looked up at Jed and caught his eyes for a second, just long enough for something to pass between them. Jed Strange got the message his twin was sending him. He eased closer to the rabbit gun, which sat leaning against the wall. Then he stopped and stood near it. Without bringing attention to himself, Jed picked the rabbit gun up and cradled it in the crook of his good arm.

In the midafternoon, Doc Eisenhower stood back from checking on Tim's leg wound and let a sigh of relief. "Well, the bleeding's stopped. I'm going to have to get over to the hotel lobby and check on them wounded rail-roaders." He turned to Sheriff Connally and said, "The day crews will start straggling in anytime now. Keep a close eye toward the tavern."

"I will, Doc," said Sheriff Connally, "and thanks for all your help."

"Oh, I'll be back in a little while, Sheriff. I want one more look at that leg before you put this boy on a saddle." Doc Eisenhower rolled down his shirtsleeves, gathered up his black bag, and headed for the front door. "What about me, Doc?" Perkins, who was still lying with the rope around his thick neck, pleaded from the floor, "I'm sicker than a dog. My guts ache something awful, the back of my neck too."

"Oh, really? I hate to hear that, Perkins," Doc Eisenhower said. Then without another word to him, Doc turned and left.

Sheriff Connally chuckled under his breath.

"I'm afraid I must also leave for a while also, Sheriff," said Willard Chapin. "I need to check for any incoming messages. But I'll be back too."

"How about bringing us some more grub, Willard?" Sheriff Connally asked. "You've been so obliging, I hate to ask."

"Not at all, Sheriff, I'll be happy to bring back some food from Gertie's." Willard put on his bowler hat and left. Watching first the doctor, then the telegraph clerk leaving, Jed Strange slipped another guarded look at his twin brother, then moved closer to the desk where Tim's gun belt lay in a coiled pile, the butt of his Colt standing against it in its holster.

When Sheriff Connally saw a road wagon full of sweaty workers roll past the window, he reached down, pulled Perkins to his feet, and shoved him toward one of the empty cells. "In you go," he said to the groaning man. "Looks like some of the workers are headed for the tavern." He locked the door to the cell, shoved the key down deep into his pocket, and took a rifle from the rack along the wall. As he loaded it, he said to Jed Strange, "Keep an eye on your brother for me. I'm going to sit on the porch with a rifle across my lap for a while, just to make a show of force for them."

Jed Strange only nodded without answering, but from his cell, Denton Perkins whined, "Sheriff, you're not leaving me alone with these two, are you?"

"Shut up, Perkins. I've heard enough of your mouth to last me a lifetime," Connally hissed, swinging his hat onto his head and a rifle under his arm.

As soon as Sheriff Connally was out on the porch and seated in a low wooden chair, Jed Strange stepped wordlessly into the open cell and handed Tim Strange the rabbit gun. "Hey, what are you fixin' to do?" Perkins asked, his eyes going wide.

Jed stepped over to Perkins's cell. "Open your mouth again, and he'll empty both barrels into your maw."

Perkins cowered back from the bars and watched Jed Strange slip out through the rear door, silently closing it behind him. After a few tense moments had passed, Perkins watched Jed Strange slip back inside and walk hurriedly to the open cell where Tim Strange was already struggling to get up from the bunk. Jed looped his twin brother's arm across his shoulder and helped him toward the rear door, stopping at Perkins's cell long enough to prop Tim against the bars and say to Perkins, "Come here, you."

Perkins came to the bars, ready to plead for his life, but before he got a word out, Jed reached through the bars, grabbed him by his hair, and yanked his head forward. Perkins's forehead struck the iron bars with a dull thud, and as Jed turned him loose, the big railroader slumped to the floor, half conscious. "Come on, Tim," Jed whispered, holding his brother's arm over his shoulder, "the bays are right out back."

Chapter 4

A few railroad workers had begun to gather out front of Copley's Tavern. They stood with beer mugs in their hands and looked over at Sheriff Connally on the porch of the new jail, a block away. Willard Chapin had to hurry past a barrage of taunts and threats as he carried the large wooden tray of food and coffee from Gertie's restaurant. He stepped up onto the porch of the jail and, looking a bit frightened, said to Sheriff Connally, "They're getting started early on their drinking. I'll get a shotgun and make a stand with you, Sheriff."

"No, but thanks anyway, Willard," said Sheriff Connally, standing up and opening the door for him. "If it gets too bad, I don't want your blood on my hands. This is the work I chose. If it ends here, then so be it."

"Oh no!" Willard exclaimed once he was inside, looking around for the twins and seeing they were gone.

"Well, I'll be," Connally said in a hushed tone, "they've lit out on us." He saw Perkins pulling himself up, another large ugly welt on his forehead. "How long have they been gone?" Connally demanded.

Perkins shook his aching head. "I don't know, Sheriff. The one with the arm wound cracked my head against these bars. I've been out cold ever since."

"Damn it!" said Sheriff Connally, walking to the rear door and throwing it open. He looked back and forth along the alley, noting the fresh hoofprints in the dirt. As he gazed off in the direction the twins had taken, he said almost to himself, "Those poor, dumb kids. They've no idea what their heading into out there." He turned back to Willard Chapin, who'd sat the tray down on the desk and slumped down beside it.

"Will you be going after them, Sheriff? They've proven they can take care of themselves with a gun, but I hate to think of them two wounded kids out there alone."

"I know," said Connally. "I feel the same. But I can't go no farther on this thing. My responsibility is to the folks in St. Joe. I had hoped to get the boys back there and get some sense talked into them before I try hunting down the men who killed Elvin Bray. Now there's no telling what'll happen to Jed and Tim Strange. Their pa sure taught them how to use a gun, but young boys being that quick with the trigger can be a dangerous thing."

"Where do you suppose they'll go?" Willard Chapin asked.

"Oh, there's not a doubt in my mind, they're headed down to Indian Territory," Sheriff Connally replied. "If they don't get themselves killed first."

West of Kansas City, June 18, 1871

Jed and Tim Strange swung wide of the Missouri farm country and took to the open wild grasslands west of Kansas City. Their first night found them camped at a thin stream beneath the cut bank of a low rising knoll. Jed's wounded arm was stiff and sore, but there was little swelling. He shed the cloth sling from around his shoulder and, soaking it in the clear stream water, used it to attend to Tim's leg wound, which was healing over but still trickling blood. "Careful you don't break it open," Tim said in the gray evening light.

"I wish Ma or Pa or somebody who knew what they were doing was here," Jed replied, sounding worried.

"Well, they're not," Tim said. "Give it here, I'll clean it myself." He reached down and started to take the wet rag from Jed's hand, but Jed drew it back.

"I'm doing it Tim," Jed declared. "All's I said was that I *wish* somebody knew more about what to do." He carefully began dabbing the wet rag at the edge of his brother's wound.

"Wishing and wanting is a thing of the past," Tim said in a milder tone. "We've both seen how easy it is to get into trouble out here. From now on we trust nobody, and we guard each other's backs, the same way we did in that gunfight. That's the only thing that's going to keep us alive. I've never seen so many people anxious to hang somebody."

"I know," said Jed. "I hated cutting out on Sheriff Connally. But it might have been the only way to save all our lives."

"He understands, Jed," Tim said. "I'll always be beholden to him for what he was trying to do. But we're not letting anybody take us back to St. Joseph until we finish what we've started. Agreed?"

Jed nodded firmly. "Agreed." He finished cleaning Tim's wound and rewrapped it in the same gory bandage. "I just hope wherever Danielle's at, she's doing better than we are."

· · ·

Fort Smith, Arkansas, June 20, 1871

Danielle Strange walked from the U.S. federal marshal's office to the boardinghouse where she'd seen the vacancy sign on her way into town. In her run-down boots, she walked with the wide gait of a drover. She carried her dusty saddlebags, chaps, and range spurs draped over her shoulder, her rifle in her left hand, her right hand always close to the tied-down holster on her hip. The palm of her hand brushed past the butt on her Colt with each step. She had wintered in Mobeetie, Texas, where a family by the name of Elerby had taken her in, helping to nurse a knife wound in her side and a deep cut on her cheek. Then Danielle joined the Elerby boys, Luke and Clinton, who along with their father, Lattimer Elerby, and a small crew of drovers had brought one of the first spring herds up to Abilene.

"Damn the luck, Buck Jordan," she said to herself, swear words coming more freely to her now than they had before spending the last year of her life as a man in a man's world. "Why did you have to go get yourself killed?" Only moments before she'd learned of Jordan's death, having heard it from some of the deputies and jail guards gathered outside the Hanging Judge's*

* Hanging Judge *was a name given to Judge Charles Isaac Parker.*

69

court. Buck Jordan, like many of the Hanging Judge's lawmen, had met his death out in the Indian Territory at the hand of killers whose whereabouts and identities were unknown.

Amid the squeaking of passing wagons and the clop of hooves on the hard rutted street, she added in a whisper to herself, "You were my only contact with the law in Indian Territory. Damn it!" Along with the cussing, other things now came more easily to her, like the biting taste of whiskey, the clicking of a roulette wheel, and the ability to swing up her Colt with no hesitancy and watch a man fall to the dirt on an empty street in front of her. This was where the vengeance trail had led her, and this was where she lived.

In her pocket she carried a wrinkled paper that listed the names of the men who had killed her father, Daniel Strange. Of the ten names she'd written down a year ago, only six remained. The other four she had crossed off one at a time after seeing to it they'd paid the price for leaving Daniel Strange hanging dead from a tree. Her quest for the killers had started with meeting U.S. Marshal Buck Jordan here in Fort Smith. Jordan was the man who'd found her father's body, and he'd given her directions to her father's grave.

From the grave site, fate and circumstance had led her wandering from town to town on the killers' trails. The first killer on her list had been Bart Scovill, who'd been wearing her father's silver inlaid custom Colt when she caught up with him at a town dance. Dressed as a woman that night, Danielle had lured Bart Scovill on, then, with the fiddle ringing light and melodious in the background, she'd left him hanging dead from a barn rafter after retrieving her father's pistol.

From there, she'd traveled on and rooted out three more of the outlaws, killing them quick and without mercy. But now, she'd been off their trail for a while and hoped that Buck Jordan might give her some sort of a lead. When Danielle had taken the knife in her side last fall, it had shown her it was time to drop out of sight for a while and let her new name cool off. She'd started to develop quite a reputation as Daniel Strange, the young gunslinger with the cold green eyes, and an even colder heart.

When the Elerby boys had found Danielle wounded along the trail outside of Mobeetie, she'd told them her name was Danny Duggin, and they had never questioned it. She had a feeling they knew she was really the young gunslinger who'd gotten shot two days before in town and had since vanished. But they never let on. All the people of Mobeetie knew was that the emerald-eyed gunslinger named Daniel Strange had ridden away lying low in his saddle and hadn't been seen or heard from since, his bones lying bleached somewhere, no doubt.

Well, she thought to herself, *so much the better.* If the killers had any idea that Daniel Strange was looking for them, they would have let their guard down by now. She would

71

get back on their trail with a new identity. Stepping up onto the porch of the boardinghouse, she paused for a moment, touching her fingertips first to the scar on her cheek, then to the thin false mustache she'd purchased from a traveling theatrical company and taken to wearing. Once assured that her true identity was well concealed, Danielle raised the brass door knocker and tapped it soundly.

When Danielle had paid the two dollars for a room to a jovial heavyset woman wearing a white full-length cooking apron, she'd introduced herself as Danny Duggin. She watched the woman pocket the money beneath her apron and run a hand across her moist brow as she spoke.

"It's a pleasure to meet you. I'm Norena Chapin, Mr. Duggin, but most of my regulars just call me Ma. Will you be staying with me for long? Because if you are, you can pay by the week or month and save yourself some money."

Danielle answered in the lowered, gruff voice she had become accustomed to using. "No, ma'am. I expect I'll be headed out sometime tomorrow. I saw your sign out front and knew I'd rather stay here than in a hotel. For my money, nothing beats a good home-cooked boardinghouse meal."

Norena Chapin blushed, obviously flattered, and raised a hand to smooth a strand of loose hair. "Why, thank you, Mr. Duggin. My son Willard always says the same thing. He used to be on the road a lot until he settled down with a job operating a telegraph office in Tracy Sidings. I expect from your clothes that you're a cattle drover?"

"Yes, ma'am, of late anyway," said Danielle. "Although, having heard about the death of a friend of mine, Marshal Buck Jordan, I suppose I might just go hunting for his killers."

Norena Chapin touched her work-worn fingers to her cheek, saying, "Oh my, wasn't that a terrible thing. And you were a friend of Buck Jordan?"

"Yes, ma'am, so to speak," said Danielle.

"He used to live here, you know," Norena Chapin added.

"No, ma'am, I didn't know that," said Danielle.

"Oh, yes. His room was the first one at the top of the stairs, the room you'll be staying in. It used to be Willard's room, too, when he lived at home. I still miss them both something awful. I'm always fearful for Willard, although he lives in a railroad siding town, and I'm sure the railroad keeps law and order there."

"Yes, ma'am, I'm sure they do," Danielle said, already anticipating a bath and soft bed before supper.

"But it's getting terrible everywhere," Norena Chapin offered, keeping Danielle waiting as she searched beneath her large apron for a room key. "Only day before yesterday, Willard wired me and told me there had been a shooting there." She spoke as she searched one dress pocket, then the other. "The sheriff from St. Joseph arrived in the nick of time to keep some of the townsmen from lynching a couple of young boys for a murder they didn't commit."

"Oh?" Hearing word of her hometown, St. Joseph, got Danielle's attention. "Was that sheriff's name Connally?"

"Willard didn't mention his name," Norena said, still searching her pocket, "but the two teenaged boys were look-alikes. Willard said the boys were both wounded, and managed to slip away that evening. Said the sheriff was upset because he wanted to take them back to St. Joe for safekeeping."

Danielle stood stunned for a second at the news, her hand at first unable to reach out for the key when Norena Chapin finally found it and offered it to her. Could the two boys be her brothers, Tim and Jed? Of course they were, she thought. What other twin boys were around St. Joseph? None that she could think of, at least not around the age Norena mentioned. Then, taking the key, she asked, "How badly were the boys wounded?"

"Well, they were able to get away, so I don't suppose it must've been too bad," Norena said. Then, seeing the look on Danielle's face, she asked, "Why? Do you know anyone from St. Joseph?"

"Uh, yes, ma'am. But it's been a while since I've seen them." Suddenly the foyer of the boardinghouse felt small and tight to Danielle. She had to get upstairs to her room, and do some thinking without Norena Chapin's eyes on her.

"Willard said two men killed the St. Joseph town tax assessor. That's what started this whole incident, apparently. At first some of the people thought it was the young twins. That's why the sheriff was following them. It turns out the boys were innocent, and the two murderers are still running loose. That's something you better be leery of if you're going to be traveling."

"I certainly will do that, ma'am," Danielle said, already heading for the stairs. "Now, if you'll excuse me, I better get myself a bath and some rest."

"Yes, Mr. Duggin, you do that," Norena said as Danielle stepped upward. "I'll come wake you for supper."

In the room, Danielle undressed, peeling off the fake mustache and taking off the binder she wore to flatten her breasts. She then threw a towel around herself and went to the bathroom for a soak in the tub. The water in the large iron tub was only tepid, but it had been changed that morning, and Danielle was thankful for that. Too often in the past year she'd had to bathe in water that had accommodated five or six other people before her. As she lathered and scrubbed, she thought about what Norena Chapin had told her, and came to the conclusion that it had to be her brothers Tim and Jed that Norena's son Willard was talking about.

"But why?" Danielle asked herself aloud, in the stillness of the bathroom. She pictured her brothers' faces in her mind, wondering who was looking after her mother. She refused to consider that something might have happened to her mother that would free the twins up and allow them to leave the farm. She finished her bath, trying to guess where the twins might be after striking out from Tracy Sidings, wounded and on their own. "You're headed this way, aren't you?" she murmured. In silence, she went back to her room and stretched out naked on the bed, letting the slight breeze through the window dry her, offering her some comfort from the scorching heat of the day.

That evening at supper, she took her seat at the boardinghouse table amid six male guests and partook of roast beef, gravy, potatoes, and corn bread. Being there for only one night, the other guests only made polite conversation with her in passing. But when one guest, a jail guard named Lee Tate, told the others about the telegram that had arrived from Arizona earlier in the week advising law officers of the release of felons who had served their time, Danielle took note. Danielle's interest began to fade until Tate mentioned the name *Duncan Grago.* She jerked her attention toward Tate in such a quick manner that all conversation stopped, and all eyes turned to her as she spoke.

"Grago, you said? What was his first name?" Her intense stare was unsettling. The name *Grago* was the name on the top of her list of her father's killers.

Lee Tate was taken aback by this young

stranger with the thin wispy mustache, the scarred cheek, and cold verdant eyes. "Why, his first name is Duncan, like I just said," Tate answered with a bemused expression. "Why, do you know him?"

"No," Danielle said, easing back into her chair, "but I've heard of Newt Duncan, and wondered if they might be kin."

As Lee Tate considered it, a whiskey drummer named Bob Dennard cut in, saying "Humph, they're kin, all right, like two rattlesnakes from under the same rock." Eyes turned to him as he continued. "I came across those two years back in El Paso. They were both young then, Newton being the oldest. They killed an old Mexican couple near there that never harmed a soul in their life. The Gragos punched their ticket for a bag of coffee and an old silver broach the woman wore." He sucked a tooth and set his coffee mug down beside his plate. "Texas has had a price of five hundred dollars on their heads for the longest time. I hope you've got no truck with the likes of them, Mr. Duggin. If I thought you did, I'd have to call you a rotten, killing animal, no different than they are."

A tense hush fell about the table. Danielle looked at Bob Dennard and realized in an instant that he was not the whiskey drummer he had introduced himself as. What was he then? she asked herself, staring into his hard gray eyes. A bounty hunter? She thought about it as she spoke.

"No, I have no truck with them—none

that's your concern anyway. But you might have asked in a less insulting manner." Danielle set her coffee mug down as well, and kept both palms flat on the table edge.

"I might have...but I didn't," said Dennard, his face pinching red as he spoke. "I saw what you are the minute you came in, Mr. Duggin, if indeed that *is* your name."

The tension thickened around the table. Chairs scooted back, the other men ready to distance themselves from what looked like a coming storm between the two. Dennard continued. "You come in here unarmed, but where you wear your holster is the only spot on your trousers that ain't bleached out from the sun. Drover, you say? Hell, I know better. That ain't no brush cut on your face, and you didn't get them backed-out eyes staring up cattle's rumps. Who are you, Duggin? Why all the questions about ex-convicts?"

As Dennard spoke, Norena Chapin had stepped into the room with a fresh bowl of potatoes. She saw the trouble brewing and stopped in her tracks. "Now, see here, both of you. I don't allow quarreling and such at my table—"

"Easy, Norena," said Dennard, who was well known at the boardinghouse from years of frequent lodging there, "this young man is about to explain something to all of us. Let's hear what he has to say."

Danielle held Dennard's stare, and thought about the derringer in her boot well. She could get to it if she needed it. That was not

an issue. Her first concern was for the innocent people around the table. Her second
concern was for Dennard himself. He was
rude and short with her, but only because
he'd mistaken her for the very kind of person
she herself was hunting for. There was irony
here, but she wasn't about to explain herself
to this man. She did not want to blow her new
name, uncovering once again her intent. "You
don't want to hear the only thing I've got to
say to you, mister," she said in a calm, even
tone. "I came to this table unarmed, in respect
for this woman's home. Now, if you'll excuse
me, ma'am," she added with a nod toward
Norena Chapin, "I'll take my leave."

"Not without answering me first, you won't,"
Dennard said insistently.

Leaving half her plate of food uneaten,
Danielle scooted her chair back, stood up, and
turned from the table. The sound of a pistol
cocking caused her to freeze in her tracks, her
hand poised, ready to drop down to her boot.
But before she made her move, Dennard said
in warning, "Hear that sound? The next time
you hear it will be when your pistol is riding
your hip. You'll answer me today, civilly, or
you'll answer me tomorrow on the outskirts
of town."

Without turning, Danielle said over her
shoulder, "Will that sound I hear tomorrow
be coming at my back? Or will you have the
guts to cock it head-on?" She walked out of
the room without another word, and retired
to her room for the night.

. . .

Fort Smith, Arkansas, June 21, 1871

Norena Chapin was up before daylight and met Danielle as she came down the stairs with her gear over her shoulder. "Mr. Duggin," Norena said, "I just couldn't let you leave without first apologizing for Mr. Dennard's behavior last evening. You poor dear, you didn't even get to finish your supper."

Not expecting anyone to be up this early, Danielle had placed her Stetson atop her head before leaving her room. She removed it in deference to Norena's presence and said with a smile, "It was not your fault, ma'am, nor was it the fault of the cooking. The meal was excellent, and I'll be stopping here anytime I'm in Fort Smith."

"I certainly hope so," said Norena. She raised a bag from behind her back and held it out. "Here, I prepared something for you, for the road. I couldn't bear to see you leave here shortchanged. I even thought about giving you back your money, but I knew you'd be too proud to take it."

"You're right, ma'am," said Danielle. "I can't hold you responsible for the rudeness of one of your guests." Danielle took the offered bag. "But I'll accept this and thank you for your kindness."

Norena Chapin smiled. "I don't know what got into Mr. Dennard. I've never see him act that way."

"Well, let's hope that's the end of it," Danielle said. She left through the front door in the gray light of dawn and looked back to return Norena Chapin's wave on her way to the livery barn.

At the barn, Danielle found the stable boy already going about his chores, tending a pile of hay with a pitch fork. Once Danielle had prepared her chestnut mare for the road and led it out into the main bay of the barn, she flipped the boy a silver dollar and asked, "Tell me, young man, does a whiskey drummer by the name of Bob Dennard keep his horse here?"

"Yes, sir, he does," the boy said, pointing a dirty finger at an empty stall, "but it's not there now. He rode out of here over an hour ago. He woke me up to let him in."

"I see," said Danielle, "and what kind of horse does he ride?"

"A big dapple gray. Not what you'd expect a whiskey drummer to ride, is it?" the boy added. "Most drummers travel by coach or buggy. But not Dennard. He carries a lot of weaponry too." The boy grinned. "My pa says maybe Dennard don't want to be sassed by some saloon keeper."

"Your pa might be more right than he thinks," Danielle said, leading the chestnut mare out the front door. Looking down at the set of fresh tracks, she stepped up into the saddle. Turning the mare and following the prints out to the main street, she headed north, but not before seeing the hoofprints lead off across the street to an alley. It was the perfect place for Dennard to sit and wait for her, she thought. She heeled the mare forward, knowing that before she rode out of sight, Dennard would be on her trail.

Chapter 5

The Old Pike Road, June 21, 1871

Headed northwest, Danielle kept the chestnut mare at a steady clip on the hard dirt and stone as the first thin line of sunlight mantled the sky. Topping a low rise in the road, she reined the mare up sharply, then held the animal still and listened to the sound of a single horse's hooves closing behind her. Danielle batted her boots to the chestnut's sides and raced forward another two hundred yards until she topped another rise and started down the other side, out of sight where the road turned through a stretch of rock. Upon entering the waist-high rocks and brush, Danielle slowed the mare down, swung from the saddle, and stepped down into cover as the mare galloped on.

She waited in the brush and rock and, in less than five minutes, saw the big dapple gray come into sight, moving at a slow trot. Dennard was looking down in the pale morning light, keeping an eye on the hoofprints of Danielle's mare. So intent was he in his tracking, he didn't see Danielle jump in front of his horse, causing the big dapple to rear up beneath him

"Damn it!" Dennard cursed as his horse's hooves touched down. His hand had gone instinctively to the pistol on his hip, but it froze there at the sight of Danielle covering him with both of her Colts drawn and cocked at him from less than six feet away.

"Raise your gun with two fingers and drop it, Dennard," Danielle demanded. Seeing the hesitancy in his eyes, Danielle added, "Try anything and I'll clip your thumb off."

Dennard replied in defiance, "I'm not going to die out here in the dirt, killed by some lousy outlaw." His pistol streaked upward, but the shot from Danielle's Colt lifted it spinning from his hand. The dapple gray shied back a step, whinnying as Dennard clasped his left hand around his now bleeding right hand.

"I'm not an outlaw, Dennard, but you will die here in the dirt if you don't do like you're told." Danielle cocked the pistol again.

As Dennard stepped down grudgingly from his saddle, Danielle whistled up the chestnut mare and by the time Dennard had turned to face her, still holding his bleeding hand, the mare came cantering up to Danielle's side. Danielle holstered her left Colt and raised a hand to the mare's muzzle, saying, "Good horse, Sundown." Then she said to Dennard, "I know you think you were tracking an outlaw. That's the only reason you're still alive. But you called this one wrong, Dennard. I'm not on the dodge. I'm on a manhunt myself."

"Yeah?" Dennard said, skeptically. "I know a hardcase when I see one. You look like one, you even smell like one. You got the jump on me, now go ahead and shoot, get it over with. I won't beg for my life."

"It's starting to sound tempting, Dennard," Danielle said. "Hold your coat open, show me what else you're packing." As she spoke, Danielle circled around him to his horse and pulled his Henry rifle from the saddle boot.

"I'm clean," Dennard said, opening his lapels with his bloody hands. "I never need a hideout gun. I face a man straight-up, or I don't face him at all."

"Is that the way you were planning to do with me?" Danielle asked, stepping back to pick Dennard's pistol up off the ground. "You were going to follow me, then ride in and invite me to a shoot-out?"

"No. I was going to get the jump on you, hogtie you, and make you tell me everything you know about Newt and Duncan Grago, or any other outlaws you ride with."

"Then you're sure in for a disappointing day, mister," Danielle said. "Now get your boots off and pitch them to me." She reached down and took up the reins to the dapple gray.

"You can't leave me out here afoot," Dennard said, steadying himself on one foot as he yanked off a boot and pitched it over on the ground. "Horse theft is still a hanging offense,

84

young man," he said, taking off his other boot.

"Not when somebody's on your trail, about to dry-gulch you," Danielle said.

"I'm a bounty hunter," Dennard said with a scowl, getting bolder now that he saw his life was not in danger. "I've got a right to do my job."

"Not on me, you don't. There's no bounty on my head. I've got business to take care of. I'm not going to have you hounding me out here."

"Then you explain yourself, young man," said Dennard. "Why were you asking about the Grago brothers?"

"I'm not explaining a damn thing to you, Dennard," Danielle said, stepping toward her chestnut mare, leading the dapple gray. "But you're going to tell me what you know about the Gragos."

"Like hell I will," Dennard said, defiantly.

"Oh, you will, Dennard." Danielle aimed the Colt at his left foot. "You can tell me now while you've got ten toes, or you can tell me five seconds from now when you've only got nine."

"All right, hold on!" Dennard placed one foot over the other, as if to protect them. "Newt Grago is holed up down in the Territory, gathering himself a gang. He's hard to get to. Some gunman killed off four of his buddies. I believe he thinks that gunman is looking for him, too."

"Name some men who ride with him,"

Danielle demanded, "and don't lie. I already know some of their names."

Dennard hesitated, then let out a breath and said, "There's Leo Knight, Morgan Goss, Sep Howard, Chancy Burke, Julius Byler, Rufe Gaddis, Saul Delmano, Cincinnati Carver, and Blade Hogue. There's others, too. They come and go down in the Territory. But that's all I can think of with a gun pointed at my toes."

"Forget Goss, Knight, Howard, and Carver," said Danielle. "Where can I find the others when they're not with Grago?"

"If I knew the answer to that, they'd already be dead," said Dennard. He thought about it for a second. "But I heard tell that Rufe Gaddis and Saul Delmano were tossing Mexican horses down near Laredo, what time they're not robbing stagecoaches and raising hell."

"And the others?" Danielle probed.

"Well"—Dennard thought some more— "Chancy Burke is border trash, a killer and a drifter. What time he's not riding with Grago, you're apt to find him in any Mexican whorehouse that'll have him. As far as Blade Hogue and Julius Byler"—Dennard shrugged—"that's anybody's guess, I reckon." Dennard eyed Danielle closely. "I'll tell you one thing, young man. If you're really not an outlaw, you best not go horning into my business. I make a living killing these dogs. Nobody messes with my livelihood."

Danielle nodded, running the names through her mind and realizing most of these men were on her list. "I'm no bounty hunter, Dennard." She'd never heard of Leo Knight, Morgan Goss, or Cincinnati Carver, but the others were the men who'd had a hand in killing her father. For a moment she was tempted to ask Dennard to join her, him taking the bounty on their heads, and her taking her vengeance. Yet she had sworn at her father's grave that she would track down his killers one by one, and this was not the time to change her tactics.

"I'm taking your horse a mile up the road with me," Danielle said. "You'll find it tied beside the trail, along with your shooting gear. I'm throwing your boots away. I figure by the time you get there, then get back to town and get yourself some boots and a hat, I'll be cleared out of here. If you're smart, you'll stay off my back. Now give me your hat."

Dennard swore under his breath, yanked his bowler hat from his head, and sailed it to her. Danielle caught it and tucked it up under her arm, turning sideways to him just enough to step up into her saddle. "What if somebody passes by before I get there and steals my horse and guns?" Dennard said.

"Then you better walk quick, Dennard," Danielle said with a thin smile. She turned the chestnut mare and heeled it forward, leading the dapple gray. If her brothers Jed and Tim were headed this way, she would find them.

Danielle left the dapple gray where she'd said she would, and taking the trail through the rocky brush country, she rode on. At noon she only stopped long enough to rest the mare while she partook of the vittles Norena Chapin had given her. Then she pressed north for the rest of the day. Evening shadows were drawing long across the land when she stopped to water her mare and make camp at a run-out spring beneath a low rock ledge.

She saw the tracks of four horses as she stepped down to fill her canteen. Two sets of tracks were older than the others. These led off upward and off the trail. The other two sets of tracks circled away from the water and wound upward toward the ledge above her. She could feel eyes on her back as she capped the canteen, stood up, and looked around while the chestnut mare drew its fill. "Easy, Sundown," she whispered, running a hand along the mare's dust-streaked side.

Danielle knew this was no time for any sudden moves. She draped the canteen strap over her saddle horn and walked slowly around the mare as if inspecting her saddle and tack. On the other side of the animal, Danielle stooped down pretending to inspect the mare's forelegs, and in doing so managed to scan the rocky slope above her. The slightest rustle of brush along the narrow ledge caught her attention. On her way back around the mare, she stopped short, yanked the rifle from her saddle boot with one hand, and as quick as a whip slapped her other hand on the mare's rump, sending the animal darting away along the stream bank as she flattened to the ground behind a low stand of rock.

Danielle aimed deliberately high, two shots from her rifle kicking up chips of rock from the terraced ledge, her third shot going low into a scrub cedar sapling. "The next shot will take some bone with it!" she called out to rustling brush where she could tell someone had just hugged the dirt, taking cover.

"Whoa now! Take it easy, mister," a nervous voice called down to her, "we mean you no harm!"

It had been over a year since Danielle had heard the sound of her brother Jed's voice, yet she recognized it instantly, and her heart leapt for joy. But she stilled herself and called back to him, lowering her voice back into a husky tone, "Then why are you up there watching me, like a bushwhacker?"

"I—That is, *we* are sorry, mister," Jed Strange replied, rising slowly from the mound of brush, his hands chest-high in a show of peace. "We thought you were somebody else. There's two outlaws on this trail. That's their hoofprints leading up into the hills. We already had trouble with them once. We weren't taking any chances."

"Whose *we*?" Danielle demanded of him, already knowing, but playing her role as a wary traveler. She had to fight herself to keep from running upward along the ledge and throwing her arms around her brothers. "How many of you are up there?"

"There's two of us, mister," Jed answered. "Me and my brother. Can we come down there? We need to finish watering our horses."

"Both of you come down here real slow-like," Danielle said. "The light's failing, so don't make no sudden moves. I might get the wrong idea."

"Yes, sir," Jed called down to her. "We'll come down with our hands in sight."

Danielle smiled to herself. She knew how fast her brothers were with a gun. Even with their hands rose a bit from their holsters they could pull iron quicker than most men. In the darkening dusk she rose from behind her cover of rock and waited, hearing the horses' hooves clack along the ledge, then down onto the softer ground and toward her. Once they were ten yards away, keeping her Stetson brim low across her brow, she said, "That's close enough," and looked Jed and Tim up and down, taking note of Tim's limp, and the bandage around his thigh. "What happened to him, a snakebite?"

"No," Tim said, speaking for himself, reaching his free hand down and trying to close the gap in his ripped trousers. "I was shot in the leg. A railroad crew mistook me for a wanted outlaw. But they were wrong, mister, just so's you don't think we mean you any harm."

"If I thought you meant me harm, young man," said Danielle, "the conversation would never have made it this far." She jerked a thumb toward the run-out stream, saying, "Go on, finish watering your horses, whilst I go get mine and picket it to graze. If you boys want to share a camp here, I have some coffee beans and jerked beef."

"Lord, mister," Tim said, "we'd love some hot coffee. We've been living hand to mouth on squirrel and possum since we left Tracy Sidings. I'm Tim Strange, this is my twin brother Jed."

"Twins, eh?" Danielle pretended to eye them closer. "I suppose the light's too dim to tell it right now. I'm Danny Duggin, a drover up from Texas. Why don't one of you gather us some fire kindling? I'll be right back with that coffee. I'd like to hear about these outlaws you had problems with."

Tim and Jed Strange looked at one another as Danielle walked along the stream to where her mare stood drinking. "He's sure a trusting sort, Jed," said Tim.

Jed let out a breath and relaxed. "Yeah. It's good to know that not everybody is out to rob or kill you."

Luckily Sundown was streaked with sweat and road dust, or else Tim and Jed might have recognized her right away, Danielle thought as she reached down and gathered the reins. She led the mare away from the stream a few feet and picketed her in a graze of sweet grass. When Danielle had taken down her saddle and saddlebags, she walked back to where Tim and Jed were already busy starting a small fire. "I'll go picket our horses with yours, mister," said Jed Strange, taking up both sets of reins. But before he could lead them away, Danielle spoke, stopping him.

"No. My horse is just up from Texas on a trail drive. He's ornery and cross," she lied.

"Besides, you never know what illness he might be carrying. Do us all a favor and picket your horses closer in, away from him."

"Thanks for the warning, mister," Tim said. "Our horses ain't in the best of shape right now, anyway."

"Oh?" said Danielle to Tim, watching Jed lead the two gaunt bays to a separate stretch of grass nearer by. "Have you young men been on hard times?"

"Not to complain, Mr. Duggin, but it's been rougher than a cob the past year," Tim said, breaking a match loose and bending down to strike it. "We lost our pa to some murderers over a year ago. Jed and I haven't been able to find work."

Before Tim could say more, Jed called over to them in the darkening evening light, saying to Danielle, "Then we ran into those two outlaws no sooner than we left St. Joe. They came near to pinning a murder on us and getting us hung. Lucky for us, the sheriff from St. Joe showed up to vouch for us, and keep a lynch mob off our backs." He walked back into the growing glow of the small campfire as it fed upward on a pile of cedar and pine twigs.

Not wanting to sound too prying, but still wanting to hear all the news they had from home, Danielle dropped her saddle and gear back out of the coming firelight, and asked, "What about the rest of your family back in St. Joe? Couldn't they have vouched for you as well?"

"We've only got one sister, Mr. Duggin," Tim said, as Jed walked back with their saddles and dropped them to the ground, "and she left home after Pa's death. That's who we're looking for out here. We've got bad news for her, but there's no telling where she's at."

"I see," said Danielle quietly, cutting him off for the moment, for she already knew there was bad news coming about her mother. She prepared herself for it, wanting to postpone hearing it for as long as she could. Her heart had leapt at the sight of her brothers, the two of them looking a little more like men since last she'd seen them. She had missed them terribly and it had taken much control to keep from revealing who she was and throwing her arms around them. Yet, for their sake, she thought, Danielle held her feelings in check, and took the small bag of coffee beans and the battered pot from her saddlebags. Pitching the bag to Jed, she said to him, "Bust us up some beans. I'll get us some water, and we'll brew up a pot."

It was a few minutes later when Danielle heard the news of her mother's death. As they sipped their hot coffee, Tim went on to say that he and Jed had buried their mother before leaving home. When Danielle heard it, she could not let on how terribly crushed she was. But as unbearable as the news was, all she could do was keep her hat brim tipped forward and down, hiding her eyes from them in the glow of the fire. Even more crushing was the fact that she could take no comfort from her brothers, nor could she offer them any in return. For all the twins knew, they were strangers here on a lone frontier trail. She dared not reveal herself to them, tempting though it was, for while she had long grown accustomed to this terrible vengeance trail, she did not wish it for her brothers. She managed to keep her tears hidden beneath her hat brim. When she could speak without her voice betraying her, she did so with a harder edge than she'd intended.

"Boys, I'm sorry to hear about your troubles. But has it occurred to you that maybe your sister wouldn't want you joining her? Has it occurred to you that maybe she isn't even in the country? If she left home hunting those kind of men, she could be halfway across Mexico by now."

"Then that's where we'll find her, Mr. Duggin," Tim said with determination. "We're not turning back, if that's what you're getting at. There's nothing for us back there."

Danielle considered it, then said, "No, that's not what I'm getting at. It's none of my business what you do. But for all you know, maybe your sister already found the men who killed your pa. Maybe they're all dead by now." She hesitated for a second, then added, "Maybe she's even dead herself."

After a silence, Jed said, "Then we won't stop until we find where she's buried. We have to tell her about Ma, even if we have to say it to a grave marker."

Danielle felt the tears well in her eyes again,

94

and she fought them back. Nothing was going to stop these two and she knew it. The best she could hope for was to get some miles between them and continue her search. Hopefully she would rid the world of the remaining men on her list before her brothers ever had to face any of them. For her money, it was even odds that one of the outlaws the boys had encountered was Duncan Grago. She wasn't about to let an opportunity like this slip by. She was too close to be dissuaded now. Come morning, she would find the outlaws' trail and stick to it.

"Well then, boys," she said in a softer tone of voice, "all I can tell you is, be careful in Indian, Territory. If you think it's tough here, you ain't seen nothing yet. There's outlaws there who'll cut your throat just to see which way you'll fall. Don't trust anybody. Don't ever let your guards down."

"Thanks, mister," said Tim. "We don't intend to."

As Tim spoke, Jed eyed Danielle's half-hidden face in the licking flames. "Mr. Duggin, I can't help thinking that you look familiar. Have you ever been to St. Joseph?"

Danielle thought about it quickly. Deciding it would better to give him some reason for recognition than to deny it altogether, she said, "Yes, indeed I have, several times over the past few years. There's a gunsmith there who did some work for me on my pistols. Did some fine custom work. Can't remember his name though."

95

"Well, I'll be danged!" exclaimed Tim. "That was our pa, for sure. Pa was known as the best gunsmith in Missouri. If he did some custom work on your Colts, you've got some good ones." He leaned slightly forward. "Can I take a look at them?"

With her riding dust still on, Danielle had made it a point to keep her father's Colt handles out of sight. Now she adjusted her duster across herself and said, "Out here, you never hand your gun to a stranger, young man, no matter how friendly the circumstance."

"Sorry," said Tim, "I should have learned better by now."

"No apology necessary, young man," said Danielle. "I only mentioned it for your own good." She finished her coffee, then slung the grounds from her cup. "I reckon we best all get some shut-eye. It's been a long day."

Jed and Tim looked at one another. "But Mr. Duggin, we've been doing all the talking. What about you? What are you doing out here?"

"Just passing through, boys," Danielle said, reaching around and adjusting her blanket. "There's nothing much to tell you about myself. I'm a drover, working the spreads up from Texas. Of course if you're looking for work, I can give you some names of ranchers and trail bosses."

"Would you, please?" Tim asked, he and Jed both leaning forward eagerly. "We'll be needing work whether we find our sister or not."

This was a good way to get them off the trail

for a while, Danielle thought. "Ever worked a herd?" she asked, already knowing the answer.

"No, but we handle a horse as well as the next, and we ain't afraid of a day's work, no matter how hard," said Jed.

"Then go down to Mobeetie, Texas, to the Riley spread," Danielle said. "Tell Jason Riley you're new at droving but you need work. Better not waste any time getting there. He'll be pushing a big herd to Dodge before long. Jobs fill up quick."

"We'll head there tomorrow," Tim said, excited about the prospect of work. "Which way is it from here?"

"Swing west from here," Danielle said. "Pick up the Arkansas River the other side of Fort Smith towards the Canadian, then follow the Canadian past the grasslands into Texas. After about a day's ride into East Texas, head due south across the Washita. Follow the cow tracks from there. Ask anybody where the Jacob Riley spread is, if you have trouble finding it."

"But what about hunting for Danielle?" Jed asked his brother.

"We need to eat, don't we?" Tim replied. "Besides, Mobeetie might be as good a place as any to look for her. Right, Mr. Duggin?"

"I would think so," said Danielle. "One trail's as good as the next when you've no destination to begin with."

"But we were headed down to Fort Smith, to talk to a marshal by the name of Buck

Jordan," Jed cut in. "He's the one who sent us Pa's belongings. We figured maybe he could tell us something about our sister."

"I'll save you both some time," Danielle said glumly. "Buck Jordan is dead. I heard about it coming through Fort Smith. The Hanging Judge loses about one marshal a month to badlands outlaws. Last month it was Buck Jordan." Danielle offered a thin, sad smile beneath the cover of her hat brim and her fake mustache. "That tells you something about Indian Territory, I reckon." She smoothed her blanket, lay back with her head on her saddle, and flipped half the blanket across herself. "Go on to Mobeetie, boys. Get yourself a stake of money. Then go hunt for your sister." She pulled her hat brim farther down over her face. "That's my advice. Good night, boys," she added with finality.

During the night while the twins slept, Danielle raised her brim and looked from one to the other of them. The news of her mother's death still stung her down deep. For a long moment she watched her two brothers sleep, longing to gather them both into her arms. She thought of happier times on their Missouri farm, and saw visions of the entire family gathered around the kitchen table. Her eyes watered again, but she caught herself and rubbed her eyes dry with her knuckles. She stood up silently, gathering her gear. From inside her saddlebags, she took out her only other pair of jeans, and slipping over closer to her sleeping brothers, laid them near Tim's head. Then she took out most of her jerked beef and the bag of coffee beans and laid the supplies atop the folded trousers. "God be with you both," she whispered to herself, resisting the urge to place a hand on their cheeks. Then, like a passing breath of night wind, she was gone.

The Old Pike Road, June 22, 1871

At dawn, Jed shook his brother's shoulder, saying, "Wake up, Tim. Duggin is gone."

"Gone?" Tim sat up and rubbed sleep from his face. "Where? Why?" He looked all around, acquainting himself with the campsite in the early light.

"I don't know," Jed replied, standing back a step. "But he left us food and coffee...and look." He held up the jeans and shook them out. "He's even left you a pair of blue jeans."

"Well, I'll be." Tim stood up stiffly on his wounded leg then snatched the trousers from Jed's hand, looking at them in disbelief. "For all his tough tone of voice, I reckon Danny Duggin is surely—" Tim's voice failed him for a moment, and he swallowed a tight knot in his throat.

"I know," said Jed, looking at the bag of coffee beans and jerked beef in his hand. "There's some decent folks out here. It just takes some sifting to find them I reckon."

Tim collected himself, holding the trousers tight against his chest. "It's charity, no matter how you look at it. He must've known that if

99

we'd been awake, I'd never accepted him giving me these trousers." He squeezed the jeans tighter. "But *damn*, I'm awfully glad he did it!"

Jed looked off toward where the chestnut mare had been picketed before Danny Duggin had slipped away in the night. "I swear, Tim," he said, "there was something I liked about that man. I know we never met him before, but he seemed almost like kin, didn't he?"

"Yep, I felt that way too." Tim gazed off with his brother, the two of them feeling small against the magnitude of the land. "If we ever get back on our feet and run into him again, I want to repay Mr. Danny Duggin for these jeans, and thank him for his kindness."

Chapter 6

Indian Territory, June 24, 1871

The hoofprints Danielle followed led her on a three-day meandering loop, southwest around Fort Smith and deeper toward the heart of Indian Territory. On the third evening she'd heard distant gunfire and followed the sound of it. Then she spotted a black rise of smoke, which guided her to the burnt hull of an abandoned wagon. The bodies of an old teamster and his four mules lay scattered among the ruins. Danielle took note of the jagged upthrust of rock standing above a sunken basin of brush and sage. The hoofprints she'd been tracking led in that direction. While there was no reason for the riders to have tarried here, she still played it safe, swinging fifty yards to the west so that she would ride in with the sinking sun to her back.

At the crackling embers that were once the wagon bed, Danielle kicked through the teamster's load of scattered bolts of cloth and hand tools. She shook her head at the pillaged remains. Whatever the old man had carried in his pockets were all the outlaws could have found any use for. What had this gotten them? she wondered—a twist of tobacco, a few dollars, maybe the old man's rifle or pistol? The senselessness of it angered her, and she kicked at the spoilage on the dusty trail.

Above the smoldering coals and the whir of the wind, Danielle hadn't heard the two horses slip in close at a silent walk until the sound of a rifle cocking behind her caught her attention. Before she could turn and draw, the voice of Duncan Grago said with the low hiss of a rattlesnake, "Go on and try it, peckerwood. We ain't above shooting you in the back."

Danielle froze for a second, then turning her head slightly, she said over her shoulder, "I'm surprised you haven't already. From the looks of that ole man, back-shooting *is* your strongest suit."

"There's only one reason we haven't," Duncan Grago said. "I want to know who you are, and why you've been breathing down our necks the past three days. I don't like people following me. It always spells law dog or bounty hunter to me."

"Following you?" Danielle chuckled, taking her chances on turning a bit farther around. Facing them now, her hands were poised chest-high, but still able to get a fast grab on her Colts. "I wasn't *following* you, I was leading you from behind." She leveled her gaze at them, inching her hands down as she spoke. "I figured if there was any bushwhackers or renegades running loose, I'd hear them killing you and get myself a head start out of here." She shrugged. "Better you than me, I always say."

Sep Howard only stared suspiciously, taking note of the cold green eyes, and the big dust-streaked chestnut mare. But after the second it took for Danielle's words to sink in, Duncan Grago allowed a grin to form on his parched lips. "Well, hell, I can't argue with that kind of thinking," he said. "There was a couple of plow jockeys back along the trail. Don't suppose you ran into them, did you?"

Danielle thought about it, then said, "Yeah, our paths crossed. They told me what you did to them back in St. Joe, then again in Tracy Sidings."

"No kidding?" Now Duncan Grago grinned openly. "What did you tell them?"

"I told them they better kill you the first chance they get, or else you'd be causing them trouble the rest of their lives," said Danielle.

Duncan Grago laughed aloud, but Sep

Howard still sat staring, his hard, unyielding gaze leveled on Danielle. Finally he cut in, saying to Duncan Grago, "I never mentioned it to you, Dunc, but last summer there was a young gunslinger kicking up dust across the Territory. He had green eyes, went by the name *Daniel Strange,* and he rode a big chestnut, just like that one right there." Sep Howard nodded at Sundown without taking his eyes off Danielle. "What's your name, mister?"

"My name's Danny Duggin, mister," said Danielle, her hand poised lower now, nearer to her pistol. "What's yours?"

"Never mind my name," said Sep Howard. His voice turned to Duncan Grago but his eyes stayed on Danielle. "That's pretty close, wouldn't you say, Dunc? His name's *Danny,* the gunman's name was *Dan.* They both have green eyes, both ride a big chestnut."

Duncan Grago's smile faded. "You're saying this is him?"

"I'm saying everything about him is awfully familiar," Sep Howard replied. "We all heard that young gunslinger got himself carved to death by Comanche Jack Pierce, but we could have heard wrong."

"You didn't hear wrong," Danielle said. "I heard all about that gunslinger myself. Comanche Jack Pierce cut him to pieces over a card game. He died outside Mobeetie." Danielle jerked her thumb toward Sundown. "For all I know, that might have been his chestnut. I bought her from a stable owner when

103

her owner never came back for her. Now that's about all the explaining I plan on doing here. Besides, if I was a gunslinger wanting to hide my name, I could do a lot better than changing it from Dan to Danny, don't you think?"

"He got you there, Sep," said Duncan Grago with a short laugh. "I figure he just bumped the pot on you. Now are you going to call him or fold? To tell you the truth, I like the man's style. He ain't afraid, standing there, knowing any second we might pin a couple of slugs to his chest."

"Yeah?" said Sep Howard. "Well, I don't believe him, and I sure don't like him. For my money he's the same one who—"

His words were cut short by the blast of fire from Danielle's smoking Colt. She'd seen the faintest movement of his hand toward his pistol as he'd spoken. As Sep Howard's body flew backward from the saddle of his rearing horse, Danielle's Colt leveled and cocked on Duncan Grago before his hand could even close around his pistol butt. "I wouldn't do it if I were you, *Dunc*," said Danielle, mimicking the name Sep Howard had called him.

Duncan Grago froze, then relaxed as Danielle's thumb let the Colt's hammer down to half cock. He shot a glance at Sep Howard lying dead in the dirt, then cut his eyes back to Danielle as she punched the spent cartridge from her Colt and replaced it with a new round. "What the hell did you do that for?" Duncan rasped.

"I could tell he was getting ready to go for his gun," Danielle said. "Why beat around the bush about it?" She spun the cylinder on her Colt, flipped it around across her palm, and slid it back into her holster. "Anyway, I knew we weren't going to be friends, he and I," she added. "Now what about you?"

Duncan Grago had never seen a cross-draw that quick in his life. He sucked a slice of air through his teeth, calmed himself, then said, "I'm Duncan Grago." He nodded at the body sprawled on the ground. "That *was* Sep Howard. I don't think he even saw what hit him, and he was more than a fair hand with a gun."

"Can't tell it by looking," Danielle said. She walked over to Sep Howard's body, stooped down, and rifled through his shirt pockets, taking out a twist of tobacco and a small fold of sweat-dampened dollar bills. She fanned the bills, then refolded them and stuck them down into her riding duster. "You want his pistol?" she asked.

"Naw, it didn't do much for him," Duncan Grago said. "What about that money though?"

Danielle looked up at him and said, "If you wanted his money, you should have shot him yourself." She pitched Grago the twist of tobacco and watched him chuckle and bite off a plug, working it in his jaw as he spoke.

"No offense, Danny Duggin, but I believe you're as crazy and wild as I am." Grago spat a brown stream of juice for emphasis.

"Too bad this fool didn't see it," she replied.

"It might have saved him a fast ride to hell."
Danielle had only gone through Sep Howard's
pockets for show. She wanted Duncan Grago
to see her as a hardcase, and it had worked.
She took her time dropping the saddle and
bridle from Sep Howard's horse and slapping it on its rump. She wanted Duncan
Grago to have the time he needed to work things
out in his mind, for she knew that was exactly
what he was thinking.

"What's your plans now?" Grago asked
over his chaw.

Danielle turned from watching the horse run
freely away in a drifting wake of dust and
said, "Well, I thought I might go invest this
money in a bottle of rye, maybe see if I can
double it on a faro table. What about you?
Where were you two headed before I stopped
his clock?"

"I just pulled me a bunch of prison time in
Arizona," replied Grago, "so naturally I've been
wandering here and there, taking the long
way around, raising myself a little hell." He
nodded at the bodies of the old teamster and
the mules. "But I've got a brother waiting on
me down in the Territory. He has a good-size
gang riding with him off and on. If you really
want to double that money, you might want
to ride along with me. We'll be making some
easy cash, quick enough. He's always looking
for good gunmen."

Danielle felt her heart leap in her chest at
the prospect of finding Newt Grago and perhaps all the other killers in one spot. But she

hid her eagerness, and said, "No thanks. I work better alone." She looked up at him with a cool, level stare and decided to see just how far she could push him. "We might not get along, you and me. Then I'd have to be going through your pockets too." She offered a tight trace of a smile, watching his eyes for any sign of a comeback. If he was smart, she thought, he wouldn't stand still for this game of big dog little dog she was playing on him. Danielle was going to ride with him; there was no doubt in her mind. But first she wanted to knuckle him under a little, just enough to let him know she was going to be in charge.

"Hell, I ain't hard to get along with," Duncan Grago said, as if having not heard her veiled threat. "Ride on down with me. We've got a stop to make along the way. Sep and I was supposed to meet one of my brother's men, a fellow by the name of Julius Byler, outside of Fort Smith. After that we'll all three head down and join my brother. It'll be worth it to you, I can guarantee it."

That's the wrong way to respond, Dunc, Danielle thought to herself, staring up at him. He should have come back with something tougher, letting her know he wasn't the least bit intimidated by this Danny Duggin with his fast draw and his sharp tongue. But it was too late now. Duncan Grago had just rolled over and shown his belly. She was the big dog now.

"Well..." Danielle paused as if considering it for a second. Then she turned and stepped up into her saddle and reined Sundown around beside him, letting him see her palm brush past the butt of her Colt. He almost flinched at the sight of it. "I hope you're right, Dunc," she said, watching him settle as her hands dropped harmlessly down onto her saddle horn. "I hate being disappointed."

"You won't be," he said, nudging his horse forward. "Once we hook up with Newt and his boys, there'll be action aplenty. You can count on it."

"I already am," Danielle said, nudging the big chestnut mare along beside him. "Just lead me to him."

The Arkansas River, June 26, 1871

Julius Byler had grown cross and restless waiting for Sep Howard and Newt's younger brother, Duncan Grago. He'd been holed up in a shack eighteen miles out of Fort Smith for most of the winter, and had run out of supplies over two weeks ago. His last trip into Fort Smith had ended in a shoot-out at a mercantile store when he'd stolen a new Winchester while the owner wasn't looking. He'd been afraid to show his face there ever since. With Judge Parker holding court there, the town swarmed with marshals and deputies. If a man didn't want to end up on the end of Maledon's* rope, Byler thought, Fort Smith was a good place to avoid.

Julius Byler had been watching the river trail

* *George Maledon was the hangman for Judge Charles Isaac Parker.*

through the dirty window, and at the sight of the two horsemen coming up into sight through a sparse pine thicket, he snatched the stolen Winchester from its spot inside the door and levered a round into the chamber.

Danielle was the first to see the movement through the dingy window glass and, upon seeing the pane raise two inches, she stopped Sundown and said to Duncan Grago, "If this is the place, you best get ready to explain yourself, Dunc."

Duncan Grago caught sight of the rifle barrel slip across the windowsill and level toward him. He called out from twenty feet away, "Don't shoot! I'm Duncan Grago. If you're Julius Byler, my brother Newt sent me and Sep Howard to meet you."

From inside the window, Julius Byler called out, "Then where's Sep? I been expecting yas the past week."

"Sep's dead," said Duncan Grago, "but I'm here. If I wasn't who I say I am, I'd never have found this place."

"How did you find it?" Byler asked, still aiming down the rifle barrel.

"My brother Newt brought me here years ago. We spent a month hiding out from a bunch of detectives out of Tennessee."

Byler hesitated, eyeing them through the dirty glass. Finally he asked, "Who's that with you? What happened to Sep Howard?"

"It's a long story, what happened to Sep Howard," Duncan Grago replied, "but this is Danny Duggin. He's a friend of mine."

Danielle smiled to herself and sat still, letting Duncan Grago set things up for her. She was back on the killer's trail now, the very air around her thick with their scent, she thought. She'd take Julius Byler down and cross off his name from her list before they ever left this place. She just had to figure a way to do it without spooking Duncan Grago.

The two of them watched the rifle barrel draw back inside the window, then they heard a bolt lift from the plank door. They stepped their horses closer as Julius Byler came out, hooking his galluses up over his shoulders, the rifle still in his hand and pointed loosely in their direction. "I don't like waiting, never did." As he spoke to Duncan Grago, he eyed Danielle, taking close note of the dust-streaked chestnut mare. "And you," he said, turning his words to her, "I don't know you from Adam. Far as I'm concerned, you can turn tail and follow your tracks out of here."

"I don't turn tail real easy," Danielle said in a low tone. She stepped the mare closer. The rifle raised in Julius Byler's hands. But Duncan Grago moved his horse sidelong in between them, speaking down to Byler in a harsh voice.

"Listen to me, Byler. Sep Howard said my brother wanted us to bring you along. Now I don't give a damn if you come or not. But you best think twice before you go shoving iron at Danny Duggin. He's with me. If he don't kill you, I will."

"You're vouching for this man?" Byler

asked. "Because if you are, I'll take it your brother, Newt, is vouching for him too."

"Damn right I vouch for him!" Grago snapped. "Think I'd ride with a man I wouldn't vouch for?"

"All right, then, take it easy," said Byler, backing off. "Once you get to know me, you'll realize I'm a cautious man."

"That's good to know, Byler," Danielle said. She swung down from her saddle, slow and easy. "Now you suppose we could get some hot grub and coffee before we head down to the Territory?"

"We could, except I don't have the makin's of a hot meal, and no coffee either. I been stored out over two weeks, living on hardtack and water, unless I can shoot a muskrat on the river-bank."

"Damn," said Duncan Grago, swinging down from his saddle and stretching his legs. "You expect me and my partner to eat a stinking muskrat? We'll have to get some supplies before we head out of here."

We're partners now? Danielle smiled to herself, liking the way Duncan Grago was implying that they were friends. She'd kept him good and buffaloed ever since she shot Sep Howard. The night before last, when Duncan had told her his grisly story of why he'd gone to prison, she hadn't shrunk from his knife fight story the way Sep Howard had. Instead, when Duncan had finished telling her, she'd only told him in a calm voice that had she been that Mexican she would have hunted him and killed him. His jaw had twitched, but he hadn't rebutted her threat in any way. His attitude would probably change once he was reunited with his brother and had more guns around to protect him. But for now, Danielle had him where she wanted him. With someone who was his match, Duncan Grago was a coward, she thought. A coward who would take her where she wanted to go.

"Me and Danny will rest here a day while you go into Fort Smith and pull up some supplies, Byler," Duncan Grago said, taking charge now that everything seemed to be settled.

"I can't do it." Byler shook his shaggy head. "I stole a rifle and shot a store owner in the leg. They see my face in Fort Smith, they'll likely blow it off my shoulders."

"Well, hell's bells," said Duncan Grago, letting out an exasperated breath. "Is there anyplace else around here? Damned if I want to ride back that way." Danielle cut in, saying, "I'll go, since you're both too afraid."

"I never said I'm afraid," Duncan Grago sneered, careful not to come back too strong at Danielle's cutting remark. "I just hate back-tracking myself."

Looking at Danielle, Byler said, "I'd prefer keeping you in my sight for a while, Danny Duggin, till I know you better."

"You don't want to know me any better, Byler," Danielle said in warning.

"Cut it out, both of you," Duncan Grago demanded. "I'll go round up supplies. Think you two can get along till I get back?"

"We'll be fine," Danielle said, keeping a cold stare on Byler. "Ain't that right, *Julius*?"

It was later that evening when Danielle decided to make her move on Julius Byler. It would take Duncan Grago most of the night to ride back from Fort Smith, if he didn't decide to spend the night camped along the river and head back in the morning. After rubbing Sundown with a handful of straw and picketing her on a hilly rise behind the shack, Danielle had sat down on a cedar stump in the dusty front yard and took her time cleaning and oiling her pistols one at a time, making sure to keep one ready and loaded across her lap.

The look she'd last seen on Julius Byler's face before he'd gone inside and bolted the door told Danielle he knew something was up between them. She kept an eye on the closed window for any sign of him or his rifle barrel. When she'd finished with her pistols, she stood up and swung her gun belt around her waist, buckled it, and adjusted it, taking her time, knowing full well that Byler was watching through a crack somewhere in the sun-bleached walls.

For a moment Danielle only stared at the shack, knowing the moment to wreak her vengeance was at hand. She let the long controlled anger inside her come to the surface now, preparing for her task. Only yards away inside the shack stood another of the men who had killed her father, and like the other murderers she had found over the past year, she would see him dead. Danielle swallowed back the bitter taste in her throat, took a deep breath, and let it out slowly. She reached down at her feet and picked up a small rock.

"Julius Byler, it's time you pay up for murder," she called out, tossing the rock against the door of the shack.

"What the hell are you talking about?" Julius Byler called out. Inside the shack, his face was streaked with sweat. "I've never seen you before in my life!" He stood with his back pressed to the wall, his eyes fixed on the front door. "I never should have let you ride in with Grago! That's what I get for being hospitable!"

"You've never seen me before, but you know who I am," Danielle said. "You had me pegged as soon as you saw the chestnut mare. I'm that gunslinger who was killing you bastards last summer. Come on out—it's time we reckoned up, just the two of us, the way it was with Bart Scovill, Snakehead Kalpana, Levi Jasper, and Brice Levan. They all died by my hand. Now you'll do the same."

"What's this about? Don't I have a right to know?" Julius Byler demanded.

"You don't have a right to nothing, far as I'm concerned." Danielle stepped sideways in the dusty yard, then took a fighting stance twelve feet from the plank door. "But I'll tell you anyway. Remember the man you and your outlaw friends robbed and hung in Indian Territory, back last year?" She paused, waiting for a response.

A silence passed, then Byler called out, "Hell, I don't remember. That's a long time ago. He weren't the only man we killed, who-ever he was."

Danielle felt her jaw tighten, her teeth clench. "That was my pa, you murdering son of a bitch. Now wipe the sweat off you palms, keep your hands from trembling near your guns, and get on out here!"

"Well, I'll be damned," Byler said, stalling as he stepped quietly over to the door, lifting the latch ever so slowly. "I remember you now. That's the reason all those boys died last summer, huh?" He opened the door just a sliver of an inch, looking out at the figure of the gun-fighter, standing to the left in shadows.

"That's the reason, Byler. That front door is the only way out for you. Let's not put it off any longer."

"So you're his son, huh?"

"No..." Danielle let her words trail. Then she said with an air of finality, "I'm his daughter."

Her words stopped Byler short and left him stunned for a second. He shook his head in disbelief. "Well, I'll be. All this time, the green-eyed gunslinger everybody talked about was just a *girl*? Now that's one worth telling about." He felt bolder now, and he grinned to himself, peep-ing through the crack. "Bart Scovill and the others, killed by a girl. They ought to have been ashamed of themselves." He took a deep breath, leaned the rifle against the wall inside the door, and loosened his pistol in his holster.

When Danielle made no response, Byler added, "Let me get this straight now. You really want a straight-up gun fight? No tricks or nothing?"

"That's right, Byler," Danielle said calmly. "You and me, no tricks." She braced her feet beneath her, knowing what was about to come.

Byler slipped the pistol from his holster, cocked it quietly, then said, "Well then, why didn't you just say so in the first—" He slung the door open and leaped out into the dirt, his pistol already out and up. Danielle's Colt streaked out in a cross-hand draw, her first shot hammering into his chest, slamming him back against the plank door frame. The second bullet hit his chest less than an inch below the first, just as his hand struggled to right his pistol toward her. Her next three shots jerked him along the front of the shack, his boots and body twisting in a crazy dance.

"There now, Pa," Danielle whispered, "I'm back in the hunt." She reached down to the hot, smoking pistol, punching out the empty cartridges and replacing them. Then she walked back to the cedar stump, sat down with a long sigh, and stared at the bloodied body in the dirt until darkness fell around her.

Chapter 7

The Arkansas River, June 27, 1871

It was midmorning when Duncan Grago rode up from the river trail. Danielle had cleaned up around the door of the shack and dragged Julius Byler's body out of sight, a few yards up the rocky slope behind the shack. She had also taken Byler's horse from the open-front stall and sent it away with a slap on its rump. As soon as Duncan Grago rode into the yard, she started right in on him in a way to keep him off balance. "What the hell took you so long?" she demanded in a testy voice. "You should have been back last night."

Duncan was taken aback and offered a weak defense. "Damn, Danny, I got caught in a rain outside of Fort Smith. Nothing to get riled about! I figured you'd realized it might be morning before I get back."

"If all you boys do is sit around and wait for one another, I ain't sure I want to be a part of this bunch," Danielle hissed. She reached out with a boot toe and kicked a rock across the yard. "I'm like Byler when it comes to waiting. I can't stand it."

Duncan Grago stepped down from his mount and looked all around the yard and the front of the shack. "Where is Byler?" His eyes stopped for an instant at the sight of a fresh bullet hole in the front wall of the shack, where one of Danielle's shots had gone through Byler and lodged there.

"How the hell should I know?" Danielle snapped in reply. "We got into it last night after you left. He said this shack wasn't big enough for both of us. Wasn't going to let me inside. I had to straighten him out."

"You—you killed him?" Duncan Grago took on a curious look.

"No, I didn't kill him," Danielle lied, "but I should have. The son of a bitch threw down on me with his rifle. I creased his scalp and he ran off." She narrowed a cold stare at Duncan Grago. "If you've got a complaint about it, get it said." Her hand rested on the butt of one of her Colts.

"To hell with him." Grago shrugged. "I only came here because Newt asked me and Sep to bring Byler with us. If he don't like our company, he can do otherwise, I reckon." Duncan Grago looked relieved as Danielle dropped her hand from the pistol. "I'm glad you didn't kill him, though. Him and Newt's been friends for years."

Her voice still tight and cutting, Danielle said, "Look at me, Dunc. Do you think I'm a fool? I wouldn't kill one of your gang unless I had to."

"I understand, Danny," Duncan said, his right hand raised as if to hold her at bay. "I was just speculating is all. There's no problem between us. We're *amigos*, far as I'm concerned."

"Good then." Danielle pretended to cool

down and spread a guarded smile to herself. "I like you, Duncan. I hope we can ride together without any misunderstandings. The last *amigo* I had went bad on me. I had to leave him lying in the dirt with his brains spilling out of his hat."

Duncan Grago wasn't used to somebody talking this way to him. This gunslinger had him rattled. He was used to being the one telling the tough stories, making everybody a little wary of him. Danny Duggin was a whole other thing. Duncan liked him, but he was scared to death of him, if the truth was known. "We'll never have that kind of problem, Danny," he said. "You and me are cut from the same cloth. We're both mean as hell, and we'll die that way, eh? Ain't that right?" He offered a bold grin, putting a lot of chin into it.

"Yeah," Danielle said, "for me, anyway. I'm still wondering about you." She said it half jokingly, leaving Duncan guessing where he really stood with her. "Now are we ready to ride or not?" Danielle stepped over to where she'd reined Sundown to a weathered post in the ground.

"Sure thing," said Duncan Grago, stepping back up into his saddle. "But don't you want to eat something first?"

"We'll eat on the trail," Danielle said, making it sound like an order. "Unless you can't go a few hours on an empty belly."

"Me? Hell, I'm fine. Had some coffee and jerked beef at daybreak."

"That's good to hear, Dunc," Danielle said over her shoulder, nudging the mare forward and taking the lead. "Get up here beside me. I don't like nobody fanning my trail."

"Sure thing, Danny." Duncan Grago sidled his horse closer to Sundown. "I was thinking on the way back here. It's a long ride to where we're headed. Maybe we ought to swing in somewhere and rob us a bank or something. What do you think?" Danielle only stared ahead. "We'll see, Dunc," she said. "We'll see."

Mobeetie, Texas, July 10, 1871

By the time Jed and Tim Strange rode into the small town of Mobeetie, Texas, they had been out of supplies for the past four days, living once more on jackrabbit and creek water, much to Jed's dismay. They found the Riley spread, but Jacob Riley and his regular drovers had ridden out a few days ago to deliver a small herd to an army encampment near the Mexican border. The old ranch blacksmith, Barney Pitts, had speculated to the boys that it would be another three or four days before Riley and his men would return. Pitts had offered Jed and Tim a spot in the bunkhouse and a place at the table, but until the two knew they would be working for Riley, their pride would not allow them to accept Pitt's hospitality.

"It would have been different if we were experienced cowhands," Tim said as the two of them rode along the dusty street of Mobeetie, "but if we ended up not getting the job, staying there would be no more than a handout." He looked sidelong at Jed. "Pa always said if a man takes one handout, he'll soon take another."

"I know we did the right thing turning it down," Jed said with a grimace, "but it sure would be nice looking at some food that didn't smell like rabbit for a change."

As Jed spoke, Tim saw something ahead of them above a boardwalk that caused him to stop his bay in its tracks. "Well, get ready to eat, Brother Jed," said Tim. He nodded at a hand-painted sign swaying on the hot breeze out front of a busy saloon. "Do you see what I see?" The sign read: EAT YOUR FILL WITH THE PURCHASE OF A FIVE-CENT MUG OF BEER.

"I see it," Jed replied in a hushed tone, "but I don't believe it."

"I do," Tim said, batting his heels to his horse and pushing it forward. "Come on, Jed, let's get in there and eat before they change their mind."

At the crowded hitch rail out front of the saloon, they jumped down, spun their reins, and started up toward the bat wing doors. But they had to jump to one side as the doors flew open and a burly bartender hurled a drunk through the air, then stood back dusting his hands as the man rolled in the dirt street and rose up onto his knees cursing loudly.

"Don't mind him, boys," the bartender said to Jed and Tim. "Go on in and make yourselves to home."

On the street, the drunk raged, shaking a grimy fist in the air. "Yeah, that's it, go on inside! See what you get for your nickel beer! These sonsabitches will rob yas blind! Look what they've done to me!" He jerked the inside lining up out of his empty pocket. "Don't think they won't do it to you, too! The rotten sonsabitches!"

"Well, you boys coming in or not?" the bartender asked, throwing open the bat wing doors for them.

"Much obliged," Tim said, stepping inside with Jed right behind him. Both of them stood in awe for a second at the sight and sound of a spinning betting wheel and the rattle of a snappy piano through a blue haze of cigar smoke.

"Find yourselves a spot and squeeze, in boys. Drink and eat your fill," the bartender said, stepping past them across the sawdust floor and disappearing around behind the crowded bar.

The twins looked at one another and seemed to snap out of a trance. "He don't have to invite me twice," Jed Strange said, eagerly moving to the crowded bar where men raised sandwiches thick with roast beef and fried chili peppers. The two of them managed to secure enough elbow room to rake up slices of bread, and had begun piling on the beef when across the bar the same bartender looked them up and down as he spoke.

"You got to order a mug of beer, boys. That's the only rule to it. The rest is on the house." Tim reached his hand down into his boot well as he chewed a mouthful of meat and bread. He pulled out the two folded dollar bills from inside his damp sock—all that was left of the fourteen dollars they'd drawn from Elvin Bray before leaving St. Joseph. He peeled the two damp dollars apart and handed one to the bartender. "Must we both buy a beer, or can we share one?" Jed asked.

The bartender snatched the dollar and smiled behind his thick, dark mustache. "Both of you have to buy one if you both plan to stuff yourselves on my wife's roast beef."

"Give us each a mug, then!" Tim said, grinning and shoving the other dollar down into his shirt pocket. Down the bar from them, a hefty man named Mose Epps, who had a reputation as the town bully, gigged his drinking buddy with his elbow and nodded at Jed and Tim Strange.

"Look at these two sodbusters, Randy," Mose Epps said, making no attempt at keeping his voice lowered. "They act like they ain't et in a month."

The other drinkers heard him above the din of the crowd and the rattle of the piano, and most ignored his rudeness. But his drinking buddy, Randy Farrel, laughed loud enough to get Jed and Tim Strange's attention. They looked up from counting their change in Tim's palm and, seeing Mose Epps's expression of disgust and the man beside him laughing, the twins gave them both a questioning look.

"That's right, you heard me," Epps said scornfully. "I said you two act like you ain't et nothing for a month. Now what about it?" He stood with his hand on the pistol at his hip. Three drinkers at the bar between Epps and the twins picked up their beer mugs and slunk back out of the way.

Tim swallowed a mouthful of roast beef and bread, then washed it down with a gulp of beer. "Mister, you're mighty close to being right about that," Tim said, making light of the insult. "My brother here claims he's been seeing jackrabbit in his sleep for the past four nights."

A couple of the drinkers offered a nervous laugh, hoping Mose Epps would see the humor of it and let these haggard-looking boys alone. But Epps would have none of it. He stared coldly at the twins as he raised his beer mug, drained it, and sat it down solidly on the wet bar top. "Give me another, Frank," he said to the bartender. "I've got enough sense and manners to not take your generosity on the cuff."

"Leave it alone, Mose," Frank the bartender said in a lowered voice. He filled Epps's mug, slid it before him, and picked up the nickel from the bar. "Lunch is on the house for one and all, you know that."

"Yeah, I know it," Epps said, raising his voice for the twins' benefit. "But it's meant to draw business, not to draw a couple of look-alike saddle tramps in so's they can line their flues."

The saloon fell silent save for the clicking of the spinning wheel. Even the piano player had to turn his attention to the bar. Tim and

Jed Strange stopped chewing their food. Jed reached out and sat his beer mug on the bar. "Tim, let's go," he whispered. "This is just a come-on, to get folks to gamble."

"Now you've got it," Mose Epps sneered. "Nickel beer and free food is for the rollers, not for a couple of—"

"Hold on now," the bartender said, cutting Epps off. "Nickel beer and lunch is for anybody shows up. Boys, enjoy yourselves," he insisted to Tim and Jed Strange. "You don't *have* to gamble to eat and drink here. You're welcome all the same."

"Much obliged, sir," Tim Strange said to the bartender, keeping a cold stare fixed on Mose Epps. In a tight, calm voice, he said to Epps, "Let's get back to what you said about look-alike *saddle tramps*."

Mose Epps was used to bullying his way around in the streets and saloons of Mobeetie, Texas. Although the white-hot fire in Tim Strange's eyes told him he might have pushed the wrong man this time, Epps wasn't about to let himself get backed down in front of the drinking crowd. "You heard me just fine the first time, sodbuster," Epps growled, his hand wrapping around the butt of the big two-handed horse pistol standing high on his stomach. "Now, if you don't want me to box your jaws, you both better crawfish out that door and—"

His words stopped at the sight of Tim's Colt, out of its holster now and cocked at his chest. The move was so sleek and fast, Mose

Epps didn't even have time to grip his pistol, let alone try to draw it. "But I want to hear you say it again, that part about look-alike saddle tramps lining their flues," Tim said. "I *dare* you to, you bag of hog guts."

"Easy, Tim," Jed whispered beside him. "He ain't worth killing."

Mose Epps stood stunned, helpless before the barrel of the cocked Colt. A few feet to his side, Randy Farrel started to inch his hand toward the pistol on his hip, but just as suddenly as Tim Strange had drawn and cocked his pistol, Jed Strange now did the same. "Don't do it, mister, please," Jed said to Farrel, "or I will kill you." Randy Farrel's hand crept back up chest-high, and stopped there in a show of submission.

"Now you," Tim said to Epps. "I'm still waiting. Are you going to say it again, or crawfish out that door the way you told *us* to?"

Epps's lips twitched as he tried to form a nervous smile. "Boys, I don't know how this got so out of hand. I was just making a little joke, you know? I didn't mean nothing by it."

"Yeah, you did," Tim said, not letting Epps off the spot. "I know your type. You like to belittle a man every chance you get. But when it comes down to guts and muscle, you've got neither one. That's when you decide to call it a joke."

"Please, buddy, I'm sorry," Mose Epps said in a low, shamed voice, not wanting the whole saloon to hear him beg.

"That's better," Tim said. He stalked forward, his eyes ablaze, and poked the tip of his barrel against Mose Epps's sweat-beaded forehead. "Now crawl out of here," Tim hissed, "before I blast the top of your head off!"

Mose Epps back-stepped across the floor, his face flaming red in humiliation, all eyes watching him. Once he had stepped through the bat wing doors, with Randy Farrel right behind him, Tim and Jed holstered their Colts and turned to the bartender. The saloon still stood in hushed silence. "Sir," Tim said to the burly man behind the bar, "I apologize if we took advantage of you here. We've been on the road awhile, and the sight of that sign out front got the best of us, I reckon."

The bartender shook his head with a sigh of relief. "Boys, that sign means exactly what it says. Buy a nickel beer and eat your fill. To hell with Mose Epps. This is *my* place. I make the signs *and* the rules. Now drink up, and eat all you want." He looked around at the other patrons, who still stood back in stunned silence. "Well, what are you all waiting for?" the bartender said, waving them closer to the bar with both arms. "Next beer is on the house."

Jed reached out and stacked roast beef between two more pieces of bread, this time eating a little slower. Tim drained his beer mug and pushed it forward for a refill. "That was some wicked gun-handling, boys," said a voice beside them. They both turned to see a smiling face, and watched the man lower a black cigar from his lips and let out a long stream of smoke. "Permit me to introduce myself," the man said, his grin widening. "I'm Arno Dunne, and I couldn't help but notice how quick you boys grabbed up a handful of iron."

Tim and Jed had both settled down now, but they still had their bark on. More interested in eating than making conversation, Tim only acknowledged Arno Dunne with a nod, saying over a mouthful of food, "He was in the wrong, mister. That's the short of it."

"I agree," said Dunne, having to speak to their backs as both the twins had turned away from him. "It's a bad mistake, getting in a man's way when he's hungry. You had very right to drop him once his hand went to his pistol butt."

Tim and Jed turned back to Dunne as the piano struck up a fresh tune. "I knew it wasn't going to go that far," Tim said. "He was a windbag and a bully, and just needed to be took down a notch." This time as Tim ate and spoke, he noticed the brace of polished Colts on Arno Dunne's hips.

"He may be just a barroom bully," said Dunne, "but I wager you haven't seen the last of him. This is his perch. He'll have to make a move to save face here."

"Well, we hope you're wrong, Mr. Dunne," said Jed. "We came looking for food, not trouble."

"Call me Arno, boys," Dunne insisted. "I didn't catch your names."

"I'm Tim, this is my twin brother, Jed.

128

We're just in town for a couple of days. We came to look for work at the Riley spread."

"The Riley spread, eh?" Arno Dunne seemed to think about something for a second, puffing his cigar. Then he said, "I hate to tell you, but Riley's not going to be hiring anybody for a while. If that's your only prospect for work, I'm afraid you've drawn a blank."

"How do you know?" Jed asked.

"Word has it him and his boys were hit by rustlers while they was taking a herd down to the army. If I know Jacob Riley, he'll be hunting down his cattle if it takes him a month. Meanwhile there'll be no work at his place."

Tim studied Arno Dunne's face, saying, "We just talked to his blacksmith earlier today. He never mentioned cattle rustlers."

"Barney Pitts is lucky he knows his own name." Arno Dunne shrugged, working his cigar between his lips. "I just got word myself, at a friend's house on my way here." He paused and blew out a breath of smoke. "I didn't catch your last names, boys."

Tim started to tell him, but before he could speak, the piano player stopped playing abruptly and dove from his bench onto the sawdust floor, shouting, "Shotguns! Look out!"

Jed, Tim, and Arno Dunne spun toward the slapping sound of the bat wing doors just in time to see Mose Epps and Randy Farrel spread two feet apart, each of them raising a double-barreled shotgun. "Nobody makes me a crawfish!" Epps raged. But he'd have

129

better spent his time shooting instead of talking, for Tim and Jed Strange both drew and fired in one blinding swift motion. Arno Dunne barely cleared leather before the sound of the twins pistols roared in unison.

A blast of buckshot fired up into the ceiling taking down a wagon wheel lantern frame as Randy Farrel slammed backward through the bat wing doors, his shotgun flinging from his hands. At the same time, two slugs from Tim's Colt drove Mose Epps back against the wall beside the doors, where he slid down to his knees and fell face forward, dead. His shotgun went off, sending a streak of fire and a spray of splinters across the floor. A death-like silence hung in the air after the blasts. Smoke curled and drifted from the barrels of the twins' Colts.

"Lord have mercy," the bartender whispered, breaking the silence. He looked at the body of Epps, then through the broken doors at Randy Farrel stretched out dead in the street.

"You all saw it!" Arno Dunne shouted, fanning his unfired pistol back and forth across the stunned onlookers. "Epps and Farrel started it, didn't they?"

"That's right," said the bartender. "When the sheriff gets here, that's what we'll say. Epps and Farrel caused the whole thing."

"Sheriff, hell," said Dunne. He shot Tim and Jed a warning glance. "If you boys are smart, you'll clear out of here. You want to take your chances with the sheriff? He's Mose Epps's cousin."

Tim and Jed looked at one another, their last encounter with angry townsfolk still fresh in their memory. "We ain't staying," said Tim. He turned to the bartender. "Mister, you saw it. Will you tell the law we were only defending ourselves?"

"That's exactly what I'll tell him," said the bartender, "but you'd be wise to stay and tell him yourself."

"Yeah," Arno cut in sarcastically, "and take a chance on him jackpotting you for shooting a couple of snakes. Come on, boys, I'm getting you out of here for your own good." He turned back and forth with his pistol covering the drinking crowd. "Any objections?"

The crowd cowered back. Jed said to his bother, "Tim, maybe we ought to stay and explain."

"No, come on, Dunne's right." He backed toward the door, limping slightly as he punched out the two spent cartridges from his Colt. "Why do we need to explain anything? Everybody here knows the truth."

Jed backed away with him as Arno Dunne ushered them both out the doors to the hitch rail. Jed stood frozen for a second when he looked down at the body of Randy Farrel lying dead in the dirt. "Come on, Jed, damn it!" Tim shouted, untying both of their reins and pitching Jed's over to him. "Let's ride!"

"Listen to your brother, boy," Arno Dunne demanded. He'd already stepped atop a buckskin Spanish barb and spun it around in the street. "The sheriff'll be here any minute!"

They rode hard and fast out of Mobeetie, Arno Dunne at the lead on a well-beaten road headed south. At a fork two miles out of town, Arno slid his barb horse to a halt and jerked it around, facing the twins as they followed suit. He laughed and slapped his thigh. "Boys, you sure know how to stir up a slow day in Mobeetie," he said. But Tim and Jed Strange saw no humor in his remark, and their expressions told him so. "Aw, come on now," Arno said, "those two got what was coming to them, we all know it. Be thankful I was able to warn you before they shot you both in the back. Ease up on yourselves a little. Life goes on."

"As I recall, it was the piano player who warned us," Tim said, still looking solemn.

"Well, however it went, just be thankful we're all alive and kicking." Arno chuckled, taking out a fresh cigar from inside his coat and biting the tip off it. "That's what it's all about, ain't it? Staying alive?" He struck a match, lit it, and flipped the match away. He propped a boot across his saddle fork and relaxed, eyeing the twins and blowing a long stream of smoke.

Jed spoke, pushing up his sweaty hat brim, "Now we have no way of seeing Jacob Riley about work for sure."

"I already told you, there's no work there for yas," Arno Dunne said, sounding a bit put out. "Besides, if work's what you're after, I know a better bunch to work for than Jacob Riley any day." He wagged his cigar at the Colts on their hips. "The way you boys swing iron, you'd be foolish eating dust and staring up a longhorn's rear end from sun to sun. Believe me, there's better ways to make a living."

"You mean gun work, don't you, Dunne?" Tim said, starting to distrust this smiling stranger and his slick style. "My brother and I ain't hired guns, and we don't intend to be. We might be young, but we ain't stupid."

"Of course you're not," Arno Dunne said without conviction. "But you're new out here, and just got a taste of how fast things can happen. There's two kinds of people in this world— the givers and the takers. This is hard country, boys. If you want to give, it'll take everything you've got, down to the hide on the soles of you feet. When it's through with you, it'll spit you in the dirt and let the wind cover you over." He grinned. "But it don't have to go that way. Look at me." He spread his arms, showing his new but dusty clothes, his fine hand-tooled holster, his well-blocked Stetson, and shiny leather riding gloves. "I drive cattle myself when I can't keep from it, only I don't do it for a dollar a day and found. No siree. If I mess with longhorns, I make as much as Riley, and don't have to stand near the expense he does."

Jed spat, crossing his wrists on his saddle horn and looking away. Tim stiffened a bit and said to Arno Dunne, "What you're telling us is that you're a cattle rustler, no different than the ones who stole from Jacob Riley."

"Cattle rustler? A thief? Naw, not me." Arno Dunne laughed under his breath. "But let's put this way, it ain't stealing if they're just running around loose. Same way with Mexican horses. If the *padrones* can't keep their horses on their side of the border, they shouldn't complain about losing them."

"We see what you're getting at, Dunne," Tim answered, barely hiding his disgust. "I reckon we'll just say *adios* here and go our way."

"Boys, you oughta think about it first," Arno Dunne cautioned them before they had time to turn their horses. "Where you going to go right now? You're broke and hungry—you said so yourselves." He reached a gloved hand back and patted his bulging saddlebags. "I've got supplies for over a week, and money to buy more once these run out."

"We don't take handouts, Dunne," Jed Strange said, now turning his bay. "Let's go, Tim."

"Not so fast," Tim said, reaching a hand out and taking Jed's bay by its bridle, stopping it. "Dunne, you said you and your bunch handle cattle when you can't keep from it. What do you do the rest of the time?"

"Tim, you don't mean it," Jed said, stunned by his brother's interest.

Dunne spread another slick grin. "At a boy, now you're starting to use your head." He tapped his cigar to his temple. "We do whatever comes up the trail to us. Most make enough money that most times we don't have to do anything at all. Think you could handle that? Learn to take life easy, enjoy the spoils of the land?"

Tim stared at him for a second, then asked, "And where are your friends? Where are you headed?"

Arno Dunne pointed southeast with his cigar. "They're waiting for me right now, boys. Right down there, smack in the heart of Indian Territory."

"That's it for me, I'm leaving, Tim," Jed murmured, "and you're leaving with me." Again Jed tried to turn his bay, but Tim held it firm by its bridle as he spoke to Dunne.

"Will you excuse me and my brother for a minute, Dunne?" Tim asked.

Arno Dunne said with a sweeping gesture of his cigar, "Take your time, boys, talk it over real good. We're in no hurry here."

Chapter 8

Arno Dunne looked on from twenty feet away as Jed and Tim Strange talked between themselves. At first Jed was strongly opposed to riding any farther with a rustler like Arno Dunne. While Dunne watched, he smiled to himself and blew long streams of cigar smoke into the hot passing breeze. He couldn't make out Jed Strange's words, but he could tell by the way the boy shook his head that he wasn't at all interested in Dunne's proposition.

"How can you even consider taking up with this man, Tim?" Jed whispered to his twin brother. "If we get tangled up with a bunch like he's talking about, we'll never find Danielle. We'll be lucky if we don't hang." As Jed spoke, he took the window shade cord from his pocket that he'd been carrying ever since St. Joseph. Out of habit now, he anxiously coiled it back and forth around his finger.

"Listen to me, Jed." Tim spoke in a firm tone, reaching out and clasping his hand down on Jed's, stopping him from toying with the window shade cord. "I've been thinking about it ever since this man opened his mouth about Indian Territory. If Danielle's down there hunting down killers, this is the kind of men she'll be after. She could be on their trail right now. For all we know, Dunne could *be* one of Pa's killers, or know of them anyway. I can see what he is, but he might have come along at just the right time to be some help to us. He knows the Territory, and we don't."

"Yeah," Jed interjected, "but remember what Danny Duggin said? There's men in the Territory who'll cut your throat just to see how you fall? That's Dunne, if you want my opinion." Jed reached into his pocket and took out his small whittling knife. He cut the length of window sash cord in half as he spoke.

"I know it is, Jed. That's why I figure nobody will bother us so long as we're with him. All we got to do is keep an eye on him. We'll stick with him and his friends until we

136

know our way around. When it comes to taking care of ourselves with a gun, we've got no problem. We just have to watch our step. What do you say?"

"I say, we ain't going to get started breaking the law, Tim. It's easy enough to get in dutch out here without going looking for it."

"I know," Tim said, "but we've got to make a move of some kind or we'll never do what we set out to. The job didn't pan out. Now I say we get to looking for Danielle before that plan goes wrong on us as well. If we ain't got enough sense to keep from becoming outlaws, we ought not to be out here in the first place. Now, are you with me on this?"

"Are you going on with him, even if I'm not?" Jed asked, his eyes searching Tim's.

Tim let out a breath, then replied, "No, brother, you know better than that. I'm just saying we better get to doing something, or else go on back home and forget it."

Jed looked away for a moment, considering it. He took one of the lengths of window shade cord and deftly fashioned a miniature thirteen-knot noose into it. He laid it on his knee, then picked up the other length and formed another small noose. Finally he looked back at Tim and handed him one of the nooses and said, "All right, let's do it. Just make sure we watch each other's backs."

"That goes without saying," Tim whispered. "But what's this for?"

"Just to remind us we're riding in the shadow of a noose," said Jed. He spun his own miniature noose around on his finger and slipped it down around his saddle horn.

"Good idea," Tim said, slipping his miniature noose down on his saddle horn the same way. "We'll always remember that it's just you and me against the rest of the outlaw world, brother." When they both turned their bays back around and heeled them toward Arno Dunne, the man smiled even wider than he had before, seeing the looks on their faces.

"All right then," Arno Dunne said jovially, jerking his horse around to the thin trail leading off to the southeast toward a stretch of low badlands hills. "Let's press some saddle leather, boys. We've wasted too much time as it is."

The Washita River, Indian Territory,
July 20, 1871

Fortunately for Danielle Strange, Duncan Grago had made no more mention of swinging out of their way to rob a bank on their way deeper into Indian Territory. Danielle would not have gone along with it even if he had. She remained ever mindful that her task was to hunt down a band of outlaws, not become one herself. Yet, the farther they traveled without any incident, the more restless and angry Duncan Grago became. He directed none of his anger toward her, for he knew better. But toward everything else, including the land itself, Duncan Grago became seething mad and hard-handed. Even his horse became a victim of his rage, and would have suffered much abuse

138

had it not been for Danielle stopping him. When the poor animal had stumbled coming down a slope of loose rock, Duncan Grago had jumped down from his saddle, picked up a hand-sized stone, and screamed at the helpless animal.

"You worthless buzzard-bait son of a bitch!" he raged, drawing his arm high and wide, ready to smash the horse between the eyes.

But Danielle had already seen the attack coming and was down from her saddle in a flash. She caught Duncan's arm with her left hand, and with her right hand swung her pistol full circle, cracking Grago across the top of his head with the barrel. It was nearly a half hour before Duncan Grago became conscious. During that time, Danielle dragged him into the shade beneath a high wide pine tree, propping him up against it.

She stood back with her hand near her pistol butt, just in case he awoke and made a move on her. But as he raised his bleary eyes to her, he only asked in dull confusion, "What—what happened?"

Danielle took a hard tone with him, saying, "I busted your head with a gun barrel, that's what happened."

Duncan Grago's eyes flashed white hot for a second, but noting her hand near her Colt, and having already seen what that Colt could do, he checked himself, raising a hand to his throbbing head and asking with a groan, "What the hell for? Last I remember, I was going to knock that cayuse's head off."

"That's right, you were, you damn fool," Danielle spat, leaning down and lifting him by his shoulder. "Then you'd be afoot the rest of the way, or else I'd be stuck with you against my back."

Duncan Grago looked bewildered for a moment, considering it. "I reckon I just saw red when the horse faltered under me."

"Well, you best start seeing some other color," Danielle said, helping him steady himself on his wobbly feet. "This ain't the kind of country to be in without a horse. Do something that stupid, and I'll leave you to the coyotes." She shoved him slightly, guiding his horse.

"I—I didn't mean to," Grago said. "I don't know what came over me."

Danielle only watched and shook her head as Duncan struggled up into his saddle and gathered his reins. Then she stepped atop Sundown and heeled the big chestnut forward, keeping Duncan beside her and in her sight. Duncan Grago was like a storm in a clay jar, she thought, aching to bust loose and destroy something at every turn in the trail. Little did she know that his opportunity would come that very evening when they met a small crew of drovers leading a herd from the Texas panhandle toward Fort Smith.

Had Danielle seen the rising dust of the herd sooner, she would have diverted around them. But by the time she and Duncan rode up a wide rocky basin, the lead rider was already in sight, moving toward them slowly with some forty head of cattle trudging a few yards behind him. "Well," Duncan said with a grin, "looks like we don't have to cook tonight."

"Yeah," Danielle replied, already getting a bad feeling. "Let's mind our manners. We don't need to draw attention to ourselves." But she could tell by the look on Duncan's face that he had no idea what she meant. She nudged Sundown forward grudgingly, seeing the lead drover raise a gloved hand toward them from a hundred yards away.

"Hello, the herd!" Danielle called out as she and Duncan Grago drew nearer and pulled their horses to one side, waiting for an invitation to approach.

"Hello yourselves," called out the lead man, waving them toward him. "Come on over, these cattle have no spook in 'em."

Danielle and Duncan moved in, sidling up to the young man who had looked more and more familiar as Danielle drew closer. "Dan?" said the young drover, peering at Danielle, "is that you?"

Danielle recognized him now through the caked dust on his cheeks and a week's worth of beard stubble. It was Tuck Carlyle, a young man her age with whom she'd worked the past summer running a herd of cattle. Seeing Tuck made Danielle's heart soar for a second. But then she reminded herself of Duncan Grago being with her, and realized she had to find a way to let Tuck know what she was up to. Luckily for her, Tuck had only called her Dan, and not *Daniel Strange* as he might have

141

done. Tuck had no idea that the person he knew as Daniel Strange was really a woman. He did know that Daniel Strange had been on the vengeance trail the last time they'd seen one another.

"Yep, it's me, Danny Duggin," Danielle said, staring intensely at Tuck, hoping he'd get the message. He did, and right away.

"I knew that was you riding in, Danny," Tuck said without a hitch. "But you do look different, having grown yourself a lip duster. And ya got yourself a scar, I see."

"Yep," Danielle replied, touching her finger to her cheek. "I had a little disagreement over a card game. How've you been, Tuck?"

"Fine as can be," Tuck said, letting his gaze drift from Danielle to Duncan Grago.

"This is Dunc," Danielle said. "We're riding together these days." The way she said it gave Tuck Carlyle an idea that the two were not close friends. "Dunc, this is Tuck Carlyle, a trail buddy of mine."

Duncan Grago only lifted his chin in a short nod and said nothing, even as Tuck acknowledged him with a howdy and a friendly smile. Tuck turned back to Danielle, saying, "What about you? Are you still—?" Tuck caught himself and reshuffled his words. He was about to ask whether she was still hunting the outlaws who had killed her father, but he changed the question quickly, and asked, "Are you still doing what you were doing the last time I saw you?" The way he said it worked out perfect for Danielle, for it sounded

142

as if Danielle might have been up to something on the sly.

"Yeah, I'm still dodging the law," Danielle said. "It's all right to say it in front of Dunc. He's had some run-ins with the law himself, right, Dunc?"

"Yeah," Duncan Grago sneered, looking away as he spoke. "And I plan on having some more before I get too old to enjoy it."

Tuck Carlyle gave Danielle a guarded nod, letting her know he understood. "Hope you'll be staying for supper, Danny," Tuck said. "Long as it's been, I reckon we ought to get caught up."

"Thanks for the invite," Danielle said, "but we best be moving along."

"What's our hurry?" Grago asked, taking on a bolder tone now that someone was around to see and hear him.

Before Danielle could come up with a reply, Tuck Carlyle cut in, saying, "Sure, Danny, what's your hurry?" He jerked his head back toward the rest of the drovers strung out along the herd. "Nobody back there knows you." This was Tuck's way of letting Danielle know that nobody would slip up and say the wrong thing. "Have supper with us. We're just a greasy sack outfit,* but we eat as good as anybody."

Danielle relented. "Well, why not then? Whose small herd is this anyway?"

*Greasy sack outfit *was a term for an outfit with no chuck wagon. Such outfits carried their provisions in flour sacks and canvas bags.*

"These hide racks belong to the old Scotsman, Connery. He lost them in a poker game to Dubb Macklin in Fort Smith. He's paying me and the others to deliver them for him. I reckon delivery was part of the bet." Tuck grinned. "Evidently the age or condition of the animals wasn't though. There's a couple in there you'd swear came over with Noah on his ark. I'll be glad to get shed of them. Keep hoping rustlers will take 'em off our hands, but so far we've had no takers."

Danielle laughed with him, then asked, "How's your sister, Carrie, and your ma?"

"Ma's fine, Carrie too." Tuck lifted a gaze to Danielle, adding about his sister, "She still talks about you all the time. I tried telling her there's more than one moony-eyed cowhand prowling the range. She won't hear of it, though."

"I wish she would," Danielle said. "There's no place for her with me."

Danielle let herself reflect back on the summer past, when there had been a peculiar situation between herself, Tuck Carlyle, and his sister Carrie. Danielle had never let the Carlyles know that she was really a woman disguising herself as a man. Because of it, Carrie Carlyle had become deeply infatuated with the person she knew as Daniel Strange. To make matters worse, Danielle had herself fallen head over heels for Tuck Carlyle for a time. Thinking about it reminded her of how much she'd learned over the past year on the trail. Becoming attracted to a man was the one thing she must avoid at all cost. There would come a day when Danielle would shed her disguise and take up the normal life of a woman. But until that day came, she would be careful not to let her feelings as a woman come between her and what she must do.

"Well, so much for wishful thinking," Tuck Carlyle said, as if in answer to Danielle's thoughts.

Danielle gave him a questioning look, and seeing it, Tuck went on to explain, "I mean, about Carrie still wanting you to come back and sweep her off her feet."

"Yeah," Danielle said, looking Tuck up and down longingly, then turning her face forward to the open land, "so much for wishful thinking."

"So, what time will this bunch be stopping to pull down some grub?" Duncan Grago asked, his tone rude and impatient.

Tuck Carlyle passed a glance at Danielle, then replied, "This is no sun-to-sun drive. I reckon we can gather down as soon as we get to the basin up ahead. Can you wait that long?"

"I reckon I can if I have to," Duncan Grago grumbled under his breath.

There were only four other cowhands working the small drive, Tuck Carlyle taking up the roles of trail boss, line-rider, and point man. At supper time, a young man named Curtis Lotts, who doubled as cook, prepared a pot of beans with pork seasoning, and a platter of what he called fried chicken, which was really nothing more than a wishful term for thick bacon rolled in flour and fried to a crisp turn. Around the campfire sat Tuck Carlyle, Curtis Lotts, and an old drover from Abilene known only as Stick. The other two men were a couple of brothers named Clarence and Tolliver Martin, who worked full time for the old Scotsman's spread. These two sat watch on the small herd, waiting to be relieved for supper by Stick and Curtis Lotts.

As soon as Danielle found a moment alone with Tuck Carlyle, she quickly explained to him about the knife fight she'd had, and how she was going by the name *Danny Duggin,* hoping the reputation she'd built as Daniel Strange would die down. Inspecting Sundown's hooves while the two of them stood a few yards away from Duncan Grago and the others, she told Tuck who Duncan was and why she was traveling with him. Tuck Carlyle only shook his head.

"I swear, Dan, the farther you ride this vengeance trail, the less I recognize you, and I'm not talking about just the mustache and the scar on your cheek."

"I know, Tuck," Danielle responded, straightening up from Sundown's hooves and dusting her hands together. "Sometimes I don't rightly recognize myself. But I'm praying it'll all be over soon. When it is, I hope to run into you again. There's things I'd tell you that I can't tell you now." She longed for the day when she could reveal her true identity to him, and settle down to a normal life.

"We're *amigos*, Dan," Tuck said, "so anytime you've got to tell me, I'll be ready to listen. Meanwhile, I've sure got some news for you. Remember the Flagg family, the ones who threw some of their cattle in on the drive we made last year?"

"Yep, I remember them," said Danielle. "Good folks as I recall."

"That's right they are. Well, ole man Flagg's sister in St. Louis passed away and her widower husband sent their daughter Ilene to live with the Flaggs whilst he works the steamers." His eyes got excited as he continued. "The thing is, Dan, she and I have struck up quite a romance. The next time you see me, there's a good chance she'll be my wife, that is, if she'll have me."

They had turned and started back toward the campfire as Tuck spoke. Now his words stopped Danielle in her tracks. She stood speechless, trying hard to hide the disappointment in her eyes. After a moment of seeing how his words had affected his friend, Tuck Carlyle laughed and said, "Damn, Dan, don't look so troubled by it! I just told you I might be getting married, not that I was about to get myself snakebit."

Danielle shook the weight of sadness from her shoulders and forced herself to laugh along with him. "I know, Tuck. It just took me by surprise for a second there. I'm happy for you, real happy. If I'm around, I better get an invitation to the wedding."

Tuck slapped her on the back. "Hell, that goes without saying. What about you, Dan? Have you met yourself a good woman yet?"

"Naw," Danielle said, "you know me. I've got no time for anything but the hunt for my pa's killers."

"Maybe once that's over, you'll run into the right person," Tuck said encouragingly.

"Yes, maybe so," Danielle said, looking away from him as they stepped in closer to the campfire so that he couldn't see the hurt in her eyes.

All went well throughout the evening meal. Duncan Grago was sullen, and while not the friendliest man the drovers had ever met, he'd at least managed to keep quiet and eat his meal. But about the time Danielle thought the evening might pass without incident, Duncan's mood took a sharp turn for the worse. Once Stick and Curtis Lotts had left to relieve the Martin brothers, Clarence Martin tried to show an extra stretch of hospitality by pulling out a bottle of rye he'd been saving in his saddlebags.

"Whoa, boys, no drinking on the trail," said Tuck Carlyle, seeing Clarence hold the bottle up in his hand. Clarence's intention had been to ask Tuck's permission before passing the bottle around the campfire. Yet the bottle of rye seemed to strike a chord in Duncan Grago's brain. He snatched the bottle as he butted in, cutting Tuck Carlyle off.

"Don't mind if I do, buddy," Grago said, already pulling the cork from the bottle with his teeth.

Tuck Carlyle saw it was too late to stop him, so he tried instead to alter the course. "Well, one drink each, boys," he said, "but only because we have a couple of supper guests."

Saying that was also a mistake, Danielle thought, watching the words sink into Duncan Grago's mind. Knowing it was going to be his only drink for the night, Duncan took a long, deep pull that drew everybody's rapt attention until he lowered the bottle and blew out a tight breath. "Lord, that's good!" he exclaimed, his face glowing red in a instant from the rush of alcohol.

Danielle had no desire for a drink. Her only purpose in reaching for the bottle was to get it out of Duncan's hand before he threw back another long guzzle. "Then let us in on it," she said, snatching the bottle from him.

"Dang it," Clarence Martin said in a half-joking tone, "I didn't mean for yas to drink it all."

"Then you shouldn't have brought it out," Duncan Grago shot back at him. There was no mistaking the lack of humor in Duncan's voice.

Danielle saw the long drink of whiskey wrap its tentacles around Duncan Grago's mood, and she almost held her breath at what she knew could turn ugly as quick as a streak of heat lightning.

"I was only joshing," said Clarence Martin, taking the bottle back and rubbing his hand across the top of it. "Whiskey's meant to be drunk, is what I always say."

But Duncan Grago took Clarence's words as a sign of weakness and gave him a look of contempt. "Is that so, huh? Then give me that bottle and watch me drink it."

"I said one drink each," Tuck Carlyle cut in. Being the trail boss, Tuck knew it was up to him to clamp down before things got out of hand. "I never allow my drovers to drink on the trail. It's a bad practice." He held his hand out for the bottle, but Duncan only looked at it with a dark chuckle as he spoke.

"I ain't one of your drovers, and I don't need no *practice*. I been drinking right handily for years." He raised the bottle to his lips and threw back a shot, but Danielle's hand shot out and once again snatched it from his lips. Whiskey spilled. Clarence Martin muttered under his breath in disapproval.

"Here you go, Tuck," Danielle said in a low tone, keeping her eyes on Duncan Grago as she picked the cork up from the ground, wiping it on her thigh and shoving it down into the bottle. She pitched the bottle up to Tuck, who stood above the rest of them seated around the fire. "It's time we shove off, Dunc," she added to Duncan Grago, seeing his eyes fixed coldly on Tuck Carlyle.

"Why?" Duncan asked, the heat of the whiskey boiling inside his head and chest. "No need in us going somewhere and making a camp when there's one right here." His eyes were still locked on Tuck Carlyle, and Tuck hadn't backed down an inch. Danielle knew Tuck wouldn't, not for Duncan Grago or anybody else. She acted quick, reaching out with her boot and nudging Duncan.

"I said, it's time we go. Now come on, or I'll leave you where you're sitting." As she spoke, her hand rested poised near her pistol butt.

Duncan Grago hesitated a second longer, then he let out a breath and said grudgingly, "Hell, all right then." Rising up and dusting off the seat of his trousers, he gave a smug parting glance to Tuck Carlyle, then turned it to Clarence Martin. "You ever need me to show you how to drink whiskey, just come looking."

The words stung Clarence Martin's pride, and as Duncan and Danielle turned to walk to their horses, Clarence rose from the ground, muttering under his breath, "By Gawd if he didn't spill as much as he drunk."

Duncan Grago let out a sarcastic laugh over his shoulder, saying in a belittling voice, "If you're going to weep over it like a woman, send me a bill for it, you steer-licking peckerwood."

That did it. Clarence Martin threw his hand to his pistol, shouting as he raised it, shouting, "You belligerent bastard!" Three shots resounded as Duncan Grago ducked to one side, turning, drawing, and firing back at the flashes of muzzle fire in the graying evening light. All Danielle could do at that split second was move aside, crouching as the bullets flew. Tuck Carlyle and Tolliver Martin did the same, for no matter what kind of man

Duncan Grago was, and no matter how he'd provoked the fight, at that moment he was within his rights to defend himself.

A total of eight shots were fired between them. Clarence Martin's shots went wild as he sank backward to the ground, one of Duncan Grago's first bullets nailing his chest. Tolliver Martin had recovered from his shock and went for his pistol, but one of Duncan's shots sliced deep into his shoulder. He flew backward across the campfire with flames licking at his wool shirt.

"You all saw it!" Duncan Grago screamed, backing toward his horse, his pistol fanning back and forth between Tuck and Danielle. "He tried back-shooting me! I had to kill him!"

Danielle and Tuck Carlyle gritted their teeth and fought the urge to go for their Colts. But they knew they couldn't dispute Duncan Grago. Clarence Martin had done the unthinkable, and it had left him dead on the ground. His brother Tolliver rolled back and forth on the ground, smothering the fire from his wool shirt, his pistol lying a foot from his hand. He tried lifting himself to his feet, his left hand clenched tight to his wounded shoulder.

"Nobody move!" Duncan Grago shouted, backing farther away to his horse. "Don't nobody try to follow me!"

"Wait, Dunc," Danielle called out to him, stepping forward. But Duncan Grago was wild and scared, not even hearing her. He swung up into his saddle with his pistol still pointed at them and batted his horse away from the campsite at a fast clip.

"Help me find my pistol," Tolliver Martin cried out, his voice strained against the pain in his bleeding shoulder. He staggered, in place. Tuck Carlyle caught him as he fell, and helped sit him on the ground as blood poured freely. "I'm going after him! I'll kill him. Look what he done to my brother!"

"Easy now, Toll," said Tuck, trying to console him as he tore open his shirtsleeve to inspect the wound. "I hate saying it, but that man was in his rights. I don't know what got into Clarence, doing a thing like that. But you getting yourself killed ain't going to change a thing."

Hearing the gunfire from camp, the small herd of cattle milled in a spreading circle, spooked. Stick and Lotts pressed their horses dangerously close to the frightened beasts, keeping a firm hold on them, folding the circle back upon itself. "Thank the Lord these old dowds ain't breech-loaded!*" Stick called across the restless tangle of horns, "They're too old to run or they'd be gone by now!"

"Reckon you've got them?" Lott called back to him. "I'll go see what's the matter!"

"Go on! These hides have no run in 'em! I'll join you once they 'plete down!"

Lotts turned, booting his horse toward

* Dowds *was a term for bulls past their prime;* breech-loaded, *a term for uncut bulls.*

153

camp. As he slid his horse to a halt, dropping from its back before it had settled, he saw Clarence Martin's body, and saw Tuck and Danielle leaning down over Tolliver. "What's happened?" Lotts shouted.

"Just what it looks like," Danielle said stiffly. "Clarence and Dunc went at it. Dunc killed him and wounded his brother." Even as Danielle spoke, she took a step back and gazed off at the lingering dust left by Duncan Grago's horse. "Damn, I'm awful sorry, Tuck," she said. "It was a mistake thinking that lunatic could go a meal without causing trouble."

"It wasn't your fault," Tuck said, looking up from tending to Tolliver's wound. "Things got said that couldn't be made right. You're wanting to get right after him, ain't ya?"

"I won't leave you short-handed, Tuck," she replied. "It ain't my style."

"I know it ain't, Dan," Tuck said with a grimace, "but go on. If there's anything good to come of this, it'll be you taking care of that bastard once and for all." Tuck looked around at Curtis Lotts and asked, "How's the herd?"

"Stick's got 'em steadied. He's coming directly."

"No, he ain't," said Tuck. "Get out there and tell him to hold tight. You too. Nothing you can do here. This is done." When he looked back toward Danielle, she had taken another step back toward her chestnut mare, a questioning look in her eyes, until Tuck nodded hard, saying, "Yes, go on. This ain't changed nothing between us. We're still *amigos.*"

"Thanks, Tuck," Danielle said in a quiet voice, taking another slow step before breaking into a run toward Sundown. In a second she was mounted and gone, Sundown's hooves pounding the hard earth beneath them.

Chapter 9

Indian Territory, July 21, 1871

Duncan Grago had gotten a good head start, and with no regard whatsoever for his horse's safety, he'd kept a good distance between himself and Danielle throughout most of the night. Danielle, keeping Sundown at a steady but safe pace in the rugged rock and brushland, kept on Duncan's trail by following the looming dust in the night air. From time to time she dropped down from her saddle and found his horse's hoofprints in the pale moonlight.

Around an hour before dawn, Danielle heard the distant sound of a horse nickering long and loud in pain. Knowing it had to be Duncan's horse, she pushed her chestnut mare a little harder toward the sound until at last she found the horse limping in a slow circle beside the narrow trail.

Swinging down from her saddle, Danielle

called out to the black shadows on a hillside to her right, "Dunc, it's me, Danny. I'm by myself. Don't do nothing stupid." Footprints on the ground wandered in a short circle, then led up into the brush on a steep slope.

Danielle gathered the reins of the limping horse, straightened the saddle hanging down on its side, and called out again, "I know you hear me, Dunc. Come on down. Nobody's going to bother you."

After a moment of silence, Duncan Grago's voice came out of the purple darkness, saying, "Nobody is with you, Danny? Are you sure?"

"Damn it, Dunc, I told you I'm alone, didn't I? Get down here right now, or I'm going to leave you behind. Why'd you keep me tracking you all night anyway?"

"I'm coming, Danny, all right?" Duncan Grago scurried down through sand and brush. "I was just afraid you'd taken their side against me."

"You were in the right back there, Dunc, even Tuck Carlyle said so," Danielle said to Duncan's dark figure as he stepped out of the inky night. She didn't mention the fact that he had provoked the fight, for it would do no good now. What she needed now was to get the two of them back on the trail, headed for the men who'd killed her father.

"I knew it was self-defense," Duncan Grago said, stepping closer in the moonlight, his pistol hanging loose in his hand, "but I wasn't sure that it would make any difference to your friends."

Danielle shook her head, saying, "Holster your pistol, Dunc. Tuck saw how it happened. He didn't like it, but he had to abide by it. He's the trail boss. What he says goes with his cowhands."

"It's because you were with me, wasn't it?" Duncan asked, slipping his pistol inside his holster. "If it hadn't been for you, they'd have been right on my tail."

"Maybe," Danielle said. She leaned down beside Duncan's horse as she spoke, and gently ran a hand along the swollen tendon in its right leg, then upward along the lumpiness in its knee. The horse whinnied low in pain. Letting out a tired breath, Danielle said as she straightened and dusted off her hands, "This poor animal's done for out here. You should have known better than to push it so hard in the dark, on this kind of ground."

"I—I wasn't thinking as clear as I should have been," Duncan said, his voice sounding ashamed. "That whiskey had me a little *loco* for a while. I drank it too fast, I reckon."

"Yeah, I reckon," Danielle said with a snap of sarcasm. "Now I have to decide whether or not I want you breathing on my back until we can find you a horse somewhere."

"I don't know what comes over me sometimes," Duncan Grago said. Danielle took note of how much he sounded like a schoolboy caught in some kind of mischief. She almost felt sorry for him, were it not for the body of Clarence Martin lying dead in the distant darkness, and the countless others who'd

157

suffered at Duncan Grago's hand. Duncan continued, "It seems like something's inside me that just busts out all of a sudden. I can't help it."

Danielle didn't answer as she reached down, loosened the cinch from beneath his horse's belly, and dropped the saddle to the ground. She dropped the bridle from around the horse's muzzle and watched it wander for a moment on its shattered leg, nickering pitifully. "Finish it," she said to Duncan in a low, solemn tone. Then she stepped away and turned to Sundown, holding on to the reins until the sound and flash of Duncan Grago's pistol filled the night, and the pain-filled nickering of his horse was cut short into silence.

When they'd both stepped atop Sundown, Duncan Grago adjusted himself against Danielle's back, his saddle and bridle resting down along his leg. "I've never liked thanking a person," Duncan said, "and the fact is I've never had much reason to." His voice softened, "But I'm obliged to you, Danny Duggin. Nobody has ever befriended me this way. I kind of wished they had over the years. You've been straight with me."

Danielle felt the slightest twinge of guilt for a second and had to remind herself of what a low piece of work Duncan Grago really was. "Well, like I said, Dunc, you were in the right back there. Once I side with a person, I try to stick with them." She gave the chestnut mare a slight nudge, letting the mare make her own pace at a walk. "From now on, though, you're going to have to act like you've got some sense," she added.

"I will, Danny... I'll try," Duncan said.

In the clammy coolness before dawn, Danielle became more and more aware of the heat of Duncan Grago against her back. The feel of him evoked an uncomfortable urge inside her that she didn't want to admit to. She had no passion for the likes of Duncan Grago, yet the closeness of a man stirred something inside her that she could not deny. As the first thin reef of sunlight spread across the horizon, she felt Duncan Grago slumber against her, his head lying over her shoulder and his warm breath caressing the side of her throat. She shifted uneasily in her saddle. Unable to escape the closeness of him, she finally gigged him gently with her elbow and said, "Wake up, Dunc. You hear me? Wake up, it's daylight."

"Huh?" As he stirred from his sleep, he became unsteady and threw his arm around her chest to keep from slipping off the mare's rump. Duncan noticed nothing out of the ordinary when his hand clutched the binder she used to flatten her breasts, but she did, and her natural impulse was the shove his hand away. Her reaction stunned him from his drowsiness for a second, and he said, "Oh sorry, Danny," before he even realized why he'd said it.

"It's time we got down and rested the mare," Danielle said, her cheeks feeling flushed. Yet, Duncan had slumped forward against her again, and seemed to have relaxed back to sleep.

"Just a few more minutes," he whispered, dreamily, too drowsy to notice the warm comfortable feeling that sleeping against Danny Duggin induced in him.

Danielle prodded him again, harder this time, saying, "Hey, what the hell is wrong with you? Wake up, I'm not your pillow!"

The shock of the situation struck a sharp note in Duncan Grago's mind, and he flung himself off the mare, looking confused and embarrassed as he staggered in place. "Oh, Danny! Damn it! I—I'm sorry! I must have been dreaming."

"Forget it," Danielle snapped. Unable to face him directly for a moment, she looked back along the trail, then at Duncan's empty hands. "Where's your saddle and tack?"

Duncan shook sleep from his eyes, and lowered his head. "Damn it, I must've dropped them both somewhere."

Danielle slumped a bit in disgust, saying, "Well, hell. You've just about lost everything but your boots." Then she swung down from her saddle and stretched her legs. "We're going to have to take turns on this mare, to not wear her out. We'll also have to rest her in the hottest part of the day."

"I'll ride the first hour," Danielle continued. "Then you take the next hour. How much farther is it to your brother and his men?"

"Not far," Duncan Grago said. "We should be there tomorrow sometime. There's an old relay station thirty miles ahead. If I'm lucky, I can pick up a horse there."

Salt Fork of Red River, Indian Territory, July 22, 1871

Traveling with Arno Dunne, Jed and Tim Strange had kept ever mindful of what they told him about themselves. Dunne had a way of trying to pry information out of them in what appeared to be normal conversation. But the twins had revealed little to him. When Dunne had asked them what their last name was, Tim told him it was Faulkner, their mother's maiden name being the first name that had popped into his mind. They had been riding their horses at a walk along a winding ridge-line when Dunne asked, and looking back and forth at their faces as he stopped his horse and let the twins drift past him, he couldn't judge whether or not they were telling him the truth.

"Faulkner, huh? Well, that's good enough for now," Dunne whispered to himself, watching the twins turn their bays on the thin trail and sit looking back at him.

"What's the holdup?" Tim asked, his hand relaxed and comfortable on his lap near the butt of his Colt. Jed Strange let his bay take a sidelong step, putting a couple of feet between him and his brother.

"Nothing," said Arno Dunne with a shrug. "Just got tired of riding lead. Thought I'd drop back for a while." He caught the look of

161

distrust in their eyes, and shook his head. "Boys, I've never saw two young men so full of suspicion in my life."

Tim offered a faint smile and spoke in a polite manner. "It's not that we don't trust you, Dunne. It's just that you're the only one who knows the way we're going."

"Oh, I see." Arno Dunne chuckled, nudging his horse forward. "I'm glad you cleared that up for me. I was about to think you didn't trust me behind your backs." He passed between them, tipping his fingers to his hat brim, once more taking the lead.

As Dunne rode a few yards ahead of the twins, Tim looked at Jed, saying, "See how easily he does things? We let down for a second and he puts us right at his advantage."

"I know," Jed replied, watching Arno Dunne's back. "But it won't happen again." As he spoke, he toyed with the miniature noose hanging from his saddle horn. "How's your leg feeling?"

Tim patted his healing wound gently. "It's mending right along," he said. "How about your arm?"

"It's almost good as new," Jed said, stretching his arm, working his fingers open and shut. "I'm ready for whatever's ahead."

"Good." Tim nodded, the two of them heeling their bays closer behind Arno Dunne.

Dunne looked back over his shoulder at them, saying, "Did you ever stop to think what a big chance *I'm* taking? Why should I be so sure I can trust you two behind me?"

"You invited us, Dunne," Tim said. "If it's not to your liking, just let us know."

Dunne let out a short laugh. "Naw, I'm only joshing with you. If I had any doubts, we wouldn't have come this far. The truth is, I can see you two haven't had as much experience as you let on. But that's okay by me," he added quickly. "I saw how handy you are with those Colts." He paused as if thinking something over, then said without turning to them, "Tell me something, though. How would you feel about an ol' fashioned duel?"

"What do you mean?" Jed asked, the two of them moving their bays up closer as the trail broadened.

"You know," said Dunne, "stepping off ten paces, looking a man in the eyes until somebody gives a signal, then trying your best to blow the hell out of him before he does the same thing to you? Think either one of you can handle that?"

"You sound like you're talking about a sporting event," Jed responded.

"Yeah," Tim interjected, "and gunfighting is not a sport, Dunne. Why would any man consider doing something like that?"

"Why, for money, of course." Dunne chuckled. "I mean *serious* money, the kind you can unroll onto your palm and feel the weight of it. The kind of money that makes women swoon, and makes men green with envy." He tossed them a glance over his shoulder, smiling slyly. "Think about it, boys. I'm talking about the kind of money that instead of pinching a nickel for a beer and a free lunch, you'd be setting up the house and leaning with your thumbs hooked under your arms."

"You're talking to the wrong men, Dunne," Jed replied. "That kind of money has blood all over it."

"Just making conversation is all," Dunne said, stepping his horse off the trail toward a ridge overlooking a wide stretch of flatland. "But in case you don't know it, blood washes right off of money. The bigger the money, the less of a stain blood leaves on it."

"But still," Jed said, "we were taught that the only time to use our Colts is in self-defense. It ain't right, what you're talking about—"

"Exactly how much money are you talking about, Dunne?" Tim Strange asked, cutting his twin brother off.

Arno Dunne had stopped his horse close to the edge of the ridge. He rose up in his stirrups, gazed out across the flatland, then backed his horse so it faced the twins. He smiled, tapping a finger to his forehead. "Now there's the proper question—*how much money?*" He winked, and looked back and forth between them. "For twins, you two sure have some different ways of looking at things, don't you?" He gestured his hand toward Jed, saying, "Jed's only concern is whether something is right or wrong. But you"—he pointed his finger at Tim—"you go right to the business end of it. You want to know what it's worth to you in dollars and cents. I like that." Arno

Dunne's smile broadened, staring at Tim Strange.

Tim shrugged. "What's the harm in asking? You said you were only making conversation. That's true, ain't it?"

"What's the difference whether or not I was just making conversation?" Arno Dunne asked. "The question is still on the table—would you fight a duel like that or not?"

"It depends on the kind of man I was up against," Tim replied, his gaze fixed right on Arno Dunne.

"Hell, boy, we already know what kind of man he is. He's the kind of man who would kill you for money, or else he wouldn't be standing there. Now that we've settled that, would you do it or not?"

Tim looked away from Dunne, saying, "You're talking crazy. I don't want to hear any more about it."

Dunne laughed and shook his head. "Then let me ask you both this. Are you tired of riding those lank-sided bays? Because if you are, we've got a fresh change of horse coming." He jerked his head toward that flatland below the ridgeline. "They should be getting here most anytime."

"What are you talking about?" Jed stepped his bay forward and peered out ahead. At a distance of less than three hundred yards, he noticed seven men moving toward them across the flatlands, leading a ten-horse string stretched out between them.

"He's right," Jed said to Tim, stepping his

bay back from the ridgeline. "It looks like a group of seven cowhands coming up from the Red."

"You counted seven," said Dunne, "but unless I've missed my guess, there's two more you didn't see."

"Seven or nine, what's the difference?" Tim said to Dunne. "We're not trading these bays. They're good horses. They're just a little bit off their weight right now. But they'll fill out once we get them on some steady grain."

"Trade?" Dunne chuckled. "Who the hell is talking about a trade? I swear, boys, do I have to spell everything out for yas? You don't trade for nothing out here, not if you've got any guts at all."

"Hold it, Dunne," Jed cut in. "We're not horse thieves and bushwhackers. Those are just some hardworking drovers down there."

"Oh, you think so? Well, you're wrong." Arno Dunne's face turned solemn, and he added, "Maybe it's time both of you decide exactly *what* you are. So far all I've heard is what the two of you *won't* do." Dunne stepped down, pulling his rifle from his saddle boot. "You can either side with me or stay out of my way. There's a fight coming up out of that draw."

"Not for me and Tim, there ain't," Jed said.

Arno Dunne turned to Tim, wiped a hand along his rifle barrel, and checked it. "What about it, Tim? You with me on this or not?"

"What are you saying, Dunne?" Tim asked. "That those men aren't drovers at all?"

"That's exactly what I'm saying." Arno Dunne levered a round into his rifle chamber. "They're headed this way because their two scouts spotted us and gave them a signal from somewhere, probably from behind us. Now you both best get to deciding where you stand on this."

"Like hell!" Jed swung his horse to the edge of the ridge, his pistol streaking up from his holster.

Seeing what his twin bother was about to do, Tim shouted, "Wait, Jed!"

But it was too late. Jed fired three warning shots into the air, the sound of them echoing out across the basin below as he yelled down, "Hello, the basin!"

"You damned fool!" Arno Dunne hissed. "Now you've done it! Get back from that edge, you've got yourself skylighted!"

But Jed didn't rein his bay horse back. Instead he turned the bay toward Dunne, his pistol covering him. Two hundred yards below on the flatland, the riders heard the shots and scattered into brush, fanning out into a broad circle surrounding the ridgeline. "I'm not moving until they're safely around us, Dunne," Jed replied.

"Then like as not, you've gotten us all killed," Dunne said. Paying no attention to Jed's pistol pointing at him, Dunne stepped away, taking a position behind a small cluster of rock and gazing down onto the flatland.

At the edge of the ridge, dirt and chips of rock suddenly sprang up at the hooves of Jed's bay beneath the sound of the rifle fire from below them. The horse shied back. "Get down, Jed!" Tim shouted. He didn't have to shout twice. A bullet whistled past Jed's head as he ducked, jerking his horse back from the edge.

From his position behind the rocks, Arno Dunne returned fire into the basin, already seeing the men moving into a widening circle around them. He tossed a quick glance at Jed and Tim Strange, watching them jerking their horses farther back out of the rifle fire. "You boys have a lot to learn," he shouted to them. "Too bad you ain't going to live long enough to learn it."

"Never mind about us, Dunne," Tim called out to him as Dunne raised his rifle and continued firing, "we'll live through this. How'd you know they weren't drovers?"

Arno Dunne shook his head in disgust. "There's some things you just know, boys, if you want to see the next sunrise."

Chapter 10

From their position in the rocks along the ridgeline, Tim turned to Dunne as the rifle fire drew closer around them. "Maybe there's still enough time for us to make a run back along the trail we came up on."

Arno Dunne let out a dark chuckle under his breath, scanning the puffs of rifle shots below them. "I've got a feeling that's what they would like for us to do." He jerked his head back toward the winding narrow trail. "Those two scouts I was talking about will be waiting back there for us, up in the rocks. They'll pick us off like ducks in a shooting galley."

"How do you know that, Dunne?" Jed asked in a critical tone.

"Because that's what I would do if I was them," Arno Dunne snapped. As a shot clipped a rock near his head, Dunne flinched back and cursed under his breath.

"Then what are we supposed to do?" Jed asked angrily, "just sit here while they get a tighter grip on us, kill our horses, then take what they want?"

"Nope," said Dunne, eyeing the two of them, "but horses *are* what they want. So they'll try their best not to kill them." He ducked slightly as another shot sliced through the air close to them. "Since you boys don't have rifles, what you're going to do is leave me here close to the horses while the two of you belly-crawl out through the firing and get behind them." He spread a thin smile. "It'll give you both a chance to use those big Colts you're so proud of."

Tim and Jed looked at one another for a second, then realized that what Dunne said made sense. "All right then," Tim responded, nodding toward the ten-gauge rabbit gun beside Jed, "we'll leave this with you in case they get in close enough for you to need it."

"Okay, leave it," said Dunne with a shrug, "but if they get that close, I'll be dead anyway."

"What if I pull the horses in closer to you?" Jed asked. "Won't that make them quit firing?"

"Naw, that'll just make 'em mad," said Dunne. "They'll know why you did it, then they'll say to hell with it and make a rush, killing everything. We got to keep the horses safe, for bait. As long as they know they've got a chance at gaining some live horses out of this deal, they'll move a little easier."

Two shots whistled past, forcing Tim to duck his head down as he asked Dunne, "Do you know these men?"

"Probably, some of them, by name anyway. But I wouldn't exactly say any of us were ever saddle mates. It wouldn't matter now if we were. They're making their play. They don't care who it is up here."

A shot whined in and blasted up bits of rock at Dunne's shoulder. He ventured a return shot over his cover of rock, then dropped back down and looked at the twins, saying, "They're moving closer. Are you going or not?"

Jed swallowed against the tight knot in his throat and looked at Tim. "Yeah, we're going," said Tim.

"All right, then," Dunne said. "Get behind them, but don't cut them off. Leave them room to fall back if they feel the urge. Keep them flanked, but be careful. You'll be firing toward one another."

"Let's go," Tim said to his brother. Jed

170

nodded, checked his pistol, then dropped down flat onto his belly beside Tim.

They crawled away in opposite directions beneath the rifle fire, which was now growing heavier and closer. Yet, Tim noted to himself as he'd put the distance of a few yards between himself and Arno Dunne's position, the rife fire had not followed him. They hadn't caught a glimpse of him crawling away. He hoped the same was true for his brother. He glanced back over his shoulder in the dirt, but saw no sign of Jed. "Watch yourself, Jed," he whispered to himself. Then he turned forward and continued crawling, gradually circling to his left.

Thirty yards on the other side of Arno Dunne, Jed Strange hugged the ground. Also noting that the rifle shots had not followed him, he breathed a short sigh of relief, then inched forward, circling to his right until he knew from the sound of the rifle fire that he'd gotten past the men's positions. He lay flat for a second, getting a feel for his next move. The sound of two rifles firing in unison lay less then twenty yards away. He crawled closer toward the sound, then stopped cold as he heard one man say to the other, "I'm reloading, keep them pinned."

"Take your time, Kelsy, I've got all day," the other voice replied.

Jed Strange held his breath for a moment, lest the sound of it be heard as he inched closer toward the backs of two men who lay beneath the cover of a short stretch of rock and

171

pale broom sage. Busy with their rifle fire, the two men never looked around, for if they had, they would have seen Jed clear as day. He crept to within twenty feet of them, his pistol cocked in their direction. The wise thing to do would be to shoot them both in the back with no warning. Yet, as he raised his pistol and aimed it dead center on a sweat-streaked leather vest, he hesitated. He could not abide shooting a man in the back.

As the two men fired repeatedly toward Arno Dunne's position, Jed stood slowly to his feet, took a deep breath, and said, "Both of you drop your guns! Raise your hands!"

"What the—?" The two men turned quickly to face him, neither of them making an attempt to lower their rifles.

"You heard me, drop them!" Jed demanded.

The riflemen would have none of it. "You bet," said one, a killing grin on his whiskered face. Their hands tightened on their rifles and, seeing the look on their faces, Jed's Colt exploded twice, bucking in his hand.

Both men went down, one pitching backward across the low stand of rock. The other man spun in place as he fell. His rifle went off, the shot going wild as his rifle jumped out of his hand and fell to the ground.

Jed threw himself to the ground as a voice called out from twenty feet away, "Hey, Kelsy, Dermot? What are you two doing over there? I heard pistol shots."

Jed hurried forward on his belly, snatched up the fallen rifle, checked it, and levered a round into the chamber. The voice called out again, "Somebody get over there, see what's going on with Dermot and Kelsy." As the voice spoke, the firing lulled for a second. Jed hurried to the covered low rock and turned himself toward the voice. Just as he did, he heard the sound of Tim's Colt bark out from across the wide circle of riflemen. "What the hell is going on out here?" the voice cried out.

"I don't know, but I'll damn sure find out," another voice responded. Jed waited for a second, aiming the rifle but holding his fire as the sound of footsteps rustled through the broom sage. When the man stepped into view, crouched and moving forward, he lifted his eyes to Jed Strange and had started to swing his rifle to his shoulder when Jed's shot nailed into his chest.

"They've gotten around us!" a voice shouted, seeing the man Jed had shot fly backward in a spray of crimson.

Tim Strange had heard the shots from his brother's Colt at the same time he'd begun making his move on one of the riflemen at the other side of the firing circle. Now he rose to his knee with his own newly acquired rifle in his hand, wiped the smear of blood from the stock, and fired toward the sound of the voices. Arno Dunne, taking advantage of the commotion, acted quickly, firing straight ahead into the center of his attackers.

With the tables clearly turned on them, the three remaining outlaws drew close together, forced to do so by the deadly accurate rifle fire from Tim and Jed on either side. Huddled in the dust and looking back longingly toward the spot they had left their horses, the leader, a man named Brenton Belcher, spoke to the two men beside him.

"How the hell did you boys let this happen? We're cut off here!" Shots spat overhead, pinning them down as Belcher raged. "Where's our scouts, Paco and Logan? I know damn well they hear all the shooting!"

Beside Belcher, a thin outlaw named Cody Renfrow raised his cheek from the dust just enough to answer. "I reckon they cut out on us, Belcher. But to hell with them, what are *we* going to do?" His words were partly drowned out beneath the rifle fire.

Belcher looked past Cody to the other man, a young Texan named Arliss Sidlo. "Arliss, crawl back to the horses and get them in here as close as you can. We'll keep you covered."

"Keep me covered?" said Sidlo. "Hell fire! You can't even get a shot off without them clipping your ears."

"Go on, damn it!" Belcher demanded. "Either get moving or I'll shoot you myself!"

Arliss Sidlo turned on his belly and crawled away, rifle fire nipping at the ground around him. When he'd gotten out of sight, Cody said to Belcher as the two of them managed to throw a couple of slugs toward the sound of Jed and Tim's rifles, "Arliss ain't coming back, Belcher, in case you're wondering."

"He better," said Belcher. "I meant what I said about shooting him."

"He knows that," said Cody. "That's *why* he ain't coming back."

Belcher thought about it for a second, then said in bitter disappointment, "Damn it all. We're really in a fix here." He took advantage of a lull in the rifle fire and called out toward Arno Dunne, "Hey, out there, any chance of us surrendering?"

From Tim's position behind a low rock, he heard Arno Dunne call back to Belcher, saying, "Not a chance in hell, mister. You bit this off, now chew on it." Two shots from Arno Dunne's rifle resounded, making sure the outlaw understood.

Belcher plastered his face to the dirt as the two shots struck the ground near his shoulder. Then he rose up an inch, spat grit from his lips, and said, "I recognize your voice. Is that you, Dunne?"

"You bet is it," Dunne replied. "Is that you, Belcher?"

"Yes, it is," Belcher called back to him. As soon as he spoke, he rolled away a few inches, for he knew Dunne was taking aim at the sound of his voice in the brush. "It don't seem right, ole boys like us killing each other, does it?"

"A while ago I might have agreed with you, Belcher," Dunne called back with a humorous chuckle. "But I see nothing wrong with it now." He levered a round and fired, the bullet thumping into the ground, causing Belcher to roll farther away.

"Hold your fire!" Jed Strange called out to

Arno Dunne. "If they've had enough, let them go."

"You're out of your mind!" Arno Dunne yelled at him. "If they had kept the upper hand, there's no amount of begging and pleading that would have kept them from killing us."

"But we're not them," Jed shouted, moving closer toward the two pinned-down outlaws as he spoke to Dunne. "We'll let you go, if you promise to ride on," he added to Belcher and Cody.

"Yes, sir!" Belcher called out. "We promise. Let us clear out to our horses and you'll see no more of us."

"Your horses are gone, Belcher," Arno Dunne said. "Your buddy is beating a path out of here right now, taking everything with him."

"Well, damn him!" swore Belcher.

From his position on the other side of the two outlaws, Tim saw his brother Jed move closer to them and called over to him, "Stay back, Jed! You can't trust these vermin."

"We're letting them go, Tim," Jed replied. "They're done for. They don't want to fight."

"He's right!" Belcher called out. "All we want is to get out of here."

Tim, seeing that Jed wouldn't be dissuaded, moved in a little closer and called out to his brother, "All right, Jed, they can leave. But stay back from them."

Arno Dunne shook his head and said to himself, "You damned idiots have no idea what you're fooling with." Then he levered his rifle and moved forward, the three of them forming a circle around the two outlaws in the brush. "Go on then, Belcher," Arno Dunne called out, "both of yas get the hell out of here."

The two scouts, a Mexican named Paco and his partner, a Kansan named Turly Logan, had not run out on Belcher and the others. They had stayed back along the trail until they caught sight of Arliss Sidlo riding off with the string of horses. Now they were riding in hard and fast along the trail. Hearing their hoofbeats, Belcher's courage returned. He stood up slowly with his rifle cocked and aimed at Arno Dunne as he spoke.

"One thing I forgot to mention, Dunne," said Belcher. "We're going to be needing a couple of your horses. Just call it a loan among ole buddies." But Tim, having caught sight of the two riders charging toward them, dropped Belcher with a quick shot, then turned to face the two returning scouts. He dropped his rifle to the ground and his Colt came streaking up from his holster. Twenty yards away, Jed Strange also saw the two riders charging and drew his pistol as well. Arno Dunne spun with them, just in time for a bullet to graze his shoulder. Tim, Jed, and Arno Dunne fired as one, their volley lifting both riders from their saddles and hurling them backward to the rocky ground.

"Look out, Dunne!" Tim shouted, spinning back toward Belcher and Cody. Belcher had managed to stand up, blood running freely from his chest. With Cody beside him, both men started to fire on Dunne from behind.

Jed and Tim responded ahead of Dunne, their shots dropping both men into the brush. Dunne stared, realizing how close he'd just came to dying. "Hell's bells, boys, I believe you saved my life."

"You're welcome, Dunne," Tim said in a clipped tone as the brothers stepped forward to the bodies in the brush. Arno Dunne stood silent for a moment with his hand pressed to his grazed shoulder.

Lying on the ground with one hand to his gaping chest wound and his other hand raised in surrender, Brenton Belcher gasped and said to Jed and Tim as they encircled him, "Don't...shoot no more. I...really am through now."

"Good of you to let us know," Tim said wryly. He reached out with his pistol pointed at Belcher's face and started to squeeze the trigger.

"Wait, Tim! Don't do it," said Jed. "He's done for. It ain't self-defense now."

"I don't give a damn," Tim hissed through clenched teeth. "Dunne was right. Show them no mercy." But still he hesitated, knowing that what Jed had just told him was true. No matter the circumstance, this man was no longer a threat.

"Shoot that lousy bastard, Tim!" Arno Dunne ranted, moving up beside Tim. He pushed his rifle barrel forward toward Belcher, seeing Cody lying dead in the dirt. "He's the last of the bunch. This way nobody comes back later on carrying a grudge!"

"No," said Tim, shoving Arno Dunne's rifle barrel away from Belcher. "Jed's right, this ain't self-defense any longer. He'll be dead soon enough."

"Not soon enough to suit me." Dunne sneered. But under Tim's frigid gaze, he made no attempt to repoint his rifle at the dying outlaw.

"We never did...like one another, Dunne," Belcher said, his voice thick with blood. "Seeing these...boys shoot. I reckon...you're headed to...the big contest with them, eh?"

"Shut up and die, Belcher," Arno Dunne snapped. "We don't have all day to waste on you."

"Yep, that's it," Brenton Belcher said in a low rasping laugh. "These boys...are your entries. You always was one...to play the angles." As his words ended, his eyes glazed over and grew more distant until a long, low breath rattled from his chest. He slumped back onto the ground and lay limp.

"Son of a bitch," Dunne cursed, leaning forward and spitting in the dead man's face. "He was right about one thing—we never did get along."

"What contest was he talking about?" Tim asked, taking a step back and holstering his Colt.

"Nothing," said Dunne. "You never could pay attention to anything this horse-thieving fool had to say." Dunne avoided any further explanation. Instead, he directed his attention to Jed, who stepped forward now and slipped his pistol into his holster. "There, Jed, you see what your little ounce of mercy almost cost us?"

"I saw it, Dunne," Jed replied, "but we still tried to do the right thing. That's all we have to answer to the Lord for."

"Ha!" Dunne said. "You keep that attitude, you'll be going to heaven all right, but it might be too damn soon to suit you."

"Back to what he said about a contest," Tim interrupted, nodding at Belcher's body on the ground as he spoke to Dunne. "He seemed to know what he was talking about."

"You just ain't going to turn it loose, are you?" Dunne asked, trying to fake an innocent smile.

"That's right, I ain't," Tim said firmly, his hand resting on the butt of his Colt, "so spit it out."

Arno Dunne took a patient breath and shook his head, saying, "All right, I'll level with you—not that it makes any difference. Newt Grago is cooking up a shooting contest, just something to see who's the fastest gun. I have to admit, seeing the way you two boys handle them Colts, it entered my mind that you might stand a chance to win yourselves some big money. To be honest, I hoped I might make a few dollars myself, betting on yas."

"That's what you were getting at earlier, ain't it?" Jed asked. "When you started all that talk about facing a man off in an old-time duel?"

"Yep, it was. But it was only speculation, boys, so don't get on no high horse over it." Dunne raised his hat brim, wiped sweat from his forehead, then lowered it and tucked his rifle up under his arm. "The more I see of you Faulkner twins, the more I realize you're not about to do anything you don't want to do. So let's forget the whole matter. I owe you both for saving my life. Far as I'm concerned, the best way I can repay you is to get on my horse and ride away from yas. You're both good boys. You've got no business out here. If you ever change your minds and decide to throw into this kind of life, look me up." He half turned and started toward his horse when Tim's voice stopped him.

"How much money?" Tim asked.

"What?" Arno Dunne looked taken aback. So did Jed Strange.

"You said maybe Jed and I could make some good money in this shooting contest. How much?" Tim's face was a mask of resolve.

"Well now." Arno Dunne scratched his jaw thinking it over. "It's what you call a matched shoot-out. Every time you beat a man, the stakes on your next fight gets higher. Take it all the way to the top, we're talking about as much as ten thousand dollars."

"That's ten thousand after you take your cut?" Tim asked.

Arno Dunne looked embarrassed, but only for a moment. "Yes, that's after I take my cut. Let's face it, you boys would never known about this if it weren't for me."

181

"And how much is your cut, Dunne?" Tim asked.

Before Arno Dunne could answer, Jed cut in, saying to his brother, "Tim, you don't mean it. We're not going to do something like this. This is deliberate murder."

"No, it's not, Jed," said Tim, staring at Dunne as he spoke. "It's like Dunne said earlier—these men are there for the same reason we'll be. Everybody knows the risk going in. Ain't that right, Dunne?"

Dunne chuckled. "You've been paying more attention than I thought, Tim Faulkner. Now see if you can talk some sense to your brother, the *deacon* here"—he thumbed toward Jed—"and we've got ourselves a business arrangement."

"You still never said how much your cut is, Dunne," Tim persisted, without taking his eyes from Arno Dunne's.

Dunne stalled for a second, then let out a resigned breath, saying, "Hell, you're going to find out anyway. The pot gets cut straight down the middle every time you win, fifty to you two, fifty to me."

"Huh-uh," said Tim. "We'd be better off leaving you to lay here in the dirt, find this Newt Grago, and take our chances with him."

"Easy now," said Dunne, his smile back at work. "You're catching on to how things work, but don't get ahead of yourself. Grago's men would kill you both, seeing you ride in without me or somebody to vouch for yas."

"You get ten percent, Dunne, not a dollar

more," Tim said as Jed stood listening in disbelief.

"Huh-uh," Arno shook his head. "Thirty or else I ride."

"Fifteen, or you can go *ahead* and ride, Dunne," said Tim.

Dunne considered it, once more scratching his jaw. "You're getting hard to deal with, Tim Faulkner. But let's make it twenty percent and get out of this heat."

Tim offered a faint smile in return. "'Okay, twenty percent every time we win."

"What about if we lose?" Jed asked, looking back and forth between the two of them. When neither Tim nor Arno Dunne answered him, he asked again. But Tim and Arno Dunne just walked off toward the horses and Jed trotted to catch up to his brother, asking him in a lower tone as they stepped farther away from Dunne to their bays, "Do you know what you're agreeing to, Tim? This is no different than being a paid assassin."

Tim replied, nearly whispering, "Damn it, Jed, you saw he was about to leave. Where would that put us as far as finding these men, and possibly Danielle? Agreeing to do it don't mean we're going to. Just stick with me on this. Once we're inside this bunch of outlaws, we can deal with what to do next."

Jed let out a tight breath of relief. "Tim, you had me worried there for a second, but now that you've explained your reasons, I see what you mean. I'm sorry I doubted you. I should have known better than to think you'd go along with something like this."

"Just keep that in mind, Jed," Tim said. "No matter what I go along with, always realize that I've got our best interest at heart."

"I know that, Tim. You was just so convincing it fooled me for a minute. I'm back on track now."

"Good," Tim said. "Now play along with things and keep quiet. Don't be asking questions like what happens if we lose. You know as well as I do—if we lose, we're dead."

Chapter 11

Indian Territory, July 23, 1871

At a remote spot along a nameless creek, Danielle Strange and Duncan Grago had spent a day in the shade of a tarpaulin lean-to, where an old horse thief named Uhl Hobbs kept a fresh string of stolen horses. Hobbs had welcomed them into his camp only after recognizing Duncan Grago. While Danielle rested and grained Sundown, Duncan Grago picked out a copper-colored Spanish barb that had gone a long time without a rider on its back. Danielle and Hobbs stood at the rail of a makeshift corral and watched Duncan get the barb used to a saddle. After a moment of studying Danielle with a guarded gaze, Hobbs asked, "Don't suppose you caught sight of any lawmen along the Red, did you?"

"Nope," Danielle answered, keeping her attention on Duncan as he wrestled with the headstrong copper barb. Hobbs looked her up and down again, and asked, "That's a powerfully good-looking Colt you're carrying, Danny Duggin. Don't expect you'd be willing to trade it out for some riding stock?"

"Not at all interested," Danielle replied, her hand resting instinctively on the butt of her Colt. She knew Hobbs was more interested in finding out everything he could about this newcomer, Danny Duggin, than he was in trading for a gun or a horse.

"Being a trader, I always like to ask," Hobbs said. Then after a moment of silence he asked in a bolder tone, "How come I've never seen you before, Danny Duggin? Dunc says you've been around Fort Smith, and down in Texas for a while. I go to both places quite often."

Danielle dealt him a level stare, saying, "I guess you just weren't looking where I was standing, Hobbs. Now if you've got any more questions to ask about me, get it done. You're starting to rub against my grain."

Hobbs jerked back a step and kept his grimy hands chest-high in a show of peace. "No offense, Mr. Duggin. You can't blame me for being a little cautious. Hell, it ain't even legal for me being here, let alone holding a string of horses with no paperwork on them."

Danielle allowed a faint smile. "No offense taken, Hobbs. Dunc and I will be moving on once he gets the air out from under that saddle. Until then, you might just as well settle down and stop wondering who I am or where I've been. You ought to know I'm not going to tell you anything I don't want you to know."

Hobbs cackled across broken yellowed teeth and shook his head. "Reckon I'm just curious by nature." He raised a crooked finger for emphasis. "But I want to tell you this, for your own good. I heard there's a whole posse of deputies from Parker's court getting ready to make a sweep through here. So the two of you best keep an eye turned back to your trail. Be sure and mention it to Dunc first chance you get."

"I will. Much obliged for the information," Danielle said, seeing Duncan Grago wrestle the barb over closer to them. "We always keep an eye on our trail."

When Duncan had paid Hobbs for the copper barb and a Mexican saddle, he and Danielle rode on. They spent the rest of the day and part of the following morning pushing forward through tangles of brush across jagged terrain more fitting for mountain goats than horses.

Robber's Rock, Indian Territory, July 24, 1871

Two shots from the smoking pistols echoed in the ledges and canyons surrounding Robber's Rock. Newt Grago tossed aside a handful of beef rib bones he'd been eating and wiped his hands on a soiled bandanna. He stepped off the porch of the newly built plank shack and

186

looked across the wide encampment of men and horses. There had to be as many as sixty or seventy men there, he estimated to himself, the thought of it making him smile. When the men had drifted in, two and three at a time over the past couple of weeks, they'd brought with them stolen cattle and Mexican horses. Two large tents had arrived a week earlier with a grifting gambler named Merlin Haas, who had come at Newt Grago's request. Along with the tents, Haas had also brought along some gaming tables, as well as six painted ladies all the way from Austin, Texas. The atmosphere at Robber's Rock was like that of a carnival, and that was just what Newt Grago wanted.

"Damn fine shooting," Newt Grago said to Chancy Burke. Burke punched out the spent cartridge shell from his pistol and replaced it with a new round. He only nodded at Newt Grago and watched him walk toward the body of Curly Lyndell lying flat in the dirt. Newt Grago finished wiping his hands, wadded up the greasy bandanna, and shoved it down into his hip pocket. Looking down at the body closely, Grago sucked at a tooth and loosened a fleck of beef from it with his fingernail. Then he spat the fleck away and turned, facing the gathering of onlookers, saying loud enough for all to hear, "Boys, Curly Lyndell is deader than hell."

Among the gathered spectators came sighs of disappointment as well as whoops and cheers for Chancy Burke. Newt Grago gave the crowd a second to spend itself down, then he raised a stack of dollars from his lapel pocket and fanned it in the air above his head as he stepped back over to Chancy Burke. "That means ole Chancy here has just made himself the easiest two hundred and fifty dollars he ever made in his life." Newt Grago handed Chancy Burke the money, then turned back to the crowd, saying, "I know damn well some of you might have made just as much, or lost just as much, depending upon how you bet. But the fact is, the only way to *win* big here is to *play* big here!"

The crowd stirred, and Newt Grago raised his hands toward them. "Boys, I ain't going to try to talk you into anything. But the man who challenges Chancy Burke and beats him gets his two hundred and fifty, plus another two hundred fifty for being the winner. I'm talking about *five hundred dollars*! Do I have any takers?"

While Newt Grago looked the crowd over for a show of hands and saw none, one of the women from Austin freed herself from an outlaw's arm around her waist and slinked forward a step. She threw her hand on her hip, striking a pose as she turned and said to the crowd, "Boys, I'd shoot any one of you here for five hundred dollars. Can I get in on this?" she asked Grago.

"Haw!" Newt laughed, throwing his head back. "You get over there where you belong, Lulu. This is man's sport."

"Man's sport, my Aunt Fannie's drawers," Lulu said sarcastically, cutting her gaze to the gathering of outlaws. "There must not be a man in the bunch. What's the matter with you bunch of gutless coyotes?"

"Shut up, Lulu," said a drunken voice, "or I'll put a bullet in you for free, just to see what color your blood is. If you've got any, that is."

The crowd roared its approval. Newt Grago silenced them down with his raised hands. "Like I said, nobody's going to talk you into anything, but go have a few drinks and think it over. Chancy Burke is now the man to beat. He'll be ready when any one of you are, right, Chancy?"

"That's right," said Burke, fanning his winnings with one hand while spinning his Colt down into his low-slung holster. "The sooner the better, far as I'm concerned. I came here to win. I plan on leaving with both boots full of money."

The same drunken voice called out again to Burke from amid the crowd, "If that kid shows up who killed Scovill, Levan, and the others, you might fill your boots with something entirely different."

The crowd roared with laughter. Chancy Burke's face flared crimson red. "Who said that?" he shouted, stepping forward with his hand near his tied-down Colt. "I want the big-mouthed son of a bitch who said that to come forward and say it again!" His eyes scanned the crowd as the laughter settled into cold silence. "Who was it? Was that you, Blanford? You're always shooting off your soup-hole. Come on out here and say it again!"

The crowd parted and Ollie Blanford, a tall Arkansan with a drooping red mustache, stepped forward. "It weren't me said it, Burke. If it was, I wouldn't be at all hesitant to saying it to your face. Now what about me always shooting off my soup-hole? I don't recall ever speaking more than a word or two to you in my whole life. We never rode together. Why'd you single me out?" His long arm hung loose but poised, his fingertips turned slightly in toward his pistol butt.

"Because it sounded like your voice, Blanford," said Burke.

As the two outlaws spoke, Merlin Haas had moved in beside Newt Grago. Now, seeing trouble brewing quickly between Burke and Blanford, Haas took his cigar from his mouth and said to Grago, "I best stop this before it gets too far out of hand."

But Grago took Haas by the arm, stopping him, saying, "Naw, what's your hurry? Let it go a minute. This might be just the thing to get this ball rolling." He chuckled and pulled Haas back beside him.

"Hell, maybe you're right," Haas whispered.

Ollie Blanford responded to Chancy Burke, "It might have sounded like me, but it weren't. As far as my bad-mouthing, I never say a damn thing I ain't prepared to back up, with knuckle or lead either one."

"Then let's do her up," Chancy Burke hissed, scraping a boot sidelong in the dirt, taking a fighting stance.

"That suits the hell out of me, boy," Ollie Blanford replied. The crowd moved aside as Blanford's hand slipped down slowly, removing the strip of rawhide from across his pistol hammer.

"Whoa now, boys," said Newt Grago, seeing his opportunity to reap some benefit for himself, "let's take a second to get the pot right. This is exactly what I was talking about. You're going to shoot one another anyway, one of you might as well make something from it— the rest of us too." He glanced around at the crowd for support. "If any of you want in on this, you better get over to Haas right away, before these two commence skinning leather." He took a step back, turned to Blanford and Burke, and said to them both, "You boys can give us just a minute here, can't you?"

"I'm ready anytime he is," Burke said, keeping his gaze fixed on Blanford.

"Same here," Blanford said. "I can wait a minute or two before killing him, if it's worth five hundred dollars to me."

"Don't start spending that money yet, Blanford," Burke threatened. "All you're buying is a ticket to hell."

"That's the spirit, boys," Grago said, stepping back and hurrying over to Merlin Haas. "This is all working out just fine, Haas," he said, leaning close to Merlin Haas's ear while the grifter counted the money being shoved at him by the excited crowd.

"It's the craziest, wildest thing you've ever come up with, Grago," Haas replied, scratching down numbers and names with a pencil stub as the wad of cash in his hand grew ever larger, "but I ain't complaining...no, sir!" He shook his fistful of money.

Lulu waded in among the bettors, waving a ten-dollar bill out before her. "Ten dollars on Burke? Anybody? What do you say?"

Newt Grago grabbed her by her arm and pulled her away from the crowd. "That's enough, Lulu, you've done your part. Now put your money away, settle back, and watch the show."

Lulu lowered her voice, speaking to him. "You said to get them stirred up and keep them that way, Grago. That's exactly what I'm trying to do."

"I know, Lulu, and you've done a good job. Between you and that loudmouthed drunk a while ago, they'll be at one another's throats the rest of the day. We'll all make a bundle on it." While he spoke, Newt Grago took out a big double eagle coin and shoved it down the front of her tight-fitting bodice. "Relax now."

Lulu giggled and patted the coin inside her dress. "Whatever you say, Grago, but I still don't see what you're going to gain, getting a bunch of your own gang killed off this way."

"It's makes good sense, Lulu," said Grago. "Even the best of herds needs some careful culling now and then. I want only the fastest and the best riding with me. This is one way of making sure I get them. At the end of this, I'll have a gang of men so tough, they'll make

192

the James-Younger Gang look like a bunch of pickpockets."

"Meanwhile, you and Merlin Haas make a tidy bankroll, covering the bets and cutting a percentage of the pot, right?" she asked.

"Of course, Lulu." Grago smiled. "Only a damn fool works for free. Me and Haas will make our money, but don't worry—you and your girls will be well taken care of in the process."

"That's all that matters to me." Lulu giggled. She shoved two fingers down into her bodice, fished out the double eagle, and flipped it, catching it sideways out of the air on its way down.

While the sun boiled white hot in the afternoon sky, Danielle and Duncan Grago crossed a stretch of land that had appeared flat from a distance. Yet, angling now toward a pair of slim rising buttes, Danielle saw that they would be moving through nothing more than a rocky maze of gulches, cut banks, and drop-offs for the next ten miles.

Once across the rugged furnace, the land leveled in between the buttes, and it was at that point that they heard the two quick pistol shots resound in the distance. Duncan only grinned, looking up among the high ledges into the shadows the buttes, saying, "Yep, that'll be Newt and the boys. We'll be running into some lookouts here any minute. So let's not make any sudden moves until they see who I am." He squinted in the sun's glare, his eyes scanning back and forth above them.

Danielle searched also, reminding herself of how dangerous and difficult this would have been on her own, without an insider like Duncan leading the way. The ledges along the slope of the buttes were perfect for an ambush, the land beneath them offering little protection. "Let's hope they recognize you," she said. "After all, you've been gone for a while."

"Don't worry, Brother Newt has them watching for me. They won't do nothing that'll get him down their collar." He gigged the copper barb forward, the horse still resisting slightly but getting used to a rider on its back. Before they had traveled another mile, two more pistol shots echoed in the distance. Duncan only smiled and nodded them forward.

As they drew deeper between the two buttes, a flash of evening sunlight glinted off a rifle barrel fifty yards above them. Instinctively, Danielle's hand went to her Colt, but a voice from behind a large rock alongside the trail called out, "Keep your hands in sight, mister," and Danielle froze.

"It's me, Grago," said Duncan, turning his horse in the direction of the voice, keeping his hands in view. "Don't shoot. This is my friend, Danny Duggin."

"Dunc?" the voice said. "I thought that was you when we saw you crossing the scrubs. It's me, Chester." Danielle watched as the man stepped in view from behind the rock, a cocked rifle in his hands. "Newt's been wondering what took you so long getting here."

"Chester Gibb," Duncan said, relaxing now and letting his hands down, "it's been a long time since I laid eyes on you. Who's up in the rocks?"

"That's Clet Eldridge," said Gibb. "Me and him's been waiting for somebody to relieve us, so's we can get a couple drinks of whiskey. Your brother's got quite a gathering in there. They've been whooping it up, sure enough." He raised an arm to the man in the rock shadows above them and waved back and forth slowly, letting him know everything was all right.

"Yeah, we heard some shooting earlier," Duncan said. "What's going on in there?"

"It's the wildest thing you ever saw, Dunc," said Gibb. "Newt's got a contest going to see who's the fastest gun. So far, nobody has beat Chancy Burke. He killed ol' Marvin Parrish this morning. Shot him right through the heart."

At the sound of the name *Chancy Burke,* Danielle perked up, remembering the name from her list of killers. Duncan looked astonished and asked Gibb, "You mean it's a contest where they're really shooting each other?"

"Yep." Gibb chuckled. "I told you, it's the wildest thing ever. A man can either make himself some money or end up dead in the dirt." His eyes went to Danielle Strange. "What about you, mister? Are you any good with that tied-down Colt, or do you wear it to keep your shirt tucked in?"

Danielle said from beneath her lowered hat brim, "Don't concern yourself about my Colt or my shirttail."

Duncan Grago cut in, saying, "Chester, I might as well tell you right now, Danny Duggin don't tolerate much guff off of nobody. As far as his Colt goes, you can take it from me—it does whatever he wants it to. He's a friend of mine, and I vouch for him." Duncan's hand rested on his pistol butt. "Is there any more that needs to be said on the matter?"

"Hell no, Dunc," Chester Gibb said quickly. "You know how I am. Sometimes I like to aggravate." His eyes went to Danielle. "No harm intended, Danny Duggin. Any friend of Dunc's is a friend of mine, right, Dunc?"

Duncan Grago stared at him with a tight, fixed grin. Danielle saw the wild look that had been missing for a while come back into his eyes. "Let's hope so, Chester," he said, "otherwise I'd put a bullet right where your—"

Danielle cut him off, saying to Chester Gibb, "How fast is this Chancy Burke?"

Chester Gibb swallowed a dry knot in his throat, glad to change the subject. "He's damn fast. Right now he's the cock of the walk. But there's others on their way here that are just as fast, if not faster."

"Oh? Who's coming?" Danielle asked, knowing she was on the verge of standing face-to-face with her father's murderers and barely able to keep from riding in with her Colts blazing. Still, she kept calm, wanting to find out everything she could about these men.

"Well, let's see," said Chester Gibb, scratching his beard-stubbled jaw, thinking about it. "There's what's left of the regulars, Rufe Gaddis, Saul Delmano, and Julius Byler, not to mention some others Newt sent for. Arno Dunne's supposed to be on his way. If I know Arno, he's gone and got himself a gunslinger he figures is fast enough to make him some money here."

"Yeah, that's Arno Dunne, all right," said Duncan, "always playing an angle." He tilted his head slightly and asked, "you mentioned Julius Byler? Hell, I figured Julius would have already arrived by now. We met up with him, but then him and Danny here had a falling-out. When Danny ran him off, I thought he probably came on out here."

"Nope, he ain't here." Chester Gibb looked from Duncan to Danielle, and asked, "You ran Julius Byler off? I don't know how you did that unless you shot him."

Feeling both Duncan's and Gibb's eyes on her, Danielle shrugged, saying calmly, "That's what I did. I shot him, six times in the chest, then sent him packing. Told him if he came back, I'd shoot him some more." She stared blankly from beneath her lowered hat brim and waited.

For a second Chester Gibb only stood with a puzzled look on his face. Then he chuckled, and said to Duncan Grago, "Well, I see your friend Danny Duggin here has a sense of humor. For a minute there he had me believing it." He waved them past him on up the narrow trail toward Robber's Rock. "You two go on, Dunc. Tell somebody to come out and relieve us. Me and Eldridge has been out here long enough. Besides, there ain't no lawmen foolish enough to ride into Robber's Rock no how."

"I'll tell Newt to send somebody," said Duncan, straightening the copper barb onto the trail.

Danielle followed Duncan Grago closely. Hearing Chester Gibb's words caused a guarded smile to alight on her lips. *Just keep believing that, Gibb,* she thought to herself as her eyes searched upward around them. In the shadows of rock fifty feet above them, a rifleman stepped forward and waved them along the narrowing pass.

Danielle hadn't said a word to Duncan Grago about the posse out of Fort Smith that the old horse thief Hobbs had told her about. She hoped Hobbs was right, but she wasn't about to mention it to Duncan Grago. As far as she was concerned, the law could have whatever was left of this band of outlaws. She only wanted the ones whose names were on her list. If the law was coming, she needed to get her killing done and clear out of here, for once the posse hit, they wouldn't know Danny Duggin from the rest of this bunch. Danielle nudged her chestnut mare forward, anxious to bring her vengeance to a head.

"Once we get to the camp, you stick close to me for a while, Danny," Duncan Grago said over his shoulder. "Just till everybody sees you're all right."

"Sure, Dunc, no problem," Danielle said, staring straight ahead, preparing her mind for the killing task that lay ahead.

Chapter 12

Standing on the porch above the crowd, Newt Grago and Merlin Haas were the first to see the two horses come into view from the trail leading down to the encampment. "Think it's your brother Duncan?" Haas asked, still holding a thick stack of dollars in his sweaty hand.

"I'd bet on it," Newt Grago replied. He stepped down and elbowed his way through the gathered outlaws who were still milling around the corpse of Ollie Blandford. "Get him away from here before he starts drawing flies," Newt demanded of the crowd.

"You heard him, boys," said Haas, stepping along behind Newt Grago toward the two riders in the distance. "Get Ollie out of here— Curly Lyndell too." He gestured toward the body of Curly Lyndell lying a few yards away. "We can't have another round until somebody does some cleaning up here."

"What are we supposed to do with them?" a voice called out from amid the crowd.

"Hell, I don't know," Haas said in passing,

199

"tie a rope around their ankles and drag them to a gully somewhere, I reckon. Just get them out of here before they turn ripe on us. I'll tell Lulu to give a free bottle of rye to the man who gets rid of them."

"What the hell are we waiting for, boys," the same voice called out, "somebody get a rope!"

A few yards past the gathered crowd, Newt Grago and Merlin Haas stopped and stood at the edge of the dusty clearing, looking out at the two approaching riders. "Yep, that's Dunc on the left," Newt Grago said, a smile spreading on his sweat-streaked face. "We'll see some action now. He was meaner than a sack full of rattlesnakes when he went to prison. He'll be even meaner now, I expect. You never met Dunc, did you, Haas?"

"Nope, can't say I ever had the pleasure," Merlin Haas replied, squinting in the mellow evening sunlight. He saw Duncan Grago lift his hat and run a hand back across his short-cropped hair. "Looks like they sheared him to the bone before they turned him loose. Who's that with him?"

"I don't know who it is," said Newt, him-self squinting in the sunlight. "But it ain't Julius Byler or Sep Howard either one, that's for sure. Damn it! I told Sep to make sure he and Dunc stopped by Byler's hideout and brought him along with them." He lifted his hat from his head and swung it back and forth, waving at his brother and the rider beside him. "Well, whoever it is, if he's riding with Dunc, he's got to be all right."

"Yeah," said Haas, grinning. "If he gets himself killed here, I've got first claim on that big chestnut he's riding."

Newt Grago had been so excited to see Dunc riding in that he'd paid no attention to the horse the other man was riding. But now he stiffened a bit at Haas's words, as a thought dawned on him. "We'll see," he said, his tone of voice changing, growing cautious now as he tried peering closer at the face of the other rider. After a moment, he called out over his shoulder to the men a few yards behind him, "Boys, get on over here. My brother Dunc is riding in. Let's make him feel welcome!"

The outlaws moved in closer behind Newt Grago and Merlin Haas, two of them dropping the rope they'd looped around the ankle of Ollie Blanford's body and leaving him lying in the dirt. "What's up, boss?" Chancy Burke said, stepping in beside Newt Grago. "You sound worried."

"Worried? Naw, not me," said Newt. "Just keep your eyes skinned on this man riding with Dunc."

"I've got him covered," Chancy Burke said, lowering his voice as the two horses cantered in the last few yards and came to a halt. Burke's right hand rested on the butt of his Colt, jiggling it in his holster.

"Hot damn, Brother Newt!" Duncan Grago cried out joyously, jumping down from the copper barb's back and running forward, his hat flying back off of his head.

Danielle instinctively touched her fingers

to her fake mustache, checking it. Then she adjusted her hat brim low and level, crossed her wrists on her saddle horn, and watched the Grago brothers throw their arms around one another as they laughed and cursed between themselves. She swallowed back the bitter taste of anger and fought the urge to swing her Colt from her holster and drop Newt Grago on the spot.

"Dunc, you don't look a damn bit different than when I last saw you!" Newt Grago said, shoving his brother back at arm's length and looking him up and down. "I take it you've been properly rehabilitated though? I'd hate to think that in all this time, they failed to teach you the error of your ways."

Duncan Grago stepped back laughing and looked all around at the gathered outlaws as he spoke to Newt. "You bet they showed me the errors of my ways. They taught me the most important lesson a man ought to know." He hesitated for a second, making sure all eyes and ears were upon him. Then he said, laughing even louder, "They taught me to never be taken *alive!*"

The outlaws whooped and roared with laughter. Danielle only smiled enough to go along with Duncan Grago's show. Even as she did so, she noticed Newt Grago and the man on his left cutting their eyes at her, then looking away. She knew they were checking out this stranger on the chestnut mare sitting before them, and she knew why. The man who'd killed some of their friends had been riding a big chestnut mare. But she stayed calm, already knowing the questions would come, already preparing herself for them.

In a moment, when the laughter and greetings had died down, Newt Grago turned toward her with his left arm looped up around Duncan's shoulder. His right hand hung loose and natural near the pistol on his hip. "So, Dunc," Newt Grago asked, his eyes hooded and his thin smile fixing on Danielle, "who is your friend here? Somebody from prison, I reckon?"

"Naw, this is my pal, Danny Duggin," Duncan Grago said. "We met on the trail coming here from Fort Smith. Danny saved my bacon. Hadn't been for him, I'd be dead."

"Is that a fact?" Newt Grago asked, eyeing Danielle. "In that case, I'm mighty obliged to you, Danny Duggin." He jerked a thumb toward Haas on his right, then Burke on his left, saying, "Meet Merlin Haas and Chancy Burke, a couple of the boys. You can meet the rest, providing you'll be sticking around for a while."

Danielle nodded at the two men in turn, careful not to let the white-hot vengeance show in her eyes as she looked upon the face of Chancy Burke. "I plan on staying awhile," she replied, "if it's all right by you. Dunc said it would be."

"Well, hell yes, it's all right with him," Duncan cut in, speaking for his brother. "Right, Newt?"

Newt Grago only gave a grudging nod, stepping forward, looking closely at the chestnut mare as Duncan Grago continued. "I had the awfulest time getting Danny here to come along with me. He mostly keeps to himself. A real loner, you might say."

"A real loner, huh?" Newt said almost to himself, running a hand down Sundown's muzzle. Sundown shied and pulled her head to one side. "A fine mare you've got here, Danny Duggin," Newt said, inspecting Sundown closely as he spoke. "Had her long?"

Here goes, Danielle though to herself, knowing she had play this just right. "A few months," she replied in an offhand manner. "I've got no paper on her, but she ain't stolen, if that's what you're wondering." Danielle pulled the reins, moving Sundown away from Newt's hand.

"It wouldn't matter to me if she was stolen or not," Newt chuckled. "Hell, most of the horses here are stolen. But I am curious as to where you got her."

Danielle took on a testy tone. "You can stay curious then. I came here with Dunc because he said there was money to be made. He forgot to mention that a man had to explain where he gets his riding stock."

"Easy, Danny," Duncan Grago said, trying to keep the air friendly. "Newt's only making conversation, ain't you, Newt?"

"Maybe...maybe not," said Newt, keeping a suspicious gaze on Danielle. "The fact is, there was a young man about your age who rode a big chestnut mare last summer. He killed some pals of mine. Rumor has it he's riding a vengeance trail—"

"Save your breath, Grago," Danielle said, cutting him off with a sigh of exasperation. "I've already heard this story." She allowed herself a slight laugh. "Hell's fire, you're the third person that's brought it up in the past few weeks. If you thought I was that man, why didn't you just come out and say so in the first place?"

Newt Grago slid a glance around to Chancy Burke, then looked back at Danielle.

Danielle noted how Chancy Burke and the others were ready to make a move at Newt Grago's slightest signal. She stayed calm, not even lifting her wrists from her saddle horn.

"If it makes you feel any better," she said, "the gunslinger you're talking about is dead. I know because I found his body. He was cut all to hell. This *was* his mare." She reached out a hand and patted Sundown's neck, then let her hand lie back on her thigh, not near her pistol just yet, but close by should the need suddenly arise. "I found this big chestnut wandering around and took her. That's as much as I can tell you about it."

Newt Grago seemed to be weighing her story. Danielle was unsure if he believed it or not. Finally he said, "You're sure that gunslinger is dead, huh?"

Danielle made a relaxed shrug in reply. "He was dead when I found him, he was dead when I left. It ain't likely his condition has changed since then."

Faint laughter rippled across the outlaws. Newt Grago even grinned a little. For a second he seemed satisfied, but then his grin faded somewhat and he said, "Yeah, that's funny. There's only one thing that puzzles me." He raised a finger and feigned a curious expression. "See, this gunslinger's name was *Dan* Strange. Your name's *Danny* Duggin. You can see the similarity, I'm sure?"

Danielle let out another breath, this time shaking her head slowly. "Yep, and I've been asked that question before by Sep Howard. I'll tell you the same thing I told him. I'd have to be a damned fool to change my name from Dan to Danny, now wouldn't I?"

Another wave of laughter stirred among the outlaws, until Newt Grago silenced it with a harsh glance backward. Then he said to Danielle, "You mean Sep Howard already asked you about it?"

"Yep," Danielle said.

"By the way, where is Sep?" Newt asked, turning to Duncan Grago.

But before Duncan could answer, Danielle said in a flat tone, "I shot him dead."

The crowd tensed as Newt Grago jerked back toward her with murder in his eyes. "You what? You shot Sep Howard?"

"That's right."

"But it was a fair fight, Newt," Duncan cut in. "Danny only did what he had to do. I vouch for him. Sep Howard tried gunning him and bang! Danny put him down."

"Sep Howard was no small piece of work," Newt said, looking back at Danielle.

"He is now," Danielle replied quietly.

"He was a pal of mine too," Newt said.

"Well, maybe you ought to pick pals who can keep themselves from getting killed," Danielle offered, knowing it to be the best answer she could possibly give to a man looking for fast and hard gunmen. She spread a flat, mirthless smile. "We both know this is a tough world we live in."

"I sure can't argue that with you." Newt Grago chuckled, seeming to loosen up. The others followed suit, one passing a bottle of rye to another as the tension seemed to lift. "Where's Julius Byler?" he asked Duncan Grago. "You were supposed to swing by his place and bring him along."

"He bad-mouthed Danny and Danny ran him off," Duncan Grago said proudly.

Again, Newt looked surprised and swung his attention back to Danielle. "The hell you say!"

Danielle shrugged one shoulder, tossing the matter aside. "Like I said about picking pals."

Chancy Burke saw that this Danny Duggin was stealing some of the thunder he'd built up among the men, and he didn't like it. He took a step forward, saying, "Sounds like you're pretty cocksure of yourself, Duggin. Maybe you need a good lesson in manners."

"I'm always willing to learn," Danielle said, answering him in a way that left no margin for doubt. "How good are you at teaching?"

"Hold on, boys," said Merlin Haas, stepping in before Newt Grago got the chance to himself. "This ain't the place for it. Anybody wants to show their fangs, let's do it by the rules, like we've been doing it."

"The rules?" Danielle asked, having used the exchange with Burke as a good reason to drop her hand back to her Colt. "What are you talking about, rules?"

Newt Grago saw the opportunity to further his shooting contest, and he took it. "Danny Duggin, if you're a man likes action, my brother Dunc has brought you to the right place." He poked a thumb over his shoulder, pointing back toward the shack. "Come on, all of yas. Let's get Dunc and Danny some rye whiskey, make them both feel at home here."

"Sounds good to me," Duncan Grago said, stepping back and swinging up onto his copper barb. "What do you say, Danny?"

"I'm right beside you," Danielle responded, nudging Sundown forward, giving Chancy Burke a cold, lingering stare as she stepped the mare past him.

As the whole motley collection of gunmen moved back toward the shack, Newt Grago said to Chancy Burke, "Kill that son of a bitch so quick he won't know what hits him. You hear me?"

"I hear you," said Burke. "But what about Dunc? He seems real taken by this Danny Duggin. I don't want Dunc coming down on me over it."

Newt grinned. "That's why we want it to be just one more part of the shooting contest. That way Dunc can't blame nobody."

"Good thinking," said Chancy Burke. "You figure this is that gunslinger from last summer, don't you?"

"I don't know. He fits the description. But whether he's that gunslinger or not, there's no mistaking that mare. Remember the man we left hanging from the tree last year? The big chestnut I wanted, before it managed to get away?" He nodded toward the chestnut mare as Danielle slow-stepped it toward the shack. "If that's not the same animal, I'll eat my shirt."

Chancy Burke nodded slowly. "If that's him, and the rumors we heard are true, he's after me the same as he is you and the rest of us."

"That's right," Newt Grago said in a grim tone. "So that's something you better keep in mind when you face him tomorrow."

"Tomorrow hell, what's wrong with tonight?" Chancy Burke asked.

"Because if he really is that gunslinger, you'll need the rest of the evening to go somewhere and practice your draw. I don't want no slipups here. I want him dead the first time he toes the mark."

"He's dead right now, Newt." Burke chuckled confidently, watching the chestnut mare move away in a low stir of dust. "He just don't realize it yet."

On their way to the shack, Danielle cast a sidelong glance at the body of Ollie Blanford lying in the dirt, a rope looped around one ankle leading to a saddle horn on a dusty paint horse standing obediently waiting. Danielle looked farther across the flat clearing out front of the shack, at the other body in the dirt. "Your brother likes some pretty tough games," she said to Duncan Grago, riding beside her. "Is he as keen on participating as he is on promoting?"

"Ha!" Duncan laughed. "Newt is the best gunman I ever saw, and I've seen plenty. The thing is he don't have to do his own gun-handling anymore, unless he wants to. Newt's the man on top now. He can get somebody else to do his shooting for him. But that don't make him soft." Duncan grinned. "That just makes him smart. I already see what he's doing here. He's getting rid of the deadwood. I figure he's making something on it at the same time. By the time this is over, he'll have the damndest bunch of killers you ever saw working for him. Then the world better step aside. Won't you be proud, pulling iron with a gang like this?"

"Yeah," said Danielle. "I can hardly wait."

At dark, Danielle slipped away from Duncan Grago long enough to go to the crowded rope corral where she had left Sundown after watering, graining, and rubbing her down with a handful of dried wild grass. To remove the temptation of anybody stealing the big chestnut, Danielle led her nearly fifty yards away from the encampment and left her at the mouth of a dry wash where long strands of clumped grass leaned in the night breeze. She didn't hobble the mare, but left her free to roam and graze, knowing Sundown would stay close by, unless someone or something came upon her. In such an event it would be better to leave the mare free of any restraints.

Returning to the camp, Danielle walked to the glow of lanterns spilling out through open tent flies. The tent on her right appeared less crowded than the one on her left, so she veered over to it and stepped inside to the sound of both profane curses and drunken laughter as the outlaws stood lined along the banks of a row of battered faro tables. Past the tables, Danielle saw Duncan and two other outlaws drinking at a bar, which was merely a long pine plank lying across two wooden whiskey casts. Seeing Danielle, Duncan motioned her forward with his whiskey bottle in his hand.

"Where've you been?" Duncan asked in a friendly tone. "You're way behind on your drinking! Newt will be here any minute. We'll go to his shack, drink some more rye, and talk about old times." He pushed the half-full bottle of rye into her hand, then gestured with a nod toward the two men beside him. "This here is Morgan Goss and Cincinnati Carver. Boys, this is Danny Duggin, my best pal."

"Yeah, so we heard," said Cincinnati Carver, a ratty-looking outlaw with a sawed-off shotgun slung over his left shoulder, and a small hatchet riding in his belt. "We was there when you rode in, remember?" Both outlaws gave Danielle a cautious but respectful nod, then attended to the dirty shot glasses of rye in their hands. Danielle knew nothing about the two men, yet she recalled Bob Dennard mentioning them the day she got the drop on him on the trail out of Fort Smith.

Morgan Goss stood well over six feet tall and was slim as a rake handle. He wore a tall black Mexican sombrero that had a bullet hole in its crown, an aged bloodstain surrounding it. His wrists were girded with tall silver-studded leather gauntlets. Bandoleers of pistol ammunition crisscrossed his chest. He leaned forward along the plank bar and spoke to Danielle in a guarded voice. "Don't want to say this too loud, but I hope to hell you shoot Chancy Burke's head off in the morning. Me and Cincinnati is putting our whole bankroll on you."

Danielle gave Duncan a surprised look, and he raised a hand in defense. "Don't ask me, Danny," he said. "I had nothing to do with it. The way you and Burke nearly locked horns earlier has got everybody speculating, I reckon. Everybody figures you two will be going at it."

Nothing would please me more, Danielle thought. But she didn't want to seem too eager about it at first. "I didn't come here for this kind of business," she said. "In fact, if I knew what was going on, I might not have come at all." She raised the bottle of rye, appearing to take a long drink, but actually only taking a short sip. "If this is what you had in mind,

212

Dunc, I might just take my leave come morning and clear out of here."

"I didn't know nothing about this, Danny, I swear," said Duncan Grago. "But you have to admit, if there's some money to be made drawing and shooting that big Colt, why not make it?"

"He's telling you right, Danny Duggin," said Cincinnati Carver. "If a man can spin a bullet out faster than the next, he'll fare well here."

"What about you?" Danielle asked him. "Are you going to be facing anybody?"

"Me? Hell no!" Cincinnati Carver patted the side of his trousers, showing he had no sidearm. "I don't even trust myself to *carry* a pistol, I'm so bad with one." His hand went to the stock of the sawed-off shotgun slung over his shoulder. He stroked it lovingly. "Now if they'd let me use Little Milly here, I'd be game as a wild mustang."

Beside Cincinnati Carver, Morgan Goss laughed and said, "The trouble is, one blast from Little Millie would not only kill his opponent, it'd also wipe out half the spectators."

"What about you?" Danielle asked Morgan Goss. "Are you going to face anybody out there?"

"I ain't a fancy gunslinger," Goss responded. "I don't kid myself about it. I can shoot as straight as the next man, but I'm not fast on the draw." He tossed back a shot of rye and wiped the back of a leather wrist gauntlet across his mouth. "Besides, I've been outlawing

213

too long to have to prove myself, and I'm slick enough at stealing horses that I'm never scarce of cash."

"You figure that's what this is all about, money or fame?" asked Danielle. She offered a trace of a smile looking into Morgan Goss's large, watery eyes.

Morgan Goss shrugged, saying, "That's all most things are about, ain't it? A man steps up to kill another man in a shooting contest, it's because he either needs to line his pockets, or wants to broaden his name."

"Or both," Cincinnati Carver added, raising his glass of rye.

"What the hell do you two horse old thieves know about any damn thing?" Duncan Grago snapped at them, somehow finding a way to take offense at what the men said. "My brother organized this whole thing. I won't have you bad-mouthing it." As he spoke, Danielle noticed the wild gleam that was back in his eyes, brought on no doubt by the whiskey and the excitement of being back among his own kind.

Morgan Goss and Cincinnati Carver both shied back a step, seeing Duncan Grago's hand drop to the butt of his pistol. "Hold on, Dunc," Goss said, "we weren't speaking ill of Newt. Hell, we're just speculating on why a man—"

"Don't tell me to *hold on*." Duncan seethed, cutting Goss off. Eyes turned from the faro tables toward the sound of Duncan Grago's raised voice. "So what if a man wants to gain himself a reputation shooting some sons-

214

abitches? So what if he wants to make himself money for doing it? This is a free country!" The longer Duncan raged, the more Danielle could see that he was spinning out of control. His hand had gripped the butt of his Colt, his fingers tightened around it. She saw him start to jerk the gun from his holster, and as quick as the snap of a whip, she drew her own Colt and swung the barrel sidelong against his forehead.

Duncan Grago crumbled, but Danielle swooped down, looping him across her back as he fell, then raised him up on her shoulders. She turned with her pistol still out, letting the crowd see it, saying, "Everybody stay calm. No harm done. My buddy Dunc just got a little too much rye in him." The weight of Duncan Grago on her shoulders was staggering, yet she managed to stand straight, and turn toward the fly of the tent. The faro players chuckled, dismissing it, and turned back to the tables.

"Damn, Danny Duggin," said Morgan Goss, "we both owe you our thanks. Dunc always was crazy as a June bug once he got to drinking."

"I know," said Danielle, "I've seen it before." She didn't know how long she could stand the weight on her back, and she wasn't about to let anybody see her have to drop him. "Tell his brother he's all right. He just needs to sleep it off a couple of hours."

"We'll tell him," said Cincinnati Carver.

Danielle forced herself to walk steady and upright beneath the crushing load until she'd

215

left the tent and gotten out of the glow of lantern light. She staggered a few yards farther to the spot where the two of them had pitched their saddles and gear on a clear spot of ground. Dropping Duncan to the ground, her breath heaving in her chest, she dragged him by his ankles the few remaining feet to his rolled-up blanket. "I don't know...why I'm wasting my...time on you," she whispered, out of breath.

When she'd finished spreading Duncan's blanket and rolling him over onto it, Danielle wet her bandanna with tepid water from her canteen and pressed it to the welt on Duncan's forehead. He groaned, and she sat down and adjusted his head over into her lap. "What—? What hit me?" he asked in a dazed voice.

"Damn it, Dunc, I hit you, you fool," she said.

"But...why?" he asked, closing his eyes and relaxing in her lap.

"Because you were about to kill a couple of your brother's men, Carver and Goss." She pressed the wet rag gently with one hand while she held her other hand beneath his chin.

"Oh, I see," Duncan said, his mind drifting. In his addled state he nuzzled his cheek against her stomach. Danielle smiled to herself, knowing that once he came to enough to realize what he was doing, this would jolt him the rest of the way to his senses. Not wanting to confuse his already unstable mental condition, she started to shift herself out from underneath him. But he managed to stop her by raising a limber arm and holding her in place.

"Don't go," he said in a dreamy half-conscious voice. "I—I could lay here...all night. Couldn't you?"

Danielle smiled again to herself without answering. She sat still for a few minutes longer, touching the wet rag to his swollen forehead. When Duncan Grago finally opened his eyes and looked up at her face with some clarity, he gasped at the realization of where he was lying and how comfortable he'd been there. "Oh, my God," he rasped. Yet Danielle noted that he still made no attempt to raise up.

"It's all right, Dunc," Danielle said, shifting her weight once more in order to move from beneath him. But before she could free herself and stand up, Newt Grago's voice called out in the moonlight.

"What the hell is going on here?" Newt bellowed. He stomped closer as Duncan flung himself upward to his unsteady feet and hurriedly dusted the seat of his trousers. Danielle stood up as well, the wet bandanna hanging from her hand. She quickly raised her fingers to her mustache, making sure it was in place.

"Nothing, Newt," Duncan said, his words sounding shaky. "Danny here was just tending this bump on my head."

"Yeah, I heard about that bump and how it got there." Newt's eyes narrowed on Danielle. "I don't know what kind of man you are, Danny Duggin. But by God, my brother's coming with me to the shack, right now!" He reached out, grabbed Duncan's wrist, and yanked him away from beside her. Behind Newt Grago, Danielle caught sight of Chancy Burke standing with his hand on his pistol, a wizened grin on his face.

"Jesus, Newt!" Duncan Grago cut in, taking a wide, staggering step away from his brother. "What the hell are you thinking? Danny and me are pals! My God! You don't think we—?"

"Shut up, Dunc!" Newt spat at him. "Get to the shack, damn it to hell, before somebody else comes along here." Before Duncan could offer anything more in his and Danielle's defense, Newt moved in and shoved him away toward the path. As Duncan staggered out of sight, Newt spun back to Danielle. But he reined himself down at the sight of her drawn Colt cocked toward him and Chancy Burke.

"Settle down, Newt Grago," she said, knowing how easy it would be right then to kill him and Chancy Burke on the spot. Yet in doing so she also knew she would be throwing away her chance at getting the rest of her father's killers once they'd all arrived. "Whatever you're thinking, put it out of your mind. I cracked Dunc's head because I figured you wouldn't want him killing a couple of good horse thieves. I was soaking his head and nothing more, when you came in here."

Newt Grago only stood broiling in his rage and shock. Finally he said in a voice barely under control, "Come morning, you're going to face Chancy Burke. We'll see what you are, once and for all."

"What if I say no?" Danielle asked, not wanting to appear too anxious. "What if I just ride out of here tonight?"

"I hope you try riding out of here," Newt Grago warned. "I've got guards at every trail in and out. You're here, and you'll die here, come morning. Don't let me see your face near my brother again." He wheeled around and left, calling over his shoulder to Chancy Burke, "Come on, Burke, leave this sorry coyote to think about it all night."

"Right, Newt," Chancy Burke said. Before turning away from Danielle, Burke said to her in a lowered tone, "See you in the morning, Danny boy."

"My pleasure, Burke," Danielle whispered to herself as they stepped out of sight. Before the sound of their boots faded, Danielle gathered her blanket and saddle and moved away in the moonlight, not about to sleep here where they would expect her to be. At any time these men could change their minds and slip up on her in the night.

Newt Grago stomped back to his shack, Duncan staggering forward a few feet in front of him and Chancy Burke moving up beside him. "Don't you ever breathe a word of this to a soul," Newt said without facing Burke, "or I'll rip your tongue out. Do you hear me?"

"I hear you, Newt," said Burke. "But I've got to ask, just between you and me, is poor Dunc gone crazy on us? Maybe from being in prison too long?"

"There ain't a damn thing wrong with Dunc!" Newt stopped in midstride and grabbed Chancy Burke by his shirt, raging close to his face, "It's that bastard Danny Duggin, or whoever the hell that pansy really is! He's got Dunc's mind all twisted out of shape. Can't you see that?"

"Sure, Newt, I see it, take it easy," Chancy Burke replied quickly, although deep down he had some doubts about Duncan Grago after seeing the way he'd acted back there.

"I want that man dead in the dirt, Burke. And I don't want to hear another word about something being wrong with my brother!" He turned Burke's shirt loose and huffed away.

Burke stood for a second grinning to himself, casting a glance back toward the spot where they had left Danielle. "Hell," Burke said aloud to himself in the darkness, "you ain't fooling me, Danny Duggin. You might be quick, you might even shoot straight. But I've got you pegged now, Danny boy. This is going to be too damn easy."

Chapter 13

Robber's Rock, Indian Territory, July 25, 1871

Before daylight, Danielle got up from her blanket, having slept on and off throughout the night without a campfire, and carried her saddle and gear to the place where she'd left Sundown. She saddled the mare, walking her closer to the encampment but not bringing her all the way in. Instead, she left the mare hitched to a white oak tree several yards away from the rope corral where all the other horses were kept. There were more horses there now. All through the night, Danielle had heard the sound of drunken laughter emanating from the big gambling tents. More than once she'd heard the sound of pistol fire. She hoped the men on her list were among the outlaws that had arrived in the night.

The clearing in front of the plank shack was almost empty now in the early dawn light. Across from the shack, three men sat on the ground out front of one of the big tents with a bottle of rye, passing it back and forth between them. Danielle recognized Morgan Goss as one of the men, his tall sombrero now slumped forward. One of Lulu's girls sat on his lap with her arms around his neck. As Danielle came closer, one of the other men gigged Goss in his ribs. Morgan Goss looked up at Danielle and blinked his large bloodshot eyes. "Danny Duggin, you best clear out of here for your own good," he said in a whiskey-slurred voice.

"I've been told I can't," Danielle said, trying to sound regretful. "Looks like I'm in this contest whether I want to be or not."

"Yeah, that's what I heard," said Goss. "Damn, I feel like it's mine and Cincinnati's fault, causing trouble with Dunc, and you cracking his head for him. I never figured he'd take it so hard."

Danielle cocked her head, curious. "I meant having to face off with Chancy Burke today. What are you talking about, Goss?"

Morgan Goss blinked his big watery eyes again, saying, "Hell, you don't know? Dunc is all stoked up over you busting his head. Came back in the tent late last night, wild-eyed crazy, swearing he was going to shoot you dead."

"Damn it," Danielle whispered under her breath. She got the picture now. Duncan was so ashamed of what his brother Newt and Chancy Burke had seen, that now he had to prove something to them. He had to turn against his friend Danny Duggin just to save face. *The poor stupid fool,* Danielle thought. Duncan Grago thought there was something wrong with himself because he felt an attraction for her. It was an attraction he could only think of as unnatural, having no idea Danny Duggin was really a woman. "Where is Dunc?" she asked Goss.

"He passed out a couple of hours ago," Goss said. "They carried him inside the shack."

"Who else is in there?"

"Nobody." Goss shrugged. "Newt, Haas, and Chancy Burke all three rode out an hour ago to check on the guards. Three more men showed up during the night. There's supposed to be more coming still."

"Who are they?" Danielle asked, hoping it was the men on her list.

"One of them is Mysterious Dave Mather★. The other two are Bill Longley† and Briley Whitfield. Briley ain't nothing, he just rode here with them. But Longley's a straight-up killer. Said he heard about this shooting contest all the way over in Evergreen, Texas, when Rufe Gaddis rode through and told him about it."

"Is Rufe Gaddis here yet?" Danielle asked, recognizing his name from her list.

"Naw, but he will be before long," said Goss, "along with Saul Delmano and the rest of them. Bill Longley says he plans to make himself a thousand-dollar grubstake here, then quit. Mather said a man had to be crazy to take part in something like this, but he'll be betting on Bill Longley. If I was you, I'd be careful. This thing is drawing gunmen like honey draws flies."

"Thanks, Goss, I will be." Danielle let out a breath, then turned and walked to the door of the plank shack. She knocked low and quietly, then seeing the door open a few inches from the touch of her knuckles, she eased inside and closed the door behind her.

"Dunc?" she inquired, taking a step forward toward the snoring figure stretched out on a bunk beneath a wad of blanket. When Duncan Grago didn't stir, she stepped closer and said

★ *Mysterious Dave Mather was a young gunman known to work both sides of the law, friend of Doc Holliday, Wyatt Earp, and other notables.*
† *Bill Longley was a young Texan who killed a black lawman at the age of fifteen, and spent the rest of his life as a gunman and outlaw.*

his name again. This time, Duncan Grago heard her and sprang up onto the side of the bunk, gathering his open shirt across his chest. His gun belt hung from a ladder-back chair beside the bunk. "It's me, Danny Duggin," Danielle said, taking a step between Duncan and his pistol belt.

"I know it's you, Danny," Duncan said in bitter voice, "and you've got no business here. If Newt sees you here, he'll kill you. What do you want?"

"I heard you were making threats against me, Dunc," Danielle said. "Don't do something stupid and make me have to kill you."

His red-streaked eyes lifted to her, full of anger. "What makes you so damn sure you'll be the one doing the killing?"

"I'm not here to argue, Dunc. I just came to let you know. I don't want us to face off out there. If it happens, it'll be your call, not mine."

Duncan looked down and rubbed his face with both hands. "I was drunk when I said it, Danny." He hesitated for a second, then added, "But I told my brother I was going to do it...so I reckon I will. He thinks there's some-thing—" Duncan cut himself off, then shook his head and held his face in his hands. "Hell, I don't know *what* he thinks. I don't even know what *I* think. There's something about you, Danny. You make me have crazy thoughts. I feel like I'm losing my mind when I'm around you."

Danielle felt sorry for him, seeing how confused he was over his feelings. But there was no way she could explain it to him. In all her time posing as a man, this was the first time something like this had happened. Somehow her womanhood had reached through her rough disguise, and although neither she nor Duncan Grago had meant for it to happen, he seemed to have fallen for her. He didn't realize that what he felt was only the natural draw of a man to a woman. All he knew was there were feelings inside him that he could not fathom.

"Dunc, listen to me," she said, almost having to bite her tongue to keep from telling him the truth, "there's nothing wrong with you. You're not losing your mind. But you need to get away from here, clear your head somewhere, get yourself a woman. You've been away all these years, everything is crowding you. Don't let yourself get tricked into thinking that you have to prove yourself to your brother or anybody else."

"Prove *what* to my brother?" He stood up from the bunk, his fists clenched at his sides. "What the hell are you trying to say is wrong with me?"

Danielle didn't back down an inch. She could tell he wanted to step forward in his rage and his shame, but she also knew he wasn't about to have her pistol come up from her holster and crack his head again. "Stand down, Dunc," she warned in a low tone, "I'm not saying anything is wrong with you. It's you who's thinking it."

"Damn it to hell! Get out of here!" Duncan shouted hoarsely at her. "This is a shooting contest! I'll choose who I want to face on the street! If you don't want a shoot-out with me, crawfish out of this camp and don't come back! Or I'll kill you, Danny Duggin, I swear to God I will!"

Danielle took a slow step back, her hand on her Colt, mindful of Duncan's pistol in the holster hanging on the chair back. She raised a finger, pointing at him as she spoke. "All right, Dunc, I've asked you not to do it. I'll face Chancy Burke in the street. I'll kill him, there's not a doubt in my mind. Whether or not I face you next is up to you. Think it over, that's all I ask."

Danielle backed to the door, opening it behind her. Before she stepped back from the shack, she saw the disturbed, hurt look in Duncan's eyes. "Danny," he said, shaking his head slowly, "I'm sorry. I've got to do it, don't you see? I hate to...but I've just got to."

"Yeah," she said, almost in a whisper. "So do I, Dunc. So do I."

Danielle walked back to the front of the large gambling tent where Morgan Goss stood talking to the three men who had arrived during the night. Other men had stirred from their blankets and they came drifting in out of the morning haze. Lulu came walking up to Morgan Goss and the others at the same time as Danielle. "What was all the shouting about?" she asked, barely stopping long enough for an answer as she headed inside the large tent with a metal cash box under her arm.

"Ask Danny Duggin," Goss said, pointing in Danielle's direction. But Lulu only tossed Danielle a glance in passing and let the tent fly fall behind her.

"Danny Duggin?" one of the newcomers inquired as Danielle stepped in among them. He was a thin, young man with small pinched eyes and a drooping dark mustache. A bottle of rye hung from his right hand. Next to him stood a taller young man, equally thin, wearing a long goatee. "I knew some Duggins back in Pennsylvania. Any kin there?"

"No kin that I know of," Danielle replied.

"Say, you're the one Burke and some of the others were talking about last night," said the one with the goatee.

"Oh?" Danielle just looked at him.

"Yep, he's the one, all right," said Morgan Goss. "He's a good *hombre*, in my opinion, and I don't say that often about anybody."

"Hell, Goss, you don't even say that about your own pa." The man with the goatee chuckled.

"Danny," said Goss, "this here is Billy Longley and Dave Mather."

Danielle gave the two men a respectful nod.

"Good to make your acquaintance, Danny Duggin," said Longley, the one with the long goatee. "I'm glad to get the chance to size up the competition." He spread a tight level grin. "Looks like one of us will soon be laying dead, while the other strikes a match on his belt buckle."

"I won't be shooting with you, Bill Longley," Danielle said firmly, "so you might just as well forget it. Go check out some other competition."

"Bet you a dollar I can goad you into it." Longley grinned.

"No bet, Longley," said Danielle. "This contest ain't my style. I'm only shooting against Chancy Burke because there's no way out of it," she lied. "Newt Grago is forcing me into it."

"Aw, come on now, Danny Duggin," said Bill Longley. "You don't look like a man easily forced into anything he don't want to do in the first place."

Danielle just stared at him.

"Don't let Bill get under your skin, Danny Duggin," said Dave Mather. "He's come here with the notion of making a thousand dollars. It's got him a little edgy just thinking about it."

"Ain't a damn thing edgy about me," Longley said to Mather, keeping a fixed stare on Danielle. "I'll make my thousand any way they want to do this thing. I'll kill one son of a bitch for a thousand, two sonsabitches for five hundred a piece, or a *thousand* sonsabitches for a dollar a head. Makes me no difference."

"Good luck then," said Danielle. "I won't be one of them."

"Are you sure, Danny Duggin?" Longley asked, leaning a bit toward her.

"Cut it out, Bill," Mather said laughingly, pulling Longley back and sticking the bottle of rye in his hand. "Here, have some breakfast." Mather turned to Danielle. "What's the story on you and Dunc Grago? Goss said he's talking about killing you."

"Talk won't get it done," Danielle said. "He was drunk, I cracked his head. I'm hoping he'll get over it before the shooting starts."

"Some men get over a head cracking sooner than others," said Mather with a wince. "Some don't get over them at all. If I was you, I'd shoot Duncan Grago as soon as his face hits daylight coming out of the shack." He grinned. "It might save you a lot of trouble down the road."

"I'll take my chances," Danielle said. "Now if you'll all excuse me, I'm going to see what this place feeds for breakfast before the morning drinkers show up."

"Better hurry then." Mather grinned. "They're dragging in already."

No sooner had Danielle stepped out of sight inside the large tent, than Bill Longley leaned closer to Dave Mather and asked, "What do you say, Dave? He doesn't look like much to me. After I trim a couple other of these gunslingers down, talk Danny Duggin into trying me, then put a couple of hundred on me with Merlin Haas. We'll make a bundle."

"He doesn't strike me as the kind of man you can talk into anything," Mather replied. "Besides, I ain't sure I'd put a hundred on you against this Danny Duggin, if that's his real name. He impresses me as a man on a mission. Get between him and whatever that mission is, I could see him killing you without batting an eye."

"Thanks for your support, partner," Longley hissed, giving Mather a rough shove.

Mather rocked back on his feet, then came forward and snatched the bottle of rye from Bill Longley's hand, grinning. "Don't mention it, partner," he replied, raising the bottle to his lips.

By the time Danielle had washed down a bowl of loose hash with a mug of warm beer, the tent was alive and kicking with outlaws still drunk or hung over from the night before. Halfway through her meal, Danielle caught sight of Duncan Grago coming into the tent. Duncan had Lulu set him up a bottle of rye and a glass. But upon seeing Danielle down the bar from him, Duncan sneered, backhanded the glass from the bar, jerked up the bottle, and left with it. Danielle stood still for a moment, just staring at the open tent fly.

"What's the matter, Danny Duggin?" said Lulu's voice behind the bar. "You and your buddy not waking up eye to eye this morning?"

Danielle turned to face her across the plank bar. "Do we know each other, ma'am?"

Lulu saw the flare of fire in her eyes before Danielle managed to conceal it. "Honey, you don't know me, but I sure know you." Lulu tossed a hand. "Leastwise, I know of you. You're the one giving Newt Grago his worst night's sleep in years."

"If that's true, then I'm glad of it," said Danielle, laying down a coin for her breakfast and beer.

"Ready for another?" Lulu asked.

"No thanks. I wasn't even ready for that one, until you said you're out of coffee." Danielle offered an amiable smile to make up for the look in her eyes when Lulu had first approached her.

"I'm Lulu Dorsey. Glad to meet you, Danny Duggin," Lulu said, returning the smile. She cocked her head to one side. "Tell me something—what is it about you that's got the Grago brothers and Chancy Burke so stirred up?"

"Beats me, Lulu," said Danielle. "I reckon they were just looking for something to get stirred up over, and I happened along. That's just my opinion." Now Danielle cocked her head in return, asking, "Why do *you* think it is?"

"I think it's because you remind them of things they'd sooner forget. Newt thinks you recognize him from somewhere, like maybe you've got a grudge to settle or something."

"If that's so, why hasn't he made a move to try and settle up with me?" Danielle asked. "Or, better yet, why haven't *I* made a move to settle that grudge if there is one?"

"Oh, I don't know..." Lulu fluffed her curly hair with her fingertips, flirting with what she thought was the handsome young Danny Duggin standing before her. "But if you're not busy tonight, we could go over all the reasons—" Her words were cut short at the sight of Duncan

231

Grago stepping back inside the tent with his pistol out at arm's length, aimed and cocked at Danielle.

"Damn you to hell, Danny Duggin!" Duncan Grago screamed, his face contorted, tears running freely down his cheeks. Lulu jumped to the side and down to the dirt floor. Men dove away from the bar and the faro tables, taking cover. But Danielle stood firm, her eyes riveted on Duncan Grago, both her hands coming up slowly and spreading along the edge of the bar behind her. "You better grab for your Colt, Danny! I'm going to kill you!"

Danielle saw the anger and the madness in his eyes. Yet, she saw something else there that told her if she didn't make a move she wouldn't have to kill him. She held firm, resisting the urge to go for her pistol, praying she wasn't calling this thing wrong—if she was, she'd surely die.

"I mean it, Danny! Damn you!" Duncan bellowed. "Go for your Colt, or I'll cut you in half! I swear it!"

Danielle never wavered an inch. The first shot from Duncan's pistol exploded, the bullet whistling past her shoulder two feet away. Behind the bar a stack of beer mugs shattered in a spray of glass. Danielle only stared. Her hunch was confirmed. If Duncan meant to shoot her, he wouldn't have missed, not by that wide of a mark. The next shot went past her other shoulder, this one father away than the first. She allowed herself a tight breath, still holding ground.

"I mean it!" Duncan raged. Two more shots exploded, one on either side of her, wood splinters showering down from where one bullet nipped the tent pole behind the bar. "What do you want from me, huh? Want me to holster up? Give you a chance to draw? All right, there!" Duncan uncocked his pistol and shoved it into his holster. His trembling hand poised close to the butt of the weapon. "Now draw, damn you! Draw, or I'll kill you in cold blood, so help me God!"

Danielle still only stared, making no effort to prepare herself for a gunfight. "All right then! You're dead!" Duncan screamed. He streaked the pistol up from his holster, cocked and pointed. In that second Danielle saw clearly what Duncan Grago was asking of his friend Danny Duggin. In his confused and tortured state of mind, Duncan was asking to be killed. Like some injured hopeless animal, his every move begged to be put out of his misery.

"I won't fight you, Dunc, not like this," Danielle said in a level, unyielding voice.

Duncan Grago's hand shook even worse, then slumped toward the dirt floor. He let out a tormented scream, firing the two remaining shots into the ground. "Damn it to everlasting hell! What's happening to me?" he sobbed, crumbling to his knees in full view of the other outlaws.

"Nothing you don't have coming, you son of a bitch!" said Bill Longley, stepping in behind him and planting a hard boot on his slumped shoulder. Duncan Grago flew forward on his face. Bill Longley jumped forward, yanking a pair of brass knuckles from his hip pocket. "What kind of low poltroon makes a play like that and then don't follow through. I'll work your head over like it's a hickory stump." He reached down, grabbed Duncan Grago by the back of his shirt, and lifted him up halfway, drawing back the brass knuckles for a good solid punch to Duncan's face.

"Turn him loose, Longley," Danielle said, stepping forward.

"Like hell," said Longley, drawing his arm farther back, widening the arc of his swing. But his arm stopped suddenly as the tip of Danielle's pistol barrel jammed against his ear and cocked.

"I said turn him loose. Nobody takes up my fight unless I ask them to." Danielle leaned some pressure into the Colt, causing Longley's head to tilt beneath the weight of it.

"For God sakes, don't beg for my life, Danny!" Duncan Grago sobbed into the dirt.

"Shut up, Dunc," Danielle snapped.

"You're making a bad mistake, Duggin," Bill Longley snarled, trying to look sideways as he spoke. "Let me lay into this piece of punkwood. I want to beat him real bad."

"You'll die, Longley, that's a promise," Danielle warned.

"Aw, come on. I saw how you just stood there, wouldn't do nothing. You won't shoot me, not really."

"Ten dollars says he will," Mysterious Dave Mather said, stepping inside the tent, his short-barreled Hood .38 caliber out of his shoulder harness and pointed at Danielle. "Of course I'll kill ole Danny Duggin here as soon as he pulls that trigger on you, if that's any consolation."

Longley stared sideways at Dave Mather, thinking about it. Seeing the small Hood pistol, he let out a sigh, saying, "Damn it, Dave, why'd you draw that little cork-popper when you see he's got a big Colt pinned to the side of my head?"

Dave Mather chuckled, dark and low. "Call it poor judgment, Bill. I dressed in a hurry this morning. What're you going to do? I'm ready to back your play."

"Well hell," Bill Longley said, relenting, lowering his arm slowly and letting the brass knuckles drop from his fingers. "I hate somebody poking a pistol in my ear, Duggin. It's cause to kill a man, I always say."

"You just can't turn nothing loose easy, can you, Bill?" Dave Mather said, stepping forward, his pistol still trained on Danielle. He bent down and picked up the brass knuckles. "Now let him up, Danny. Let's all move slow and easy, keep from splattering brains all over the day drinkers, what do you say?"

"Sounds good to me if you really mean it," said Danielle. "If this is a setup, we're all going to die here."

"It's no setup, Danny Duggin," said Dave Mather. "If I was going to shoot you, it wouldn't matter whether or not you held a gun to Bill's head. Show a little trust here." He grinned.

When Danielle stepped back and relaxed her grip on her Colt, Bill Longley raised Duncan Grago to his feet and shoved him through the fly of the tent. "Here, don't forget this." He snatched Duncan's pistol from the ground and pitched it out behind him. "You might need it to go somewhere and blow your brains out." He turned back to Danielle, dusting his hands together. "No hard feelings, Danny Duggin, but the next time you point a pistol at me, you better make sure it comes out smoking." He smiled flatly and without expression. "Come on, Dave, before I change my mind and wipe this whole place out."

"In a minute, Bill," said Mather. He stood beside Danielle and watched until Bill Longley left the tent. Then Mather turned to Danielle, holstering his Hood pistol up under his arm. "Tell me, Danny Duggin, does this sort of thing happen everyplace you go?"

"Lately it seems like it," said Danielle. She stepped back to the bar and slumped back against it. "Am I going to have to watch my back with Bill Longley around?"

"I doubt it. In his own way, he thought he was doing you a favor. He might challenge you in this shooting contest. Otherwise, like he said, no hard feelings."

"That's good to know," Danielle said. "I've got enough trouble here as it is. I don't need any more."

No sooner than she'd spoken, Morgan Goss stuck his head inside the tent, announcing to the drinkers who were now getting back to the

236

bar and the faro tables, "New riders coming in, boys. Looks like Arno Dunne brought a couple of shooters with him. Reckon we'll be starting the contest again most any time."

"Is there anybody else you recognize?" Danielle asked, hoping to hear some of the names on her list.

"Nope, just these three, Arno Dunne and couple of look-alikes on a pair of bay horses."

Danielle stood stunned for a second, knowing it must be her brothers Jed and Tim.

"What's wrong, Danny?" Dave Mather chuckled. "You look like you just fell down a long, dark hole."

"It feels like it, Mather," Danielle responded, and leveling her hat low on her forehead, she walked toward the tent fly.

Chapter 14

"Stick close to me, boys," Arno Dunne told Jed and Tim Strange as they rode into the encampment, "and say no more than you have to." The twins only nodded, looking all around at the grizzled faces, the tents, and the lay of the rugged land, in case they had to make a quick getaway. "None of these men know you, or how good you are with those Colts." Arno laughed under his breath. "We want to keep it that way as long as we can. By the time they find out, we'll have most of their money in our pockets."

"We understand," said Tim. He recalled the events of the morning as they rode along. They had met up with Newt Grago, Merlin Haas, and Chancy Burke along the trail. When Arno Dunne explained how he'd brought these two along to join the contest, Chancy Burke looked them up and down with a sneer, sizing them up as a couple of greenhorns fresh off of the farm. "What's the story on those little deadman's knots hanging from your saddle horns?" he'd asked, pointing at the two miniature nooses made from the window blind cord. Before either Jed or Tim could respond, Arno Dunne cut in.

"That's a secret, Burke," Dunne said. Then he looked away from Chancy Burke and at Merlin Haas and Newt Grago. "In fact, everything about these boys is a secret, except their names." He nodded toward Jed and Tim. "This here's the Faulkner twins, Tim and Jed. Anybody wants to know more about them will have to step up face-to-face and find out for themselves."

"Are they any good with them Colts?" Burke asked. "You must think so or you wouldn't have brought them here."

Arno Dunne gave a playful wink to Newt Grago as he answered Chancy Burke. "Of course I think they're good. The question is *how* good? And that's the part that'll cost you to find out."

Newt Grago had caught the glint in Arno Dunne's eyes, and knew he was up to something. That was fine with Newt, so long as there was a way for him and Haas to make their money as well. Arno Dunne had some crack shooters here, and Newt Grago knew it. He'd smiled and swept a hand back toward the encampment. "Any friends of Arno Dunne's are friends of mine. Head on in, Arno, we'll be back as soon as we check on the last guard position."

That had been over an hour ago, and now, drawing closer to the encampment, the twins had prepared themselves for anything. "I hope we ain't made a bad mistake here," Jed Strange whispered to Tim, the two of them dropping their bays back a few feet behind Arno Dunne. Less than fifty yards ahead, men began to gather along the edge of the camp clearing. These were tough-looking men, Jed thought, men who stared at them with eyes like vultures. Thumbs hooked into gun belts as Dunne led them forward.

"Get on up here with me, boys," Dunne said to Tim and Jed over his shoulder. "Don't get bashful on me now. We've got some work cut out for us."

Jed and Tim gigged their bays forward. "Notice how he keeps saying *we*, or *us*?" Jed asked under his breath. "He makes it sound like he's the one going to be doing the shooting."

"Yeah," Tim replied. "If this thing goes wrong or he double-crosses us, he *better* be ready to do some shooting. I'll kill him if it's the last thing I do."

At the line of gathered men, Arno Dunne sidled his horse the last few steps and said down to Cincinnati Carver, "Heard some shooting a while back. Have you started. the contest before Newt and Haas get back?"

"Naw," said Carver, "Newt would have a fit if we did something like that. All you heard was Dunc going crazy, shooting at an ole boy named Danny Duggin. They got into it last night, and Duggin cracked his head. Dunc's acting like the world came to an end because of it. Hell, you know how Dunc is." Cincinnati Carver looked the twins over, noting right away how young and inexperienced they looked. "Who's your friends, Arno?"

Dunne spread a crafty smile, looking from Carver to the rest of the faces. Bloodshot eyes looked back at him. "Boys, this is the Faulkner twins, Tim and Jed. Newt met us along the trail and welcomed them in. I told him these two were about half good with a pistol. He said, bring them in and we'll see what they can do."

Carver said, "Dunne, this thing has gotten big. Bill Longley has shown up, claiming he's going to make himself a thousand dollars here."

"Bill Longley, huh?" Arno Dunne reined his horse back a step, looking over the heads of the men and toward the two big gambling tents.

A voice laughed amid the gathered men, calling out, "Does that change any plans you might have had, Dunne?"

Arno Dunne collected himself, took a cigar from his coat pocket, and stuck it into his mouth. "Hell no," he said after a short pause, "the more the merrier. "Come on, boys," he said to Tim and Jed, jerking a nod toward the big tents, "let's go cut some dust from our throats."

The crowd of men parted and Arno Dunne and the twins stepped their horses through them. As the men dispersed behind them, Tim said to Jed, "Did you hear them mention Danny Duggin? I wonder if Danny is in on this shooting contest?"

Hearing Tim, Arno Dunne cut in, asking, "Who's this Danny Duggin? Does he know how fast you boys are?"

"We met Danny along the trail, back before we rode to Mobeetie. He's the one who gave us a tip on where to find work."

"Okay, okay," Dunne said impatiently, "but does he know how good you are with a gun? That's what I need to know."

"Not really," Tim replied. "We only met him, shared a camp and coffee with him. He seemed like a good enough *hombre*. Never thought he'd be a part of something like this. He didn't strike us as being an outlaw."

"You'd be surprised who's an outlaw and who ain't. People can fool you," Dunne replied.

"I don't want to face Danny Duggin if he's a part of this," said Jed.

Dunne sighed in exasperation. "Boys, if he's in the contest, and wants to face you, doesn't that tell you something? If he's willing to kill you, shouldn't you be just as willing to kill him?"

Jed started to speak in protest, but Tim saw it was pointless and cut him off, saying, "Damn right, Dunne. Whoever's facing me has just as much to think about as I do. So to hell with them. I'm out to win." As he spoke, he cut Jed a guarded glance, letting him know he was just going along with Dunne.

"Tim," Dunne said over his shoulder, drawing his horse to a halt outside the first large tent, "you are a joy to behold. I believe in time, you'll have your mind straight and be as good an outlaw as ever outran a rope." He reached a hand out and jiggled the miniature noose on Tim's saddle horn as the twins stopped their horses beside him. "But you, *deacon*," he added, looking at Jed, "I don't know what we'll ever make of you."

"Never you mind about me, Dunne," Jed said as the three of them swung down from their saddles, "I'll handle whatever flies at me."

Watching from beside the large tent, Danielle listened to the sound of her brothers' voices. Hearing and seeing them gave her mixed feelings. She wanted to run out and fling her arms around them both. At the same time she felt like running out and cursing them and sending them packing. But no matter what she felt, this was no time for her to divert from her course. She would have to deal with her brothers being here, keeping out of their sight as much as possible and going on with her plans once the rest of her father's killers arrived.

"Damn it, Jed and Tim," she whispered to herself, seeing them spin their reins around

242

a makeshift rail and step inside the tent, "why couldn't you just be content to stay in St. Joe?" In saying it, she felt a little guilty, for they could have very well asked her the same question last year when she began her journey. Reminding herself of this fact caused her to take a deep breath and not judge her brothers too harshly.

When she'd first heard Morgan Goss mention Arno Dunne and a couple of look-alikes riding a pair of bays, she'd gone straightaway to where she'd hitched Sundown, and moved the mare back to where she'd left her last night. She couldn't risk Jed and Tim seeing Sundown. That would destroy everything.

Now with the mare safely out of sight, all Danielle could do was wait. She moved quietly back alongside the tent, then cut away toward the shade of a white oak, where she planned to watch the camp for any sign of Newt Grago and Chancy Burke. As soon as the contest started, she wanted to get her shot at Burke and take him down. That would mark one more name off her list. Then she would find a way to stay off to herself and keep an eye on the trail leading in. She repeated the other three names on her list to herself, knowing them by heart now: Rufe Gaddis, Saul Delmano, Blade Hogue. Once these other killers rode in, she would no longer care about Jed and Tim recognizing her. Nothing else would matter then, as she'd gun them down, every one of them, and Newt Grago too. Or else she'd die trying.

It was high noon when Newt Grago, Merlin Haas, and Chancy Burke rode back into camp. By that time the outlaws had grown restless and eager for the shooting to begin. Several of the lesser gunmen had taken to drawing names among themselves, fearful of facing the likes of Chancy Burke or Bill Longley. A couple of fistfights and a knifing had broken out in the clearing of Lulu's gambling tent, and shots had erupted over one of Lulu's girls, leaving a Montana outlaw by the name of Herk Evans with a bullet in his thigh. Bill Longley had gotten a little drunker than he'd intended to, and he'd starting shooting beer mugs from atop one of the girls' heads until Dave Mather came along and stopped him.

Now Mather and Longley stood at the center of the clearing, drinking strong coffee, the rest of the outlaws giving them wide berth as they watched Grago, Haas, and Burke ride into camp. "I don't know about you," Longley said, "but the more sober I get, the worse this pigsty starts looking to me."

"You want to head out?" Mather asked, sounding astonished. "What about the thousand dollars you promised yourself?"

"Oh, I'll stand a couple of rounds if they got anybody who'll try me," Longley said, stroking his goatee. "But I've been thinking. The only man here who's game for all takers is Chancy Burke. If he kills this Danny Duggin, nobody else will be bold enough to face up to him, except me." Longley shrugged. "Then, once I kill Burke, there won't be a soul here who'll face me. That means I can only make five hundred or seven hundred at the most."

"That's not bad money," said Mather, "and who knows, when some of these others show up from Newt Grago's old bunch, you might even get some other challengers." A guarded smile came to Mather's face. "Do me a favor, lay off of Danny Duggin if you can. There's something I like about him."

"Yeah, what's that?" Longley asked.

"I can't say," Mather replied, looking away from Longley's questioning gaze. Then as if dismissing the subject, he pointed at the group of outlaws who had drawn names among themselves and were getting itchy to start the contest. "You've also got to figure, some of them will get more bark on once they commence facing one another and winning. That's just human nature."

Bill Longley nodded, thinking about it. "Yeah, I reckon you're right. We'll just have to play this thing by ear for a while. Think you better get over to Merlin Haas right away, get us a few dollars bet on Danny Duggin?"

"Sure thing," said Mather. He reached inside his coat, took out a stack of bills, and headed over to the shack where Newt Grago, Haas, and Burke had just stepped down from their horses.

At the shack, eight or ten outlaws had crowded around Newt Grago, each of them waving dollars in his face. "Hold it, boys!" Newt shouted, shoving them back from him. "One at a time." Beside him, Chancy Burke butted a man back with his chest, keeping a hand on his pistol butt.

"You heard him, damn it!" Burke shouted. "Newt ain't the one taking the bets, you need to get with Haas." He nodded at Merlin Haas, who stood clasping his coat lapels, a black cigar standing straight out from his teeth.

"But he won't take our bets unless Newt here okays it," a man named Quince Matine said. "This ain't about the regular pot. This is some matching a few of the boys have done on their own."

"The hell are you talking about, Matine?" Newt Grago asked, looking around at the gathered men.

"Edwards here has challenged his cousin, Bennie, to a shoot-out." He pointed around at the others. "Cotton Pate has challenged Anderson. Hell, we've got enough matches here to last into the night, if you'll just give us the go-ahead."

"No kidding?" Newt Grago chuckled. "So, some of you have gotten together and done a little figuring on your own, eh?" He looked at Merlin Haas and laughed. "What do you say, Haas? Want to cover some extra bets? Looks like we're going to have a whole other level of shooters here. Everybody's wanting to get into the action."

"Bring 'em on," Haas said, reaching into his coat and pulling out a pencil and paper. "We ain't turning nothing away. Step over here and give me the information. Who's fighting who?"

The men hurried over and surrounded Merlin Haas. Chancy Burke saw Dave Mather coming toward them, and he leaned close to Grago, saying, "What about these two, Newt? What are we going to do about Longley wanting in on this shooting contest?"

"I told you last night not to worry about it when him and Mather rode in, didn't I?" Newt Grago whispered, seeing Mather draw closer. "You're starting to sound like you're afraid of Longley."

"Hell, Newt, I ain't no damn fool," Chancy Burke whispered in reply. "There ain't a man here can beat Bill Longley."

"Maybe not one man," Newt said, "but I bet a few men can handle the job." He winked at Burke, then stepped forward as Dave Mather arrived with the stack of dollar bills in his hand. Chancy Burke smiled and let out a breath of relief.

"Howdy, Mather, what can I do for you?" Newt Grago asked.

"I got five hundred dollars says the kid, Danny Duggin, is going to put your boy Burke here in the ground. No offense, Burke," Mather added, casting Burke a glance. Chancy Burke's face reddened, and he looked away without reply.

"You need to see Haas, Mather. He's the one what handles the betting," said Grago.

"Huh-uh." Mather shook his head. "Merlin Haas has been known to disappear come pay-up time. I'd rather you hold the bet. It might keep me from chasing Haas down and putting a bullet in his eye."

Newt Grago laughed thinly as he took the money. "Hell, okay then, even money on Burke and Danny Duggin. We'll be starting as soon as Duggin shows up. Meanwhile, have you seen Dunc?"

"Nope," Mather said. "He hasn't shown his face after what happened over at Lulu's earlier."

"What happened at Lulu's?" Grago asked in stunned surprise.

Before Mather could answer, they recognized the voice of Danny Duggin calling out from forty yards away. "Chancy Burke! Let's get to it!"

The men gathered in the clearing stepped away at the sound of the voice. They formed a wide path for Danielle to walk through. She came forward slowly but steadily, her right hand passing close to the big Colt on her hip with each step. Among the crowd, she caught a glimpse of Tim and Jed standing beside Arno Dunne. Jed stepped forward, saying, "Danny? Danny Duggin? Remember us?"

"Not now," Danielle said, staring straight ahead. "There's killing to be done." Tim reached out and pulled Jed back, while Arno Dunne shook his head in disgust at Jed's action.

"You've been wanting it, Burke, now come and get it!" Danielle said with finality, stopping at ten yards and planting her feet a shoulder-width apart. A few feet to one side of the crowd, Bill Longley sipped back the last of his coffee and moved forward, watching with keen interest.

Beside Newt and Chancy Burke, Dave Mather chuckled, saying to Burke, "Well, Chancy, here's where the bullet meets the bone. Don't let the fact that you're about to die throw you off your game none."

"Go to hell, Mather," Chancy Burke hissed, stepping past him, and starting a wide, slow half circle to his left, wanting to get to where he could put the sun in this young gunman's eyes.

"Take your time, Burke, get it where you want it," Danielle called out to him. "It's a high-noon sun, so it won't help you much. Get your hand steady and your mind clear. I'm ready when you are."

"That's real obliging of you," Burke replied, moving sidelong, one slow step at a time, putting wide clearance between himself and Newt Grago and the others. Then he stopped, seeing the noon sun was indeed no help to him at all. "This will do just fine for me, Duggin." But Burke raised a hand toward Danielle, putting the fight off for a moment as he half turned to Newt Grago, calling out to him, "Are all the bets in place, Newt?"

Newt Grago nodded. "That's all I wanted to know," Burke said, keeping his left hand raised toward Danielle. Without lowing his left hand, Chancy Burke spun suddenly, his hand coming up with his pistol, cocking it on the upswing. The crowd gasped, unprepared for his surprise move. But Danielle was ready. She'd known his play when he'd raised his hand and turned toward Grago. Her Colt exploded before Burke even got his pistol all the way up.

One loud burst of fire filled the clearing, followed by a grunt from Chancy Burke as he staggered backward, turned a full circle, then sank to his wobbling knees. Danielle could tell his world was spinning around him as she stepped forward with her Colt hanging in her hand.

"That's what it feels like, Burke," Danielle said, bending down with him as he rocked back flat on the ground. His pistol spilled from his hand, and his fingers tried clawing at it. "Go ahead, pick it up. Die with it in your hand." She bent down face-to-face, and whispered in his ear, "That was my pa you and your rats killed last year. You left him hanging from a tree. I just wanted you to die knowing that there's one killing you didn't get away with."

"You...you son of a bitch," Chancy Burke gasped. His fingertips managed to wrap around the butt of the pistol, struggling to raise it.

"Wrong again," Danielle said. "I'm no *son* at all. I was his *daughter*." She paused for a second letting it sink into his fading eyes. Then she said, "Be sure and tell the devil it was a *woman* who sent you to hell." Straightening and taking a short step back, she waited until the pistol in his hand moved forward, shaky, trying to level up on her. She fired a round down into his forehead, then opened the cylinder on her Colt, punching out to the two spent cartridges and replacing them. As she closed the cylinder and spun it down her forearm, Newt Grago, Dave Mather, and Merlin Haas stepped in beside her.

"You didn't have to do that!" Newt Grago said angrily. "You could see he was dying!"

"It's your contest, not mine, Grago," Danielle said. "One man dies, one man wins. What's next on today's events?" She turned, facing him up close, resisting the urge to unload her Colt into his belly. Grago held her stare. She could see he was on the verge of going for his pistol, and she almost hoped he would.

"Well, now," Dave Mather said, seeing trouble about to erupt between them and moving forward to stop it, "I believe you owe me a thousand dollars, Newt." He snapped his fingers, grinning at Newt Grago. "I'll have it now, if you please."

Newt Grago pulled back a step and forced his eyes away from Danielle to Mather. He took out a huge roll of bills and counted them off into Mather's palm. The crowd sifted forward toward Chancy Burke's body. Tim and Jed looked up from the bullet hole in Burke's head, and stared at Danielle. "Lord, Danny Duggin," Jed whispered, shaking his head slowly. Danielle could not face him, so she turned and walked away toward Lulu's tent.

"So I guess that's that," said Bill Longley, giving Newt Grago a sarcastic smile. "We all see who's the man to beat now, don't we?"

"You're up with Danny Duggin anytime you want it, Longley," Newt Grago growled. "Just say the word. I want that man dead, for reasons I ain't even going to explain."

But Longley only laughed, taking half of the thousand dollars Dave Mather handed to him. "What for, Newt? I just made half of the amount I came here for without having to fire a shot. I might double it up at Lulu's tonight and head out come morning. Never let it be said that I ain't a man of peace."

Bill Longley turned to walk away with Dave Mather, but Grago stopped him, calling out, "Don't rush off, Bill, I might have a proposition for you."

"Oh?" Longley turned back, smiling toward him. "Why, Newt, I'm always pleased to listen to anything you've got to say. Go on to Lulu's, Mysterious Dave... I'll be along directly."

Chapter 15

Danielle had Lulu's tent to herself for a few moments while all the outlaws and gunmen milled around the body of Chancy Burke. The first person to arrive a few minutes behind her was Dave Mather, and he did so with a look of respect in his dark eyes as he sidled up to the bar and tipped his hat back. "You're not drinking, I see," Mather said to Danielle, flagging down Lulu to order himself a whiskey with a beer chaser.

"No," Danielle said in a flat tone, standing with her back against the bar and a boot propped up behind her. "You might not want to stand too close to me, Mysterious Dave. I've got a feeling Newt Grago ain't real happy with the outcome of the first match of the day. There could be a hail of gunfire come through this tent any minute."

"I'll take my chances," Mather said, raising the whiskey and sipping it. "But you're right, Newt ain't at all pleased." He savored the taste of the whiskey for a second then took a drink of beer and wiped his hand across his mustache. "I have no doubt he's out there right now, trying to get Bill Longley to challenge you into a match."

"Bill Longley can challenge all he wants to, I'm not fighting him," Danielle said.

"They'll goad you down, Danny Duggin, and you know how that goes." Mather smiled. "They'll call you a coward, try to get under your skin."

"Yep, they can do that." Danielle cocked her head toward Dave Mather. "But I don't fall for kid games. Newt Grago made threats on Chancy Burke's behalf, and Burke made some on his own. I didn't do it for the money or the name of doing it. I did it because I was told by both of them that I would have to if I ever wanted to leave here alive. Now Burke's dead and I'm still standing. That's as simple as I can call it. To hell with Newt Grago and what he wants." She wasn't about to tell Mather the truth—that she had come here for the sole purpose of killing not only Burke, but Grago and the others as well.

"I'll say something to Bill Longley if he goes for Grago's deal, whatever it is," Mather said. "If I can, I'll keep him from raining down your back."

"I appreciate your offer, Dave, but don't worry about my back, it's rainproof. I know Bill Longley's reputation. If he makes a move on me, I'll burn him down—same as I did Chancy Burke, same as I would anybody else."

"By God, you sure ain't short on confidence, are you, Danny Duggin?" Mather chuckled.

"Nope. If I was, I'd have been dead a long time ago." Danielle turned her head and spoke down the bar to Lulu. "Maybe I'll take a beer, after all. Bring Dave another one, too."

Lulu quickly filled two mugs and slid them down the plank bar. Danielle hooked one and raised it to her lips. When she lowered it, she looked at Mather curiously, asking, "Why would you do that for me, Dave?"

"What? Speak to Bill Longley on your behalf?" Dave Mather shrugged, raising his fresh beer. "Hell, I don't know. If I needed a reason, I reckon I'd say it's because you strike me as a man on a mission. I don't believe you belong here in this bunch, and I don't believe you're here by choice. Something brought you here, Danny Duggin, some task you can't let go of till it's finished." He sipped his beer and sat it down. "Am I right?"

Danielle didn't answer right away. Instead she looked off for a moment. "If I was here on some sort of mission like you say, do you think I'd admit it?"

"Of course not," Mather said, getting the message. He raised his beer in salute. "But all the same, here's to missions, and those of us who carry them out."

They drank their beer as others began arriving at the tent in twos and threes, talking about the shooting, and speculating on the matches coming up. Lulu got busy behind the bar, setting up bottles of whiskey and sliding frothing beer mugs into eager hands. When Bill Longley came in, he walked straight to Danielle and Dave Mather. A few drinkers scooted away, giving him plenty of elbow room, something Longley had grown accustomed to, owing to his deadly reputation. "I don't know what the trouble is between you and Newt Grago," Longley said to Danielle, "but he's sure bent on seeing you dead."

Danielle stared at him for second, then said, "I notice he's not bent enough to come do it himself."

Bill Longley laughed under his breath. "I noticed that myself. Still, the fact remains, you are the man to beat now. If I'm the only one here who has the grit to challenge you, I reckon that means it's you and me, first thing in the morning. That'll give these boys the rest of today to kill each other off." He nodded toward the other drinkers, who were hurrying with the beer, some of them headed back out into the clearing with a mug in one hand and a bottle of whiskey under their arm.

255

"What if I say no?" Danielle asked.

Bill raised a finger as if trying to work something out in his mind. "See, that's the same thing I just asked Newt Grago. He said if you refused to face me, he'd go ahead and pay me to shoot you down where you stand."

"Whoa now, Bill," Dave Mather said, seeing that Danielle wasn't backing down an inch. In fact, she straightened from against the bar with her hand poised near her Colt. "Danny and I were just talking about that. Danny Duggin here won't admit it, but there's something between him and Grago that we don't know about. I told him if he wanted to drop out of the contest, that was his business. Don't you agree?"

Longley looked as if he couldn't understand why on earth a gunman with the skill he'd just witnessed would turn down a chance to better himself. He glanced at Mysterious Dave Mather, then looked back at Danielle. "Didn't you come here for the contest?"

"I came here with Duncan Grago because he said his brother was looking for new men to ride with him. I had no idea about this contest." Danielle looked hard at Mather, adding, "And I never admitted there was anything between me and Newt Grago."

"Well, it's easy enough to see," said Bill Longley. "Speaking of Dunc Grago, that's one more thing that's got Newt Grago all worked up in a latter. He ain't been able to find his brother since he came back. Seems to think you might have dealt ol' Dunc some dirt."

Danielle shook her head. "Then he should be standing here asking me about it, instead of you. Fact is, I haven't seen Dunc myself, not since you tossed him out of here earlier. The shape he's in, he might have rode out, not wanting anybody to see him. But that's no concern of mine. What about this offer Newt made you, Longley? Did you take him up on it?" She stood firm, knowing she was looking into the eyes of one the fastest, most cold-blooded gunmen in the West.

Longley rubbed his neck with his left hand, apparently having a hard time deciding. "Damn," he said finally, "I knew if I turned it down, Newt'll have no trouble at all getting a few of his regulars to gang up on you. I hated turning down hard cash." He looked at Dave Mather. "Do you see my point, Mysterious Dave?"

"Yep"—Dave Mather nodded—"but you're the one who always says you have no respect for a man who hires somebody to do his fighting for him. Danny Duggin here says he don't want to fight you, and we both saw it ain't because he don't know how. Turn it loose, Bill. We made some money. It's not as much as you wanted, but once some of the other gunmen show up, you might still get your chance at your thousand-dollar mark." He smiled, polishing off the last drink from his mug and added, "Meanwhile, if you want to do something that makes good sense, buy us all a beer."

Bill Longley looked Danielle up and down again, then spread a thin, crafty smile. "I turned Newt's offer down. I just wanted to see how you reacted. I came here for the match, not to get into Newt Grago's favor. Let him do his own shooting. I never liked the coyote that much to begin with." He looked past Danielle, to Lulu behind the bar, waving her over to them to order a round. At the tent fly, Cincinnati Carver stuck his head in and said to the remaining outlaws still waiting to be served, "Better get a move on, boys. Cotton Pate and Little Joe Anderson are getting ready to face off!" As the men hurried out through the fly, Cincinnati Carver stuck his head back in and said to Mather, Longley, and Danielle, "What about ya'll? Ain't you gonna watch it?"

"Naw, get on out of here, Cincinnati," Longley said in a bored tone. "Once you've seen one hog killing, you've seen them all."

The sound of distant pistol fire caused the horses to twitch their ears, but the six riders only passed knowing glances back and forth at one another as they rode on slowly between the two slim buttes and turned off the main trail toward the encampment. Once off the narrow trail they rode abreast, Rufe Gaddis in the center. On his right rode Blade Hogue; on his left, Saul Delmano. The other three men were Jack Pitch, Max Dupre, and Billy Joe Earls, hardcase gunmen who'd been riding with them in South Texas the past few weeks and welcomed the chance to throw in with Newt

Grago's gang. When word of a shooting contest had reached them, Jack Pitch had bought himself a new customized model Remington, and had been practicing with it at every opportunity. Seeing they were turning off the main trail and eager to get to the encampment, Jack Pitch asked the others, "What the hell are we being so cautious for? There's nobody there but ole boys like ourselves. Nobody could have snuck past the guards."

Rufe Gaddis barely turned a glance at him, saying, "I'm always cautious. I'd rather swing wide by a mile than ride with the sun to my face. Have you got a problem with that?"

"Just asking," Jack Pitch said, spurring his horse forward.

They rode on, circling wide of the encampment and turning back toward it from the west once the afternoon sun was at their backs. They rode in silence until they entered a stretch of scrub oak surrounding a small basin. The riders fell back into a line as they rounded the edge of a tall stand of rock. Then, where the stand of rock ended and the trail began to widen again, Rufe Gaddis stopped his horse short with a jerk on its reins and said in a stunned voice, "Good God almighty!"

Staring at the body hanging from the rope tied to an overhead branch of a white oak tree, the men pressed their horses close together. "That poor hombre ain't been hanging there long," Blade Hogue said under his breath, scanning the area. "Reckon them lawmen we heard about managed to slip in here?"

Rufe Gaddis stepped his horse to one side, looked around at the other riders, and said gruffly, "Damned if I know. But the way we're squeezed up here, one shot would just about hit every one of us."

Billy Joe Earls and Blade Hogue traded confused looks with one another for a second.

Rufe Gaddis swung an arm through the air impatiently. "I mean, spread out some, damn it! Take some cover somewhere."

The men yanked their horses apart as Rufe Gaddis stepped down from his saddle. Drawing his rifle from its boot, he said over his shoulder to Saul Delmano and Jack Pitch, "You two come with me. Watch my back."

The three men walked the twenty-yard distance slowly, casting glances all around the small clearing surrounding the white oak. When they stopped ten feet back and looked up once more at the body swaying in the air, its blue hands hanging limp at its sides, Rufe Gaddis reached down and drew a knife from his boot well and pitched it over to Saul Delmano, saying in a low guarded tone, "Get over there, Saul, and cut him down." He nodded to where the rope led down from the limb and was drawn tight, tied off around the bottom of the trunk.

Gaddis and Pitch took a step backward, watching as Saul Delmano sliced through the rope. When the body thudded on the ground at their feet, Rufe Gaddis leaned down close and looked at the purple swollen face, its black tongue bulging.

"Who is it, Rufe? You recognize him?" Jack Pitch asked, seeing the look on Rufe Gaddis's face as he pushed up his hat brim and shook his head.

"Yeah, I recognize this poor bastard," Rufe Gaddis replied without turning to face Jack Pitch or Saul Delmano. Instead, he spoke down to the blank dead face in the dirt, saying, "Dunc, you crazy son of a bitch. You look even worse than the last time I saw you."

"Whooee," Jack Pitch said in a hushed whisper, staring at Duncan Grago's dead hollow eyes, "there's something about a man stretching hemp that always runs a chill right through me. How's Newt Grago going to take somebody hanging his brother?"

"I don't think anybody hung ole Dunc," Rufe Gaddis said, looking around in the dirt. "There's only one set of hoofprints. His hands aren't tied. I got a feeling Dunc hung himself. He always was on the verge of blowing his stack. Looks to me like he finally did it."

"You might want to tell Newt that," Saul Delmano said, reaching a hand up to the others, who watched from the cover of rocks and scrub oaks. He waved them in, then looked back down at Rufe Gaddis. "Newt thought a lot of Dunc, crazy bastard that he was. He's going to go blind, staggering wild over this. I damn near rather leave ole Dunc laying here and not mention it at all."

"No, we've got to take Dunc in and let Newt know about it," Rufe Gaddis said with a wince. "Let the chips fall where they will,

261

I reckon. Let's scout around for his horse, and get him up on it. We ain't taking him in to Newt until after dark. If this was my brother done something like this, I wouldn't want everybody in camp knowing about it."

"Damn," said Saul Delmano, "this is turning into a rough day."

In the tent, Arno Dunne had directed the twins away from Bill Longley and Mysterious Dave Mather and to the far end of the bar. Like most people, Dunne walked a little lightly around Longley. Evening had started to darken, and with the shooting matches over for the day, the outlaws had converged on the tent to talk about the four gunfights they'd seen and the money they had either won or lost on them. In spite of Arno Dunne cautioning them against it, as soon as Jed and Tim got themselves a mug of beer, they moved down to where Bill Longley stood slightly back from the bar with a thumb hooked in his gun belt, speaking to Duggin and Dave Mather.

They stood back politely until Bill Longley finished what he was saying, then stepping closer, Tim said, "Pardon me for interrupting, but we saw Danny Duggin and wanted to—"

Bill Longley stopped him short, blocking him from joining their private circle with a raised forearm. "Hey, boy, can't you see we're talking here?"

Tim Strange's eyes flared. Seeing it, Danielle

cut in, saying to Bill Longley, "It's all right, Longley, I know these two."

"But I don't," said Longley, "and I can't stand a person waltzing right in and including themselves." He looked Tim up and down, then turned his eyes to Jed, giving him the same cold look. "Who are you look-alikes anyway? If it weren't for those big Colts on your hips, I'd swear you just fell out from behind a plow somewhere."

"That's right," Danielle said quickly, knowing by the look on Tim's face that the next words out of Longley's mouth would be all it took to spark a fight between them, "these boys are straight off of a farm over near St. Joe. Let me handle this, Longley," she said, stepping in between Bill Longley and her brother, Tim. "Look, you two farmhands. I met you along the trail, and we had some coffee together. Don't go thinking that makes us friends. I'm here on business, *my* business." Her eyes cut from Tim to Jed. "When you called my name out in the clearing a while ago, you could have diverted my attention for just a split second and gotten me killed. Didn't you know that?"

Both twins looked stunned at Danielle's words, and she hated talking to them that way. But the shock of her gruff demeanor toward them diverted Tim from saying anything to Longley, which was all she wanted. "Danny," said Jed, "I wouldn't have done it if I thought it might cause you trouble. You was decent to us back on the trail. I was

263

pleased to see you and just spoke before I thought."

"Yeah," said Danielle, reining in her anger somewhat, "that's the trouble, you didn't *think* first. Out here, if you don't think the first time, it's usually the last chance you get. Now go on back down there with your friend. And stay the hell away from me."

Arno Dunne had been watching from his spot down the bar, and seeing Danielle nod toward him, he picked up his mug and moved down among them. "Excuse me, gents," he said. "I'm Arno Dunne. I couldn't help but notice that my two men here seemed to have rubbed you the wrong way."

"Now we've got another one crowding in," Longley said. "I bet I have to start clearing us a place here any minute." Drinkers scooted farther away along the bar as Longley's right hand dropped from its perch on his gun belt and rested near his tied-down holster.

Dave Mather allowed himself a muffled laugh, and said to Arno, "We know who you are, Dunne. You're the flushingest saddle sore Texas ever scraped off its backside. What brings you to our end of the bar?"

Arno Dunne jerked a thumb toward Tim and Jed. "I've got a couple of shooters here that I believe stand a chance in the contest. I saw that you seem to be having some cross words with them, and just wanted to remind you that if any iron gets drawn, let's make sure it happens tomorrow out in the clearing, where we all stand to make some money on it. Once these boys prove themselves, they might be the ones you have to face off with."

"I draw iron when and where it suits me, Dunne," said Bill Longley. "You don't tell me a damn thing."

"Easy, Bill," Dunne responded. "I'm just their promoter, you might say. Have you got anybody lined up to shoot against? If not, let's talk business, and think of the possibilities."

Danielle seethed, hearing Dunne talk about her brothers this way, knowing he couldn't care less if they lived or died, and knowing that right here and now there wasn't a thing she could say about it, except, "Mr. Dunne, if you're so interested in this contest, why don't you stick your own name up for tomorrow's matches? I wasn't going to enter against anybody, but in your case I'll gladly make an exception."

Still stinging from Danielle's words a moment earlier, Tim said firmly, "Danny Duggin, you've made your opinion of me and my brother clear. We don't need you speaking on our behalf." He looked at Bill Longley, then Dave Mather. "If anybody wants to call on me or my brother in the morning, we'll oblige them. You might all be surprised at what a couple of farm boys can do."

"Twenty dollars on Bill Longley," a voice called out, the drinkers obviously listening to what was being said and wanting in on the action.

"You're covered," another drinker replied.

"Wait just a damn minute," Arno Dunne

called out above the din of the excited crowd. He stilled the drinkers, then turned back to Bill Longley. "I didn't mean one of them might face you first thing tomorrow. They still have to prove themselves. I meant if all goes well, maybe you and one of them—"

Longley cut him off boldly, saying, "To hell with *one* of them, and to hell with later on. If these sodbusters are as game as they talk, I'll face them both at once, come morning, when the sun peeps over the rooster's ass."

Arno Dunne felt pressed now, knowing if somebody like Longley killed the twins first thing, he'd have no chance to make any money putting them up against some of these lesser gunmen. "No way," Arno Dunne said, "not tomorrow leastwise. They're not ready yet."

Tim had been listening, barely in control after Longley's insults and Danny Duggin's rejection. "I'm ready," Tim said. "But not two on one. First thing in the morning, I'll sign up to fight you. I'm not afraid."

Danielle winced, saying to herself, *No, Tim! Think about what you're getting into!* But she was helpless to make her thoughts known. She had to keep silent and wait. Hopefully, she prayed, she would find a way to stop it before the match tomorrow, even it meant facing Bill Longley herself.

"Where'd you say you found him?" Merlin Haas asked Rufe Gaddis. Both of them looked at the body of Duncan Grago, which Newt Grago had placed on a blanket in the corner of the shack. Newt Grago stood directly over his brother's corpse, staring down at it, shaking his head slowly in the glow of the lantern clenched tight in his fist.

Rufe Gaddis answered Merlin Haas in a near whisper. "We found him about two miles west of here when we swung wide out of the sun. Looked liked he'd been hanging there most of the day."

"Who would have done this?" Haas asked. When neither Gaddis nor Grago answered, Haas asked again, thinking they hadn't heard him. This time when he asked, Newt Grago turned toward him, the lantern's light causing Newt's face to look even grimmer.

"Go get yourself a drink, Merlin," Grago said in a low, controlled voice.

"No thanks, I'm fine," Haas replied, not getting the message that Grago just wanted him to leave.

"I *said,* go have a drink, *damn it!*" Newt repeated, this time his voice rasping like a file on hard metal.

"Oh! Why yes, I believe I will." Haas backed to the door, took his bowler hat from a peg, and leveled it down onto his forehead with nervous fingers.

"And keep your mouth shut about this," Newt Grago added. "I mean don't breathe a word to a soul about it, or I'll rip your tongue out of your head."

"No sir, Newt! Not a word," Haas stammered, "I swear it!" His hand trembled as he opened the door just enough to slip through and disappear into the night.

As soon as Merlin Haas was gone, Rufe Gaddis gave Newt Grago a knowing look, saying quietly, "You see how it happened, don't you? Dunc did this to himself."

"Yeah, I see," Newt murmured in a low, tortured voice.

"I knew you wouldn't want the word out," said Gaddis. "That's why I waited till dark and slipped in by myself. Delmano and the rest are camped a mile out, waiting for me."

"You did right bringing him in to me this way, Rufe," said Newt Grago. "He ain't acted like his old self since he rode in. I reckon prison made a mess out of him."

"Prison's rough," said Gaddis, "but damn." He shook his head, looking over at the body on the floor. "I can't imagine ole Dunc doing something like this. He must have really lost his mind."

Newt stood in silence for a second, then said, "Yes, he did, but he had some help. That snake Danny Duggin he's been riding with caused this. He's what pushed Dunc over the edge."

"Who's Danny Duggin?" Gaddis asked.

"Some two-bit gunslinger Dunc brought here with him," Newt hissed. "I've got some sneaking suspicions about that bastard."

Gaddis looked confused. "I don't get it. How'd this Duggin cause Dunc to do this?"

Newt Grago snapped his eyes onto Gaddis in the flicker of lantern light, saying in a sharp tone, "Never mind how he caused it. But he did, sure as hell. Dunc got his head screwed on wrong some way, and this Danny Duggin took advantage of it."

"Damn, Newt," said Gaddis, "I reckon some crazy things have been going on. Why's this man Duggin still alive if you saw he was causing Dunc trouble?"

"It's a long story, Rufe. But I'll tell you something else about Duggin. The first time I laid eyes on him, I suspected him to be the young gunslinger that was shooting everybody up last summer."

"My God, Newt," Gaddis said, stunned at the fact that Newt hadn't killed this Danny Duggin outright.

"I know, Rufe." Newt rubbed his lowered forehead. "I shoulda killed him right off, but he was a friend of Dunc's. I didn't want to make a move till I was dead sure of it. Now, my waiting has cost Dunc his life."

"Where is this Duggin?" Gaddis asked. "I'll just go put a bullet into his brain."

"No, it's not that easy tonight," Newt Grago said. "He's over at Lulu's with Dave Mather and Bill Longley. You never know who those two will side with."

"Longley and Mather are here?" Gaddis looked worried all of a sudden and stepped away from the door.

"Yes, both of them are here. Longley heard about the contest and came here saying he was drawing himself a thousand dollars' worth of blood then moving on." Newt rubbed his forehead again. "Things ain't gone quite the way I planned them to. But don't worry about Longley. He wouldn't go along with what I had planned for Duggin. So I've got four men all set to cut his boots out from under him, soon as he leaves Lulu's tonight and heads to his bedroll."

"What do want me and the boys to do? Just tell me, Newt. We're ready for anything," Gaddis said.

"Ride in come sunup," said Newt Grago. "Longley will be dead, Mather too, if he gets in the way. You and the boys will have Danny Duggin all to yourselves. We'll tell everybody he ambushed Dunc. Then we'll take our time and kill him good and slow."

"Sounds good to me, Newt." Rufe Gaddis backed to the door and opened it a crack, looking out into the darkness, then turned to Grago. "See you first thing in the morning. Me and the boys will all have our mean on."

Chapter 16

Robber's Rock, Indian Territory, July 26, 1871

It was in the dark hours of morning when Bill Longley and one of Lulu's girls left Danielle and Dave Mather in the gambling tent and headed to where Mather and Longley had set up a campsite for themselves. No sooner had Longley and the woman left, than Danielle looked around the tent at the few remaining bleary-eyed drinkers. Arno Dunne and the twins had left over two hours ago. Only three old hardcases stood at the faro table, arguing in a drunken stupor, one of them with an arm looped around one of Lulu's girls. Lulu herself had retired to a cot in the back corner of the tent, leaving another one of her girls tending bar. Danielle looked at the girl tending bar, seeing she was half asleep as she poured Mather a shot of rye.

"Something's not right, Dave," Danielle said suddenly.

Mather gave a drowsy smile, saying, "There's a lot of things not right, Danny. But who are we to question the workings of the universe?"

"No, Dave, damn it! Listen to me," Danielle demanded. "That woman who left with Bill Longley. Did you notice how wide awake and sober she was?"

Mather perked up a little, his shot of rye in his hand. "Yes, come to think of it." He sat his glass down, a look of consternation washing over his face.

Danielle continued, "And how she just seemed to pop up out of nowhere all of a sudden? It was like she'd been biding her time, waiting just for Longley."

"You're right, Danny," Mather said, pushing his glass back with his fingers. He turned quickly to Danielle, but Danielle was already headed out of the tent. Mather hurried, his hand coming up with his pistol. "Longley's being set up!" he said aloud to himself, swinging the tent fly back with his forearm.

Mather caught up with Danielle a few yards from the tent as rifle fire streaked out of the darkness toward the path Longley and the woman had taken. From the center of fire, Longley's pistol exploded repeatedly, fighting back. The woman screamed in pain as Mather and Danielle hurried forward, firing at the muzzle flashes, trying to give Longley some cover fire. Two of the rifles streaked lead toward them, Danielle diving in one direction and Mather in the other. But they only stayed down for a second, then both of them came up in a crouch, firing and moving forward.

"Bill!" Dave Mather called out to Longley through the roaring gunfire. "Are you all right in there?"

Longley's only reply was three shots from his Colt, one of them causing a loud whimper followed by the sound of breaking brush as one of the riflemen toppled down from his perch a few feet above the clearing.

"Good, he's holding his own," Mather said to Danielle while rifle fire flashed like heat lightning. "I'm going around to the right. You circle left. Don't fire on me if you can help it."

Danielle and Mather moved quickly, their pistols blazing their way in the darkness. Of the three remaining riflemen, only two were firing, their shots centered on Bill Longley. Danielle held her fire for a second, hearing the sound of running boots breaking through the brush toward her. Seeing the outline of a man in the pale moonlight, she stood straight up in his path and fired one well-placed round into his chest. He grunted, rolling and sliding to a halt almost at her feet. She fired another shot into him for safety's sake, then crouched back down and hurried forward.

Dave Mather, seeing the two rifles firing at Bill Longley, stood up and stalked forward, two pistols now in his hands, both of them pounding like drums. Joining Longley's fire, Mather saw one rifle cease to fire in the darkness. To his left he heard Danielle's Colt and saw the flashes of flame as Danielle moved forward, the three of them forcing the last rifleman to make a run for it.

"Bill," Mather called out to Longley, "it's me and Danny Duggin! Hold your fire, we're coming in."

"Then come in slow," Bill Longley replied in the darkness. "Let me get a good look at both of you."

Danielle moved in with caution, letting Mather arrive a moment ahead of her as she scouted the darkness for any more ambushers. She heard Mather and Longley talking as she finally stepped in closer and saw the two of them bent down over the woman. "You're hit pretty bad," Longley said down to the gasping figure on the ground. "Newt Grago put you up to this, didn't he?"

"Yes," she said, struggling for breath. "Them...cowardly bastards. They was...supposed to wait, till you were lying down on your blanket."

"They should have warned you first, honey," said Longley, brushing a strand of hair from her fading eyes. "I'm one hard ol' dog to kill."

"Well," she rasped, "it looks like I'm not..." Her words trailed and ended in a spent breath. Longley let her head down from his forearm and folded her arms across her stomach wound. "That does it," Bill Longley said with venom. "I'm going over to the shack and shoot Newt Grago's eyes out." He grunted, trying to rise to his feet and not making it. "Damn it, give me a hand here, Dave, get me on my feet."

"Bill, you're hit?" Mather asked, taking him by a shoulder and lifting him up. Bill Longley came to his feet, staggering to one side, and went back down.

"Yes, damn it all! I caught a bullet in my hip. But I'm still game. I'll get him. I hate an ambusher worse than anything."

"Hell's fire, Bill," Dave Mather said, he and Danielle both moving in to take a closer look at the flow of blood from Bill Longley's hip wound. "You're not going anywhere if we don't get this bleeding stopped."

"It's clean through, ain't it?" Longley asked, his fingers searching the wound in the darkness.

"Yeah, but it's bleeding bad," Mather replied.

"Bleeding never hurt nothing. Get me to my feet, damn it!" Longley demanded. "I've got time to kill that skunk yet."

In the darkness behind them, voices called back and forth asking one another about the gunfire. Boots thrashed through the brush toward them. "Listen back there, Bill," Mather said. "Every one of them is Newt Grago's man in some way or another. We don't stand a chance against all of them, especially with you shot up."

"Mather's right, Longley," Danielle joined in as she punched out her spent cartridges. "Let's get you away from here. We'll get your blankets and gear and get off a ways. It'll be daylight in another hour. You can come back for Newt Grago once we get you taken care of. I'll even help you kill him."

"I don't need no help killing him," said Longley, again struggling to stand up. On his feet with an arm looped across Mather's shoulder, he asked, "What tipped you off that it was a setup, Dave?"

"You can thank Danny Duggin here for that, Bill," Mather replied, adjusting Longley's weight against his side. "He caught on to it no sooner than the two of you left the tent."

"Much obliged then, Danny," Longley grunted. "I reckon you're right. Let me get patched up. Then we'll go kill us a whole slew of rats."

"What about this poor woman?" Danielle asked as Mather and Longley lumbered away toward their dark campsite.

"What about her?" Longley said over his shoulder. "She played the hand Grago dealt her. She lost. Burying her ain't my responsibility."

Danielle sighed under her breath, looking down at the dead woman on the ground. But then she shook her head and caught up to Mather and Longley for a moment. "I've got something to take care of. You two go on. There's a little creek down over the rise. You'll see my mare along there. I'll meet you there."

"Where are you going, Danny?" Mather asked. "This place is going to blow wide open once Newt sees his boys didn't get the job done. He'll try to kill you the second he lays eyes on you."

"I know," Danielle said, "but I've got to take care of something. It's important."

"Part of your *mission*, I take it?" Mather asked.

"Yeah," Danielle said, backing away, "You could call it that."

Inside the shack, Newt Grago seethed at the wounded rifleman who had fled there to escape the hail of gunfire once his companions had fallen. "Tanner, you cowardly cur!" Grago shouted in his face. Grabbing him by his shirt and yanking him in close. "You mean to tell me that *four* riflemen couldn't handle Bill Longley?"

"It weren't just Longley, Newt, I swear!" the frightened Lloyd Tanner insisted. "There was that gunman Duggin, and Mysterious Dave Mather! I heard them call out to one another!"

"Damn it to hell!" Grago raged, shoving

Tanner away from him and pacing back and forth, needing to think.

"They'll be coming, Newt," said Tanner. "What are we going to do?"

"Shut up, Tanner!" Newt Grago barked at him. He paced some more, rubbing his temples. Then he abruptly stopped. "All right, here's the plan. You ride out a mile along the west trail. You'll find Rufe Gaddis and some others camped there. Bring them back here as fast as you can. Get back before sunup. I'll round up the whole camp and tell them what that bastard Duggin did to my bother Dunc. We'll get this straightened out, you can count on it."

"What did he do to your brother Dunc?" Tanner asked, holding his left hand tight against the bullet graze on his right shoulder.

"I'll show you what he did!" Grago screamed, dragging Tanner to the body of Duncan Grago lying in the corner. "There, take a look at him! That's what he did! Duggin killed him! Left poor Dunc hanging from an oak limb. Now get out there and get Rufe and the boys and get back here pronto!"

"But, Newt, what about my shoulder? I'm bleeding like a stuck hog," Tanner pleaded.

"You haven't seen bleeding yet, if you don't get moving," Grago said through clenched teeth. He stomped across the shack, picked up his gun belt from a chair back, and slung it around his waist. Before he got it buckled, Tanner was out the door and running toward the corral, snatching a saddle and bridle up from the

277

ground out front of the shack on his way. The gunfire had awakened the encampment, and as Tanner fumbled with the rope, loosening the corral gate, Arno rushed up beside him.

"Tanner, what the hell's going on?" Dunne asked, seeing the blood on Tanner's shoulder.

"Get away from me, Arno! I've no time for you. All hell has busted loose here!" He hurried into the milling horses, grabbed one by its mane, and pitched the bridle around its head, tossing his saddle up across the horse's back. "Duggin kilt Dunc Grago and left him hanging in a tree! Newt's coming now to get everybody after Duggin, Mather, and Longley!"

"Mather and Longley?" Dunne asked. "Did they have something to do with it?"

"I don't know!" Tanner yanked the saddle cinch tight. "But I'm gone to bring in Rufe Gaddis and the boys. Now get out'n my way!" He shoved Dunne back, then hurled himself up onto the saddle and kicked the horse forward. Dunne watched him ride away, then closing the rope gate, he cursed to himself, "Damn it. Today was my day for making a killing here."

Danielle stood back out of the chaos in the encampment clearing, searching among the torch-lit faces for her brothers, Tim and Jed. Around the corner from Lulu's gambling tent, she saw men strap on their pistols and check their rifles while others came running forward hitching up their galluses, rubbing sleep from their eyes. Danielle finally spotted Tim and Jed as Arno Dunne came hurrying up to them, standing too close for her to say anything. She hunkered down against the side of the tent and waited, feeling precious seconds tick by. In another few minutes the first rays of sun would begin peeping up over the horizon, shedding her cover of darkness.

She listened to Dunne, only making out part of what he was telling the twins. But she did manage to hear him tell Tim and Jed that Tanner had gone to get Rufe Gaddis and the boys, and that they would be here in just a few minutes. Hearing it caused her blood to race. In the glow of lantern and torchlight, she saw Arno Dunne step back from the twins. "Stay here," Danielle heard Arno Dunne instruct her brothers, "I'll get my rifle and be right back."

As soon as Dunne moved away, Danielle called out in a hushed voice, "Tim, Jed, over here, by the tent."

They looked around at the sound of her voice. "Danny Duggin?" Jed asked, barely lowering his voice.

Tim caught the secretive manner in which Danny Duggin was addressing them and poked Jed in the ribs, whispering, "Keep it down, Jed."

Looking all around first to make sure no one had heard them, Tim nudged Jed toward the side of the tent, where he saw Danielle's green eyes flashing at them from beneath her lowered hat brim. "Hurry up!" Danielle hissed at them.

279

"Danny!" Tim said as he and Jed hunkered down out of sight. "Arno Dunne said you killed Newt's brother Dunc. Is it true?"

"No," Danielle whispered, "but it might as well be. Now listen to me, we don't have much time. Duncan Grago is one of the two outlaws who killed Elvin Bray back in St. Joe and tried to ambush you on the trail."

"What the—?" Tim and Jed looked at one another, stunned.

"Don't talk—listen!" Danielle said, cutting them both off. "The men who killed your pa are on their way here. I heard Arno Dunne just tell you they would be here anytime now."

"Hey!" Tim said, interrupting her, "What do you know about our pa? Or about Elvin Bray?" His hand went to the butt of his pistol.

Danielle lowered her head, seeing she wasn't going to get by with the explanation she had planned to tell them. "All right, Tim," she said, "just pay attention. We're in a bad spot here." She peeled the fake mustache back from her lip and looked up, pushing her hat brim up for a better view. "It's me, your sister...Danielle." Then she stared in silence for a second, letting it sink in.

"Oh Lord God," Tim finally whispered in astonishment.

"My goodness gracious, it *is* you," Jed murmured, his voice beginning to tremble. "Danielle... we came looking for you! We were going to snoop around, see what we could find out, try to find you—" Jed's voice stuck in his throat, and they both leaned forward. Tim joined him, and all three of them, kneeling in hiding, threw their arms around one another.

"I know...I know," Danielle whispered, holding back her sobs, taking up extra precious seconds to hold her brothers to her bosom. "It's been hard on you...on all of us. I wanted to tell you sooner, but I couldn't risk it." Tears streamed down her cheeks. She smelled the road dust and dried sweat on her brothers and found comfort in it, knowing that they smelled the same scent on her, and that it was the scent of their long journey bringing the three of them together. "My brothers," she whispered, "at last I can say those words...*my brothers*." Even in their stunned surprise, Jed and Tim Strange looked at one another, each knowing that their venture had just taken a change for the better. Their family was reunited now, their destinies the same.

At the sound of boots running past them, close to their position, Danielle held them back at arm's length. She ran a sleeve across her eyes, then said, "Listen to me. We'll talk later. Right now, Bill Longley and Dave Mather are hiding out down by where I hid Sundown. You two can walk right into the corral while everybody's busy wondering what's going on. Get your horses, and get back here with them. We've got lots to do this morning."

"Danielle," Jed asked, "you mentioned the men who killed Pa are coming? Shouldn't we wait here for them?"

"Come on, Jed," Tim said, before Danielle

could answer, "Danielle knows what she's doing. Let's get our horses and get them back over here. It's turning daylight on us."

Danielle hunkered down and watched them hurry to the corral. On their way back with their horses, Arno Dunne ran up beside them, trying to grab Tim's reins, but Tim shook him loose. Dunne ran behind them on foot, cursing and waving his rifle in the air. As Tim and Jed turned their horses in alongside the big tent, Arno Dunne followed right behind them, ranting, "You lousy plowboys! You're not going to run out on me! I came to see you make me some money, or else watch you die trying! You think you're gonna run out on me?" He levered a round up into the rifle chamber and raised it. "You low-down—"

At the sound of the rifle lever, Tim and Jed had both swung around in their saddles, their pistols out and aimed. But they froze, seeing the knife handle sticking out of Dunne's chest, Danielle's hand wrapped around it as she stood behind him with her left arm wrapped around his throat. "I'm sorry I don't have time to kill you proper-like, Arno Dunne, you rotten snake," she rasped in his ear, "for using my brothers, turning them into the likes of you and your kind." Across the clearing behind them, Newt Grago had stepped out onto the porch and called out to the gathering outlaws, waving them in closer to him. Danielle looked around over her shoulder at the sound of Grago's voice but knew that killing him would have to wait until she returned. "I haven't forgotten you,

Grago," she whispered to herself, tightening her grip on the knife handle in Dunne's chest.

Tim and Jed both winced, seeing Danielle twist the knife blade deeper into Arno Dunne's heart. Dunne's mouth opened in a silent scream. "Lord, Danielle," Tim whispered, watching Arno Dunne's gloved hands jerk and quiver, then fall limp at his sides. Danielle let Dunne drop to the ground, leaving the knife still sunk in his chest.

"Let's go," she said, wiping blood from her hand as her brothers stared at her as if in disbelief. Danielle stepped forward, tossed herself up onto the rump of Tim's horse, and threw her arm around Tim's waist. Before Tim or Jed could respond, she batted her heels to the horse's sides and sent it lunging into a full gallup.

Jed Strange looked back at the body of Arno Dunne lying on the ground in a dark circle of blood. "I'm glad you got the killing you've been looking for, Arno Dunne. I just wish it had of come from me." He jerked the horse away and kicked it out behind his brother and sister.

Chapter 17

The last few yards, riding double to where Dave Mather and Bill Longley stood waiting for them, Danielle looked over Tim's shoulder and saw the bodies of two outlaws lying on the ground.

283

Mysterious Dave Mather stood back in the silver gray light of dawn, waving her and her brothers in. He smiled, a rifle hanging from one hand and a pistol from the other, as they rode in closer and sidled their horses up to him.

Longley sat on a mound of earth with his right leg stretched out before him, a blood-soaked bandanna pressed against his hip. Sundown's reins were in Longley's other hand, along with his pistol. "Well," Dave Mather said, grinning up at Danielle, noting that her mustache was gone, "I see you took the time to shave before returning."

"It's a long story, Mather," Danielle said, dropping down from behind Tim. "These two are my brothers. I didn't tell you before, but I'm telling you now, so you'll know they're both on our side."

Mather's grin widened. "Nothing like a little surprise on the verge of a gun battle, I always say." He nodded at the two bodies on the ground. "Now here's a surprise for you. We caught three of them coming in from the buttes, riding like hell. Said there's a forty-man posse coming down on this place." He nodded at one of the bodies, saying, "This one told us before he died. They were hightailing it back to Newt Grago. The one who got away should be getting to Grago about now. I felt bad having to shoot these two"—Mather shrugged—"but we needed their horses worse than they did."

"A forty-man posse?" Danielle glanced back in the direction of the tall, slim buttes.

"Damn it, why now? I've got things to take care of!"

"Oh, the mission?" Mather asked. Behind him, Bill Longley struggled to his feet, dusted his seat, and walked forward, leading the chestnut mare, not looking at all happy about it.

"Yeah, the mission," Danielle said. She let out a breath. "Well, I've sided with you, Mather. Tell me how you two want to handle this thing. I won't back out on it."

"Far as we're concerned, there's nothing to back out on," Bill Longley said in a gruff tone. "Do we look like fools to you? Dave and I ain't facing no forty-man posse, not with all the charges I've got hanging over my head. They'd have to hang me eight or nine times just to get caught up."

"Then what are you going to do?" Danielle asked, looking back and forth between the two. "A posse that size will leave some guards at the passes. How do you plan on slipping past them, especially when Longley's wounded?"

Mather looked off in the direction of the buttes, then looked back at Danielle. "Oh, I'll think of something. They don't call me Mysterious Dave for nothing."

Bill Longley cut in, saying, "Hope you've got no objections, but I'll be taking this chestnut mare with me. You can ride one of those dead mongrels' horses." He nodded at the two horses they'd taken and hitched to a stand of scrub cedar.

Danielle's first impulse was to throw her hand

285

to her Colt and tell him he'd have to kill her before he'd ride away on Sundown. But she held herself in check, seeing something in Bill Longley's eyes that said he was just testing her. "Be my guest, Longley," she said. "There's nothing I'd like better than to send you off on that mare."

But Longley hesitated, looked at Mather, and said, "This peckerwood thinks he's tricking me into something, don't he?"

"It appears that way to me, Bill," Mather said. "If I was to guess, I'd say Danny Duggin here knows that somebody in that posse is going to recognize that mare. Am I right, Danny Duggin?"

"Yep, you guessed it," Danielle said. "Hell, I can't do you this way, Longley, not even as a joke. If anybody in the posse spots that mare, you'll never shake them off your tail."

"A joke, huh?" Bill Longley flung Sundown's reins over to Danielle. "I don't see a damn thing funny about it." He turned to Mather, adding, "Let's get out of here, before I take a notion to start shooting everybody around me. I hate killing a man after he helped me out of a tight spot." He eyed Danielle closely for a moment, then grumbled, "Watch your backside, Danny Duggin, I'm beholden to you." He turned and limped over to the other two horses.

Mather spread a playful smile at Danielle. "I think Longley has taken a liking to you. You're the first person I've ever seen that he's let talk to him this way." Mather took a

286

step closer, looking into Danielle's eyes. "It's too bad about this mission of yours, Danny Duggin," he said, close to her face.

"Why's that, Dave?" Danielle asked, not backing up an inch, but getting an uncomfortable feeling from him standing so close. Mather's eyes searched hers in a way she hadn't felt for a long time.

Mather leaned nearer to her and whispered close to her ear, "Because without that mustache and low-slung Stetson, you are one fine-looking young woman...whoever you are."

Danielle felt her cheeks flush. She stepped back, ready to issue her denial and make some tough-sounding statement. But before she could say a word, Dave Mather's lips found hers and pressed a deep kiss on her, muffling her protest. Then before she could do anything else, he had moved back away from her. She stood enraged, yet powerless, and somewhat pleased that he had seen through her disguise. He was the first one who had done so in all her time on the outlaw trail.

"You bastard," Danielle cursed him in a whisper, trying to sound like she meant it.

But Mather winked, seeing that her heart wasn't in it. "If I'm wrong, may lightning strike me dead on the spot. But there's some things a beautiful woman just can't hide. And even if you could, there's some men you just can't hide it from." He then added in an even lower tone, "Don't worry, Mysterious Dave knows how to keep a secret like nobody's business. I won't tell if you won't."

On the bays behind her, Tim and Jed Strange lowered their hat brims and chuckled to themselves. Bill Longley stood to the side with the two horses' reins hanging from his hand, his mouth agape at what he'd just witnessed. He stared at Dave Mather as Mather walked over nonchalantly and took a set of reins from his hands. "Come on, Bill, thought you was in a hurry to leave," Mather said as he swung up into the saddle.

"God almighty, Dave!" Longley said, still staring in disbelief as he struggled into the saddle, taking care not to further aggravate his wound, "What the hell is the matter with you?"

"Let's just say I got caught up in the moment." Dave Mather chuckled, tasting his lips.

"Caught up in the moment?" Longley said, having to shake his head in order to clear it. "I'll be dipped and dragged! That's the damnedest thing I ever saw you do! Am I going to be all right riding with you?"

Mather looked back at Danielle, who still stood in silence, watching him tap his horse forward. He tipped his dusty hat brim to her, then turned to Bill Longley, saying, "Yeah, Bill, you mud-ugly yard goat...you don't have a *thing* to worry about."

Rufe Gaddis, Saul Delmano, Jack Pitch, Max Dupre, Billy Joe Earls, and Blade Hogue followed Tanner around the last turn along the trail into the encampment. Coming in from the west, where they'd spent the night, they now spread out single file, riding the last quarter of a mile through a narrow rocky pass that opened into a stretch of rolling flatlands. On the other end of the flatland, the top of Lulu's tent stood visible above a rise of clump grass and scrub cedar. In the distance beyond the encampment a rise of dust stood high, drifting sidelong in the air. It was the plumes of dust that prompted Rufe Gaddis to pull back on his reins and cause his horse to rear slightly as it came to a halt.

"What is it, Rufe?" Jack Pitch asked, his own horse spinning in place as Pitch reined it down harshly. The other men bunched up behind them.

"I don't know," said Gaddis, "but I sure don't like the looks of it. The last time I saw that much dust that high in the air, it turned out to be a whole company of Yankee cavalry, come to clean up our gun smuggling down along the border." He backed his horse up a step.

"Think the law got word of Newt's contest?" asked Blade Hogue, moving in between Gaddis and Pitch. "Figured this was a good place to round up a bunch of us at once?"

"It wouldn't surprise me," said Gaddis. "Newt didn't mind letting the word out."

"What do you think, Rufe?" asked Pitch. "Want to ride on in, take our chances?"

Gaddis gave him a sarcastic look. "You really are itching to use that new Remington, ain't you, Jack?"

"Tanner said Newt Grago needs our help," Pitch responded, red-faced, "that's all I was getting at. I don't want to be looked at as ducking out on trouble."

"Just shut up, Jack, before I wear that shiny new Remington out over your head," Rufe Gaddis snapped at him.

"Rufe," said Blade Hogue, hoping to divert Gaddis and Pitch from locking horns, "maybe a couple of us oughta swing around and—"

"Quiet, Hogue!" Rufe Gaddis said, listening closely with his head cocked toward the flats. "Did you hear that?"

"Yeah," said Saul Delmano, stepping his horse forward through the others, "that was rifle fire." As they all sat focused toward the distance, the sound of gunfire resounded in a long, hard volley. The men looked at one another with wary eyes.

"It damn sure is rifle fire," Rufe Gaddis said. Then he turned to Tanner and asked, "How many men was Newt talking about killing?"

Tanner stared wide-eyed at the distant explosions, saying, "Just three that he told me about. There's that gunslinger Danny Duggin, then there's Bill Longley, and Dave Mather, if'n he got in the way, is what Newt said."

"Well, that's not the sound of three rifles," Saul Delmano said, moving his horse in beside Jack Pitch.

"Damn right it's not," said Gaddis. He jerked his horse around and forced it into the other riders, making them part for him. "Come on, boys, we're going to sit this one out for a while, see what that's all about." He gigged his horse forward into the narrow rock pass.

Jack Pitch called out to Gaddis, "Maybe that's all of Newt's boys firing at those three men. Did you stop to think of that?"

"No, I didn't, Jack," Rufe Gaddis called back over his shoulder to Jack Pitch as the others turned their horses and fell in behind him, "but why don't you go check it all out for us. You seem to be the one so interested in finding out." He spurred his horse into a trot before Jack Pitch could answer. Beside Jack Pitch, Saul Delmano stepped down from his horse and lifted its right front hoof, inspecting it closely.

"Ain't you coming?" Jack Pitch asked Delmano.

"I'll be right along," Delmano replied, "soon as I see why this horse is favoring its hoof." He watched as Jack Pitch shook his head and kicked his horse forward. As soon as Pitch caught up to the others, Delmano dropped the horse's hoof, swung up into his saddle, and rode off in the opposite direction. With a posse coming, he wasn't about to get caught riding with Rufe Gaddis, Blade Hogue, and the rest of them. Delmano had had a bad feeling all night about riding in and killing this Danny Duggin, especially after Gaddis said Duggin was riding with Bill Longley and Dave Mather. Delmano decided he'd rather take his chances slipping around the posse on his own.

A hundred yards back into the narrow rock pass, Rufe Gaddis stopped his horse again, this time at the sight of the single rider atop the chestnut mare sitting sideways across his path. "Now what do we have here?" Gaddis said to Tanner, who reined down beside him. Tanner's hand went to the butt of the rifle in his saddle boot as the other riders stopped behind him.

"Something we can do for you, mister?" Rufe Gaddis called out to Danielle from thirty feet away, already having a pretty good idea what was about to happen. Gaddis was only talking to give the men behind him a chance to spread out as much as possible in the tight space of the pass. He knew it was no coincidence that this rider met them at this spot. Above them on either side, rock walls rose up fifty feet, providing for a perfect ambush.

Danielle raised her hand, and in it was the worn list of names she'd been carrying so long. Not having to look at the list, she recited the names from memory. In a flat tone, she said, "Blade Hogue, Rufe Gaddis, Saul Delmano."

"Yep," said Rufe Gaddis, "that's us, all right." He could tell where this was going. His hand drifted to his pistol butt.

"You know why I'm here," Danielle called out. "If the rest of you want to live, back your horses and get out of here."

A couple of the men stifled a short laugh at the thought of one rider sounding to sure of himself in the face of these odds. But Rufe Gaddis didn't laugh. Neither did Blade Hogue. As Gaddis replied, Hogue ventured a glance along the rising rock to their left and right.

"You're that gunslinger from last summer, ain't ya?" said Gaddis.

"Yep," Danielle replied. And that was all she said.

"You're name's not Danny Duggin though, is it?" Gaddis asked, hoping the men behind him were ready for what was coming.

"Nope," Danielle said. Then she fell silent again.

"I heard somewhere that this is all about somebody killing your pa, and leaving him hanging from a tree," Gaddis said.

As Gaddis spoke, Danielle stepped down slowly from her saddle and pushed Sundown on the rump, sending the mare out of harm's way. "You heard, right," Danielle said, stepping forward slowly, fanning her riding duster back behind her holsters.

"What if I told you me and these boys had nothing to do with it?" Rufe Gaddis asked, his right hand poised near his pistol butt.

Danielle ignored his question. "Let's get to it," she said, coming closer yet.

Rufe Gaddis offered a tight, edgy smile, not sure if he should step down from his saddle or not. Uncertain how many men were atop the rock with rifles pointed down at him, he said, "I'm no fool. You think I don't know an ambush when I see one. Who's up there? Longley? Mather?" He allowed himself to turn his eyes from Danielle just enough to call up along the rock ledges, "Is this your style? Come on down and face us like men!" His words echoed along the narrow pass.

"We already have," said the voice behind them. Gaddis and the others jerked around in their saddles and saw the two figures standing afoot in the trail behind them. Tim and Jed Strange stood five feet apart, their gun hands poised, their eyes level and determined.

Jack Pitch grinned. "Ragged-assed farm boys, wearing guns too big for them," Pitch murmured. But nobody seemed to hear him as he sized the brothers up. *These two are mine,* he thought to himself. All that practice with his new Remington wasn't going to waste, after all. He sat staring at Tim and Jed as Rufe Gaddis turned his attention back to Danielle.

Now that Gaddis had some idea of what he was facing, he swung down slowly from his saddle. Had there been men covering them from above, he would have been better off staying mounted, maybe being able to make a run for it once the rifle fire got too hot and heavy. But this was no ambush. These three wanted it face-to-face. *So be it,* he thought, getting some solid earth beneath his boots. This was going to work out fine. Didn't these fools realize they would be shooting into one another in a cross fire like this? He smiled again and spread his feet a shoulder-width apart, facing Danielle, knowing Hogue and the others would take care of the two men behind them.

"All right, boys," Gaddis said over his shoulder without taking his eyes off Danielle, "Let's hurry up and get this over with. We ain't got all—"

Danielle's first shot tore Rufe Gaddis's words from his chest and sent him reeling backward. Her next shot slammed into Tanner, who had drawn his rifle from its boot but seemed confused as to which way to point it. Behind him, Tim and Jed's pistols exploded, taking Blade Hogue from his saddle as his horse reared high with him. Tanner's horse reared as well. Danielle's shot flung him from his saddle into Max Dupre. A loud curse came from Dupre as Tanner's blood splashed on his face. Before he could raise a hand and wipe his eyes, two shots hit him front and rear. He spun from his saddle into a tangle of frightened hooves and falling bodies.

Jack Pitch had gotten off three shots from his new Remington before a bullet from Jed's big Colt went through Billy Joe Earls's neck and sliced through Pitch's shoulder. Jack Pitch dove from his horse and rolled away from the heart of the melee to where he could find room to rise up onto his knees and use his new pistol to its best advantage. He raised the Remington, taking his time even as the battle raged. Getting a perfect aim on Tim Strange's chest, Pitch said to himself, "Got ya!" and pulled the trigger. But the hammer didn't fall. Wild-eyed, Pitch shook the gun, then slapped it against his palm, desperately trying to dislodge the dirt inside the open hammer that had been scraped up as he'd rolled across the ground.

"Damn it! Wait!" Jack Pitch screamed at Tim and Jed, seeing both of their pistols swing around toward him, trailing smoke. He shook the Remington again as if to show them that his pistol wasn't working. But neither of them seemed to care, he thought, feeling the hard blasts of .45 slugs pound into his chest.

In seconds it was over. Silence moved in beneath the drifting echoes and settled onto the narrow trail. With the smell of burnt gunpowder heavy around her, Danielle poked out the spent cartridges from her smoking Colt and replaced them. Doing so, she kept an eye on Rufe Gaddis, who lay writhing back and forth on the ground, his hands clasped to his bleeding chest. His right hand still held his pistol. "Tim, Jed!" she called out across the fleeing horses through a swirl of dust. "Are you okay?"

"We're all right," Tim answered, sidestepping the frightened animals as they pounded away along the trail. "Jed got a bullet through his shirt, but he's fine. What about you?"

"I'll do," Danielle said, feeling the warm blood seep down her side. She looked back at Rufe Gaddis, who had managed to squirm upward onto one knee, his blood-slick hand grasping his pistol tighter, trying to raise it.

"I'll...kill you," Gaddis rasped, "you lousy...good-for-nothing...gunslinger."

"Come on," Danielle said, stepping toward him, "you can do it. Raise that pistol. Come on! Raise it!" she bellowed.

Gaddis struggled, using all his waning strength. "Damn you...to hell!"

Danielle's Colt hung in her hand at her side. She raised the barrel just enough to send a fatal slug between Rufe Gaddis'd eyes. His pistol flew from his hand and he pitched backward in the dirt.

Tim and Jed had stepped forward through the swirl of hoof dust and looked down at Gaddis, then over at Danielle. "You're hit," Tim said to her. Both of them rushed forward, but Danielle stayed them back with a raised hand.

"I'm all right." She nodded toward the distant sound of rifle fire, noting that it had moved closer across the flatlands. "We need to make tracks. That posse is heading this way."

"But we ain't outlaws," Jed offered. "We've got nothing to worry about."

"They don't know what we are," Danielle said. "Anyway, we've got no time for their questions. If Newt Grago's still alive, I want him. He's the last of Pa's killers." She pressed her hand to her wounded side and limped toward Sundown, who stood off to one side of the narrow trail. "Get your horses. Let's go."

Tim and Jed looked at one another, then Jed called out to Danielle, "At least let us take a look at your side first, Danielle. You can't go around bleeding like that."

"It'll dry," she said, picking up Sundown's reins. "Grago's not getting away from us."

"Danielle, for God sakes," Jed started to plead.

But Danielle cut him short, saying, "Listen, there's horses coming! Now get ready!"

As soon as she said it, two horses rounded the pass into sight. "Whoa!" Morgan Goss shouted to his horse, which slid almost down onto its haunches in stopping. He looked around at the bodies on the ground, then at Tim and Jed, who stood on either side of the trail. His hands went up in surrender. Behind him came Cincinnati Carver lying low in his saddle and staring back at the trail behind him. When Carver turned forward and saw Goss's hands in the air, he reined his horse down and flung his shotgun away.

"Don't shoot! You've got us!" Cincinnati Carver shouted, still not recognizing them from the encampment.

"Settle down, Cincinnati," Danielle said, stepping into better view, flipping her Colt back into its holster, which caused Carver and Goss to breathe a little easier. "It's me, Danny Duggin."

"Duggin?" Cincinnati Carver looked surprised. He looked at the bodies on the ground, then back to Danielle. "What's going on here? Who shot Gaddis and these boys?"

"I did, Cincinnati," Danielle replied.

"Damn it, you're the law," said Morgan Goss, "and to think I trusted you, even drank with you...bet my money on you!"

"I'm not the law, Goss. I just had something to settle with Newt Grago and this bunch."

Goss lowered his hands as Danielle stepped forward and picked up his shotgun from the dirt, dusting it off against her leg. "Danny Duggin, you're shot there," Goss said, nodding at the blood on Danielle's side.

"I'm all right," she said. "How far back is that posse?"

"Not far enough," said Cincinnati Carver. "They're sweeping through here like a hay sickle any minute. Me and Goss decided we best get down to *Mejico*, where folks have better manners. You're welcome to come, all three of yas."

"Naw, we're not wanted by the law," Danielle said, handing Carver's shotgun up to him. "Is Newt Grago dead?"

"Humph," said Cincinnati Carver, "not unless he fell off his running horse and broke his neck. The snake cleared out of there first thing. Left all of us to face that posse alone." He looked back along the trail as he spoke. "Don't mean to appear rude, Danny, but we best get our shanks in the wind. They're awfully close."

"Which way did Newt Grago head?" Danielle asked.

"Hell, the same way he always heads when things get too hot for him. He's got a woman named Bertha Stillwell he always runs to. She's opened a saloon in that whistle-stop town they just named Newton. She's got lots of connections there with men from the Atchison, Topeka & Sante Fe Railroad. Newt says they just named the town after him. Says it'll bring him luck. The damned fool—the town's really named after a place in Massachusetts! Are you going to kill Newt too when you find him? Because if you are, tell him I said good riddance before he dies, the no-good yellow bastard."

Danielle didn't answer. Hearing the rifle fire moving closer, she stepped back and said, "Good luck down in Mexico, boys," then slapped Morgan Goss's horse on its rump. The two outlaws wasted no more time. They bolted off along the trail, leaving a wake of dust behind them.

When they were out of sight, Tim asked, "Do you think they're telling the truth about Grago?"

"Yep, I think so. If not, we'll find out in Newton." She stepped toward Sundown without another word, swinging up into her saddle and heeling the mare forward.

"I've heard of that place, Newton, Kansas. It's already supposed to be the toughest place in the West," Jed said to Tim as they walked to where they'd hitched their horses. "If Newt Grago has a lot of friends there, we'll be in for a rough time."

"Then we both best be ready for it," said Tim, staring straight ahead, "because it looks like that's where we're headed, come hell or high water."

Chapter 18

Leaving the narrow trail and riding wide of the encampment to the northwest, Danielle, Tim, and Jed Strange avoided the posse, keeping close to a stretch of low rock cliffs along a dry creek bed. For the first half hour they'd pushed the horses hard until they were sure the sound of rifle fire had turned away from them, following a more southerly direction. Most of the outlaws who had managed to get away from the encampment had fled southwest toward Texas. From there they would head for the Rio Grande, crossing into Mexico the way Cincinnati Carver and Morgan Goss planned to do.

When Danielle and her brothers stopped to rest their mounts, they did so atop a rock ledge that faced the encampment from less than half a mile away. From there, the site of the encampment looked like a place struck by a cyclone. Danielle, Tim, and Jed gazed out across the wavering heat toward the flattened tent. Gambling tables lay broken and scattered. Bodies of outlaws lay strewn within the wide clearing across a fifty-yard stretch of surrounding land. Lulu and her girls were handcuffed and sitting on the ground, along with four wounded outlaws who sat with their heads bowed. Two Cherokee trackers stood guarding the prisoners with their rifles propped on their hips.

Danielle stood up, dusting her trousers, and backed away from the rock ledge. "Well, that does it for Newt Grago's shooting contest," she said. "All he managed to do was get a bunch of men killed."

Jed and Tim both stood up and backed away from the ledge beside her. "One good thing came out of it though," Jed said. "If Arno

Dunne hadn't been so eager to bring us here, we might not have found you."

"That's right," Tim joined in. "Plus, we got to meet up with some of Pa's killers face-to-face." He looked at Danielle. "Of course, Jed and I didn't know which one was which, but I reckon you did, didn't you?"

Danielle shook her head, saying, "No, I never laid eyes on those men back there. But don't worry, they're Pa's killers all right. One of them gave me all their names last year before he died. Newt Grago is the only one left."

Just saying Grago's name caused her to grow anxious, wanting to get back in the saddle. She walked to Sundown and took up the reins. "Come on," she said to Tim and Jed, "time's a-wasting."

The three mounted up and rode away. In a thicket of scrub cedar not twenty feet from where they had stood, Saul Delmano lowered his rifle and watched their backs until they disappeared around a turn in the trail. Delmano had heard every word they'd said. It would have been easy to take aim and ambush them, but a shot from his rifle would have alerted the Cherokee guards and any other deputy who might be in the encampment.

"I'll get my chance," Delmano said to himself. He waited a few minutes longer, then led his horse from the thicket, and followed their tracks wide of the slim buttes toward the northern boundary of Indian Territory. For the next three days he managed to stay within a mile of them, keeping to the brush and dry washes, cautiously keeping an eye on the rise of dust Danielle and her brothers left in their wake.

The Canadian River, July 29, 1871

Newt Grago had not traveled alone these past three days. At the first sign of the posse converging on the encampment, he'd collected Merlin Haas and three other hardcases to ride with him. He'd taken Merlin Haas along because Haas still held most of their winnings. Once Newt Grago took the large roll of money from Merlin Haas, it became apparent to Haas that Grago had no more use for him. Merlin Haas kept as quiet as possible, hoping to get away from the outlaw leader as soon as they crossed into Kansas. The three other men with Grago were the two Stanley brothers, Hop and Renfrow—both former guerrilla riders from the old Quantrill Raiders days—and a Missouri stagecoach robber named Willis McNutt, who had ridden off and on with Newt Grago over the past few years. Grago had left the Stanley brothers along the Washita River the day before, to ambush anyone who might be following their tracks. He'd promised the Stanleys two hundred dollars apiece once they met up with him later in Newton, Kansas.

"The Stanley brothers won't have a chance in hell if they get into a shoot-out with a posse that large," McNutt said in a guarded tone to Merlin Haas as the two of them huddled near a low fire. Newt Grago stood a few yards away at the river's edge, checking his horse's hooves.

Merlin Haas whispered to McNutt in reply, "I'm thinking it ain't so much the posse he's concerned about now as it is that gunslinger, Danny Duggin. Grago wants Duggin dead awfully bad. Says he's the one what left Dunc hanging from a rope. Besides, the posse most likely has their hands full with everybody headed across Texas for the border."

McNutt looked Merlin Haas up and down, a trace of a cruel grin showing through his red beard. "You think you know so much, Haas? Then think of this. Newt's going to close his trail behind him once he gets on over to Kansas. He don't like leaving witnesses behind him. When he leaves here in the morning, only one of us will be going with him. The other is going to be sitting here with a rifle waiting for whoever comes along."

"You're wrong, McNutt," Haas said, but his voice lacked conviction.

McNutt stifled a laugh, saying, "Yeah, you hope I'm wrong, Haas, but you know better. When Grago gets to Newton, he won't need neither one of us. He's got protection there. He'll be walking the streets in a suit and tie, smoking a big cigar."

Merlin Haas swallowed back the dryness in his throat and said, "Well, he knows I can make him money. He'd be foolish to let something happen to me."

"Yeah?" McNutt patted the pistol standing in a holster across his stomach. "Maybe you can grift and gamble, but I can help him stay alive. Which one would you pick if you was him?"

Merlin Haas started to respond, but then stopped himself and sat silent as Newt Grago walked back to the small fire and crouched down on his haunches, saying, "Boys, the horses are in bad shape, us pushing them so hard." He picked up a short stick of kindling and stirred it around in the bed of glowing embers. "Resting tonight will help them some, but we'll be lucky if they make it all the way into Kansas."

"Then what do you suppose we do?" McNutt asked Grago, giving Merlin Haas a knowing glance as he did so.

"I don't know," said Grago, shaking his head slowly. "I've got to think about it and figure something out." He stood back up and stepped over to unroll a blanket on the ground. "Meanwhile, let's get some rest ourselves. Tomorrow's going to be a long day."

But Merlin Haas got very little rest that night. In spite of his long day in the saddle, he rolled back and forth from one side to the next in his blanket. More than once he thought about easing over to the horses, cutting one out, and slipping away into the darkness. His hand went now and then to his share of the winnings in his coat pocket, reassuring himself that it was still there. At one point he came close to rising up and making his move to the horses, yet before he got to his feet, McNutt's voice spoke to him from across the campfire.

305

"What's the matter, Haas, can't sleep?" McNutt murmured, a dark, playful tone to his voice.

"I—I thought I heard something out there," Haas replied.

"You didn't hear nothing, Haas," McNutt said. "If you did, don't worry about it. That's why I'm sitting guard."

"Oh, all right then," Haas said, feeling his heart pound in his chest. He lay back down and turned away from McNutt, his hand resting inside his coat on the small Uhlinger pistol he kept there.

The Canadian River, July 30, 1871

In the gray hour before dawn, Merlin Haas had finally dozed off when he felt Newt Grago's boot nudge him roughly in his side. "Wake up, Haas," Grago said, standing above him, "I've made us a plan that'll work out best for all of us."

Merlin Haas rolled onto his back, his hand still beneath the blanket, on the pistol inside his coat. "What's the plan?" Haas asked, suddenly aware of the tip of Grago's rifle barrel hovering near him. The rifle was not pointed at Haas, but it was close enough that he got the message. Behind Grago, McNutt sat stooped over the low glowing embers, his face shadowed by the low brim of his hat.

"Like I told you last night," said Grago, "these horses are blowing out on us. I figure it's best you stay behind here on the Canadian and keep an eye on the trail. Me and McNutt will take your horse as a spare. If we find fresh horses up ahead, we'll come back for you. If not, you take up with the Stanleys when they come through here."

"But—but what if they don't come?" Haas asked, getting a sick feeling low in his stomach.

"Then somebody has killed them," Grago said, leaving no room for questioning in his voice. "You'll take a horse from whoever comes along next." His rifle barrel tipped slightly closer to Merlin Haas's face. "Do you see any problem with that?" he asked.

Merlin Haas knew better than to push it, so he said, "Well, no, anything you say, Newt. Leave me a rifle though, won't you?"

Grago seemed to think about it, then said, "No, that's probably not a good idea. You've got that little Uhlinger. It'll do the job for you." He paused, then added, "It'd be best if you gave me your share of the winnings, just for safekeeping till we meet up again, don't you think?"

Merlin Haas reached his free hand inside his coat pocket, feeling his legs tremble, knowing better than to resist. "Yes, that's a good idea, Newt." He handed the thick roll of money up to him. "Here, take it all. I want you to have it... I mean, to keep for me, that is." He knew his voice sounded shaky. Behind Grago, Haas heard McNutt chuckle under his breath.

"What's so funny?" Grago asked McNutt, turning a wary eye toward him as he shoved the money down into his pocket.

"Nothing," said McNutt. "Just recalling something that happened to me once a long time ago."

"Well, keep it to yourself." Grago sneered. "Go get the horses. We've got a long ride ahead."

As McNutt stood and moved away to where the horses stood saddled and ready, Newt Grago turned back to Merlin Haas. "We made some money together, Haas. If you make it to Newton, just look me up." He smiled in the darkness. "I won't be hard to find. Hell, the town's named after me."

Merlin Haas tried to calm himself, unable to speak without his voice betraying him. He only nodded, trying to return the smile, but finding his lips stiff, he was unable to do so.

When McNutt walked the three horses over to the low circle of firelight, he looked down at Haas and winked, saying in a hushed voice, "I told you, didn't I?" Then he turned to Grago, handed him the reins to one of the horses, and in a moment all that remained of the two was the low drumming of hooves moving along the bank of the river.

It took Merlin Haas a few minutes to collect himself and stand up without his knees feeling too weak to support him. Once he was sure the two men were gone, he staggered in place and rubbed his face in his hands. Then he took a deep breath, pulled the Uhlinger pistol from inside his coat, and turned it over and over in his hand. What were the odds of his staying here and picking up a horse? Even as he asked himself, he already the answer. "Slim to none," he said aloud, his voice sounding hollow to him in the still dawn air. He sighed and sat back down in the low glow of the firelight and looked around bleakly at the deserted camp.

The Washita River, July 30, 1871

It was not anything that Danielle heard or saw riding closer to the rise of ground near the banks of the Washita. It was something she felt, something she'd learned to pay attention to this past year on countless trails through the lawless frontier. The tracks they'd been following swung to the left, toward a low spot where the river crossing would be shallow. Yet something told her there was trouble waiting behind the low rise forty yards to the right. From the low rise, the crossing lay bare and unprotected. It was the kind of spot that was perfect for an ambush. Once at the crossing, she and her brothers would be in the open, helpless in the sights of a good rifleman.

"Hold up," she said suddenly to Tim and Jed riding beside her. She reined Sundown to a halt and scanned the low rise and the river crossing a hundred and fifty yards ahead of them.

"What is it?" Tim asked, the three of them squinting in the midmorning sun's glare.

"We're not going in there just yet," Danielle said, stepping Sundown back and forth. "Don't let your bays stand still. Keep them moving. I've got a hunch there's rifles looking at us from that rise."

"So do I," said Tim, as he and Jed kept their bays moving back and forth now, "but I've been feeling like there's somebody behind us too. Maybe it's just nerves."

"Nope," Danielle said, "there is somebody behind us, probably has been ever since we left the buttes. I caught a glimpse of dust a while ago. But this is different. Keep moving. Let's cut west, see if we can tip their hand. If they see us leaving, they'll take a long shot instead of letting us get past them."

"Good thinking," Jed replied, gigging his bay quarter-wise, not letting it stand still beneath him. When Danielle cut west on Sundown and heeled forward, Tim did the same, Jed dropping in behind him. Before they had gone ten yards, two rifle shots thumped into the ground at the hooves of Tim and Jed's bays, causing the horses to rear sideways as the sound of the shots echoed around them.

"Hurry up!" Danielle called out behind her, giving Sundown more heel. "They're still too close for comfort!" Sundown bolted west, and Jed and Tim's bays followed, all three of them staying back from the riverbank until Danielle had put another hundred or more yards between them and the crossing. When she cut back toward the river, she slowed enough to let Tim bring his bay in beside her as he spoke.

"What now?" Tim called out above the sound of hooves beneath them.

"They've got to come out of their cover if they want us," Danielle said, drawing her Colt as she shouted to him. "Let's see if they will!"

Behind the low rise, Hop Stanley stood up, dusting his knees, cursing aloud to his brother Renfrow. "Damn it to hell! Look what we've brought on. Can't you hit anything with that Winchester?"

"Me? What about you?" Renfrow shouted, jerking his horse's reins up from the ground and swinging up into the saddle. "I didn't see you doing so hot yourself! You was afraid they'd get out of range, and now by God they have!"

"Come on," said Hop Stanley, also snatching up his horse's reins and levering another round into his rifle chamber, "if we don't get them now, they'll be all over us. Keep them on the run!"

Bringing up the rear behind Tim and Danielle, Jed Strange looked back over his shoulder as they headed into a wide, sloping turn toward the riverbank. He saw the two riders pounding hard on their trail and shouted forward to Tim and Danielle, "Here they come— looks like there's only two of them!"

"Good!" Danielle shouted without looking back. "Make this turn out of sight, then stop!"

Hop and Renfrow Stanley pressed their horses flat-out along the trail, the dust of the other three horses still looming in the air, stinging their eyes and faces. Hop Stanley had his rifle cocked and ready to raise as soon as they made the wide turn toward the river. But straightening out around the bend, both Hop and Renfrow sat back hard on their reins, trying to slide their horses to a halt. They failed to do so before the blasts of pistol fire lifted them from their saddles. Danielle, Tim, and Jed stood in the center of the trail, their pistols smoking as the Stanley brothers rolled dead to the ground, a red mist of blood seeming to hang in the air for a second, then settling with the dust.

The twins stared, their pistols still trained on the two lifeless bodies. Danielle stepped forward, watching one of the Stanley brothers' horses stand up from where it had faltered and tumbled in the dirt. The horse nickered and shook itself off, then trotted to one side, its saddle loose and drooping beneath its belly. "Get those horses," Danielle said over her shoulder, "we might need them for spares."

"Are they Newt Grago's men?" Tim asked, stepping forward beside her and nodding at the two bodies.

"You can bet on it," Danielle replied. She cut her gaze off along the rise and fall of the land behind them. "That takes care of them. But we've still got somebody trailing us."

Two hundred yards away, lying on his belly in tall grass, Saul Delmano cursed to himself, seeing the two bodies lying on the trail. He wasn't sure from this distance, but it looked like it was the Stanley brothers riding in, making a stupid fatal mistake. *Well, so much for that,* he thought, sliding backward to where the land sloped down behind him. Once behind the cover of the rise, he walked over to his horse and shoved his rifle back into its boot. He wasn't about to get those three on his tail. He would stay back and play it safe. They still had a long way to go.

Chapter 19

Newton, Kansas, August 7, 1871

The town of Newton sat on the Chisholm Trail, where only a year before there had been nothing but a few dust-blown shacks, stacks of cross ties and steel rails, and a crew of determined gandy dancers*. Judge R. P. Muse, an agent for the Atchison, Topeka & Santa Fe Railroad, had chosen the spot as a likely site for a rail terminal, owing to the big herds of cattle coming up the trail from Texas, and the settlers and businessmen coming in from the East. The stockyards and loading chutes seemed to swell with long-horns from daylight to dark. With the long-horns came the men who drove them, good, hardworking men for the most part. Yet among them came the lawless element; the grifters, the thieves and killers, whose only

* Gandy dancers *was a term for men who worked in a rail-laying crew.*

interest in cattle lay in the large amounts of cash that the industry generated. Newton, although still in its infancy as a rail town, had already been labeled the wickedest city in the West.

Newt Grago stood on the boardwalk out front of Bertha Stillwell's saloon and looked at the stir of passerbys in the morning heat, chewing a cigar. With his thumbs hooked to the lapel of his new swallow-tailed dress coat, he smiled. "Damn, Berth," he said to the big woman standing beside him, "I do believe you've hit the jackpot here." A shot rang out from the direction of another saloon at the far end of the street. A woman screamed. The crowd outside Bertha's only looked back over their shoulders and hurried on about their business.

Bertha and Newt Grago glanced across the top of the moving traffic toward the sound of the shot, then looked away. "I knew you'd like it here, once you arrived," Bertha replied. She was a hefty woman who carried herself well, and dressed in the latest fashions. She fanned looming dust with a delicate flowered kerchief and smiled at Newt Grago. "As far as anybody bothering you here, leave that to me and the boys. I sent Jake Reed up to Cottonwood Station last night. He'll be back this evening with Spurlock, Quince, and some of the others by this evening. There should be as many as seven or eight guns in all. Think that's enough to keep you out of trouble? If not, we'll hire more. I aim to please," she added in a coy tone.

Newt Grago blushed a bit, then said, "I

just hope Spurlock and his boys ain't forgot who's always in charge when I'm around. I'm the one who'll be calling the shots."

"I told Jake to be sure and make that clear to Spurlock," Bertha interjected.

"If I ain't mistaken," Grago went on, "there's a gunslinger on my trail that's going to require my strictest attention as soon as he gets here."

"Whatever you need, Newt," Bertha replied, reaching over and squeezing his hand. "I already put the word out—anything you want, you get, including the use of my two body-guards, George Pipp and Star-eye Waller."

"You are a jewel, Berth." Newt Grago smiled. He ran a clean hand down the front of his white boiled shirt, and looked himself up and down, realizing that he hardly resembled the man who'd ridden in here two days ago, dust-streaked, leading a gaunt, spare horse behind him. When he and McNutt arrived at the outskirts of Newton, Grago instructed McNutt to hang back awhile, and then come into town alone. No one had any idea they were together, except for Bertha Stillwell. McNutt had kept close to Grago and watched his back. There was no sheriff in Newton at present, but lawmen came and went on an almost daily basis, hunting wanted fugitives who'd broken the law inside their towns and jurisdictions across Kansas. Newt Grago always liked to play it safe when he could. Willis McNutt was his ace in the hole.

But neither Newt Grago's watchful eyes from the boardwalk, nor Willis McNutt

315

standing across the street leaning on a hitch rail, caught sight of the four riders who had slid around the perimeter of Newton and slipped in from the other end of town. Danielle led the way, followed by Merlin Haas, then her brothers Tim and Jed, who had kept a close eye on Haas since they'd found him along the banks of the Canadian River.

Amid the busy cattle chutes at the far end of town, Danielle reined Sundown to a halt and pressed a hand to the tender, swollen wound throbbing painfully in her side. Tim and Jed both knew what was bothering her as soon as they stopped beside her, and Tim said, "We've got to get that looked at before we do anything else, Danielle."

"I'm all right." She looked at each of them in turn, then looked at Merlin Haas and asked, "Are you good for your word, Haas? You said you'd do some scouting around for us. Can we trust you?"

"Damn right you can," Haas replied without hesitation. "After what that bastard did to me, left me afoot, took all my money, I've got no qualms whatsoever about handing him over to you. Let me get going and see what I can find out."

"Go on then," Danielle said, "check things out. We'll meet you here this afternoon." She nodded toward a drover's shack where saddles hung along a rail fence and blankets and gear lay piled on a plank porch. In a circle of stones, fire licked beneath a tin coffeepot sitting atop a greasy blackened roasting rack.

"We'll stay here. It looks like there's room for a few more blankets on the ground."

"I'll be back," Merlin Haas said. "You can count on it."

Tim and Jed both turned to her as soon as Merlin Haas drifted away from the chutes and onto the crowded street. "Think we can trust that cur?" Tim asked.

"Nope, not much," Danielle replied. "That's why I want you two to keep an eye on him from a distance. I'm going to take your advice and get this wound looked at. It's paining me something awful. I just didn't want to say anything in front of Haas." She stepped Sundown back from between her brothers, then said as she turned the mare away, "Both of you be careful. I'll find a doctor and meet you back here."

Tim and Jed nodded and watched her ride off toward the busy street.

Danielle made her way along the rutted dirt street, keeping the mare near the boardwalk, where she hoped to be less noticeable should the eyes of Newt Grago or any of his outlaw friends be searching the crowd for her. Without the fake mustache, and keeping her hat brim low on her forehead, the only thing recognizable about her was Sundown, and even the mare would be hard to spot, all covered with road dust and streaked with sweat. At a hitch rail she pulled the mare in beneath a freshly painted sign which read: DOCTOR LANNAHAN.

Casting a glance back and forth along the street, she stepped down from her saddle, hitched Sundown, and walked up the boardwalk and in through the single wooden door.

Inside the empty office, a thin, young doctor looked up from his desk in a corner and put on his wire-rimmed spectacles as he stood to face her.

"I'm Dr. Philip Lannahan," he said, adjusting his vest, "may I help you?" No sooner than he asked, he saw the dark circle of dried blood on her side and moved forward as Danielle swayed a step before catching herself.

Danielle moved her hand from her side, saying, "I took a bullet a couple of days back, Doctor. It's still inside me. Got me feeling weak and fevered all over."

"Oh my goodness!" Dr. Lannahan said, moving with her, ushering her past the front office into the next room, where a gurney stood covered with a clean white sheet. "You can't let something like that go unattended, young man. What on earth were you thinking?"

Before Danielle answered, the doctor pressed her back onto the gurney and began unbuttoning the bib of her shirt. Danielle raised a hand and stopped him. "I'll tell you why I had to let it go for a while, Doctor," she said. "I'm in the midst of a manhunt and the men I'm hunting were too close for me to take the time to stop."

"I see," the doctor said. "That's foolish of you, but I suppose I understand." His finger went back to the buttons, but again she stopped him.

"There's something you're about to find out that you must promise never to mention to anyone," she said.

The doctor looked deep into the serious eyes demanding secrecy of him. "I treat wounds, young man. I don't harbor fugitives, if that's what you're about to tell me."

"No, Doctor, that's not it at all." She sighed and let him open her shirt, knowing that as soon as he saw the binder around her chest, he would begin to understand.

As he pulled the open shirt back across her shoulders, he caught sight of the binder and hesitated for a second. Then he continued undressing her, saying, "I see what you're asking me now. Don't worry, your secret is safe with me, Miss...?"

"I'm Danielle Strange," she said, letting out a breath and trying to relax. "I go by the name *Danny Duggin*." She pointed to the binder around her breasts. "This is also why I couldn't stop and get the bullet taken out. By the time my brothers and I had a chance to stop and attend my wound, we ran into another man who traveled on with us. I couldn't risk him knowing I'm a woman."

"Well," said the doctor, stepping over to a metal tray where shiny instruments gleamed in the sunlight that streamed through a window, "I hope you haven't waited too long. You're burning up with fever." As he spoke, he reached out and gently pressed her back flat against the gurney and touched a finger to the swollen flesh surrounding the bullet hole.

319

"This is infected," he said almost to himself, studying the condition of the wound. "It's not the worst I've ever seen, but it's certainly not the best either. I hope you have nothing planned for the next few days, Miss Strange. It looks like you're going to be boarding right here."

"Don't get into the habit of calling me Miss Strange," Danielle said in a firm tone. "Call me Danny Duggin. And yes, I'm afraid I do have something planned for the day. Something most urgent."

"But, Miss—I mean, Danny Duggin," the doctor said, quickly correcting himself, "you won't be able to be up and around for a while once I remove this bullet! To attempt it would be insane."

"Then what can you give me for the fever and the pain until I finish my business and get back here?"

"No, that's out of the question," the doctor said, shaking his head. "I must insist you stay here right now, get the bullet removed, and then rest and recuperate. Whatever you have to do in Newton will simply have to wait."

"It can't wait, Doctor," Danielle said, rising slightly onto one elbow, the pain of her wound throbbing deep inside the inflamed flesh. "Give me something to take, and send me on my way."

"Anything I give you for the pain is only to put you to sleep. Anything I give you for the fever and infection isn't going to have a great deal of effect until we get that bullet out of you.

I can clean it, soak it in alcohol for now, and dress it in a bandage. But the alcohol is going to burn like the dickens."

"Let's get to it, Doctor," she said with resolve. "It'll have to do for now."

"Are you certain about this?" Dr. Lannahan asked. "I assure you this will burn like nothing you've ever felt."

"Stop talking about it and get it done," she demanded. "I can stand the pain."

"As you wish," said the doctor. He stepped back over to the tray and returned in a moment with a fresh dressing and a bottle of alcohol. Danielle lay clutching the sides of the gurney with both hands as the white-hot liquid seem to sear the flesh from her bones. She kept herself from screaming aloud until finally through the pain came a queasy numbness. As the doctor finished soaking the wound and wrapping it in clean gauze, she lay shivering beneath a clammy patina of sweat.

"There now," the doctor said at length, stepping back from her. "If you think that was bad, wait until that infection gets worse. I've seen men beg someone to shoot them."

"I'll keep that in mind, Doctor," Danielle said, forcing herself to sit up on the gurney and swinging her legs down over the edge. Stiffly she pulled on her shirt, closed the bib shut across her chest, and began buttoning it up. "How long before this fever starts knocking me off my feet, Doctor?" she asked.

The doctor shook his head in exasperation. "Oh, a couple of hours, a day. Who knows? I'm surprised you're on your feet right now."

Danielle gave him a stern gaze. He relented, saying, "Oh, all right. I'd say by this afternoon, you should expect it to get to its worst stage. But mind you, once you get to that point, I can't promise you're going to pull through. Blood poisoning is not a pleasant death."

Danielle finished buttoning up her shirt, thinking of her father's death and saying, "Neither is hanging from a tree in the middle of nowhere, Doctor." She stood up and took a second to clear her head before taking a step. Then she said, "I'll be back tonight, I promise," and walked back across the front office and out the door.

It was already afternoon when the twins came back to the shack beside the rail chutes. Danielle sat near the rail fence, her face looking ashen and drawn. Tim noticed that she shivered a little as they stepped down from the bays and walked over to her. "What did you find?" Danielle asked them right away.

Before answering, Tim asked a question of his own. "What'd the doctor say? Are you doing all right?"

"He said I'm fine," Danielle replied. "What did you find out? Did you see Newt Grago?"

"Yep, we saw him from a distance," said Jed. "Merlin Haas went right up to him. You couldn't tell anything had ever happened between them. They even shook hands. We saw

Grago give him some money. Then they went inside a saloon, and that's the last we saw of them."

"How many men are hanging around Grago?" Danielle asked.

"None that we saw," Jed answered.

"Good," Danielle said in an expelled breath. "This time it's just me and him. Then it's over," she added, looking up at her brothers. "We can go back home."

"Are you sure you're feeling all right?" Tim persisted. "You don't look so good."

"Yes, I feel fine," Danielle said, a bit testy. "It's just a graze like I told you before," she lied. "The doctor cleaned it and bandaged it. Told me to come back tonight, and he'd take a closer look at it."

"What for?" asked Tim. "If it's only a graze, what else is he going to do?" He looked suspicious.

"How do I know?" Danielle snapped at him. "I told him I had business to take care of. He said I'd be fine, so long as I came back tonight and had him look at it again."

"All right," Tim said, backing off, "take it easy. I'm just worried about you, is all."

Danielle took a deep breath, calming herself, then said, "I know, but we don't have time for your worrying. As soon as Haas gets back, if his story sounds real enough, you two are going to watch my back. I'm going to call Newt Grago out in the street and settle all accounts."

Tim and Jed both nodded, but Tim saw

the glazed, hollow look in Danielle's eyes. He knew better than to say anything right then, yet he couldn't help but wonder if she was really up to doing what she'd come so far to do.

At the bar inside Bertha Stillwell's saloon, Merlin Haas wiped foam from his upper lip and sat his mug of beer back down on the bar. He looked at Newt Grago standing beside him and resisted the urge to pull the Uhlinger pistol from inside his coat and put a bullet between Grago's eyes. But killing Newt Grago was not why he had come here, he reminded himself, managing a smile. That was something Danny Duggin would do, once Haas got back and told him that Newt Grago was here alone, with nobody around but a couple of Bertha's bodyguards. From what Haas had seen of Danny Duggin's gun handling, the two bodyguards wouldn't bother him a bit, especially since he had a couple of helpers of his own.

"I have to admit, Newt," Merlin Haas said, still managing a tight smile, "I was pretty damn sore at you, leaving me that way. To tell the truth, I never believed you'd give me my money back even if I made it here."

"Well," Grago responded, "to be honest myself, I never thought you'd make it. I figured there was no sense in that money laying out there in the dirt somewhere while the buzzards picked your bones. But since you did make it, here's to you." He raised a shot of rye in salute to Merlin Haas. After he threw it back, smacking his lips with a hiss, he asked, "Now tell me again, how was it you got a hold of one of the Stanley brothers' horses?"

Haas shrugged. "Just like I said. I was hiking back along the trail toward the Washita, and first thing you know, there it came trotting up to me. All's I did was raise my hands, stop it, and step into the saddle." He raised his beer again, and this time when he sat it down he added, "Of course, I figure it must mean that either Hop or Renfrow, or maybe even *both* of them, are dead."

"But you saw no sign of either the posse or that young gunslinger, Duggin?"

"Not a trace," said Haas. "I figure he must've got in the wind with everybody else and headed for Texas. That's the last you'll see of him, I reckon."

"Yeah, I think you're right," Newt Grago said, eyeing Haas closely. "So, where are you headed now, Haas?" Grago asked, refilling his shot glass from the bottle on the bar.

"Wherever the action takes me." Merlin Haas shrugged. "I hate losing all the gambling equipment. Sure hate seeing Lulu carted off in handcuffs that way. But she'll show in Texas before long. They've got nothing worth holding her on. I figure me and her'll be back in business before you know it." He finished his beer in one last long swallow, then slid the empty glass across the bar top. "Well, it's been a hell of a spree, Newt. I 'spect I'll push on now."

"Glad you made it, Merlin," Grago said, slapping Haas on the back with a laugh. "You watch your backside out there."

"I'll do it, Newt Grago," said Haas, "and you do the same. Thanks for taking care of my money for me." He patted his coat pocket.

"My pleasure, *amigo,*" said Newt Grago. Now that he had heard what Haas had to say, Grago's hand swept upward with his pistol cocked. "Come to think of it, I might just hang on to it awhile longer." He spread a nasty grin. "Give it back, Haas, all of it."

Haas knew that to resist would bring himself sudden death. "I should of known better," he murmured, lifting the money and handing it back to Grago.

"Yep, you should have," Grago agreed, stuffing the inside of his coat. "Now clear out before I shoot you for the hell of it."

As Haas slunk out the door, Bertha Stillwell came up beside Newt Grago as he watched Merlin Haas disappear through the swinging doors. "Is everything all right, Newt?" Bertha asked, slipping a fleshy arm around his waist.

"Naw, everything is not all right at all," Grago said, rolling the cigar in his lips, considering things as he stared at the swinging doors. "I don't believe a word that grifter said. He didn't get this far on his own, and he didn't just walk up and find one of the Stanleys' horses trotting along the trail."

"Then how did he get here?" Bertha Stillwell asked.

"I don't know, but I'd sure like to," Grago

said, still staring at the doors. "What time did you say those boys will be here from Cottonwood Station?"

"This evening sometime," Bertha said. "Why, are you expecting trouble before then? Did you tell Haas that Spurlock and his boys are coming in from Cottonwood Station?"

"Hell no, I didn't tell him about Spurlock and his boys. But as far as *trouble* goes, I've been expecting it since the day I was born," said Newt Grago, tossing back a shot of rye and banging the empty glass down on the bar. "Why would today be any different?"

Chapter 20

Saul Delmano slipped into town, using the same trail Danielle, her brothers, and Merlin Haas had ridden in on earlier. When he saw the familiar horses hitched along the rail fence, he quickly ducked his own horse away and stepped it in between two holding pens full of steers. From there he sat watching for a moment until Merlin Haas came riding in from the main street and stepped down from his saddle. Delmano realized that Merlin Haas was the only one of the four who could recognize him. After seeing the way these three young gunmen fought, Delmano debated whether or not to stick here and side with Newt Grago, or get out, hoping that these three thought him dead along with Blade Hogue and Rufe Gaddis. He weighed his decision as he sat watching them talk among themselves.

"What did you find out?" Danielle asked Haas, listening closely for any waver in his voice or any sign of him lying. "Did you see Newt Grago?"

"Yep, I saw him, all right. Even drank a beer with him," said Merlin Haas.

The twins stood watching his face, listening along with Danielle. "How'd you tell him you got here?" Tim asked.

"I told him one of the Stanley brothers' horses came along while I was hiking back toward the Washita. Since I am riding one of their horses, I figured if he saw me on it, the story would match up." Haas grinned. "I know how to stretch the truth some when I need to. I ought to know how—it's been my occupation my whole life."

"I know," Danielle said. "Did he mention having any men here? Was there anybody around him? Don't forget, we followed two sets of hoofprints here. What about this McNutt you told us about?"

"Didn't see hide nor hair of McNutt. Maybe he lit out. As far as any others, there's only a couple of Bertha Stillwell's bodyguards hanging around. But they'd be around anyway, if Bertha's nearby." He paused for a moment, then looked at Danielle and the twins with sincerity, saying, "Listen, I know you've got some doubts about me, but I'm talking straight to you. What Newt Grago did to me, leaving me stranded that way. There's no patching that up, as far as I'm concerned. I don't care what you do to him. You can believe that or not."

Danielle considered what he'd told them. It went along with what the twins had seen, Haas and Grago going into the saloon. "If you are lying, Haas, there's not enough land out here to keep us from finding you."

"You think I don't realize that?" Haas said. "I gave it all some good thinking before I ever went looking for Newt for you. That's the God-honest truth."

Danielle looked at the twins, then back to Merlin Haas. "All right, Haas. You're free to take off. Keep the horse. But once you leave, don't come back sticking your nose into things."

Stepping back to the horse and collecting the reins from the ground, Merlin Haas said, "Don't worry, I'm already gone. If you shoot that bastard more than once, tell him the second one is from me."

They watched Merlin Haas step into his saddle and turn the horse away toward the trail they had had come in on. Danielle stood up and brushed the dust from her trousers. A feverish shiver wracked her body, but she held firm until it passed. Then she took her Colt from her hip, checked it, and spun it back into her holster. From between the rail chutes, Saul Delmano couldn't hear what Merlin Haas and the others had been saying, but seeing Haas leave on such friendly terms was all Delmano needed to see. Knowing that went a long way in helping Delmano make up his mind. He leveled his hat brim low on his forehead, then turned his horse and slipped along between the rail chutes until he found a place where he could get past any watching eyes and get onto Merlin Haas's trail.

From the northwest, on the trail from Cottonwood Station, Bertha Stillwell's bartender, Jake Reed, and a group of eight riders moved along at a steady trot. At the head of the riders beside Reed, Mace Spurlock rode with a rifle across his lap. Behind Spurlock rode Quince Evans and six gunmen who'd thrown in with them four months ago, robbing banks and stagecoaches. They were thieves and killers to the man. In riding order behind Quince Evans, they were: Earl Peach, Richard and Embrey Davenport, Duke Sollister, Joe Stokes, and Slim Early. There was no talk among them. They knew why they were headed to Newton when they left Cottonwood Station. They were going there at Bertha Stillwell's request, to protect Newt Grago. That was good enough for them.

Coming onto the dirt street as the afternoon traffic had just begun to settle, the riders spread wide and rode abreast slowly, forcing people aside and out of their way. A young boy whose mother pulled him out of the horse's path picked up a lump of dried horse droppings and hurled it at the riders. Duke Sollister turned in his saddle, his hand on the butt of his pistol, and almost drew and fired before realizing it was only a child. "Teach that kid some manners, woman," he hissed. "Nobody's too young to die."

The woman gasped, jerked the child away, and ducked inside a mercantile with her kid under her arm. At the far end of the street, Danielle, Tim, and Jed had stopped for only a moment, long enough for Danielle to look around and form a quick plan for them to cover her back in case of a surprise. She nodded at an alley on one side of the street, and Tim veered off toward it without a word. She looked at the rabbit gun in Jed's hand, then jerked her head toward a stack of nail kegs standing on the boardwalk across the street from Bertha Stillwell's saloon. "You be careful, sister," Jed whispered before moving away and leaving her in the middle of the dirt street. Danielle only nodded, knowing the raging fever inside her would not let her speak plainly without her voice wavering in her chest.

With the twins in position, she stepped to the middle of the street out front of the saloon and planted her feet squarely in the dirt beneath her, a shoulder-width apart. She did not see the riders pushing their way slowly through the traffic along the rutted street, fifty yards away from the other end of town. She saw only in her mind the vision of her pa swaying in the breeze at the end of a hangman's rope. "Newt Grago!" her voice boomed through the waning afternoon pedestrians toward the swinging doors. "Come out, you murdering son of a bitch! It's time I put you facedown in the dirt!"

At the sound of her words, boots shuffled out of the way on the boardwalk, and a lady's parasol fell to the ground. Buggy and freight wagons squeaked to a halt, both teamsters and businessmen alike abandoning their seats and running for cover. Even at forty yards away, over the street traffic, Mace Spurlock heard the voice and saw the commotion of people getting out of the way. He raised a hand and brought the others to a halt. "Give it a minute," he said over his shoulder. The horsemen milled in place, pistols coming out of holsters and eyes riveting on the lone figure in the middle of the street.

From his spot in the alley, Tim Strange saw the riders more clearly as the street emptied. He could tell Danielle hadn't seen them, her eyes pinned as they were on the saloon doors. He drew in a tense breath, stepped up onto the boardwalk, and moved unseen along the front of the buildings, hoping for a better position before the nine riders made their move. Behind the stack of nail kegs, Jed Strange had seen the riders as well, and knew instantly why they were here. He flashed a glance across the street toward Tim's alley position, but saw Tim moving forward along the boardwalk. Then his eyes caught sight of McNutt's red-bearded face venturing a peep from around a tall striped pole in front of a barber shop. "Oh Lord, Tim, look out," Jed whispered to himself. For a split second

McNutt's eyes locked on Jed's from across the street. Then McNutt drew back out of sight behind the barber pole.

"I'm coming, Danny Duggin!" Newt Grago's voice shouted out above the saloon doors. But watching the saloon, Danielle didn't see him. Instead, in the open windows above the saloon, she saw the glint of evening sun flash off of a rifle barrel, and she dove sidelong, whisking out both her Colts, one firing on the window to her left, the other to the right. White lace curtains streamed forward and down as one of Bertha Stillwell's bodyguards tumbled to the overhang above the boardwalk and fell to the street. At the same time, from the other window, a body slumped forward, a rifle falling from its hand and sliding down the overhang.

Danielle spun back toward the saloon doors in time to hear the pistol fire from inside. Her fever was playing tricks on her eyes, causing the front of the saloon to sway like reeds in a breeze. As Newt Grago burst through the doors, her shot only clipped his shoulder and sent him spinning along the front of the building. He dove down behind a wooden cigar Indian and fired back at her. Jed Strange saw that McNutt had spotted Tim moving along the boardwalk. "Look out, Tim!" Jed shouted, coming up from his cover. The blast of the short-barreled rabbit gun rattled the store windows along the street, the impact of the heavily loaded buckshot slamming McNutt full in his chest and leaving little of him in its wake.

At the saloon, Grago fought hard from behind the wooden Indian, chunks of the thick statue flying in all directions as Danielle's Colts riddled it with holes.

"Come on, boys, enough sightseeing," Spurlock called out, waving the men forward, batting his heels to his horse's sides. The riders charged forward with a loud yell, their pistols gunning for Danielle in the middle of the dirt street. But coming into the play now were Tim and Jed Strange. Each of them stepped into the fray from their side of the street, centering themselves toward the oncoming riders like statues of iron, their big customized Colts bucking in their hands. As each shot rang out, another rider flew from his saddle. Catching the brunt of their fire, the riders broke rank and dove for cover, leaving their confused, terrified horses to fend for themselves.

As the riders collected themselves and returned fire from safer positions, Jed and Tim could not withstand that many guns. "Come on, Danielle, run for it!" Tim shouted, stepping forward, one gun empty in his left hand, his right hand pounding out shots as bullets whistled past him. "For God sakes, Danielle!" he screamed. The searing pain of a bullet through his shoulder only caused him to flinch as he continued to cover his sister in the street.

But Danielle fought on as if in a trance, unhearing, unresponsive to anything save for the sight of Newt Grago lying dead at her feet. And Newt Grago was proving himself to be no easy kill. He'd rolled from behind the wooden Indian and scurried along the board-walk, blood spewing from his shoulder, his ribs, and his forehead. Still he fought on, pitching down from the boardwalk as Danielle's bullets kicked up splinters behind him. He hugged the side of a water trough for cover while he hurriedly reloaded his pistol. In the street, a shot had caught Danielle high in the back and spun her to the ground. "You dirty bastards!" Jed Strange screamed in rage, seeing his sister down and his brother Tim propped up on one knee, still firing, blood matting his chest, arm, and one side of his face.

The blast from Jed's shotgun didn't hit any of the men, but it blew away the side of the abandoned freight wagon in which three of them had taken cover. They fled like roaches, Jed's Colt coming into play, taking two of them down just as a bullet sliced through his side. He fell to the ground, a hand pressed to the wound for a second as his Colt continued firing. He saw one of the men rise up and aim at him, taking his time, getting it right. But just before the man fired, a bullet sailed in above Jed and punched out the man's right eye, letting Jed know that Tim was still back there, still fighting, helping his brother all he could.

Jed reached a bloody hand inside his coat pocket and took out two fresh loads and poked them into his rabbit gun. Then he fired both barrels, lifting a cloud of splinters and glass from the front of a store. He heard Tim's Colts bark behind him in the street, taking two men down in a spray of blood.

"Pull back, boys!" Mace Spurlock shouted to his men, hurrying backward in a crouch toward where his frightened horse stood in an alley, away from the gunfire. Taking a quick look around, he saw none of the men standing except for Earl Peach, who wandered aimlessly with an empty gun clicking over and over on empty chambers in his right hand. Peach's left hand clasped tight against his stomach, keeping his innards from spilling out.

"To hell with this! I'm quits here!" Mace Spurlock shouted, flinging his pistol aside as a bullet whistled past his ear. He ducked his head to one side, his hands held high in the air. "Damn it! I give it up! Don't shot!" Blood spread down his raised arms and ran in a thin stream from his elbow. "Lord God almighty!" he shouted, looking around at the carnage in the street. "What's got into you people?"

Using all her strength, Danielle managed to roll up onto her knees, keeping the Colt in her left hand aimed toward Newt Grago's position behind the water trough, her right Colt cocking toward Mace Spurlock as he stepped closer. Ten feet behind her, Tim rose up and staggered forward, only to collapse back down onto his knees. "Watch him, Tim," Danielle warned in a shaky voice, the fever taking its toll on her, getting worse by the minute now, it seemed.

"I—I can't," Tim rasped, trying to raise his pistol, but failing to do so. Jed Strange limped forward using the empty rabbit gun now as a crutch, his right hand raising his pistol toward

Spurlock. He, too, was having a hard time keeping it steady in his blood-slickened hand.

Around the edge of the water trough, Newt Grago ventured a look at Danielle, seeing the big Colts weave back and forth in her unsteady hands. He cut a glance to Mace Spurlock. Their eyes only met for an instant, yet at that moment each of them understood the other. They made their move in unison. Spurlock jumped to one side out of Danielle's aim. His hand went to the hideout pistol behind his back as Newt Grago flung himself up from behind the water trough and fired at Danielle. Grago's bullet ripped the Colt from her left hand, spinning it high in the air. "Get him, Spurlock! Kill that bastard!" Newt Grago screamed.

But Danielle's right Colt exploded just as Spurlock swung his pistol from behind his back. The bullet ripped through his heart and dropped him backward, dead before he hit the ground. Grago fired again, his shot grazing Danielle under her arm, slicing through the binding that held her breasts flattened to her chest. She fell backward to the dirt with the impact, but fired up at Newt Grago as he tried pulling off another round. He let out a loud grunt as the bullet lifted him from behind the water trough and up onto the boardwalk. Danielle collapsed for a moment, then shook her head to make the street stop spinning. Through sheer will alone, she struggled up to her feet and stalked forward toward Newt Grago, one halting step at a time. Tears streamed down her drawn, fevered cheeks.

"Tim?" she asked over her shoulder. "Jed...?" Her words trailed.

"Yeah," Tim said, gasping, "I'm alive...so's Jed. Ain't you, Jed?"

"So far," Jed replied, his words squeezed out through the pain.

Danielle made it to the water trough, catching a hand to it for support, her other hand raising the Colt toward Newt Grago, who lay trying to catch his failing breath. Along the street, townsfolk began venturing forward from hiding, a hushed murmur of voices rising up as if from the dirt.

"At last," Danielle sobbed, "I've killed you...you and every one of your murdering son-sabitches who killed my pa."

"Yeah, so what?" Newt Grago rasped, the hole in his chest stifling his breath, the flowing blood sapping his last moments of life. "You've...got yourselves...killed too. You...ain't going to make it, none of you are."

"You're wrong, Grago. I'll live. So will my brothers," Danielle said, the Colt wobbly in her hand.

"Your brothers?" Grago tried to focus on Tim and Jed as they managed to move forward, holding one another up. But by now all Newt Grago could make out were dark images. He heard the gunslinger Danny Duggin go on to say something close to his face, something that didn't make any sense to him. Danny Duggin was a woman? That couldn't be right, Grago thought, trying to sort it all out as the darkness circled in closer around him.

Grago heard Danny Duggin's voice again, this time faintly above the cocking of the big Colt close to his face. Grago tried to speak, but couldn't as he caught the smell of burnt powder still curling from the pistol so close to his face. "Dunc," he finally managed to whisper. "You was...all right after all." Newt Grago's world stopped as a silver flash rose up and exploded in front of his closed eyelids, then all turned black, black and silent, as Danielle Strange stepped back, faltering, poking out the spent rounds from her Colt and trying with all her strength to replace them.

Newton, Kansas, August 14, 1871

A full week had passed before Danielle fully opened her eyes and looked up into the faces of her brothers, Dr. Lannahan, and of all people, Tuck Carlyle. She was still drowsy and weak. The bullet from her side had been removed, and the fever that had nearly killed her had broken only the night before. There were parts of the aftermath of the gun battle that she remembered, but most of what had happened was still a blur. She remembered dropping down on the boardwalk with one Colt still in her right hand, her reloads spilling from her left hand and rolling around on the planks beside her. After that, she recalled the doctor appearing through a gray fog and carefully scooping her up. Then she heard some mention of a bed in a separate room off the

339

doctor's office. Her last thought had been of how good a soft bed would feel beneath her. She offered a tired smile now as she spoke.

"Tuck, is that really you?" Tim and Jed gave one another a knowing glance, feeling not the least neglected that her first attentions went to the handsome young drover.

"Yes, it's really me, Danny," Tuck said. "I was just pushing a short herd to the holding pens when I heard what had happened. I'm sorry I wasn't here in time to lend a hand, especially once I heard the Gragos were part of it. Damn, you gave us all a scare."

"Dunc's dead, Tuck. This was his brother and some other outlaws."

"They told me about Dunc," said Tuck, nodding toward Tim and Jed.

She looked over at Tim and Jed, who stood bandaged and bruised two feet back from the bed. "I expect you know by now that these two scarecrows are my brothers, Tim and Jed." She offered the twins a smile as Dr. Lannahan looked her over, carefully making sure the blanket covering her stayed up close to her chin, hiding her breasts.

"Yep," said Tuck. "They told me everything."

"Everything?" Danielle gave Tim and Jed a look, asking them in a guarded manner.

Tim cut in, saying, "Yep, we told him you're our older brother. Told him how we've all been searching for our pa's killers."

"Good." Danielle sighed. Then she turned to Tuck. "You told me on the trail that you're interested in a young woman named Ilene."

340

"Yep, that's right," Tuck said, "why do you ask?"

"Because as soon as I get out of this bed, we need to go someplace and talk. Now that I'm coming off this vengeance trail, I've got something I need to tell you."

"Really?" Tuck asked, looking curious at the serious manner she'd used. "Is it something important? Because if it is—"

Jed cut him off, saying, "It'll have to wait. Not to be rude, but Jed and I really need to talk to our brother alone for a few minutes, if you don't mind."

Tuck Carlyle looked back and forth between them, then said, "Sure. Family business. I understand." He looked back down at Danielle. "We'll talk later then, Danny. I'll be in town a couple of days till the train arrives and loads these steers for St. Louis. Meanwhile, you take it easy." He raised his hat in his hands, nodded to Tim and Jed, and stepped back to the door. "Glad you're doing well, *amigo*."

Danielle smiled, lifting a hand toward him as he turned and stepped out the door. She knew something was up from the way Tim had acted. She waited until she heard the outer door close behind Tuck Carlyle, then she turned her face back to her brothers, asking Tim, "What was that all about? What's going on?"

Tim and Jed hesitated, looking down at the floor for a second before Tim finally said, "I was afraid you were about to tell him you're really a woman, Danielle. We couldn't let you do that without first making sure you really wanted him to know."

"Why not?" she asked. "This whole mess is over now. I'm free to get back to living my own life." She looked at their grim expressions, then added, "Ain't I?"

Jed spoke now, in a quiet voice, saying, "Some drovers found Merlin Haas lying alongside the trail three days ago. They brought him here and he asked for you before he died. We told him the shape you were in, so he told us instead." Jed paused, then went on, "He said the man who shot and robbed him was Saul Delmano."

Danielle looked away. A silence passed as she let the news sink in, feeling the familiar tightness once again growing inside her. When she looked back at her brothers, she asked, "How's Sundown and the bays doing?"

Jed and Tim looked at one another. "They're all three fine. The bays are filling out in the flanks now that they've been on steady grain for the past few days. What are you thinking, Danielle?"

She felt her eyes grow moist, but she struggled against her emotions, and swallowed a knot in her throat. "You already know what I'm thinking." She looked at each of them in turn, adding, "I'm thinking you best keep calling me Danny Duggin."

"You don't have to go, Danielle—I mean, Danny," said Jed, correcting himself. "Me and Tim can finish up from here. You've more than done your part."

"I made a vow standing beside Pa's grave," she said. "It's not even a choice I can make. I'll be there when Saul Delmano dies, or else I'll die in the trying."

"I told you so," Tim said to Jed in a lowered voice. He looked back at Danielle, asking, "What about this Tuck Carlyle? We saw how you looked at him. It ain't right, you having to deny yourself this way."

Danielle didn't answer. Instead, she turned to Dr. Lannahan, asking, "How soon can I ride, Doctor?"

"It all depends," he said, cutting a glance to Tim and Jed, trying to get a feel for what they wanted him to say. "A week maybe? Two weeks if you don't get your strength back the way you should."

Danielle gave him a solemn stare, saying, "My strength is coming back right now. Don't stall me, Doc. Tell me the truth—when can I ride?"

He shrugged, and offered a slight smile. "In that case, as soon as you pay your bill."

Danielle returned his smile and struggled up onto the side of the bed. "Tim, go get the horses. Jed, go into my saddlebags, get some money and pay the doctor. Are you both able to ride?" she asked in afterthought.

"Yep," Tim said, taking a step back. "But there's something else we need to tell you. There's a bounty hunter named Bob Dennard. He was also there when they brought Haas in. He says he knows you. Said you and him had some trouble back near Fort Smith."

"That's right, we did. What about him?" asked Danielle, taking the freshly washed but bullet-riddled shirt Dr. Lannahan handed her and stiffly putting an arm into it.

"He says he wants to forget the trouble between you. Said if we go after this Saul Delmano, he wants to go with us. He knows a lot about Saul Delmano, says Delmano will duck into Mexico where he has lots of friends and connections. Dennard says we'll be out-gunned if we face Delmano down there."

"Dennard's not riding with us," Danielle said with finality. She slipped the shirt the rest of the way on and stood up on weak legs, reaching for her clean trousers as the doctor draped them across the foot of the bed. "He's only in it for the blood money." She paused, considering it, then said, "There's a big difference between him and us." She pulled on her trousers, stepped into her boots, and reached for the gun belt and the pair of matched Colts hanging on a ladder-back chair beside the bed. Strapping on the gun belt, she looked from Tim to Jed, saying, "The three of us are riders of judgment."